WHAT PEOPLE ARE SAYING ABOUT *DAUGHTERS OF THE WILDERNESS*

A promising debut from first-time author Lisa Larsen Hill, *Daughters of the Wilderness* brings the story of Zelophehad's daughters to life in a fresh and engaging way. What inspired me most was the courage these five women showed as they stepped forward to claim their inheritance. Larsen Hill's natural storytelling shines through in the sweet family moments and wise insights about holding on to faith when life is hard. Full of heart, this novel is filled with feel-good moments of healing and restoration.

—Tessa Afshar, *Publishers Weekly* bestseller
and author of *The Queen's Cook*

Lisa Larsen Hill has taken an often-overlooked section of the Book of Numbers and woven an exquisite story about the daughters of Zelophehad. *Daughters of the Wilderness* is rich in historical detail and ripe with compelling characters, giving readers an imagination for what the Israelites' time in the wilderness might have been like. Lisa explores the complicated relationship between sisters in a truly authentic way, bringing light to both the humanity and the divinity of the Scriptures as only a faithful follower of the Lord can. A story full of God's overwhelming grace that extends beyond even our own expectations, this novel had me pondering my own faith and challenged me to go deeper in my walk with God. Well done!

—Heidi Chiavaroli, Carol Award–winning author
of *The Orchard House* and *Draw Close to Jesus*

Breathtaking. *Daughters of the Wilderness* is a compelling read set in a little-explored biblical time. Noa is a riveting character, all the more interesting as a child of the generation of Israelites sentenced to die in the wilderness outside the promised land. Noa and her sisters take on issues of family loyalty, women's rights, and God's plan for each life, as relevant today as they were then. This story will both capture your imagination and send you to reread your Bible.

—Lori Stanley Roeleveld, speaker, coach, and author of *God's Abundant Mercy and Graceful Influence—Lessons from Women in the Bible*

Daughters of the Wilderness is a beautifully written biblical novel that brings the story of Zelophehad's daughters to life with heart, imagination, and reverence. Author Lisa Larsen Hill weaves rich historical detail with emotional depth, giving voice to women who wrestle with faith, family, and obedience in the wilderness. Her storytelling, built on a foundation of solid biblical knowledge, is immersive and compassionate, drawing readers into the tension, hope, and courage of these remarkable sisters. This compelling debut doesn't just retell Scripture—it invites readers to experience it, reminding us that God has always worked powerfully through faithful women willing to trust Him in uncertain seasons.

—Edie Melson,
director of the Blue Ridge Mountains Christian Writers Conference,
author of the *Soul Care* series

Daughters of the Wilderness offers a delightful and faithful expansion of each sister's backstory, helping the reader imagine how their relationships, birth order, and even the meanings of their names prepared them to carry out such an unorthodox and dangerous plan. The result is a captivating tale of five amazing, resourceful, and brave young women who may just inspire modern-day "daughters" to "come forward" themselves in acts of justice, equality, and faithfulness.

—Dr. Tracy Radosevic,
dean of the Academy for Biblical Storytelling

Lisa Larsen Hill expands upon the biblical story of the daughters of Zelaphchad with great insight and imagination. In so doing, she brings these often-overlooked characters to life, reminding us that God and religion possess the capacity to change with the times.

—Rabbi Irwin Huberman,
spiritual leader of Congregation Tifereth Israel,
journalist, and author of *The Place We Call Home*.

Larsen Hill's major contribution to the genre of biblical fiction evokes the background of Zelophehad's daughters' protest against their exclusion from the division of the promised land. It is a masterful retelling of the dawn of justice for ancient Israelite women and a potential source of empowerment for women today.

—Dr. Tom Boomershine,
founder of the Network of Biblical Storytellers,
author of *Story Journey:*
An Introduction to the Gospel as Storytelling.

DAUGHTERS OF THE WILDERNESS

DAUGHTERS OF THE WILDERNESS

FIVE SISTERS, ONE BOLD REQUEST, A GOD WHO LISTENS

LISA LARSEN HILL

Published by Seeds of Faith For Women, Inc.

This book was produced in collaboration with Redemption Press, which provided design, proofreading, and production support. Redemption Press provided its imprint seal representing design excellence, creative content, and high-quality production.
Distributed by Redemption Press

ISBN 13: 979-8-9954196-0-0 (paperback)
979-8-9954196-1-7 (ePub)
Library of Congress Catalog Card Number: 2026908611

In loving memory of my mom, Marjorie Larsen,
who inspired my faith through her words and actions
and inspired me to always "Remember the lilies."
Consider the lilies, how they grow: they neither toil nor
spin; and yet I say to you, even Solomon in all his glory
was not arrayed like one of these. (Luke 12:27 NKJV)

To Roger, my love, my life, my best friend.
You encouraged, walked, and sup-
ported me every step of this journey.
My beloved is mine and I am his. (Song of Songs 2:16)

THE DAUGHTERS OF ZELOPHEHAD
CAME FORWARD.

NUMBERS 27:1

MAIN CHARACTERS

The following are the characters in *Daughters of the Wilderness.* Names marked with an asterisk (*) belong to historical figures from the Bible. All other names are fictional but have been carefully chosen from ancient Hebrew roots to fit the cultural and narrative setting. The Hebrew meanings of names are included in parentheses to illuminate the story's cultural and spiritual depth.

THE DAUGHTERS' FAMILY

Mahlah*: Oldest daughter, 21 (*Sickness* or *Fat*)
Noa*: Second-oldest daughter, 19 (*Motion/Movement*)
Hoglah*: Third-oldest daughter, 17 (*Circling/Dancing*)
Milkah*: Fourth-oldest daughter, 15 (*Queen*)
Tirzah*: Youngest daughter, 13 (*My Delight/Pleasing*)
Zelophehad* (zeh-LOH-fuh-had), nicknamed Zelo: Only son of Hepher and father of the daughters (*Firstborn* or *Protection from Terror*)
Jeska: Zelophehad's wife (*God Beholds* or *Foresight*)
Sara: first wife (*Noble*)

ZELOPHEHAD'S YOUNGER COUSINS

Emet: Older brother of Abel (*Truth*)
Adina: Emet's wife (*To Judge*)
Jonathan: Emet's grandson and son of Zebediah (*God Has Given*)
Abel: Younger brother of Emet (*Breath*)
Leora: Abel's wife (*My Light*)
Simon: Abel's adopted son (*One Who Hears*)

LEADERS AND PRIESTS

Moses*: God's chosen leader of the Israelites from Egypt to the Promised Land (*Drawn Out*)
Aaron*: Moses's brother, designated by God to lead the Levites (*Mountain of Strength*)
Eleazar*: Aaron's son, who became high priest after Aaron's death (*God Has Helped*)

KORAH'S LINE

Korah*: A Levite assigned by God to the movable Tabernacle; led a rebellion against Moses and Aaron (*Baldness* or *Ice/Frost*)
Assir*: Firstborn son (*Captive* or *Prisoner*)
Elkanah*: Second son (*God Has Created*)
Abiasaph*: Third son (*My Father Has Gathered*)
Reba: Daughter (*Fourth Born*)

OTHER CHARACTERS

Abiram*: One of Korah's followers (*My Father Is Exalted*)
Dathan*: One of Korah's followers (*Belonging to a Fountain*)
Josiah: A mentee of Abel in the workshop (*The Lord Supports*)
Kenan: Betrothed to Mahlah (*Possession*)
Nahash: A potential husband for Mahlah introduced by Emet (*Snake*)
Tikva: Midwife (*Hope*)

For the glossary of terms, see page 303.

THE ENCAMPMENT OF THE ISRAELITE TRIBES

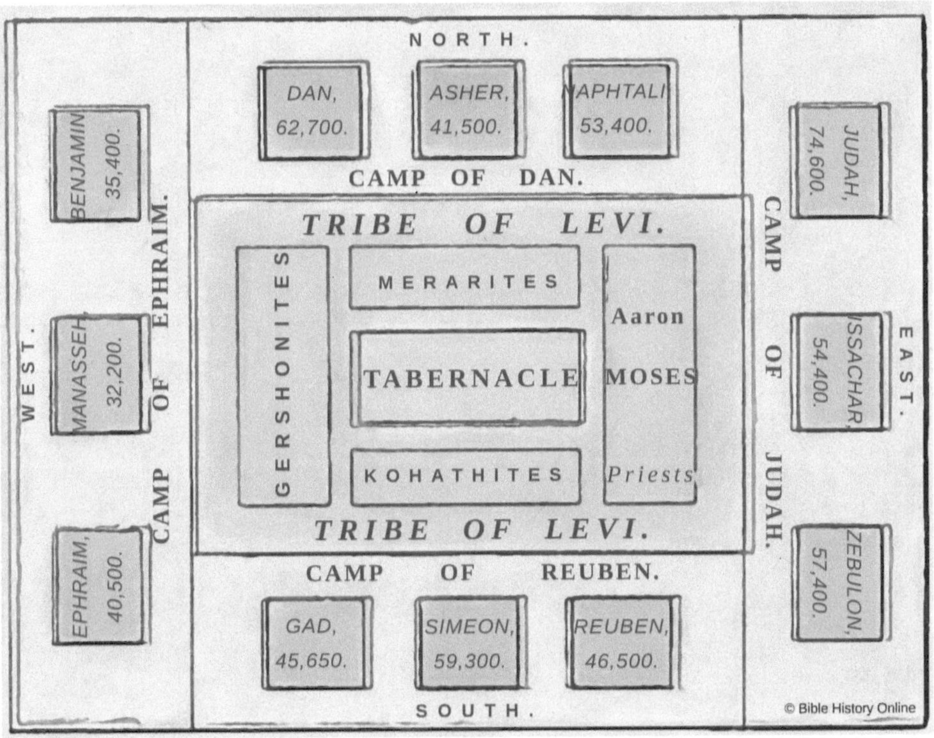

NORTH.

DAN, 62,700.
ASHER, 41,500.
NAPHTALI 53,400.

CAMP OF DAN.

WEST.

BENJAMIN 35,400.
MANASSEH 32,200.
EPHRAIM, 40,500.

CAMP OF EPHRAIM.

TRIBE OF LEVI.

GERSHONITES
MERARITES
TABERNACLE
KOHATHITES
Aaron
MOSES
Priests

TRIBE OF LEVI.

EAST.

JUDAH, 74,600.
ISSACHAR, 54,400.
ZEBULON, 57,400.

CAMP OF JUDAH.

CAMP OF REUBEN.

GAD, 45,650.
SIMEON, 59,300.
REUBEN, 46,500.

SOUTH.

PROLOGUE

SINAI PENINSULA, 1407 BC

Noa clawed at the tent ties, desperate to escape. She couldn't breathe. She ripped at the seam of the tent and dashed outside. The scorching sun greeted her like a heat front that vaporized the morning's cool air. A thunderstorm of tears cascaded down. It's all my fault, that inner voice she'd tried to suppress for years roared. She peered back inside the tent and scowled at the wedding dress her ima had labored on all evening, finishing the embroidery with her fragile hands. Wedding dress? More like a prison garment—a slave's tunic.

She clasped her hands behind her head, bringing her elbows in tight and shuffling her feet back and forth. She couldn't abandon her sister Mahlah on her wedding day. Wiping her cheeks, she reentered the tent. This should be the happiest day of Mahlah's life, but instead, her appearance was stoic—a mask of calm. Her older sister couldn't love Kenan, her intended, as she'd professed to Abba. *She must be doing this for my sisters and me.* Kenan was thirty-three years older than Mahlah, a widower with no children, and he never expressed genuine warmth to her or anyone else. Even his name's meaning, *possession*, indicated what this marriage would be about. Noa's younger sisters Hoglah and Tirzah interrupted her thoughts as they rehearsed a song for the wedding. Normally, their harmonious voices were pleasing, but today they grated on her ears as they were sharp and not in sync. Yet Milkah, her fourth sister, giggled and bubbled while braiding Mahlah's hair. Since the betrothal, Milkah couldn't hide her delight.

Noa's face turned scarlet, remembering how she'd hushed Milkah's raving. "Finally, my oldest sister will be wed, and you will be next, Noa and Hoglah. Then it's my turn."

It was all wrong. And it was all her fault.

Zelophehad lumbered toward Kenan's tent with his younger cousin, Emet. He carried Mahlah's dowry and would receive the groom's mohar, the bride-price for the loss of Mahlah's work to the family. He ran his hand through his hair, asking, "Am I doing the right thing?"

"Cousin, yes, certainly, this is the right thing for Mahlah. Kenan will be a good husband to her. He comes from a good family, and he will not be demanding."

"He is so much older! If they conceive, which he didn't with his first wife, he will be seventy-four when the child is twenty! Emet, I don't know how you talked me into this! This was not how I imagined it would be for my daughters. I wanted them to marry for love, not duty. It is about honoring each other."

"Love? Zelo, what are you talking about? Marriage is about a woman's safety. She'll be cared for and won't have to worry about how she'll live. Kenan has been careful with his father's inheritance, and he will provide for her. And let's not forget, you have four more daughters who need to be married." Emet coughed. "And you must admit that Mahlah was a challenge because of her limitations."

"Stop. Do not talk to me about her limitations. Mahlah is an excellent weaver, skilled in both clothing and tent-making. She is loyal to our God and family. She has also learned a great deal about herbs and plants for healing remedies. But why am I defending her to you?" Zelophehad raised his hands, a torrent of sweat dripping from his forehead. "She is worthy of a loving and good man. Their hearts are a far distance apart. Why did I allow this marriage to take place?"

Emet lowered the pitch of his voice. "You forget, cousin, that Mahlah had a chance to refuse this match, and she didn't. She said she would love him and stand by him."

Zelophehad swatted a hand toward him, muttering, "Yes, because your wife consistently reminded Mahlah that she was preventing her sisters from marrying, which set Milkah to repeating it daily." Why couldn't the girls' aunt stay out of Zelo's affairs? He turned to the right and trudged down an alley of tents at the Reubenite standard, the tribe's banner. *How did I let this happen?*

"I can hardly keep up with you, Zelo. We don't have to march over there. But it proves me right. Your daughters should all be married, save Tirzah."

"Emet, you don't know what you are talking about."

Emet started to speak, but the sight of the priest a few paces away quieted him.

"Shalom, Zelophehad." The Levite priest's face was solemn.

"Shalom on this momentous day. Shall we go in and finish the betrothal promises?" Emet took a step toward Kenan's tent.

The priest stepped even farther to the side, cautioning, "No, I can't go in or I'll be unclean."

"Unclean?" Zelophehad's whole body shook. Only death or illness would prevent a priest from entering.

The priest placed his palms together. "Oh, my dear man, Kenan is dead."

"Dead?" Zelophehad leaned forward, straining to understand. "What? What happened?"

Kenan's two brothers, dressed in their finest tunics for the wedding, wobbled out of the tent. "I'm sorry, Zelophehad. He had his wedding clothes set out. He was happy and looking forward to this day. None of us expected this, today of all days," one of the brothers said.

"How could this be? I saw him yesterday." Emet crossed his arms, his accusatory tone demanding an answer. "He must be only sleeping, perhaps too much to drink from last night's festivities."

"Emet, be calm, cousin. Do not add to these brothers' grief. I … I am sorry. None of us expected this." Zelophehad saw the hurt in the brothers' bent stances as they leaned on each other's shoulders. If his favorite cousin, Abel, passed away, he would be the same. Yet could they see the mixture of not only compassion but, shamefully, relief in Zelophehad? *Is this a strange blessing for my daughter?*

The second brother glowered at Emet. "The midwife came and said he died in his sleep. Let my brother's life go in peace."

Zelophehad stepped in front of Emet, blocking his cousin's view. "We are sorry, and we are both in shock. Please forgive him."

The first brother who had spoken extended his hand to Zelophehad's outstretched arm. "We understand. We are in shock as well. Kenan intended to give a bride's gift to Mahlah. We think it is right that she should receive it."

The second brother handed Zelophehad a cloth-wrapped package, opening it to unveil a large pottery bowl.

"Kenan said this was to let Mahlah know her bowl would never be empty. We had hoped he would have at least a little time with her."

Zelophehad lowered his head, sorting both comments. "Thank you for thinking of this. I will share these thoughts with her. May I ask what you meant by 'at least a little time with her'?"

The brothers' cheeks bloomed red, their eyes widening and bushy gray brows arching above them. "Ah … ah … Emet?"

Emet stepped around Zelophehad. "We join you in mourning Kenan. *Nechama*, may you find comfort from heaven. As you said, cousin, let us leave these brothers to their mourning. Come, Zelo, let us go. Shalom." Emet extended his arm around his cousin's waist and ushered him away.

Zelophehad swatted at his arm. "When were you going to expose that Kenan was twenty when we fled from Egypt? I knew he was older than Mahlah, but I thought he was like you, nineteen when he entered the wilderness. You lied to me, Emet!"

"They can hear you. Be mindful of their situation."

"I don't care if I wake their entire tribe. When were you going to—"

"This was for Mahlah—for all your daughters. Once Mahlah and your blunt-spoken Noa are married, your other three will be relatively easy to arrange. You know the prophecy. You have little time yourself."

Zelophehad abruptly halted. "You remind me of this now, at this moment—that I will never be allowed into the Promised Land? It is fortunate for you that I only have this bowl in my hand. This is not about me. It's about Mahlah marrying a man who will die here in the wilderness. What were you thinking?"

"I was thinking his younger brothers would care for her. She would be settled and would live with them."

"Emet, you will not talk to my daughters. You will not bring me any more"—he gestured in a circle with his hands—"of your ideal men for Mahlah or any of my girls. I don't want to see you in the workshop or at my home for at least a fortnight—not you or your five sons. Leave. Leave now."

"It was for the best. You know I am only trying to help you with the challenge you have about Mahlah."

"Enough. If you say one more word, I will let my fists show my fury. Go!" Zelophehad barreled to the furthest end of the camp, afraid he would be sick. His gut twisted like a choking vine, squeezing the breath from his lungs. He would welcome the cold water to bathe in to clear his mind. But first, he needed to pray. He squatted, sitting on his calves, and began his lament. *Lord, please quiet my soul. I feel I should thank You, but I do not want to wish any family a death. Thank You for passing this cup away from my precious daughter. Help me find those men who will love my daughters, keep them safe from harm, and love them the way I love Jeska before I, too, join Kenan.*

CHAPTER 1

SIX MONTHS LATER

Noa slid out of her sleeping mat and rolled it up quickly, her heart already thumping. Dressing in her light tunic, she lifted the empty manna basket with handles over her back. She moved slowly so as not to wake her sisters, slipping outside and quietly closing the tent flap behind her. When she breathed in the cool morning air, the sweet scent of flowering rabil engulfed her. She picked a handful and tucked it into her basket. Perfect! Today had to be special to celebrate her baby sister's return from the Women's tent. It would help to pluck out the remaining barbs from the injurious Kenan debacle, which was never spoken of though its tenacles strangled the air.

Humming one of Hoglah's tunes, she thanked God for his daily provision of sweet manna sprinkled like white flakes on the shrubs that sprang out in the arid desert. She collected the family's omer portions and hurried back. As she neared the tent, the excited voices of her four sisters rose, inviting her to pause. They were finally sharing something that each of them could feel good about—even Milkah.

After removing her sandals, she approached Tirzah and, with a flourish, bowed and presented the manna and flowers to her. "Welcome, sister, into the circle of womanhood. Would you do the honors and give everyone's morning share to break our fast? Mahlah and I agreed that this morning, she will forgo any cooking."

Tirzah also bowed and began circling to each sister.

Milkah waved Tirzah to put hers on the low table. "Yes, welcome, Tirzah, to our daily water chore. Now I won't have to journey to the river or milk the goats as often." She picked up her comb.

"More time gazing at your mirror, Queen Milkah?" Noa smirked at her winsome sister.

"You're jealous of the looks I get from men and boys."

Mahlah, always the peacemaker, interrupted. "We recall our first time, don't we, sisters?" Leaning on her cane, she approached Tirzah.

Queen Milkah, her hands folded together, started tapping her two thumbs together and muttered under her breath. "I was two years younger than Tirzah when I had to fetch our daily water and help with all the other daily chores, but as she's the youngest, she's coddled. When is it my turn to—"

Noa sprang in front of her. "Don't spoil it." She spun around. "Tirzah, you've everything you need, especially Mahlah's woven head disc for stability and Hoglah's beautiful painted water jug."

"I wish Ima was here." Tirzah stooped over her prized gift from Hoglah.

Noa prayed she and Mahlah had made the right decision not to share with their younger sisters how ill Ima was. She also asked God to forgive her for the lie she was about to tell.

Noa clasped Tirzah's hands. "Little sister, Ima left us a message for you. She's with Aunt Leora, preparing ointments should the Lord summon our men into battle."

Tirzah stared at her feet and murmured, "Ima has a message for me?"

Noa stepped back, smiling. "Ima said, 'Fathers and sons come to water their livestock, but they also scout potential brides, seeking a strong girl who is pretty and comes from a large family, which they believe means she will bear many children. You deserve only the best. Remember who you are.'"

Hoglah and Tirzah reached out to Milkah and Mahlah to complete a circle. "We are the daughters of Zelophehad, son of Gilead, son of Hepher, son of Makir, son of Manasseh, belonging to the tribe of Manasseh, son of Joseph." At their father's insistence, they emphasized Joseph as a reminder of their remarkable lineage of strength and courage.

Mahlah beamed. "Ima also hinted, 'After all, Moses met his wife at a well.'"

Her sisters giggled, enveloping Tirzah in a warm embrace.

"We will be back." Noa handed the water jug to Tirzah, who deftly positioned it on her head. "Ready?"

The tents of Zelophehad's Manasseh tribe were positioned between the Benjamin and Ephraim clans, making any venture a long walk. But who could complain on this beautiful morning? Moses had decreed that the Lord positioned the twelve tribes into four camps around the sacred Tent of Meeting, spread out like a small city with wide alleyways designed for traffic. Even with God's careful design, maneuvering required watchful steps to avoid tent ropes, large looms, stone firepits, and drying laundry.

They cleared the end of Manasseh's tents and were passing by the Ephraim camp, but Tirzah slowed her gait, then stood several steps behind.

"What's wrong, sister? Is it too heavy for you?"

"Why don't we ever talk about it?"

Noa held her breath. This conversation she wished to avoid, especially on this day. "Because it's too painful to speak of for Mahlah." *And for me.*

"Until today, Mahlah's been withdrawn. And Milkah has been in a foul mood since that day. I worry about both." Tirzah's shoulders sank, momentarily wobbling her water jug.

Like a bandage that's ripped from a sticky wound, her ugly thoughts exposed more fears. Noa hoped it wouldn't lead Mahlah to yet another wrongful match. "I know when even one of us is hurting, we all hurt. Abba will find Mahlah a much more suitable betrothal. But this is your day. It's all about you."

"Milkah thinks so, too?" Tirzah's half smile showed off her rounded cheeks.

"She did come close." Noa winked. "I'll share a little of the surprise that will make not only you, but Mahlah, thrilled. Abba has something special planned for later today, which I hope will bring us together and return joy to our tent. Now, let's proceed with your day, and by doing so, you'll bring some joy back to us."

The trill of female voices made the river's location no secret. From grandmothers to women Tirzah's age, they all waded into the cool flowing water, tucking long tunics into their girdle belts. The younger girls splashed and played games, while the older women lingered to relish a respite from the daily tasks of weaving, tending the animals, washing clothes, and watching over the children.

Noa guided her past the boisterous gatherings. "Do you see the various colored awnings with the tribal flags? Those are here to distinguish our tribes. Do you see our Manasseh tribe emblem?"

"Yes, it's over there. The one with the ripe olives sitting on its branch. Will we go there today?"

"The awnings provide a shady place for the older women to rest." Tirzah would soon discover that younger women lounged under the shade too, but Noa never visited since the accident. The memory had not eased with time. Noa shifted her sister around. "Look. Over there, see the flock of ibises?"

"Oh, they're beautiful." Tirzah sighed.

"Father said they have the same will to survive as us."

They made their way to the water's edge, and Noa lifted the water jug and set it down. She took off her sandals and tucked her tunic into her belt, showing her sister how to do the same. "Tirzah, you will remember this moment. Soak it all in. Welcome to your place within the circle of women."

Tirzah hoisted the water jug and took her last steps to the river.

A young woman ahead of them, her elbow pointed out, gyrated and bumped Tirzah's precious jug. Both sisters sprang to grab it, but it tumbled through their hands, shattering onto the rocks.

"I am sorry. I heard someone calling my name and turned around." The young woman appeared to be the same age as Milkah. "Is this your first time?"

Tears welled in Tirzah's eyes. She croaked, "Yes."

"If you only watched where you were." Noa laid her arm around her sister's shoulder.

"I am Reba, daughter of Korah, tribe of the Levites. I'll restore it to you and bring you a new one. It's my clumsy misstep." Reba nodded.

"No, you don't understand. My sister Hoglah made this special. You won't be able to replace my sister's handiwork. Hoglah will need to make another one. I am only sorry for Tirzah." Noa could feel her face burn fiery red. A clumsy girl had destroyed her plan for a perfect day, but she didn't mean to be so harsh. *And what a mistake to upset a Levite daughter.* Korah's daughter. Heat spread through her body, and her palms turned moist. Would there be consequences?

Tirzah squeaked, "I am Tirzah, the youngest of the five daughters of Zelophehad from the Manasseh tribe. This is my second-oldest sister, Noa. It's kind of you, Reba, to offer a replacement. I admire your design."

Noa's heart swelled with pride at her little sister's poise and instincts.

"Then you should have this one." Reba, without hesitating, positioned it on Tirzah's head disc.

Tirzah wobbled from the weight, raising her hands to steady the heavier jug. "Are you sure?"

Noa bent forward. "Tirzah, this jug is much larger. Should you have a more manageable size?"

Her jug in place, Tirzah eased her shoulders back and stood erect. "No, this one is so lovely, but Reba, I didn't mean for you to give me yours."

"Truly, it would make me feel better, and I hope it will replace this blunder with a better memory." Reba pressed her hands together.

"I'm honored." Tirzah beamed.

A woman's low voice called out. "Reba, what's taking you so long?"

"I must leave. I hope this will work for you, Tirzah." She turned and rushed toward an ample woman dressed in a lavender linen tunic, who scolded her.

"Thank you, Reba," Tirzah called after her, then turned toward Noa and sighed. "I hope she's not in trouble."

"I'm sure once she explains, her mother will understand." Could her little sister handle the extra load? She lifted and lowered the weightier jug. "Don't fill it too much until you get accustomed to it." Even at half full, it would be strenuous.

When Tirzah finished, Noa lifted and steadied it on her head.

"I didn't realize it would be so much heavier." Tirzah swayed but managed her balance after they passed the incline back from the river.

She patted the small of Tirzah's back. "Not only did you get this afternoon's water, but you received a lovely gift. And you made a new friend." She pushed away her unpleasant feelings for Reba and the possible repercussions.

"I know you tried to protect me, and I'm sorry Hoglah's special jug broke, but I wanted to do this for myself."

"And you did, Tirzah. You're standing so tall and straight. You're the epitome of grace. It's your first watering day, and nobody would guess it."

"I couldn't have done it without all your lessons. I especially liked it when you told me I was royalty with a crown on my head and needed to walk with dignity. Thank you for all you've done to prepare me for today."

"You did it all on your own." Her little sister was growing up.

Assir, engrossed in his tenor solo for the evening praise, flinched when he spied his father, Korah, pacing with his hands behind his back. As soon as Assir sang his last note, Father beckoned. He clutched Assir's elbow and hastened him to their family tent. *Why leave the Tent of Meeting so early?* When they entered the tent, Reba, his sister, rushed to remove Father's leather sandals and affix his linen ones. He motioned for Assir to sit on his right and waved Reba to a worn reed mat.

Father tapped his long, spiderlike fingers in front of his mouth. "I understand you've become friendly with one of Zelophehad's daughters. Tirzah, I believe? Your mother mentioned it to me."

Why would Father bother with Reba's new friend?

"Yes, Father. I met her at the riverbank today. I learned little about them, except she's the youngest of five sisters," she stammered and glanced at her oldest brother.

Father leaned forward with enthusiasm, grabbing her chin. "I would like you to befriend her and inform me about the family." His stare bore into her like a snake, ready to strike.

Reba froze, her voice quaking. "What's important about the sisters?"

Assir pitied her. Father took no interest in her friends or much else about her. Since Assir was the oldest son, his father granted him privileges his two brothers didn't enjoy. Assir relished these privileges and made a point of never disappointing him.

Father relaxed his probing eyes and released her chin. "I want to know more about the daughters and how their father raises them. What he teaches them, especially about Moses."

"I'll head out to the river to search for her but will stop by their tent first." She sprang up and struggled to pick up the giant jug.

Assir recalled his mother's anger at Reba for giving away her favorite vessel. Mother forced her to use an unwieldy, larger one for punishment. Poor Reba, scared as a rabbit, would do anything to gain Father's love. *Why does Father want to know what he teaches his daughters about Moses?*

A messenger arrived. "Korah, they requested you at the Tabernacle."

His father cursed under his breath. "Yes, yes. I'm coming. You may leave now, Reba." With a regal flair, he rose from his chair. "Come, we will return to our duties." He swung his hand and caught Assir's shoulder in a hearty smack, calling out, "And so it begins."

Noa poked at the olives on her plate, holding her breath for the celebration to begin of Tirzah's rite of passage and a surprise for Mahlah. Her mother's fever hadn't improved, extinguishing Noa's hopes that she could join them.

After dinner, Abba led Ima back to bed and smoothed out her blanket. Then he turned to the rest of them, his large frame dancing with mischief. "Your ima and I have prepared a special outing for tonight."

Mahlah didn't move. Noa tensed her shoulders, reliving the accident scene she wished she could change. It didn't matter that Mahlah and Abba never spoke of it. Noa's regret never entirely left her body, like a sheep's fleece she wished sheared off. *If only I'd controlled my emotions.* But tonight, Abba's gift could be a new beginning.

Wearing an ear-to-ear grin, she watched Abba grab a bundle hidden under the bed. "Mahlah, I constructed something for you with help from both Simon and Jonathan." Abba's thick fingers fumbled with a long object wrapped in a thin goatskin wrapping. Unfolding it as if he were handling a newborn, he unveiled two sticks of equal size. Flax stuffing under a smooth piece of leather secured by leather ties encircled a curved piece of wood. "Simon suggested they'd be better than your cane. My dear, stand up and let me see if I gauged them right."

"Simon did?" Mahlah rose, placing one hand on Noa's shoulder, squeezing it.

Noa wasn't sure if Mahlah blushed from being the family's center of attention or from hearing Simon's name.

Abba arranged the walking sticks. "These will go under each arm. Place your fingers over the crossbar. Here, advance your good leg and let your other leg follow." Abba hovered over Mahlah.

Noa sensed her sister's hesitation. She willed Mahlah to try. Mahlah inched forward, then another step. Would this work? Her gait had become more arduous lately, a painful slap in Noa's face. Would Mahlah gain her freedom and release Noa's guilt?

A snag in the carpet caught Mahlah's right stick, and she wobbled toward the floor.

Noa dashed behind her. "I have you, don't worry. I'm here. Let's try again." Motioning to her sisters, she ordered, "But first, straighten out this rug."

Tirzah and Hoglah hopped to each side of the large rug and pulled it straight. When Milkah didn't move, Noa glared at her.

Queen Milkah sneered so only Noa could see, then swirled back, giving the brightest smile to her father. "Abba, what a wonderful thing for Mahlah."

Abba stretched out his hands as a lamp, leading Mahlah away from darkness. "Now let's try it. Noa is behind you, and I'm in front of you."

Mahlah edged from one side of the tent to the other. "Abba, this is the best present."

When she steadied herself, she hugged her father, the sticks falling to the ground. "I'll manage so much more now. Thank you, Abba, thank you. Ima, aren't they wonderful? Please express my gratitude to Simon and Jonathan for how much I'll use these."

Noa's mouth tipped, confirming Mahlah's feelings for Simon. She wondered if she looked the same way when Jonathan's name was spoken. Simon was clever, calm, and built like an ox, but he felt inferior because he was adopted. It didn't matter to Mahlah or her. They'd make quite a pair. *Why hasn't Abba thought of this? Why haven't I?*

Abba clapped his hands. "Now, we have an adventure to embark on. Bring a warm shawl with you." The temperature plunged when the relentless desert sun descended. "Kiss your ima. We will miss you, my darling. I'll bring you back five stars." He winked at his daughters. "Mahlah and I will lead the way."

Thrilled for her sister's movement, Noa thrust open the tent flap and waved her forward. She held the flap back for all her sisters as they filed out, and she lightly pinched Milkah's arm. "After you, Queen Milkah."

Noa couldn't wait to see her sisters' reactions.

"This way, daughters." Abba waved his hands.

The brilliant light of fire emanated from the Tabernacle, becoming a beacon for their path. A soft white glow rested over the encampment. God's light burned all night, reassuring the Israelites of His presence.

"Abba, how many tents are there for the Manasseh tribe?" Tirzah asked.

"At the first census over thirty-nine years ago, we counted thirty-two thousand men over twenty. We may be over fifty thousand now. That's why you and your sisters are in high demand for your expert tent-making."

"I think it has something to do with the loom you made us, Abba." Milkah grasped Abba's hand and squeezed it.

Noa opened her mouth to retort, but Mahlah's cough cautioned her to swallow her words.

They passed by some tents with their flaps partially open before the cool desert chill of the evening set in, allowing the group to overhear conversations. Noa noticed Abba's distraction when he heard Korah's name. He stopped to adjust his sandals.

A man's deep voice grumbled, "Did you hear Korah's claim about Moses and Aaron today? He says Moses places himself above our Lord. He claimed what Moses says isn't from God, but from Moses."

"Maybe he's not so wrong. But be careful, this sounds dangerous," another man warned.

Their discussion became muffled.

Noa tapped Abba's arm. "What is it, Abba? What is Korah saying about Moses and—"

"Not now." Abba signaled his daughters forward. "Almost there, ducklings, not far now."

At the edge of the last tents, they arrived at a clearing.

"Here we are." He waved to a large, plush rug the Egyptian chief had insisted he take when the Israelites fled. Earlier, Noa had assisted her father in setting up two stools, a pitcher of water, and six cups.

The daughters spread out on the extravagant rug, exclaiming among themselves. Mahlah maneuvered onto one of the wooden stools, and her father onto the other.

"Daughters, I want you to look. Look up." He gazed at the broad expanse of stars, the half-moon giving an extra glow that surrounded them. "The tall pillar of fire that burns so bright from our Tabernacle is where God deems to live among us, giving us light so we can find our way. And He also graces us with these jewels." The stillness swaddled them as if a blanket smothered the din from the camp, leaving a quiet solitude.

He extended his long, powerful arms and pointed to the heavens. "Your grandmother declared these stars display God's love pouring out to us. They will remind you how God watches over you, even when I'm not around. My daughters, sometimes we need to contemplate why we're living, why we should give thanks to our Lord.

Remember, look up, and you will know. Whatever you're feeling, be it happy, confused, or frustrated, especially with each other"—Abba peered at Noa and Milkah—"you can look up. Day or night. When I do, it calms my soul. I experience God's creation, which changes my feelings to gratitude and hope. It's a lesson I'm grateful for. I ferried you out here to remind you of this."

Tirzah crawled over next to her father's stool. "Abba, why are there so many stars?"

"Ah, Tirzah, I'm glad you asked. When Abraham was quite old, God took him out to see the magnificent firmament and asked him to count all the stars if he was able. Could you do that?"

Tirzah cocked her head. "Is there a number that large?"

"That's right, too large to count. God told Abraham that as numerous as they are, 'so shall your offspring be.' God was blessing him, even though he and his wife, Sarah, were past the age of child-bearing. In a way, it was a test of Abraham's faith. The stars were an encouraging reminder, a sign for Abraham to trust God's promise. And that is part of our lineage, which is why it is so important to learn and tell the stories of our ancestors. I want you to remember that with God, all things are possible."

"Do you have an encouraging sign, Abba?"

Noa smiled at Tirzah's question. Tirzah's moss-green eyes melted her heart. Not yet a grown woman, her willowy frame had begun to fill out. She grew more like their ima with each passing day.

"I have two. The first I learned from my father, who chose an eagle because of its majesty. When he glimpsed one, he felt genuine comfort, as if a message of hope and assurance came from above. Our Lord knew when he needed encouragement. And now, when I spot an eagle, I, too, am comforted. The second one is from your grandfather, Gilead. Tirzah, will you assist me in demonstrating?"

Tirzah sprang up and stood abreast of Abba.

"He would stand beside me just like this and lay his hand on my shoulder, sometimes whispering something important or sometimes just a squeeze. He told me that God is this close to me, encouraging me. That I should always talk to him, to bring him my gratitude, but also my troubles. From time to time, I touch my shoulder to remind myself. When I am not here, I want you to know that God is always with you."

Noa's back stiffened. Why did Abba say he wouldn't be here? Was he not well? Recently, Abba had been walking more slowly. Noa froze at the thought of her parents leaving them too soon. Her mind raced. That would leave Uncle Emet in charge of them and dash all hopes for life in the Promised Land with Jonathan, Emet's grandson. *Oh Lord, please protect both Ima and Abba. Please hear my prayers.*

CHAPTER 2

Noa piled the laundry in the reed basket, grateful that the solitary task would offer her time to think and pray over last night. The entire night was exactly what she had hoped for, finally diminishing the memory of Kenan. Abba's thoughtfulness in creating Mahlah's gift, his recognition of Tirzah's day, and his inspiring words of awe and comfort about God's creation inspired them all. It reminded them of what is essential. She hoped her sisters felt the same and didn't dwell on his words about being gone.

Tirzah slid next to her, causing Noa to halt in mid-step. Cupping her hand over Noa's ear, she whispered, "I need your help."

Sensing her sister's need for privacy, she said, "Tirzah, we're low on zahoor. Can you gather some? The flowers will be good to give Ima strength."

Tirzah snatched a basket and departed with Noa.

"I hoped Abba's surprise would make you happy. What worries you, Tirzah?" She hated to see her baby sister's stooped posture. Sun-streaked brown tresses lined her scrunched-up face.

"Oh, it was. Yes. All of it was. But this morning, well, it's not about me, it's about Reba. I chanced upon her getting the water."

Noa softened at her sister's age of vacillating emotions. "Reba? The Levite area is out of the way."

"I was hoping to express my gratitude for her gift."

"Gift? She broke Hoglah's beautiful jug." Noa scowled.

Tirzah grabbed Noa's sleeve. "Let me tell my story."

"Forgive me. I won't interrupt."

"We stood talking when we heard Reba's name. She put her finger to her lips for me to hush. Three young women were mocking Reba."

Noa stopped abruptly, venting a large sigh. "Oh, Tirzah, that is so painful. I don't linger by the tribal women's awnings at the water because of the gossip and unkindness. I hope you both ignored it and left." Noa flushed red at the memory of the Manasseh girls teasing Mahlah.

"That's just it. I marched around to stop them. But ..."

She waved Tirzah to go on. She envisioned Tirzah's strong little body, head erect, striding to defend her new friend. "But?"

"Reba stopped me. She *wanted* to hear it."

"What did they say?"

"They don't like her, mocking how she wears her headdress, exaggerating her actions as if she's nervous and desperate for friends. One declared, 'The only reason I pretend to be friends is because of her handsome brothers, to whom I wouldn't mind being betrothed. The only drawback is her as a sister-in-law.'"

"How awful. What happened next?"

"My anger consumed me. Reba begged me to pour my water into her jug so she could leave without seeing them. She said, 'Do nothing, please. I would rather they don't know I heard them.' So, I did nothing, and I feel I should have. What would you have done?"

"You're a sincere friend, Tirzah. We can't know Reba's mind, but you did what she asked. Perhaps we can all try to befriend her. We may not have the prestige of a Levite father or handsome brothers, but we've got quite a reputation because of Abba's workshop and our tent weaving." Noa lifted her shoulders. "And we are the heirs of Jacob, the daughters of Zelophehad. We can quiet those Levite girls, and they'll view Reba differently."

"I knew you'd have a solution." Tirzah reached up and kissed her sister on the cheek. "I can always count on you." She lingered, shifting on her feet. "Noa, there's one more thing ..."

"Something else?"

"It's about Milkah. Will you promise that you won't get mad?"

"I'll try not to. But what could be so bad?"

"She doesn't want Mahlah to go out of our tent with her walking sticks. She complains it will bring more attention to her limitations for heavy tasks." Tirzah looked away. "And … and …"

"And?" Noa sensed what was coming.

"She worries about how Mahlah will ever get married. Three of Milkah's friends are already planning their weddings, and one has a baby on the way."

"Did she say this to Mahlah?" Noa gritted her teeth.

"No, she was talking to Hoglah, and I overheard it."

"What did Hoglah do?"

"She laughed and told her to worry more about her mirror and, like you said, to believe Abba will soon find the right betrothal for Mahlah. She suggested that it would be Simon because he made the sticks, and for you, Jonathan. I think Hoglah was clever. She asked Milkah to help Abba find a suitable intended for her. Immediately, Milkah started talking about potential young men from her girlfriends' brothers."

Noa twirled Tirzah twice, both chuckling. "She certainly was, and since Hoglah counseled such good advice, I'll keep quiet. But we must watch to make sure she doesn't speak of this to Mahlah." Noa cradled Tirzah's hands. "It was good you told me, though." She winked. "Now you must find some zahoor berries for Ima."

As Noa ambled to the water, her laundry bundle somehow felt lighter. Tirzah was wise beyond her young soul. *I wish you had been born in my place, and I could've learned maturity from you.* If only she could relive a similar moment with Tirzah's poise.

Like a nightmare, she recalled the entire scene. A spring day just like today, but in a different campsite full of imposing date trees. The daily water errand had become arduous because of the river's location, so she and Mahlah tackled it together. Laughing about a story Abba told, the trees had hidden them and, just like Reba, they stopped when they heard a few Manasseh girls laughing about Mahlah's name.

"Who would want a name like Mahlah? Why would her parents call her 'weak' or 'sick'?"

"Doesn't it mean 'fat'?" They laughed.

Yet another quipped, "'Let me introduce you to my wife, ... ah ... ah, Mahlah.' What man would dare say that?"

Noa's jaw tensed. Her headdress fell away as she bolted into the middle of the girls' circle, swirling around several times with her water jug and shouting, "Stop! Stop!"

Mahlah chased after her, pleading and trying to halt Noa's actions. As she did, Noa's jug careened into Mahlah, who collapsed backward, slamming onto a sharp boulder that injured her hip. Noa sank to her knees. "No, Mahlah! No!" The Manasseh girls scattered.

Noa gave her head a quick shake, trying to forget that day. Would this memory ever leave her? She heard a gentle voice within her. *Look up, and you will know*. She inhaled and beheld the blueness of the sky, the fluffy cloud shapes providing cover from the searing sun. *Thank You, Lord, for reminding me of Your presence. Forgive me and lay Your healing touch on Mahlah.*

She laid aside her brooding over the past to focus on Abba's anxiousness to make good marriages for them. Without marriage, they would not have inherited land. *Why is that?* What if he couldn't find the proper suitor who would accept and love Mahlah as she was? Would Queen Milkah become more vocal about having three sisters marry before it's her turn? *Lord, please help Abba in his search for someone who will appreciate my sister Mahlah.* Noa reached the river, where the bedlam of gossip and cackling surrounded her. She shrugged, trying to ignore the tidbits of other people's lives she heard. Her worries were enough for today.

The day after the Sabbath was important for the Levites to restore the sacred elements. Assir hurried to answer Father's summons to meet at their family tent when no one was there. It was a quick walk, since God honored the Levite tribe by designating them to live adjacent to the sacred Tent of Meeting. *What is consuming Father? And why keep a secret from my younger brothers?*

Assir, proud of the tall physique he'd inherited from his father, still felt dwarfed by his father's towering height. When he entered the tent, he saw Father pacing at the far corner. Father jerked his hand toward himself, gesturing for Assir to join him. He offered neither a greeting nor a seat.

"Make an acquaintance with one of Zelophehad's daughters. I believe her name is Milkah. Be cautious. We must stay within the boundaries of propriety, so you must arrange to meet her by coincidence. I must be certain of her father's stance on Moses and know if we can persuade him to see things my way. I doubt your sister will bring any light to my quest."

"Yes, Father, I understand. Why Milkah?" He wouldn't mind, as it was rumored she was the fairest of the sisters. But what did it mean to see things Father's way?

With a mocking smile, he responded, "Assir, she's young and won't be aware of your true purpose. Don't lose your head, and don't get any notions of marriage. That will not happen."

"Of course, Father. What makes you think Zelophehad will want to join you?" Father spent most of his time with the tribal leaders and their inner circle, but why Zelophehad, a carpenter?

"It will be clear when I point to Moses's poor leadership and how I command the respect of the people. From what I understand, his workshop is respected by many of the tribes, and he can be an influence." His father tapped his hand over his heart. "Then, instead of Aaron, they will anoint me as high priest with all the honors."

Cautious with his question to avoid igniting his father's temper, Assir ventured, "So that I'm certain, you desire to know about

Zelophehad's opinion of Moses?" Recently his father's efforts had grown, with his gatherings composed of his devotees and others curious about his speeches—events his father didn't invite Moses to attend.

"Does Zelophehad realize what Moses is doing? He creates edicts that are not from God because his ambition is to govern over us. He crowned himself and his brother supreme rulers, even perverting our looks. Your mother harped about our bodies needing to be shaved. She cried about our adulterated appearance and complained that I looked like an Egyptian servant, not the man she knows." Father paced back and forth, flailing his hands.

"This distinguished us as the men God appointed in the Levite initiation. Father, all the Levites had to do this, including Moses's brother, Aaron." *How could Father interpret it this way?*

His father spat as he snarled. "Yes, that is how cunning Moses is, subjugating his own brother with such pretentiousness. I should have been selected due to my heritage. Aaron's son, Eleazar, is half my age, yet Moses appointed him chief leader over the Levites. Aaron dons the priceless robes and bejeweled breastplate representing the twelve tribes, his little bells tinkling at the bottom edge of his tunic. I should wear it, not Aaron!"

Sweat dripped on Assir's forehead as he loudly coughed, hoping his father would lower his voice. What if other Levites heard this? What if Aaron heard it? The previous evening, his mother had not only concurred with Father but also goaded him with her nagging, blaming Moses for all the rulings she denied were coming from God.

Father tapped Assir on the shoulder, steering him to the tent opening. "I'll rejoin the tribal leaders and continue to plant seeds about Moses and his domination. Son, there's urgency to my plan. Moses portends that God will forbid anyone age twenty or older at the first census from entering the Promised Land. I should enter the Promised Land. I should hold the holy staff and perform the miracles, entering the Holy of Holies."

Assir prayed his father would come to his senses. Instead, his heart seemed to harden. What would come of this? Assir assured his father to avoid angering him. "I will seek Milkah."

"Shalom, Noa." Reba strained under the weight of her jug while keeping her balance and her jug steady on her head.

"Greetings, Reba." Noa slowed so the girl could catch up.

"I was hoping to meet you. I apologize again for breaking Tirzah's new jug and hope you've found a place in your heart to forgive me."

"Yes, Reba, you gifted Tirzah a special jug. Do you need help to take that down?" Noa softened her tone, remembering Tirzah's story.

Reba nodded.

Noa lowered her basket of clothes and stretched over for Reba's water jug. "My, even empty, it's a large jug to manage."

Reba's headpiece slid, her long, straight hair hanging in tangles. She stretched her neck from side to side. "Thank you. My mother insists I use it."

"Was the jug you gave Tirzah her favorite?"

She dropped her chin further. "Yes. We own several, but she insists I carry this." Like a light went on, she changed the subject. "Is Tirzah with you today?"

"No, it's my day."

Reba's shoulders dropped. "Oh, would you say I asked about her?"

Noa couldn't imagine being punished like this by her parents. Poor Reba, on top of rejection from her so-called friends. "Do you want to take a rest? I know of a lovely place." They picked up their burdens, and when they arrived at the clearing, Noa stopped. "Here we are, away from the hens. My father led us here last night to teach us about God's stars."

Reba caught her breath. "You're fortunate to have such a thoughtful father. My father plans nothing for me, only for my brothers."

Noa laid out her shawl with enough room for both of them. "Your father is an important man with formidable Levite duties." God set all Levite males apart instead of making priests of all the firstborn sons from every tribe. She knew from their travels that Korah and his sons transported the sacred Ark of the Covenant on their shoulders.

"My father is part of the Kohathites clan. He relishes his many responsibilities, as well as those of my brothers. He's been very busy with meetings. He forbids me from being in our tent when the tribal leaders come. One night, when the temperature dropped, I entered as quietly as I could, and he yelled at me to leave. Assir, my brother, threw me a wrap, and I waited another hour outside."

"Oh, Reba, I'm sorry. That must have been hard. Did your father allow you to stay any time?"

"Yes, but he says these meetings aren't to be disturbed." Reba's pale face turned crimson. "I've said too much. He wouldn't like me talking about what he does. If I were a son, it would be different, but who would do all the daily chores? My mother spends most of her time in prayer, or so she says." Reba raised her shoulders and twisted a corner of her mouth. "But with four sisters, it must be easier to divide the work. Would you share with me what your sisters are like? Maybe I can dream of having daughters someday."

Her heart went out to this single daughter whose father sounded so cruel. And she wondered ... What was Korah hiding that he made his only daughter stand in the cool night air? "We certainly differ from one another. It's a relief, though, as each of us contributes. It must be quite a burden for you. Do your brothers help at all?" It now made sense why Reba appeared so thin and haggard.

"They don't have time because of their roles at the Tabernacle. My oldest brother, Assir, is one of the singers. My other brothers will join him when they're older. For now, they are learning from the Levite elders."

"That leaves you with a notable amount of responsibility." Noa's compassion stirred.

Reba rubbed her calloused hands. "My mother says it will make me a better wife. What she means is that because I didn't inherit the charm or looks of my brothers, I must learn to run a household. From my family's complaints, I'm not sure I do that well."

"You know the story of Joseph and his brothers?"

Reba squeaked. "Yes."

"The most important lesson of that story is God's presence in our lives. 'You intended to harm me, but God intended it for good.' Don't give up hope for what God has planned for you."

"It's a beautiful story to remind me."

Noa wedged closer as if sharing a secret. "About my sisters. Mahlah is the oldest. She's twenty-one and is an amazing story of resilience. She was born too early, and Abba worried he might lose both my ima and Mahlah, like his first wife and only son."

"I'm sorry to hear your father lost them both. That must've been hard on him."

"It was. He grieved for ten years. Only when he met my ima did he start living again." Noa surprised herself with how comfortable she felt around Reba.

"Your father is also an important man. Everyone knows of his workshop with his abilities to create tools, his sharing of his trade secrets and skills."

"Most kind of you to share." Warmth spread throughout Noa's chest.

"What happened with Mahlah?"

"My parents beseeched Moses and the priests to pray, hired extra midwives, and fasted. It was a miracle she survived. She's quiet and so wise and loves listening to Abba, especially about our lineage. Mahlah's gait prevents her from doing the heavy chores, but she's an amazing weaver."

"Why did your parents name her Mahlah?"

Noa put her hand behind her neck and looked toward the horizon. Her sister had not only her name to contend with but also the limp Noa had caused. "It may seem strange, Mahlah meaning *sickness*. My ima acknowledged gratitude for her firstborn and, even when an illness passed through the community, she thanked God for Mahlah's survival."

"Your mother sounds devoted to our Lord."

"She is." *I pray her faith will guide her now through her illness.*

"You're the next sister in age?"

"Yes. I'm like my father in temperament. He's serious, organized, and loves teaching. My sisters would say I'm demanding, perhaps bossy. I hope my actions show my devotion to our family." Noa avoided revealing her tendency to be impulsive.

"Now, my next sister, Hoglah. She loves to compose songs, plays the harp, and sings like what an angel might sound like. But Abba worries she isn't as skillful with running a household."

As soon as Noa stopped speaking, Reba leaned closer. "That brings us to your next sister." Reba's excited attention showed which sister she was most interested in.

"Now, Milkah, if it were up to her, we'd be her servants arranging her hair all day."

They both laughed.

"Milkah means *queen*, and from the moment of her birth, she has made it clear she is special. She complained about wearing tunics worn by Mahlah or me and begged Mahlah to embroider a design so it appeared new."

Reba shrugged. "I receive accusations about my desire to be queen, but never am I indulged. My brothers outshine me. I never seem to please either my mother or father. What about Tirzah?"

"I'm sure your family appreciates you, but perhaps they forget to convey it." Noa took on an even softer tone. "Now, Tirzah. Her name means *she's my delight*. Ima knew Abba's dire hope for at least one son.

She wanted him to see Tirzah as a gift from God. Tirzah feels she's not a gift because she's a daughter—as if she could change that."

"Such a blessing from your mother. My mother named me Reba, meaning *fourth born*, nothing so pretty as 'she is my delight.'" Reba slumped. "Despite your differences with Queen Milkah, it sounds like you all work together. That's something to treasure." Reba rose slowly. "I must be on my way, as I don't wear a queen's crown in my family. I appreciate that you didn't once ask me about getting to know my brothers in hopes of an introduction. Seems that's all the interest I get from supposed girlfriends."

"Shalom, Reba. Remember Joseph." Noa sighed as the girl retreated. She wouldn't be asking for information about Reba's brothers. Her heart, long ago, was given to Jonathan, Uncle Emet's grandson. She watched Reba wobble from side to side, balancing the heavy load. She thanked God for her parents and a reminder of all her blessings, even with a sister like Queen Milkah.

Reba stumbled into her family's tent. Perspiration ran down her face and arms.

"Not used to it yet?" Assir hauled the massive water jug off her head. Mother could be harsh in her punishments.

Reba frowned, rubbing the small of her back. Released from her burden, she scurried around the large tent like a caged animal. "Is Father with you? I've much to offer him."

She must've met Tirzah. "Careful, our neighbors can hear you clear across to the Tabernacle. What's so exciting? Why not enlighten me, little sister?"

"I'm waiting for Father." Reba reached for a brush to detangle her hair. As if frustrated with the slight improvement, she donned a clean headscarf.

"Perhaps you should practice with me. I can guide you about him." Assir led her to a special Egyptian cushion Father had received from his overseer while in Egypt.

"Only if you promise to let me relate the entire story. Promise?"

He laid his hand over his heart. "I wouldn't dream of taking it away from you."

"I learned about Zelophehad's daughters by describing some of my sad circumstances. I didn't lie. I just made some of it up. Some, not all."

"From who?" Assir reclined back, knowing this was going to take some time.

Reba raised her voice as if he were deaf. "Noa. She's Zelophehad's second daughter. I suspect she doesn't open up often as she stays by herself, not mingling with the other Manasseh girls."

"Maybe you'd better get your best parts in before approaching Father. He may not be interested in every detail."

"They're all accomplished in something: Mahlah for weaving, Noa for overseeing her sisters. She says she's most like her father. Hoglah for her personality and storytelling. Or was it singing? Tirzah for her innocence. Milkah, though, stands out."

Father would've dismissed her by now and wondered why Assir hadn't prepared her better. Patience. *How can I help her? What nugget can come of all of this?*

"Milkah thinks she's a queen with her feminine charms and her ravishing hair. She saunters with gentle grace as if she were an Egyptian princess. I noticed each time she fetches water, she wears a new decoration on her sandals, or an embroidered mantle, or a beaded belt."

He read the envy from Reba's description. "Little sister, we must refine what you report to Father."

Reba wrinkled her brow. "That wasn't good? What does Father deem important? It may help if I understand what he wants?"

Assir also wondered what Father would do with this knowledge about Zelophehad. From the way Father acted, he seemed consumed. *This is a dangerous path he is pursuing.* A sour taste rumbled up from his throat. “As I stated, he’ll be back soon. You should wait so I can help you prepare.”

CHAPTER 3

Noa relished Friday nights when Abba challenged her and her sisters to memorize a commandment and explain it with a personal story. She offered to prepare her younger sisters, and all but Milkah appreciated the practice sessions. Tonight, Milkah's turn was the ninth commandment. Would Milkah bring up the incident at the river earlier in the week? Tirzah had finally admitted that Milkah was one of the hecklers that she and Reba overheard.

Tirzah whispered to Noa. "I know Milkah's favorite is 'Remember the Sabbath day and keep it holy,' so she doesn't have to do any chores."

Abba shot both of them a look and then began as he always did. "Knowing the commandments isn't about memorizing the words, but about what the commandments mean and how we live our lives. You also learn from one another how to defend your point of view."

"It may aid you with your husbands someday." Ima's smile was like an upturned sliver of a bright moon.

"Yes, and that too." Abba covered his wife's hand. "Milkah, let's begin."

Milkah had brushed her hair one hundred times and dressed in her finest tunic. Her graceful movements, even when standing still, provoked Noa. *Why do I react this way?* She shifted her feet, vowing to forget her pettiness, and focused on being receptive.

Milkah positioned herself at the end of the table in front of Abba and Ima. She looked down and to the side, acting demure, then met her parents' gaze. "The ninth commandment is 'Thou shalt not bear false witness against your neighbor.'"

"What does this commandment mean to you, Milkah?" Ima inquired. Despite her illness, Ima had insisted on participating. Noa had helped her to the table, holding her waist to steady her.

"It means we should say nothing dishonest about another person or gossip behind someone's back," Milkah said.

"Does that include your sister's friends?" Noa dipped her chin, her brows raised, and focused on Milkah.

"Of course it does." Milkah spread her palms out to her sides.

"Noa, do you have something to share with your parents and sisters?" Abba's mouth twisted.

Why did she become so perturbed? Noa fought to gain perspective and be neutral. "It's a good commandment for Milkah to explain."

"Why is that? You're so righteous, sister."

Noa didn't hesitate. "What happened at the river three days ago?"

Milkah's face blushed. "I said nothing wrong."

"Be honest. What about Reba?" Noa didn't reveal she was Korah's daughter, knowing it would add more tension. *I only want her to see the wrongs of her actions.*

"Abba, Ima, Noa is exaggerating." Milkah rose on her toes.

Ima rubbed her lips with her forefinger and studied both girls. "Daughters, this commandment is about awareness of how we're connected. And if we harm someone, we harm ourselves."

"Your ima is right. We have two concerns here. Milkah, did you or did you not say something hurtful about Reba?" Abba angled his head toward her.

"I didn't mean it to be. At least that's not what I intended."

Noa opened her mouth.

Queen Milkah cut her off, "I … I …"

"If Reba or her mother were to hear what you said, would it harm her?" Her mother spoke in a low tone to Milkah.

Milkah stood erect with her fists clenched. "I don't know. Perhaps. I felt my friends expected me to say something."

Ima tapped the place next to her for her to sit. Milkah plodded over. "All of you will experience this situation. You're visiting with friends. Then, somehow, your conversation starts about someone not in the vicinity. Here's your chance to show who you are."

Abba nodded to their mother. "Do you listen or not? Add to it? Do you keep silent because you don't want anyone to think less of you? Or do you find the courage to defend that person?"

Milkah stared at her hands.

He continued. "What you believe shows through your words and actions. We must learn from our mistakes and take responsibility for them. Milkah, I want you to ponder your actions." Then Abba beckoned to Noa. "Let's go outside."

Noa trudged behind him. *Milkah is gloating because I'm about to get a lecture.*

When they arrived at a clearing of tents, he stopped. His shoulders slumped, and he let out a quiet moan.

Noa emulated her father's posture—another disappointment to her parents for her judgment and impertinence. *Will I ever learn?*

"Noa, you know how young girls can be. You're older than Milkah and should set an example."

"Yes, Abba, which is why I mentioned it. Reba needs friends, not more ridicule. I may have overreacted, but I thought you would want me to stand up for Reba."

Her father pulled at the bridge of his nose. "You're right. You're right, but you're wrong. Do you understand? You created a wedge between you and your sister by showing her faults to us. What will happen when your mother and I aren't here? Do you listen and learn from any of your sisters or anyone besides me and your mother? And what makes you listen?"

Noa hated this. She'd rather be yelled at, even punished. Her abba always made her see something she never recognized. "I listen to Mahlah for her keen observation and gentleness. Tirzah, I listen to her innocence. Hoglah, her joy of life."

"But not Milkah. So why would your sister ever listen to you?" Abba let his last question hang for a moment before continuing. "You should reflect on it. Remember when Joseph reunited with his brothers? He tested them. You can't blame him for being skeptical or angry, but God put love and forgiveness into his heart. Your sister is a woman-child trying to grow up. It may even surprise you how much she admires you. You have a tremendous influence on your sisters. I need you to use this for their good." Abba shuffled a few feet farther. "Now come, let's gaze up at this sky tonight.

"God wishes us to absorb the sacredness of this place, where all is stripped away, leaving only its essence. I am in awe of the beauty of the stars. Is anything more beautiful than our celestial sky? Watching the heavens is as sacred as our observance time and, if I admit it, even more meaningful. Do you sense our Lord all around us? I hope you do."

Her father leaned over and kissed her forehead. "Think about your judgment, what is right and wrong. Sometimes the right thing is what you did tonight, to bring out in the open what has transpired, and sometimes a better way would be to bring your sister aside, mentor her, and show by your actions proper judgment."

Abba let out a wet cough and leaned heavily on her for a moment as she edged closer to him. Her heart ached at his loving words. *Please, Lord, don't take him away.*

Assir arranged the seating for his father and three brothers inside their oversized, luxurious tent—a reward from Pharaoh's overseer for Father's spying on the Hebrew slaves. Ready to hold court, his father perched on the throne-like leather chair and scrutinized his daughter, who stood before him.

"Reba, did you meet with your little friend today?" His voice struck a note between a sneer and a snarl. "Assir, what's her name? Zelophehad's youngest daughter?"

"Tirzah, I believe." Assir knew his father to be strict and prone to anger, but lately, he seemed to be a different person. He'd never heard this tone from him.

Assir had run a couple of practice sessions with Reba, which revealed she possessed little insight into Zelophehad, so this would be over quickly. He hoped Father would not be harsh with her.

"What have you learned?" He laid down his scroll and motioned for her to sit at his feet.

Reba tugged her tunic in place, kneeled, and peeked at Assir, then Father. She resembled a lamb about to be sacrificed.

When Reba finished, Father massaged his temples. "Go visit your aunt. I wish to confer with your brothers." He flung his hand, dismissing her.

Reba's shoulders curled forward. She took one last look at Assir and lumbered out.

He surveyed each of his sons. "Certainly, you've more to share than your sister. Let's begin with Zelophehad. I've heard enough about his daughters."

Assir spoke first, knowing his father expected no less. "At a young age, he became a foreman in Egypt, forged a good relationship with his overseer, and received extra rations for himself and his men."

Elkanah, his middle brother, interjected, "Not just an overseer. He fixed the chariot of Pharaoh's chief temple builder when the wheel broke loose on an inspection tour. Because he did it so quickly, he received a permanent assignment mending chariots and equipment. He convinced the chief temple builder that he required more slaves to keep pace with the work. He amassed over fifty Israelites in the workshop, where there were no whips."

Assir had shared this information with his brother, but due to Father's mercurial moods, he couldn't blame him for competing to be in his good graces. "As I was saying, he's clever in figuring things out and has the art of persuasion. It wasn't easy to convince an Egyptian officer."

Grimacing, his father seemed to dismiss this information. "What else? I've heard all this, which is why I'm targeting him."

Elkanah dove in. "He's well known for his workshop, big enough to hold forty men, along with his two younger cousins, Emet and Abel. Zelophehad mentors apprentices from all tribes, gaining a favorable reputation with leaders. I overheard a Judah leader say, 'Because of his training, my men will possess the skills to honor our new land.'"

"Interesting. He maintains respect with both the leaders and the men." Father stroked his bare chin.

Abiasaph, the youngest brother, shifted on his reed mat. "There's a rumor that Emet fell out competing for Zelophehad's first wife. And as overseer of the workshop, Zelophehad also assigned Emet the grueling, foul task of leather making. Lastly, Emet strongly disapproves of the way he is raising his daughters."

"He's right in his assessment. Why aren't most of them married?" He nodded to his son to continue.

Abiasaph straightened, glowing from his father's desire for more. "He insists on marrying his eldest daughter, as is our custom, but she was injured in an accident that limits her ability to walk. She was to marry an older man, Kenan, but he died the day of the wedding. It was challenging before, but now that seems to deter any prospective husband from showing interest. I also learned his first wife died giving birth to a son. He took the loss badly and waited some years before marrying again. His current wife, Jeska, isn't well."

Father softly drummed his fingers together. "Your information is insightful. Zelophehad is someone we must influence, and you must convince him to cooperate with me. He will extend my reach with the other tribes to challenge Moses."

Outside their tent, someone said, "Shalom, dear one." Assir sprang up. *Who is spying on us, and what have they heard of this dangerous discussion?* He flung open the tent cover and saw Reba as she scurried away. "It's only a child playing."

CHAPTER 4

Noa sat outside the family tent, out of the sun under a flap, staring at her completed reed mat. She longed to be in the workshop, continuing her secret lessons with Jonathan, but the strain between Emet and Abba weakened him. She hoped that in the Promised Land, she would not be under her uncle's constraints concerning what a woman was allowed to do. Her dream included being at Jonathan's side, building things together. He always encouraged her and applauded her efforts.

Abba boasted about her and her sisters' craftsmanship, which drove up their bride-price. If only that were enough for Uncle Emet to consider a betrothal of her to Jonathan. A shadow covered her, disrupting her thoughts and causing her to peer up toward the sun. Jonathan's arrival caused her stomach to flip. She blushed, thinking he could read her thoughts. She hadn't seen him since Uncle Emet discovered and forbade any more teaching lessons in the workshop.

"Shalom, Noa." Jonathan knelt in front of her.

"Shalom, Jonathan, it's been a while. Good to see you." She tucked wisps of hair under her headscarf. She'd known Jonathan, who was four years older than her, for her entire life.

"I wish it had turned out differently with my Grandfather Emet."

"I'll always be thankful for all you taught me and that Abba trusted you with my desire to learn. The stool and the walking sticks you and Simon finished for Mahlah turned out so well."

"You helped make them, too." Jonathan seemed to find the ground more interesting to view. Finally, he looked at her. "What are you working on?"

"We don't have any orders for new tents or repairs, so I assigned each of my sisters tasks to allow Ima some quiet rest. Mine is this seating mat. It isn't the best I've made, but I want to finish it and seek new tent orders."

"It seems functional." Jonathan examined it, brushing Noa's fingers, which deepened the heat over her body. "And sturdy, too. I will ask in the workshop if anyone has a tent to repair."

She nodded her thanks, though she wondered if Jonathan's asking at the workshop would irritate her uncle. When she looked up, his black curly hair reflected the sun, his hazel eyes exuding warmth. *Why keep dreaming about a future with Jonathan? Uncle Emet will never allow it because he thinks I'm so outspoken.* Something squeezed tight around her heart.

Milkah appeared with her headscarf nestled around her neck, allowing her luxuriant hair to flow down her back. The top part of her tunic was loose fitting, and a scent of lavender wafted toward them.

"Shalom," breathed Milkah. She bent low before him, setting down her water jug, and flipped the sides of her silky brown mane. "How good to see you, Jonathan. Is that a new leather mantle you're wearing?"

"Shalom, Milkah. On your way to fetch water?"

Jonathan's tone was throaty—more resounding than before. *Hmm. Did Milkah inspire that?* Noa hadn't noticed his mantle fitting snugly around his waist, but could see why Milkah had spotted how it accented his athletic shape.

"It's my task today. Want to escort me, Jonathan?"

Milkah's coyness grated on Noa's ears.

"I watered my animals earlier. And from what I hear, you women have quite an exchange there."

"Maybe some other time, then." Milkah arranged her golden-colored headscarf over her hair. Bending to grasp her jug, her drooping tunic revealed her curvaceous chest. She sauntered away, her ankle bracelet tinkling.

A sharp pang struck Noa—one she hadn't experienced before. Was there a spark there? Did Jonathan reciprocate it? Could Noa be jealous? *And isn't that my headscarf?*

She scooped up her mat, darted toward the tent, and muttered, "I've other chores to do. Shalom, Jonathan."

As she lowered the flap, she heard him say, "What did I do?"

Mahlah set aside her weaving as Noa entered the tent. "I heard Jonathan. He usually makes you happy, but your face doesn't say so. It's bright red."

"Milkah pushes me to where my blood steams like a boiling pot." Noa kept her voice low as she tossed the seating mat onto the table, glad to see only Mahlah. The curtain separating Ima's and Abba's bed was lowered. Ima must be sleeping. Seeing Queen Milkah and Jonathan had stung more than she wanted.

"That makes me even madder because I can't hide how Milkah affects me. I'm reduced to acting like a child. Why do I let her control my feelings? She knows I'm close to Jonathan, yet she purposely flirts with him. The brazen way she dipped so he could view her ... her flawless bosoms." She bent down, her eyes cast to one side, demonstrating.

"Noa." Mahlah pointed to a seat next to her. "Could you be exaggerating a little?"

"When I saw Milkah be so ... so ... She shouldn't act that way."

"Perhaps she didn't know it was so revealing. It's such a hot day. She wore one of my old tunics, which was a little large on her."

"So, for once, Milkah deigned to wear an old one without complaint. She knew exactly what she was doing."

"She knows she affects you, which is why she continues. You may be surprised that she envies you and wants your attention. You dote on Tirzah, embrace Hoglah's singing, and are always there for me.

Perhaps Milkah's teasing is to get some of your light. Why don't you pray about it and her? And to be fair, Noa, you haven't shared your feelings for Jonathan with her."

Noa chewed the tip of her thumb. Mahlah always highlighted the honorable thing, simple and fitting. Noa's behavior broke her obedience to God and her love of family. Why couldn't she control these emotions?

"You're a passionate person. It can be a blessing because you care, and it shows in your actions, but taking it too far can become a hindrance."

"Hindrance? What are you saying?" Noa valued Mahlah's opinion as much as their father's.

"You regard others' behavior from your point of view, and sometimes it's hard for you to consider others' ways."

"How can I perceive Queen Milkah's actions any differently?"

"And yours, sister?"

She spoke so softly that Noa strained to hear. If it were anyone else but Mahlah, she would've quipped back, "Do you chastise Milkah, too?" But she corralled her tongue, and as hard as it was to hear her words, she knew her sister's guidance might be true.

Assir set out for the river, passing several young women who slowed their pace to catch a glimpse of him. Reba often relayed the latest gossip about his handsome features and impressive physique. She said they spoke incessantly about how he carried himself with such dignity in his flowing robes, his upright posture prompting them to check their own so he might notice. He absently greeted many as he strode by, searching for Milkah. He recognized an opportunity when an older woman stopped to rest. "Can I help you?"

The old woman with gnarled hands laughed. "Oh, son, sometimes I need a moment to catch my breath."

Assir bent down. "A good thing for all of us. I'm seeking a daughter of Zelophehad. Her name is Milkah. Any chance you've seen her at the river?"

The old woman winked. "You're fortunate, as I am from the Manasseh tribe. Many young men come to gaze on her." She tittered with laughter, raising interest from those passing by.

He composed his most charming smile. "I'm blessed then to meet you, dear woman, as I don't know her. My mother has something for Jeska, Milkah's mother."

"Of course she does." The old woman snorted. "She's by the river, wearing a golden headscarf that sets off her crown of radiant hair. She's clothed in a light blue tunic with a black leather belt and a silver bracelet on her ankle. Something to make herself stand out. It will be hard for you to miss her."

"Thank you for your thorough description. My mother will appreciate it."

"Yes, that's what many mothers say." Another boisterous chortle came forth as Assir trotted away.

He hadn't anticipated how challenging it might be to find her among hundreds of women at the river. Their high-pitched chatter pained his ears. He positioned himself far enough away with a clear view and finally spotted Milkah amid the throng of women. Her headscarf shone like the sun at midday. It would be best to intercept her on the way back to her family's tent, so he calculated the path she would most likely trek.

Heading toward the river as if on an errand, he slowed his approach and greeted Milkah. He now understood why the old woman teased him. She was breathtaking. All he'd heard about her was true. The old woman's words played in his head. It'd be hard not to notice her lithe frame, a tight belt about her waist, and the silky hair flowing down her back from her headscarf.

Milkah appeared amused. She glanced up at him. "Sir, you stand between me and my destination, or perhaps you wish to assist me with my heavy burden?"

He caught himself staring at her. "Yes, may I?"

She dipped her chin, and although he guessed she could easily lower the water from her shoulder, he reached out, placing it on the ground. As they were in clear sight of the camp on a common walkway, nothing amiss would be construed. "My name is Assir. I am the oldest son of Korah from the Levite tribe."

"My name is Milkah. I am one of five daughters of Zelophehad of the Manasseh tribe." She toyed with her graceful, long tresses. "What brings you to the river today? Surely not to draw water?" Milkah shifted her hip to the side, her hand resting on it.

"I'm seeking my sister, Reba. Do you know her?" Overwhelmed by her sensuous pose, he found it hard to concentrate.

"I've made her acquaintance. She befriended my little sister, Tirzah."

"I seem to recall her mentioning it."

"Was it something important? After all, men usually come to water their animals."

She disarmed him with her stance, her voice ... *Focus on Father's mission*. "It's not important. Five sisters—that must be challenging."

"It can be." Milkah's rose-colored lips pursed.

"Including your mother, six lovely females surround your father. He's rich in treasures."

"We're very grateful. My father is a special man, and when I marry, I hope my intended will love me like my abba loves my ima. Theirs is a match of souls."

"That's a blessing. My parents are more partners than lovebirds."

"I'm sure your father appreciates the loyalty and support for his important role. I trust my parents' relationship won't spoil me for what my future holds."

With beauty like hers, what man wouldn't desire to grant her everything? "I would imagine finding five worthy suitors is a formidable task for your father."

"Hmm." Milkah huffed. "My sister Mahlah must marry first, and—"

"I've been searching everywhere for you, Milkah." A young girl, about thirteen, strained, carrying a large jug. "Noa wants to know why you're not back yet. She sent me for water as Ima needs it."

"This is my fault." Assir shifted to view the young girl. "I've kept you from your duties. Please forgive me."

"This is my sister Tirzah. Tirzah, this is Assir, Korah's son and Reba's brother."

Tirzah shifted her feet from side to side. "Please tell Reba I'll see her tomorrow."

"Come, Tirzah, let's go quickly."

As they left, he overheard Milkah plead, "We don't need to inform Noa of Assir. Let's keep it a secret."

Assir watched them until they were out of sight. He hadn't thought about how easy it would be to talk to her. Perhaps there was more to admire than her enticing appearance.

CHAPTER 5

Noa's stomach growled, her body empty, but she hadn't felt like eating this morning. Thoughts rolled in like a dense fog. Did Milkah have feelings for Jonathan? *When Milkah caught his eye the other day, why did I feel threatened?? I need to find Abba and talk.*

She headed to the workshop and paused at the entrance, inhaling the pungent odors of men, the warm honey scent of acacia wood, and the tang of olive oil. She scooted to the edge of the tent where, when she was younger, she'd not be noticed studying the men's creations. Why couldn't Uncle Emet see not only the tent craftsmanship that she and her sisters were known for but also all the woven baskets and flax rope they'd created to organize the workshop's apparatuses? Why not work alongside the men? If it were up to Abba, he'd have allowed it and even encouraged her. But Abba acquiesced for the sake of harmony when Uncle Emet reported that many of the men agreed with him.

Abba had assigned her uncles and cousins to different areas of the workshop and required them to memorize the location of their tools. With the Israelites' many moves, he didn't want anyone wasting time. She knew Jonathan and Simon kept score, competing to be the first family to finish their work. She smirked at men's natural instincts, but had to admit—it made quick work of reconstructing the shop when they moved.

She hugged her elbows into her sides, warmth inching up her arms as she recalled Jonathan explaining the tools and their functions: chisels, mallets, axes, planes, and squares. She would listen carefully and, on subsequent visits, repeat what she retained. If she hesitated, he'd pantomime the use. But Uncle Emet's complaints put an end to her learning.

Now, as she looked around, Abba was nowhere to be found. Uncle Emet clasped a long pole of acacia wood while one of his sons measured it against another. She waited until they finished. It allowed her to marvel at the works in progress: stools, low collapsible tables, chests, and looms, both small and large. Their extended traveling demanded all the items be as compact as possible. A fine layer of sand and sawdust seemed to blanket every crevice of the surface. *If Uncle Emet ever allowed me to work, he'd make me sweep.*

"Did you hear what Korah said?" A man stopped his chiseling to talk with a man opposite him.

"Yes, I heard and don't believe a word of it. He craves what he doesn't have."

"I don't know. He's making sense to me. He says Moses thinks too highly of himself."

"Let's speak no more of this." The second man veered his head, indicating Noa.

The other man scowled at her.

Noa glanced away to see Jonathan flexing his arm muscles with precise blows as he hammered a wheel spoke.

He looked up and met her gaze, then dropped his hammer and hurried over. "Noa, I didn't see you there. Is everything all right?"

"What brings you here, Noa?" Emet barked, inspecting her from head to toe.

"Greetings, Uncle Emet. Is my father here? Have you seen him?"

Emet picked up a sandstone and began rubbing and smoothing out the acacia pole. "Your father and Uncle Abel went to the Tent of Meeting some time ago. Noa, what have I said about being here unaccompanied?"

Emet constantly reinforced his thoughts about the separation of men's and women's roles.

"Would you let him know I came by?" Used to Emet's disdain, she wondered if he would relay the message.

Jonathan slid by her side. "I'll escort her out."

Emet grunted, continuing to focus on his project.

Noa dipped her head to hide the heat flowing into her cheeks.

Jonathan was covered in sawdust, and his hands glistened with oil. His eyes were full of mischief. "Can you still recite all the tools' names?"

Those eyes. It was like a dip in the river on a hot day. "I was just reminiscing about how much patience you had with me. Someday, I'll use what you taught me without requiring permission." She nodded her head toward the tent. "When we own a home in our Promised Land ... I mean, we all have a place to call home. I mean ..."

Jonathan lowered his head. "I know what you mean."

"Jonathan," Emet shouted.

"I'd better go. Be happy, Noa. You sparkle when you're happy."

When we ... own a home. Did he think I was suggesting we would be married? Yet he'd walked her out and said she sparkled. She grinned even as she admitted she'd acted on impulse again. *Lord, if you mean me to be with Jonathan, guide our paths.*

Zelophehad and Abel ambled back from yet another meeting with the Levite priests and tribal leaders. "I detected some disparaging remarks about Moses. Did you notice them as well?" Abel spoke softly.

Zelophehad swallowed a sour taste in his mouth. "Korah, such an arrogant man. He sows discontent in the tribes, and how they listen." His muscles relaxed as he confided in his younger cousin.

"All the talk is about Moses. Some people are in awe of him, some say he's self-important, and some worship him instead of our Lord." Abel waved his hands. "It's so volatile with Korah stirring up passionate resentment."

"Korah waxes on about Egypt and exaggerates our captors' care. Our fellow Israelites forget their cruelty." Zelophehad twitched, trying to shut out the memory of the excruciating pain from the whip stings.

"We experienced a different life in Egypt, thanks to you and your quick thinking in fixing that chariot for the chief temple builder, Zelo. You even convinced them they needed more workers, saving many from their brutal tasks."

"Emet may not see it that way."

"Leather production is a nasty job, but still, you kept him from the whip of the Egyptians, and with his temper, he was easier to manage there. But Zelo, I have confidence that God is leading Moses. We'll get to our Promised Land."

"I dream of seeing my daughters settled and married in that land. There's an entire generation that knows nothing but navigating this desert." *But I won't see them settled. I will expire before that, just as God foretold of our unfaithful generation. I must arrange these marriages.*

"But that isn't Moses's fault."

"Certainly not. We've wandered for many years because we didn't trust our Lord. I didn't trust, cousin."

"About our Promised Land?" Abel jerked mid-stride.

"No, but I, too, was lost. We learn much from the dark times in our lives. I didn't care any longer about reaching the Promised Land, so I neither voiced approval nor rejected what the spies said. I wasted ten years when I could've chosen to live again. It was as if I'd been blindfolded, thinking about myself and not trusting God. When God opened my eyes, I realized what a fool I'd been." Zelophehad rarely mentioned Sara, his first wife, and the only son he had lost. He extended his hands out as if weighing something. "Abel, it still haunts me. I didn't recognize Emet's interest in Sara. What if he had married Sara? Would she have lived? Would she have survived childbirth with him as the father?"

Abel clutched his cousin's shoulders, "Zelo, Sara loved *you*, and even if you had stepped aside, she was yours. It is sad that Emet can still be bitter over a love he would never have had. I know it's like a thorn sticking through your sandal, but you need to stop reliving this. You found your way. God said, 'Enough, come back and see My plans for you.' Jeska was His messenger about one of your inventions, no less." Abel nudged him with his elbow.

"Ah, yes." He fondly remembered the scene. "She marched into the shop, saying, 'Some man named Ze-lo-phe-had made this. If he asked a woman's opinion, it would work much simpler.' 'Oh?' I responded, and she explained what was wrong with my tent loom. And you know, she was right."

Abel chuckled. "She didn't know you made it until that morning when she approached your tent with what you'd guessed was a peace offering. Instead, she created a miniature example of how to correct your creation. How we laughed at that."

"That's when I fell in love with her. Sure of herself, her manner, her forthrightness. So different from Sara, who was charming in her shyness. It permitted me to open my heart to pursue Jeska. I didn't think God would give me a second chance, but how blessed I am! She's my best friend—more than a wife. She's a part of me. I don't know what I would do without her."

They trekked the rest of the way to the workshop in silence. He valued his close relationship with Abel. Why couldn't it be the same with Emet? *He continues to think we are in a race that he wants to win. He even thinks it's a race to get my daughters married.* Emet didn't see what he had—five sons who had given him grown grandchildren. He never seemed to show his love for them. *And he never misses a chance to remind me that my name will be forgotten without sons.*

A chill gripped Noa as she stomped back home. Emet's dismissal replayed in her head, along with her embarrassment of saying *we*

about owning a home to Jonathan, and no soothing talk with Father. Agitated, she burst into the family tent and threw off her sandals.

"Can you hold it a little higher and keep it steady?" Milkah murmured.

Hoglah hummed while swaying to her tune. She shifted an artisan bronze mirror so Milkah could brush her long tresses.

"Can you tear yourself away and do your chores?" Noa poured water into a cup to bring to Ima and some for herself. Thankful for the curtain's thickness, she hoped their mother couldn't hear them.

Hoglah tossed the mirror to Milkah, giggling toward the door. "This is where I will leave. Don't want to get between you two."

Queen Milkah continued to brush her hair, pursing her lips. "You're just jealous. I tend to my hair, and it shows. If you would heed your wild tresses, you could look half decent."

Noa was tempted to throw something at her, but restrained herself. *I'm older, more mature*. She took another sip of water. "Milkah, we ought to show Ima we can carry on while she's not feeling well."

"Ima also wishes her daughters to plan for their lives. Don't you ever wonder about marriage? You seem to be interested in Jonathan. Shouldn't you make yourself attractive? He's very eligible."

Noa shifted her hands to her hips. She wouldn't fall for Milkah's goading, but the queen's comment met its target. "You must intend to marry someone with many riches. Who will do all the cooking, herding, mending clothes, milking of goats, weaving baskets, sweeping, and tending the fire—not to mention bringing up children? And that's a short list."

"Either I'll marry a man who will give me servants, or I'll have many daughters to do chores." Milkah curled up on the silky plush blanket she claimed was hers.

"Well, now you don't have either, so you must do your chores." She sprinted over to clutch Milkah's mirror, tripped, and knocked the afternoon water over the rug.

Mahlah limped over. "Why are you both arguing? Do you have no regard for Ima?"

"We were just—" both said.

"Never mind. Milkah, please go. Noa, I would like to speak with you."

Milkah wrapped the mirror in the leather pouch, pushed up from her pallet, and stuck her tongue out at Noa as she left.

Mahlah grabbed both sides of her head. "What's wrong with you? You're better than this. Why are you so relentless with her?"

"I know. I don't understand it myself. She infuriates me." Noa straightened the water jug, the whole afternoon's water spilt.

"Why does she irritate you so much?" Mahlah sank beside her.

"Her life centers on Milkah, no one else."

"Noa, she likes her feminine ways. Maybe in a family of five sisters, she's trying to be recognized."

She shrugged. "I understand what you're saying, but ..."

"What if your mother-in-law or sister-in-law is like Milkah? Will you find a reason to fight with them too? Shine some light on her. Season her with love. By doing so, she'll feel more comfortable and less likely to emphasize her appearance. She's family—your sister."

"I want her to be herself. One day, her looks won't be there. But you're right, Mahlah. And I'm thankful for how you've treated me after what I did to you." Noa waved her hand at Mahlah's hip.

"Stop. You promised we wouldn't talk about this. It was long ago."

"I don't deserve your kindness."

"It was an accident. You didn't mean it to happen. We've been over this. Please stop. What you can do is fill this again." Mahlah pointed to the water jug. "And show your love for Milkah."

"I will, sister." Noa's head throbbing, she picked up the vessel, thankful to be alone.

CHAPTER 6

Assir sat outside at the back of the family tent, staring absent-mindedly into the camp of Ruben, lost in his thoughts, when Elkanah interrupted him. "How long have you been here? What's so important to keep you away from the Tent this morning?"

"Sorry, I got distracted. I'm wondering how to gain Milkah's trust."

"My brother, unsure of himself? Never seen you like this. Perhaps you were thinking about her in other ways? Mind you, I couldn't blame you." He crouched next to Assir.

"I can't just keep approaching her with a simple greeting and small talk about her sisters if I'm to discover anything about her father." But Elkanah was right. Assir knew how to approach a woman. *Why is Milkah different?* His thoughts grew darker. *What will happen if Zelophehad doesn't join Father?* Would this bring danger to Milkah's entire family? *How can I satisfy Father and keep her safe?*

"Brother, describe what we do here. Being a Levite has its mysteries. I've tried it myself and enthralled girls with its prestige. Wish father had charged me with your task. I wouldn't mind befriending Milkah, with those arresting brown eyes and her figure. It'd be difficult to turn away from her. I'm sure you'll find the words."

As Assir walked to the river, mulling over his brother's words, an idea sparked. *Men do like to brag. Why didn't I think of this?* He'd glean information at Zelophehad's workshop.

Assir found the workshop outside the Manasseh tribe's area. As he entered the large tent, at least forty men labored around several wooden tables arranged in an orderly fashion, concentrating on projects. Zelophehad's genial cousin, Abel, greeted him.

"Shalom, Abel. My father's Egyptian chair needs mending. Perhaps you can show me how you do things here."

Abel droned on about their techniques. Assir bit his tongue so as not to rush him. "And is it only you who runs the workshop?"

"Oh no, my cousin Zelo started it." Abel swelled with obvious admiration for his cousin's prowess in the shop and the mentorships he extended to all tribes except the Levite due to their duties, as well as the way they set it up with all the moves. Assir's attention drifted when he overheard his father's name from a man at a nearby working bench.

"I just came from listening to Korah. I think he says many interesting things."

Men crowded around the man, listening and some nodding at his words.

Assir hoped it would be a different way to find out about Zelophehad. Perhaps Abel would share his and Zelophehad's stance on Moses. Distracted by the man's review of his father, he hadn't seen Abel disappear. Once the man finished boasting about Korah, Assir still didn't have his answer.

He darted to the family tent, picked up a small basket, placed into it some of the dried apricots his father had received from a follower, and set out for the Manasseh tents.

Assir walked west to the camp of Ephraim's standard and then continued until he found the Manasseh tribal flag. Friendly neighbors directed him further. What were the chances? Milkah sat alone under the shade of their tent flap, protecting herself from the sun's beating rays.

He stood for a moment watching her delicate fingers in a hypnotic dance. Her left hand secured a bundle of black goat fleece at shoulder height, with a single strand attached to a wooden spindle, while her right hand spun the thread, keeping it taut. Her concentration and sureness added more heat to his already sweltering body.

"Shalom, Milkah. Is that for yet another tent?"

Milkah toyed with her headpiece to display more of her face and greeted him with a brilliant smile. "Yes, yet another one."

"I've come to drop off these apricots for your mother and hope they will make her feel better."

"Oh, Assir, how thoughtful. Where did you find dried apricots?" Milkah picked one out to accept his offering.

"Father sometimes is given gifts for helping someone. I'm sure your abba has the same. Have you been working long?"

"The intricate work has exhausted my fingers, but at least I don't have to wash or card the goat's wool. My youngest sister does that." Milkah waved to the basket at her feet. "Before we start on the loom, my job today is to twist the goat hair on this spindle."

"I appreciate how much talent this takes. You've not lost your streaming thread or dropped your spindle once. I know that it is hard to do, having seen our Tabernacle weavers who created the inner curtains for the Holy of Holies. I believe your sister Mahlah has worked on the outer curtains." Assir bent to be at eye level with Milkah.

He studied the tight weave of the tent panel behind her. "You and your sisters have earned quite a reputation. Even my mother, who has benefited from some of your tent panels, commented on the quality, the water resistance, and the durability."

"The Lord helps with that by sending the rain. When the fibers get wet, they expand, tightening the weave so it resists the rain." She pointed to the seam on the tent flap.

Assir ran his hand over the seam. "After all this work, can you take a little rest?"

Milkah laid down her spindle and the basket of fluffy black goat fibers. "Yes, that sounds just right." She spread her fingers, flexing them.

"I also have unfinished tasks at the Tabernacle, the mundane chores I don't like to do."

Milkah touched her throat. "Even though that's God's work?"

"I'm twenty-six, so I have a junior role now. Some of it is not that exciting. But I'll have an elder position with far more responsibility when I'm thirty."

Milkah seemed to hang on to his every word. "What do you do differently in a senior position?"

His brother was right. Talking about his duties at the Tabernacle piqued her interest, and he loved sharing what they were called to do. "God assigned each Levite family to different roles for the Tent of Meeting. I am a descendant of the Kohath family. My father says God assigned us the most important duties compared to the others."

"Most important?"

Assir had appreciated his father's in-depth teachings, except for his recent rants about Moses. "We preside over the most holy items, every piece of the gold-encrusted furnishings, including the most sacred Ark of the Covenant." He didn't disclose that they only moved the Ark and couldn't see or touch its precious items.

"Do you enjoy what you do?"

"My brothers and I are in training to praise God through song. We take turns chanting both night and day. I enjoy composing new songs and hope they will be worthy of being included in worship. A few older Levites routinely perform their tasks, but I wonder why God requires us to perform certain rituals. I ask many questions. It instills more reverence in carrying out each duty. My father has proudly instructed me because he knows I'm serious about my work." *I only wish he were still concentrating on that.* He flinched. *I must focus on questions for her.*

"People say your father departed from Egypt laden with gold. Did he relinquish it all to the Tabernacle?" Milkah bent her body toward him.

He stiffened and looked at her askew.

Milkah sat back and bowed her head.

The blistering desert sun sank closer to the western hills surrounding the camp when a young woman approached. She suddenly laughed. "Here you are. Noa wondered why you've not brought the goat's thread to the tent loom set up near Abel's tent, but it seems you've other priorities."

"Hoglah, this is Assir, Korah's son. Reba is his sister. He was describing his role at the Tabernacle. Assir, this is my middle sister, Hoglah."

All thoughts of her impertinent question disappeared with her simple introduction. Milkah's silky way of expressing herself danced in his head and tugged at his heart. He bowed slightly. "Shalom, Hoglah. It seems we both should return to our tasks."

Hoglah picked up the completed spindles. "Let's hope this is enough."

Milkah got up, linking arms with Hoglah, and swung halfway around. She flashed a coy grin. "Thank you, sir, for my lesson on your role in the Tabernacle."

A mixture of defeat and heat stirred his body, but he'd earned a sliver of her trust. *The next time should be easier.* But did he even want the answer?

Zelophehad shuffled over to Abel's tent after visiting Emet.

"Zelo, why so pensive? Are you concerned about the meeting?"

Zelophehad dug his fingers through his curly mane. "I still have trouble forgiving Emet's meddling for the disastrous betrothal. I thought it would be good to talk with him and see if we could find a way forward. But what's irritating him now? He barely spoke to me."

Abel chided, "What isn't bothering him? You know how he is. What happened?"

"Indifference—neither warmth nor disregard."

Abel coughed. "I debated whether to tell you, but it may shed light."

"You know why he's even more aloof?" Something in Abel's glance alarmed him. "Tell me."

Abel nervously stroked the nape of his neck, twisting his mouth. "Noa came to the shop without you. Emet told her to leave and then droned on about how you raise your daughters."

"My daughters? What've they done to deserve his wrath?"

"He objects to you filling their heads with anything more than being a wife. You're teaching them the duties of men—how to barter for their tent-making and defend points of view in Sabbath discussions." Abel imitated Emet's low, gravelly inflections. "Mahlah at least learned to weave well. And what good is Hoglah's singing? What about cooking? I would've married them off if they were mine."

Zelophehad put his hands up. "Yes, he would've. But he doesn't understand the importance of what I'm doing. The Manasseh tribe has grown the most, so we will have a larger territory, and I want them to be near each other, which is why I want them to marry within our tribe so they can settle near each other in the Promised Land. What do we have but family? They must count on one another."

Abel opened his mouth to speak and looked away when he said, "You want them to marry within our tribe?"

"Yes, Abel. Why do you look surprised?" Zelophehad was on the verge of revealing the secret that Emet had sworn him not to discuss about Abel's resistance to Simon being betrothed to Mahlah. *Is his reaction because of Simon and Mahlah?*

Again, Abel looked as if he would speak, but grimaced and raised his shoulders instead.

Zelophehad sensed his resistance and decided not to ask him about it. It seemed Emet was right. "I also want them to marry for love, like I have. God has graced me twice, and I know what it is to love and be loved deeply, to be yoked evenly. It may sound impractical. I want a future son-in-law who can support a wife and household, but who also appreciates and does not treat a wife like a servant, which I think Emet believes is their role. I must first find a suitable marriage for Mahlah, as she is my firstborn, but not force her into a marriage that isn't right.

"They have learned a great deal here in this wilderness. I don't think God would want them not to be who they have become. I want someone who will cherish them like I have both Jeska and Sara. Emet doesn't understand how different it is having only girls. Without a son ... without a son ..."

Abel breathed deeply. "I shouldn't have brought it up."

Zelophehad's hands hung at his sides. "I must prepare them, as I won't always be here. The skills they learned will sustain them should all else fail. I taught them negotiation and numbers, but trust me, not much. They're all better than me, Noa especially. If it weren't for the issue with Emet, I would've had her handle the shop's accounting. And what's wrong with teaching my daughters our laws? Isn't that what our Lord asks of us? Teach our children when we're at home, when we walk, when we lie down, and when we rise?"

Abel tucked his arms. "Emet doesn't admonish the schooling of the law but the discussions about them. He says defending a point of view and learning how to argue should be reserved for males. He thinks this will threaten a husband and certainly a mother-in-law."

"He would think this. I encourage them to be curious about life, to form their own opinions, and to speak their mind. I didn't need to teach any of that with six women in my tent." Zelophehad chuckled.

"I will find sons-in-law who'll appreciate a woman who can be a partner, as I have with Jeska." *Simon would do so for Mahlah. Why don't you agree, Abel?* Zelophehad rubbed his nose. "I'm afraid Emet and I will long be at odds. So much for trying to talk with him. It makes me glad that if one of us should have all daughters, it is I."

Assir's muscles tightened. He'd missed his turn to sing for a sick fellow Levite. Waiting for his father, who curtly told him to meet back at the family tent, he imagined the talk that was about to ensue.

No one was in the family tent, which Father would've arranged. Assir was no longer asked to attend the many secret meetings his father had conducted. He paced, unable to sit still, then heard singing. *Father is singing?*

Father entered, humming, while he took off his sandals. "Ah, Assir, let us sit, son." He pointed to the reed cushion in front of him.

Assir flinched. He couldn't read his father. On one hand, he seemed relaxed, even happy. On the other, he hadn't seated Assir in his usual ornate chair. He wiped the sweat from his forehead, tucking the cloth into his tunic. "Father. All is well?"

"Yes, but more about that later. Now, what's this? I hear you missed your chanting time. What happened?"

"I went to Zelophehad's workshop to glean information."

"Ah, I thought it would be a good reason. And what did you learn?"

Assir's body tingled with relief. "Abel showed me around. I told him that your chair may need repairs."

His father nodded. "Good ruse, and ..."

"Abel is very loyal to him and proud of what they've accomplished there. The important part is that your reputation grows."

"Did Abel say that?" Father's fingers danced on his mouth.

"I overheard a man give an impassioned review after listening to you speak. He said you are a prominent leader and hinted at the current leadership's impediments. He garnered quite a crowd." Assir leaned back on his cushion. He wasn't going to mention that Abel hadn't heard the discussion.

"Did anyone else speak about Moses?"

"Not by name, only as the 'current leadership.'"

Father cocked his head to the ceiling tent. "Hmm. A good thought to go there. The workshop is an excellent place to conquer. What was Abel's response? Did he give any sign?"

"He didn't remark. He didn't stay long." Assir hoped his truth stretching was not wrong. It reminded him of his sister. *"I didn't lie. I just made some of it up."*

"Well, some headway at least. Anything else?"

"I will report more soon." He left unspoken his conversation with Milkah, as he had not advanced much to report about her father. His chest burned, worried about his father's fierce anger toward Moses and the role he was playing in ferreting out information.

"My son, it was clever to go directly to the workshop. Next time, I want to know the definitive version of Zelophehad's stance. However you can obtain it ... from Milkah, the workshop, or any other way. This is a key to my plans." His temple veins throbbed. "Don't disappoint me."

CHAPTER 7

Noa breathed in the solace of the arid landscape stretching for miles. Unlike many of her fellow wanderers, she never tired of the rugged terrain's beauty—the sharp, ragged mountain peaks surrounded by clouds in the spring and snow in the winter. God's palette of colors ranged from dark clay to a tan so light that the sun's reflection caused the illusion of undulating sand. How did that lonely, feathery acacia tree survive? Was it to provide shade? How creative and majestic was God's beauty!

She wished she could draw like Jonathan to capture her appreciation of this wilderness. A few days ago, she'd dared to arrive early at the workshop to avoid Uncle Emet's disapproval and inspect the repairs of their tent loom. And ... to see Jonathan. She watched him hover over his station, his intense concentration evident as he held a charcoal stylus. When he spotted her, he stashed the precious parchment he worked on under the table.

Noa drew near. "What are you working on?"

"Nothing, it's plans for another loom."

"Let's see what you have."

Jonathan blocked her, and the drawing dropped to the ground. He bent to retrieve it, but she snatched it first.

"It's not worth looking at." He winced.

Noa's grip stayed steady, even though Jonathan tugged it. "This is beautiful. How did you learn to draw?" The charcoal sketch depicted a flowing river with the sun beating down on a single girl who stared into the water as she leaned against a blossoming almond tree. It perfectly captured a moment of serenity. The girl wore a headdress, the same style as hers. Could it have been her?

"No, it's nothing, I don't ... Please." Jonathan stuck out his hand, his chiseled face blossoming into a sweet red.

Seeing his distress, Noa released her grip. He rolled it up, tied it with a leather strap, and tucked it away with other scrolls.

"What's wrong? Why are you hiding this?"

"My father and grandfather disapprove. They both find drawing a foolish pastime. My father insists it interferes with work. Don't tell anyone." Jonathan hung his head, then sheepishly raised his eyes to her. "It was to be a surprise for—"

Zebediah and Emet emerged from the back entrance.

"Good morning, Father, Grandfather." Jonathan fiddled with an awl.

Noa slunk back from his station. She hadn't seen Jonathan's father, Zebediah, in a long time. He was the overseer of animal husbandry for the Manasseh tribe, keeping busy by tending to the animals to be sacrificed. "Shalom. I came to see the loom my father was mending. I was anxious about how far he'd gotten."

Emet scowled. "You shouldn't be alone in the workshop with any man. I've stated this on several occasions, one just recently. You're a young woman now, and there are proper practices to follow. If you're curious, then have your father accompany you. This is my final warning to you. We've got a lot of work to do. Good day to you."

She bit her lip. Her mind froze. Finding no words, she stormed out but hid behind a tent fold, waiting to hear what they would say.

"Son, you should know better. Noa's the most brazen sister. She would prove a difficult wife," Zebediah said.

Emet added, "My cousin encourages all his daughters to speak their minds and so much more. It'll lead to trouble, and as you notice, they've no suitors. I was almost successful in getting Mahlah married to Kenan, but even that didn't work. Poor man. But has Zelo done any more to help get this remedied? They should all be married by now, except for Tirzah, and she will be ready soon. It is coming to a point where I'll need to step in again."

Noa stifled a scream. *That's not the reason Father's waiting! Father doesn't need your help.*

"You listen to Grandmother. She speaks her mind to you," Jonathan countered.

"But not like Zelophehad's daughters. Be wary. Let's start our day. Give me a hand with this."

She winced. Uncle Emet had nothing to worry about. Who would wed such an opinionated woman as Noa? *Yet, I've never experienced these strange feelings.* Milkah said her stomach churned in the closeness of a handsome man. Noa had always felt comfortable with Jonathan. *But now a passion is rising within me.*

Oh, how Noa wished he might feel the same way. Jonathan listened to her and made her laugh at herself. He had such patience with everyone, including her sisters. He was kind and cared for his family despite their differences. He was his own person, even if it meant doing something he believed in despite being told not to.

Will we end up near each other in our Promised Land? One thing was sure—she couldn't imagine her life without him.

Zelophehad rose early, hoping to talk with Emet before the workshop reached its daily noisy activity. He'd had a dream of being back in Egypt as a boy, where he and Emet were inseparable. In his dream, his father told him it would be a friendship for life. Was God giving him a message? *Lord, help me forgive Emet. Let me find a bridge where we can meet. Give me patience.* He marched back to Emet's work area, but no one was there. He inhaled deeply and exhaled through his mouth. He may not have spoken with Emet, but the intent of forgiveness entered his heart. With a release of all his pent-up anger, he returned to his work and assembled the pieces needed for the loom.

Early afternoon, Emet tapped him on the shoulder.

"Ah, Emet, I came to talk with you early this morning. What makes you come at such a late time? Is all well with Adina?" Zelophehad turned to face him, concerned for Emet's wife.

"Zelo, I've something important to talk to you about. Can you stop working for a moment? I want you to meet someone."

Zelophehad laid the acacia wood down. "Why are you wearing your best tunic? Who are we meeting?"

"I want to introduce you to Nahash from the Reuben tribe." Emet straightened.

"Nahash? Does he wish to work at our shop?"

"Come, it won't take long." Emet took Zelophehad's elbow to guide him out.

"Cousin Zelo, this is Nahash from the Reuben tribe." Emet bowed his head.

Zelophehad's mind whirled. Why was Emet treating Nahash as if he were a dignitary? *What is he up to?* "Shalom, Nahash." Zelophehad nodded.

"Shalom, Zelophehad." Nahash shuffled forward, his hair a tangled web with a potbelly sticking out of his tunic.

"Zelo, Nahash has lost his dear wife. He has six wonderful children who need tending to. I thought it'd be good for you to meet him as a prospective groom for Mahlah."

"Sir, I can provide well for your daughter, and although my children are somewhat rambunctious, with the right direction and discipline, Mahlah will have them helping her with all the chores. Their mother was ill for quite a while and couldn't supervise, and I was away attending tribal meetings. I understand Mahlah has an impediment that makes walking difficult, but she can direct them. With six children, she won't have to worry about being childless from ... from her accident." Nahash proffered his palms together.

Zelophehad ground his teeth. *How dare he! Six churlish children for my oldest?* Nahash appeared to be twice her age. *How dare he condemn her for not having babies just because of her hip?* His body stiff, he shoved his fists behind his back. He deepened his tone for protocol. "I'm sorry for your loss, Nahash. How long has it been?"

Nahash looked down. "Four months. But by the time I pledge, a betrothal will take another eight months, honoring my year of mourning time."

"It's thoughtful of you to approach me with this introduction, as family is also very important to me. I want my five lovely daughters to stay together as a family. I wish to find betrothals where all five husbands' families will live near one another, meaning I'd want them all to come from the same tribe. How is it going with the Reuben tribe census?" Zelophehad would beat Emet at this game.

"We're still bringing forth our men to register. It isn't finished yet." Nahash looked down at his feet.

"From what I understand, the Manasseh tribe has increased substantially, giving our tribe the biggest allotment of land, which gives me a sense of comfort. Again, I thank you for your kind proposal, but this betrothal wouldn't be deserving of your respected lineage. Now, please forgive me, but I must get back to my shop. Emet, please see your guest home."

Nahash narrowed his gaze at Emet, who turned to Zelophehad. "Zelo, please, Nahash is a respected leader in the Reuben tribe. Your daughters won't need one another—especially Mahlah, who'll have an already-built family of six beautiful children. She'll never be lonely or worried."

Nahash unfolded his arms. "Zelo, I've saved more than enough gold. She also will never be in need."

"Dear sir, I meant you no affront. My cousin wouldn't have made the introductions unless he thought it a fine match. But I am certain my daughters will live near each other. Family is all we have. With no sons of my own, I must do all I can to ensure they can count on each other. We have a saying in our family, 'Look up, and you will know.' Somehow, the answer will come forth for you. I, too, pray God will find you the perfect match for you and your children."

Zelophehad quickly began to gyrate back, his nostrils inflamed by an audible breath. His muscles tensed with fury. *Lord, that is not what I expected when I asked you for forgiveness and patience for my cousin.* He wouldn't go back to the workshop. He lumbered the long way to the family tent to calm himself, his heart feeling like a twisted knot in his chest. He headed for his only true remedy, his wife and daughters.

Assir drifted down the worn river path to bathe. The walk was familiar to all Levites, who were required to be fastidiously clean. He spied Milkah from a distance and changed direction to cross her path. Assir shuddered at the voice of his father saying, *"Don't disappoint me."* He must find out if Zelophehad believed God's messenger was Moses. Assir fought a battle within himself, hoping he'd be able to please Father, but doubting that Zelophehad believed Father's thoughts—like most of the Israelites, including himself.

"Shalom, Milkah, I was just thinking of you."

"Me? Why were you thinking of me?"

"About our talk the other day."

"Oh." Milkah pouted.

Assir easily corrected his blunder as he couldn't stop thinking about her. "And how much I appreciate conversing with not only a beautiful woman but one whose curiosity emanates from her very being."

Milkah angled her chin slightly away, a hint of a smile on her lips.

"I'm also curious about how you spend your time when you're not doing all your many chores. What are your evenings like?" His hands sweated. Was it from her closeness or his nerves?

Milkah beamed. "We sing and weave while Father recounts stories to us. He describes in incredible detail. You dream you're there."

"Does he tell fables and make-believe stories of fair maidens and handsome warriors?"

Milkah giggled. "No, he teaches us about his time in Egypt, our family heritage, Moses, and the Tent of Meeting. They always end in a lesson."

His heart melted. "A lesson?"

"Father is passionate about us living our faith. He doesn't expect us to memorize every word, but to understand what the story means."

Her father is a faithful Israelite. Assir's cheeks burned. "A thoughtful father. I wish there were more like him. What stories they must be. Can you repeat one? Any about Moses?" Every muscle tightened, torn between what his father wanted to hear and what he already suspected. His desire to hear her every word impelled him to lean forward.

Milkah didn't inch away. "He talks about how things have happened here in the wilderness. All parents talk to their children about them. Don't they?"

"I trust they do, knowing God's desire. You were saying, about Moses?"

"A story about Moses? I recall that he explained the first story, how Moses begged God to choose someone else when God instructed him to lead the Israelites out of Egypt. But God promised He would put the words in Moses's mouth and his brother Aaron's mouth and teach them what they were to say. Abba told us that God will always be with us and provide the means to accomplish our journeys, especially with the people God puts in our lives. Whether we believe we have the skills or knowledge to do His will, He will make our paths straight. I'm sure your father does the same."

Here stood before him a sincere young woman of God, and one whose beauty shone inside and out. Assir was captivated. *She angles her head just so. Then she looks sideways with those downcast eyes. She's innocent and so alluring at the same time.* His breath was hoarse. "Who knows what God's plans can lead to?"

"I can't imagine conversing with God and refusing Him. Would you dare defy God and ask Him to choose someone else?"

Assir dropped his chin to his chest, ashamed of what he was pursuing. "I heard that story from my father. Father said, 'Moses shouldn't have said no.'" His nerves tightened, and his tone became high. "He wonders if Moses continues to defy God and then makes up his own mind, and others have told him Moses puts himself above others. Has your father ever said anything like this?"

Milkah slinked back. "No, he hasn't. Father exalts Moses and says God anointed him to teach us, especially when people go astray. He's recounted stories of the early days and the many times Moses guided all the Israelite tribes, who kept testing and not trusting God. What a strange thing for your father to say."

From her changed expression, he knew he'd gone too far and wondered why he was even doing this. "You admire your father very much and take the fifth commandment to heart. It is beautiful to see."

"Yes, Assir, I do, and I would hope your father is also teaching all these things to you and not doubting Moses. I must be on my way. Perhaps the next time we meet, you'll find something more appropriate to discuss." Milkah spirited away, her hips swaying.

He'd gained the answer. Zelophehad praised Moses. Now Father would expect Assir to convert him. *What will happen if I fail?* His stomach lurched. *I know Father would never harm me, but he could disown me. I'd be an outcast.* Yet Milkah was tugging at him to distraction. *Do I apprise Father, or do I stall, saying I need time to find out more?* He headed to the river, glad for the cold water.

"Abba, are you too tired to tell us your promised story?" Tirzah asked after dinner.

"You encourage your father, but what about Mahlah and Noa, who have heard my stories so many times?" He wouldn't breathe a word of Nahash, not even to Jeska.

"We love them, Abba, because you always add something new. So, it's as if we hear it for the first time." Noa and her sisters plumped up their seating mats, their upright posture brimming with anticipation.

Zelophehad settled onto his seating mat with an exaggerated sigh, but he knew the spark in his eyes would reveal how pleased he was to be coaxed by them. "This is an important story about how we received our Ten Commandments. Moses ascended Mount Sinai at God's direction and disappeared for forty days, leaving Aaron in charge. We wondered if Moses had perished. We were consumed by fear and doubt, its poison slowly expanding in our minds like yeast when added to flour. Korah convinced Dathan, a man from the Reubenite tribe, to be his mouthpiece, saying we had wronged God and needed to make amends by creating an edifice like the Egyptians had done to appease their gods. Aaron relented, coerced by the demanding mob, and he summoned the men. 'Take off the gold earrings from your wives, your sons, and daughters and bring them to me.'"

"I wouldn't part with my gold earrings." Milkah touched hers.

Noa smirked. "Not because of the edifice, but because—"

Zelophehad frowned and interrupted. "Milkah, you're right."

Milkah lightly nudged Noa.

"Aaron used this as a delay. He expected a drawn-out negotiation to remove precious gold jewelry from their loved one's ears. But fear overcame our community, and a stunning pile of gold mounted. Korah incited Aaron to fashion a golden calf."

Zelophehad stared ahead. "It isn't a wonder they made a fatted calf that resembled the Egyptian god Apis, the god of fertility. Since we'd lived in Egypt for over four hundred years, some of us assimilated or were contaminated by their culture. A large group believed they were honoring God by representing Him as the supreme god. The Egyptian ways surrounded us, and some, I would say, still secretly pray to Egyptian gods."

Ima coughed. "Zelo ... please ..."

Zelophehad nodded. "Hopefully, we've learned to honor our one true God, but back then, not so. My fellow Israelites blindly followed Korah's idea. Goaded by him, Aaron shouted to the ranting throng, 'These are your gods, O Israel, who brought you up out of the land of Egypt.'"

Noa pushed forward from her comfortable pillow. "But that isn't true."

"No, it isn't, and many paid for their sin. At dusk, Moses emerged from the darkness of Mount Sinai carrying heavy stone tablets. On beholding the hideous idol, his fury and anger raged. He hurled the sacred stone tablets, shattering them into pieces. I trembled with fear, believing we might all perish. Moses jerked Aaron aside, berating him. 'What did these people do to you, that you led them into such great sin?' And, Aaron did what people do. He defended his actions and then, sadly, blamed the people."

"But Aaron became our high priest. Why would God honor him?" Noa said.

"Why indeed? Ashamed that even his brother succumbed, Moses begged God for forgiveness. Our ways are not God's ways. He sees into our hearts. Perhaps God saw Aaron's weakness and dependence on Moses and understood Aaron's intent with his delay tactic. Whatever the reason, God assigned him to the priesthood. We make mistakes, but it's how we repent and what we carry in our hearts that's important."

"But what about Korah and Dathan?" Noa asked, glancing at Milkah.

"I don't know where their paths lie. We all must choose. I hope they will choose what is right."

"What good are these commandments when we continue to roam as nomads? Why have we been wandering so long?" Milkah's shoulders sank. "Doesn't Moses have a clear direction from God on when we will arrive at our Promised Land?"

Zelophehad put his arm around her shoulder. “Oh, my daughter, our commandments are not just for our life here in the wilderness. They are essential for how we should live no matter where we are. We have wandered here because the twelve spies, including a member of our Manasseh tribe, reported that the inhabitants of our Promised Land were giants and their cities were heavily fortified. Only Caleb and Joshua said we should go forward. God was angry that we didn’t trust Him to lead us and decreed that we would wander for forty years, one year for each day the spies scouted the land. Yet still in God’s compassion, He’s moved us from place to place so we could have fresh water, grazing fields, and manna every day.

“Our God is good to us, even when we go astray. It’s why I’ve nurtured you on our Lord’s commandments, so you keep these in your heart always. Be patient a little longer. Each tribe is almost finished with counting the new census to apportion our Promised Land. Soon you’ll have a home and a family of your own.” Zelophehad squeezed Milkah.

He hoped he could protect his daughters from learning his age. *What will be my fate? And when? Lord, help me make these marriages soon.*

CHAPTER 8

No amount of rehearsing could calm Assir, as the information he gained from Milkah about her father wouldn't please his.

Father uncharacteristically raised his voice and picked up Assir's tunic by his neck. "What I want to know is where you are with this Milkah. It's been weeks now. I know nothing more than she is taking up much of your precious time. What've you learned?" He let go of Assir.

"I … I've been gaining her trust." Dread gnawed at his insides. His father never treated him this way. How could he dare confirm Zelophehad's loyalty to Moses?

"Have you fallen for her?" Father came inches away from him.

"No. She's beautiful but doesn't seem to have much more to offer." Assir dug deep to submit his lie.

"Son, I want to know where your loyalties lie." Spittle built up in the corner of his father's mouth.

"Of course, Father, with you." Assir's parched throat struggled to swallow.

"I hear the mother is very sick, and her time is close. Help Milkah through this time of grief. I want you to befriend her. Help her see we want what is best for everyone. But I'll work on my way of getting to Zelophehad."

His middle brother entered the tent but didn't retreat when he saw them. Did his father ask him here, too?

"Elkanah, why don't you sit here?" Korah waved to the chair where Assir used to sit. His father had directed him on the worn reed mat he usually allocated to Reba.

Elkanah threw back his shoulders. "Yes, Father."

"You may go now, Assir. I've things to discuss with your brother."

The status of being the firstborn son slipped away. *Even if I'd wanted to inform him about Zelophehad's view, he didn't give me a chance.* And what good would it do? *He'd be angrier that I haven't done enough.* Would Milkah help him meet with her father? He needed to convince Zelophehad that his father was right. But he felt so wrong about it.

The next evening, Noa gathered her sisters around Ima's pallet and invited Abba to sit beside her. "We have a surprise for you tonight. Hoglah composed a song for you, and we realized it's for us, too. It's called 'Look Up.'"Noa winked at Tirzah, who began in a clear, soft tone.

"Look."

Hoglah joined next, harmonizing with a third higher note. "Look up."

Then the others joined in with complementary harmony.

Look up and you will know.

View God's canvas before you.

The Lord's presence surrounds you.

His magnificence inspires you.

Look up, and you will know.

They repeated it from the beginning. Their vocalizations soared with lively reverence. Tirzah sang the last verse alone with a catch in her throat that sacrificed the diction of the last word.

Ima had swayed from the first note Tirzah sang and waved them to join her on the pallet. "What a gift you've given me. A gift of love, a lullaby of hope. Whatever may happen, you'll know He is always there for you. What joy for your ima's heart. Thank you, my beautiful daughters."

Zelophehad caressed her mother's hand with a loving graze. "Such treasures in one family."

Noa's spirit lifted at the joy emanating from her mother. Her illness was now apparent to all. Ima enfolded Hoglah in her arms as all the sisters gathered around them.

Over the last three weeks, Zelophehad had prayed that Tikva, the most talented Hebrew midwife, could somehow ease Jeska's ailments. Tikva had served a famous wabau, an Egyptian physician. She had signaled that they meet alone. Fearing the outcome, he insisted they meet near the workshop.

Zelophehad watched Tikva's nimble body maneuver toward him. How could this seventy-year-old woman with her gnarled hands and lined, deep crevices be so spry? On her chin sprouted little stubble spikes like a young man's beard. Could she say something to give him hope? Was he only fooling himself?

On her back, Tikva lugged a basket overflowing with mint, hyssop, mustard, anise, cumin, and other spices he didn't recognize. "I'm sorry. As you can see, I've tried all my known methods. I even found some balsam. I have no more cures."

"Is there nothing else to be done? She seems to be in pain. My daughters and I can't bear to see her suffer."

"You and your daughters should make the best of the time left. I'll leave you with some rabil that will calm and comfort her body."

"How much longer will she be with us?"

"She is in our Lord's hands."

His heart pounded in his throat. "Please, not a word of this to my daughters."

Zelophehad slept apart from Jeska most nights to ensure her sleep, but tonight, she wanted him to remain by her side. Once everyone had settled, he lowered the curtain for privacy. He cradled her face in his rough hands, searching her eyes for any pain.

She moved his hands from her face and set them on her chest. "My darling, you're everything to me—my life's desire. You've been wonderful with our daughters, showing them how they are wanted and loved. I have only one regret." Her throat caught before she convulsed into sobs. She was barely breathing as the torment wrenched from her. "I didn't give you a son."

"What is this? You are the light of my life, my beloved in everything. You've been there for me in my darkest hours and my brightest." His head and stomach reeled. The light in her eyes, always full of joy, was dimming.

Jeska inched up, her voice low, her breathing unsteady. "You must be strong for the girls, for they'll rely on you more than ever. Leora will support you. Even though she's Abel's wife, she's like another mother to our girls, and Abel reveres you and will be by your side. Emet and Adina will also be there. He'll make amends."

"I ... I've so cherished our life together. You've given me bliss from your love of life, always finding something good even amid our challenges. The girls became better women because of your lessons and actions." About to lose control, he forced himself to bring some levity. "And your humility for the inability to finish a joke because you forget the end line."

Her mouth curved into a weak smile as she nudged him. "It's the thing I love most about you. You always make me laugh, no matter what, and sometimes, it's what saved me. I've felt treasured by you every day. Now lie close to me, as I'm tired and must rest a little."

He cuddled Jeska, feeling her body relax in his arms. "I love you, my darling." *God, give Jeska rest now. Let her know how much she is loved. Please provide me with strength.* Exhaustion lay on him like a heavy plank. He joined her, his breathing slow and sure.

In the morning, Zelophehad woke with Jeska near his chest. He gently touched her arm, but it was cold as stone. His soulmate had left this world. He let out a grief-choked wail, waking his daughters.

Noa jumped to cover Tirzah's ears. "My sweet, get dressed and rush to both aunts and ask them to hurry here, and then you should stay at Aunt Leora's."

"Is it Ima?" Tirzah tried to look behind the curtain.

Noa scrunched up a tunic and held it for Tirzah to poke her head into, then she pulled it down over Tirzah's body. "Tirzah, you must go now. It's important. I'll come for you soon." She blocked Tirzah's view and led her outside.

Tirzah stared down, her neck bent forward, and shuffled a few steps. She turned and pleaded, "You promise you'll come for me?"

"I promise, dear one." Noa's insides ached. Tirzah turned several times to see if she was still watching. Noa waved until she saw Tirzah enter their aunt's tent.

She returned to see Abba, cradling Ima, rocking her back and forth as he wailed, "My love."

"Why? Why Ima?" Milkah pleaded.

With hot tears burning down her face, Noa took Milkah aside. She tugged her sister's convulsing body and then directed her toward Mahlah.

The anguished cries of Abba filled the tent. Noa turned toward him and tried to pry him away. "Abba, we will prepare her. Go to your cousins and stay with them until we send for you."

His voice hitched. "Please go to your aunt's tent. Leave me, and let me say goodbye."

Noa hooked her arm around Hoglah's back, nodding her head to Mahlah to move their sisters away. Her vision blurred as she laid out her younger sisters' tunics, ushering them to dress. "Hoglah and

Milkah, go to Aunt Leora's and be with Tirzah. Mahlah and I will wait outside for our aunts."

Hoglah and Milkah leaned on one another and seized each other's hands as they left. Noa and Mahlah fought back their tears until their sisters entered Leora's tent.

Uncle Abel raced to embrace Mahlah and Noa with his long arms like a bird covering fledglings with its wings. "Oh, daughters, I know this is a terrible loss, and how very painful this is. Your abba is like a brother to me. He lives as a beacon of faith. I know he taught you to be strong, but grief can overtake us. There is no right or wrong way to feel, but try to help one another and your younger sisters. They look to you for solace. I am here for you, and your Aunt Leora is here for you."

"Thank you, Uncle." Noa raised her arm, wiping her tears and nose. "Abba wishes to be alone with her."

Abel comforted them each with another hug. "I understand. Go to Leora to get what you need for the burial."

Abel knelt beside Zelophehad. "I am here, Zelo."

"I thought I'd have one more day, one more waking hour. Why did I fall asleep? Her time was nigh. I should've been awake, been there when she ... she ..." Zelophehad's hands shook as he covered his mouth.

Abel embraced him, but Zelophehad was too numb to return it. "She always knew you were there for her."

Emet entered, and his color drained from him, looking ashen. He touched his cousin's forearm and firmly moved him away. "Come, the women will prepare her." Zelophehad collapsed, convulsing with weeping as Emet's body sagged under his weight.

Zelophehad tipped his head heavenward and then let it drop. "Why did He take her? She's done everything in His honor. She's an exemplary mother, a devoted servant of the Lord, my light, and my compass in this world. Why now? Why has God forsaken me?"

Emet patted Zelophehad like a child.

Zelophehad pulled away and fell on some cushions.

Emet put his arm under his waist, lifting him to a sitting position. He carried a wooden basin of water, setting it in front of him. "Zelo, come wash your face. Come, now, Zelo."

Abel crept to the chest at the end of the bed, pulled out Zelophehad's favorite outer tunic, and laid it next to him with his knife.

Zelophehad tore the garment and cried into it.

Emet raised his cousin, and Abel took the other side of Zelophehad. "The women are here, let us leave and let the women in. Come, now, come."

Noa mechanically lifted the two baskets of aloe and myrrh that her aunt had asked her to bring to the bedside, tears spilling down her cheeks. Their woody aroma permeated the room as she set them on the side of the sleeping pallet, averting her gaze from her mother.

Leora drew a sharp knife from her leather sheath, waving Mahlah and Noa to her. "I helped your younger sisters tear their outer tunics to honor our tradition of keriah. I will start the tear on the left side with a knife, and then you will shred the rest of it by hand, stopping at your heart. After mourning, we will stitch it back together. It will be a tear that recognizes that your mother has joined her ancestors. Just as we mend your tunic, in time, your heart will heal as well. You'll carry your mother with you always."

After rending their garments, Noa dropped her parents' bedroom curtain in case her sisters returned. She shifted around to her mother's lifeless body, and the room began to spin.

Leora stepped in front of Noa. "I understand this is very difficult for both of you. It is hard. My mother advised me that what we are about to do is a gift to your mother. We prepare her to be gathered by her people, just as our relatives were before us. May this help to calm you as it did for me. We will remember her as she was, not as she is now."

"I wish to help, I just, just ..." Noa rubbed her hands back and forth. Her haunted eyes beseeched Leora.

Her aunt, with a sympathetic nod, twisted her away. "Why don't you choose her tunic and headdress?"

Noa lowered her head and squeezed her aunt's hand. "Yes, I can do that." She retreated to her mother's wooden chest opposite the bed. Raising the lid, the scent of her ima surrounded her. She fought back the tears and crumbled into a ball.

Mahlah knelt beside her. "We will never see Ima wearing these things again or hear her lyrical voice."

Leora lowered the stone mortar and pestle for grinding the myrrh and bent down, laying her hand on their shoulders. "Why don't you choose the clothes together?"

Noa and Mahlah wiped their hands on a cloth and fingered their mother's tunics.

"This was her favorite. The light gray one." Noa held it up to Mahlah.

"This mitpachat headscarf she wore on special occasions, and this purple beaded headband Abba had given her when they married."

"Beautiful choices. They are beautifully woven. Did you make the tunic, Mahlah?" Leora dried her hands after washing Ima and touched a corner of the tunic.

"Yes, it's the finest she owned. Mahlah infused it with love." Noa hugged the tunic to her chest before handing it to her aunt.

Leora brushed Ima's long silver-gray hair with a wide-tooth comb and arranged the mitpachat and headband. "In my basket is the linen cloth that your mother and I worked on together. She entrusted it to me for safekeeping and asked me to let you know I would be here for you. Will you bring it over?"

Noa fingered the soft ivory cloth, and a sob caught in her throat. "Mother thought of bringing us comfort and solace even in death." She laid the cloth at her mother's feet and dared to look up at her. "I miss you so much it hurts. I will try to be the daughter you want me to be. I will love you always."

Their aunt laid out the linen cloth, the final step to wrapping Ima's body, leaving the head uncovered. The head covering would be added later. She assembled the remaining burial preparations. "I will go now and let the men know we are ready. Emet was to hire the singers and flutists. Keep the curtain down, and you can prepare for the visitors who will be coming after the purification week. You did well, my nieces."

Noa nodded. "Thank you, Aunt Leora, for your tender care of Ima and for choosing to join us in our grief."

"It is what we do for family, my dear niece." Aunt Leora lowered her voice and crossed her arms in front of her.

When her aunt left, Mahlah limped her way to Noa, and they collapsed into each other's arms.

Noa's lips trembled. "I don't believe she's not here."

Zelophehad bent over, holding his head, his glassy eyes tearing.

Abel accompanied him outside the camp, since they both were now unclean. "I will sit with you, cousin, till we hear them calling for us. Emet is making the arrangements."

He couldn't bring himself to accept Abel's words. Zelophehad's hands and feet were numb. He'd lost track of time, dazed with an emptiness he wasn't sure would ever leave him. Not knowing whether an hour or hours had gone by, Emet bent down and murmured, "Zelo, we have completed the preparations. I have hired two mekonenot and the two male flutists for the procession."

Zelophehad knew the mourning women singers would honor Jeska with songs of lament, but he felt rooted to the spot. Why did he have to move?

Abel inched closer to his cousin, raising him to his feet. "Zelo, it is time."

Zelophehad barely acknowledged his extended family and the mourners who had come to show their respect. Eyes glazed over, he turned to his cousins. "Please help me carry her."

Abel, Emet, and Jonathan followed him into his tent. Jeska's body seemed so small in the ivory burial linen wrap. He traced the outline of her hands, which crossed over her heart in a gesture of prayer. "I will always love you." He bit his tongue to keep from crying and laid the head covering over her face.

Abel extended his hand and gently led him back. Emet nodded to Zelophehad, Abel, and Jonathan, directing them to lift the bier's four corners.

Zelophehad dipped his head as he passed his daughters. They followed, shuffling five abreast. His extended family, Emet's and Abel's sons and Emet's daughters-in-law and grandchildren proceeded behind the daughters in a somber march.

He passed hundreds of men from various tribes who stood on the path to the burial site. The support of his workshop's old and new generations tugged at his heart. The two flutes whispered hauntingly reverent, emotive tunes, accompanied by a soft, mournful duet for a woman's life well lived. Those not attending the burial lined the outside of their tents to convey respect.

As they left the tent area, Korah, his sons, and Dathan stood at a distance with their heads bowed to remain ceremonially clean.

Zelophehad, in a daze, yet because they stood out, noticed the Levites' robes. Why would they bother to come to pay respects? He couldn't recall when Korah attended a funeral that wasn't a tribal leader's.

"Look past them, cousin. Don't let them take this from you. Look up, and you will know," Abel said.

Zelophehad nodded, a tear escaping. *They will not take my spirit of love from me for this woman.* He heard her voice say, *"Zelo, my love, I will always be with you."*

Finally, some distance away from the community, they arrived at an open rocky field chosen by the Levites for the burial site, as there were no caves nearby.

Zelophehad's chin trembling, he signaled to his cousins and Jonathan to lower the bier onto a large layer of stones next to the open grave. He slowly kneeled and spoke his last words of love.

The music stopped, and Shemida, one of the Manasseh elders, lifted his arms. "We come to bid farewell to Jeska, wife of Zelophehad, as she is gathered to her people. She was a faithful wife who raised five loving and industrious daughters. She, with Zelophehad, taught them the meaning of our commandments and laws, which will guide them throughout their lives. It is appropriate and right for us to commend Jeska with our Shema as she carried out her duties with diligence and joy.

> Hear, O Israel: The LORD our God, the LORD is one.
> Love the LORD your God with all your heart
> and with all your soul and with all your strength.
> These commandments that I give you today are to be on your hearts.
> Impress them on your children. Talk about them when you sit at home and when you walk along the road, when you lie down and when you get up.
> Tie them as symbols on your hands and bind them on your foreheads.
> Write them on the doorframes of your houses and on your gates.

"And now, may we honor Jeska in our hearts by supporting her husband and daughters."

Zelophehad, Emet, Abel, and Jonathan picked up the bier and lowered Jeska's body into the grave. They covered her with the mound of large stones staged there. Jonathan presented the matzevah, a thin two-foot-high rectangular limestone marker that Zelophehad had engaged him to carve. Zelophehad anchored it in the ground at the top of her grave. He then knelt, laying a small stone on top of it. His daughters, one by one from oldest to youngest, also laid small stones, touching their father's shoulder as they did. Zelophehad remained at the graveside, telling his daughters to go to their temporary tent.

Noa clasped Tirzah's hand, and the other sisters joined her, plodding side by side from the desolate spot. Dozens of people had stood outside their homes as they had walked to the grave site, speaking the traditional words of condolence, "May God comfort you."

"There were so many people." Tirzah drew her limbs close to her body.

Noa squeezed Tirzah's hand. "It was to honor Abba also."

Milkah scratched her arm under the rough-hewn sackcloth. "Can we wear something else after the burial? This is so itchy."

"Sister, we don't mention our discomfort." Noa was about to give her more of a lecture, but Mahlah interceded.

"Milkah, you will carry this memory with you your whole life. Let us not dwell on the irritation. Let us be here for each other and our abba." Mahlah carefully negotiated the uneven ground with her sticks. Milkah lowered her head and didn't utter another word.

"It should give Abba some solace that so many people accompanied us to the ceremony," Tirzah added, always trying to be the peacemaker.

"So right, Tirzah. It is a comfort to us, too, to know our parents are respected," Noa said. *How could my sisters be so different? Tirzah's kindness and thought for others. Milkah again only thinks of herself.* Mahlah's sensitive counsel had been more effective than Noa's chastising, though. Perhaps Milkah didn't accept Ima's death, and Noa should be more helpful to her. *Please, Lord, guide me with my sisters.*

Assir sighed. *Even in sackcloth, her nose red, Milkah is beautiful.* Would as many people come to honor his father if his mother passed? Assir coughed to shift his thoughts, straining to overhear Dathan's whispers during the funeral procession. He didn't hear every word, but Dathan told Father something about his followers working on a sure way to convince holdouts like Zelophehad. Father asked not to know the details but encouraged him to do whatever it took. *I wish Dathan would leave Father alone. He only fuels this threatening course of action.*

On his sweating fingers, Assir twirled the heritage ring that Father hadn't taken away … yet. What could Dathan be up to now? *Perhaps Father is right. I don't want to know.* Would Milkah even meet with him again? She dodged him every time, keeping herself surrounded by her sisters. She'd once disclosed her mother was very ill and she couldn't spend any time other than being at home, and now she would be in grief. Perhaps soon she would need someone to lean on. *I hope it will be me—and not because of Father.*

CHAPTER 9

Noa left the tent early. With a fortnight passing after the official seven days of mourning and with no storytelling at night, the grim quiet suffocated her. Her father, depressed, didn't lead them in their daily prayers and called upon each daughter to take turns for their devotions. He had not set foot in the family tent since Ima's death, staying with Uncle Abel and Aunt Leora. Her aunt said her father had returned to the workshop and assigned Emet and Abel to oversee the tutoring and running of the day-to-day activity. He'd lose track of time and often skipped meals. Aunt Leora would bring him food. She always found him sequestered in the back of the tent.

Noa feared he would never conquer his grief.

If I can show Abba I'm helping my sisters, maybe he'll find the courage to return to us. With the commission for some new tents that Noa had secured that morning, all of their minds would be kept off their sorrow with the intricate work. The slightest remembrance of Ima's smell or touch set a cascade of sadness from one sister to the next like spring water running down a wadi. Every time she entered the tent, she imagined seeing Ima, but the empty bed cruelly reminded her of her loss. Why couldn't she accept it?

Zelophehad sat in his favorite place on the outskirts of the tribe, where he had taken his daughters so many weeks ago. The ethereal light of the half-moon illuminated the rest of its circular disc, with additional light added from the pillar of fire. He laced his fingers behind his head, tipping back against a boulder. When he saw Josiah approach, he handed him a skin of water and indicated for him to sit. "Shalom, Josiah. Thank you for coming tonight. This is my favorite place to come to be restored, to appreciate our Lord's grandeur. It is the only thing that has given me solace. I've come here every night since Jeska's death."

"I can see why, Zelo. Again, I'm so sorry for your tremendous loss."

"I've been staying with Abel these past two Sabbaths, but it's past the time for me to return to my daughters. I wanted to be strong for them, and I needed the time to gather my strength. It is why I've asked you here. Jeska's death reminds me how very precious life is, and my duty as a father is to ensure that my daughters have a worthy future, one that will be fulfilled with God's promise of a land with milk and honey."

"Zelo, your daughters are lovely, but you know I am engaged." Josiah took a large gulp of water.

"Yes, I know this well. May God bless you on your wedding day and all the days of your lives. I was hoping you could help me with something else. Abel has been a good mentor to you in the workshop. He is very fond of you, as you listen so well."

"He's a very good teacher with lots of patience and encouragement. He speaks very highly of you, too."

"I have no brothers, but he is like one to me. This last fortnight, he showed me how much he cares. I don't think I would be able to return to my daughters without his understanding and compassion leading me forward."

"I know he cares very much for you and your daughters."

"Yes, that is what I hope you can help me with. I have been sworn to secrecy about a possible marriage between my oldest daughter, Mahlah, and his son Simon. Emet says that Abel doesn't want a marriage between them because she is damaged. You know she has a limp, which impairs her ability to do some chores, but Mahlah, my oldest, is so special. She is like her mother, exemplary in her devotion to our

God. Her skills and knowledge of weaving, cooking, and herbs for medicine are outstanding, and she is so gentle of spirit, but strong."

The corners of Zelophehad's mouth pulled down. "Please, Josiah, I believe Simon would be an excellent match for her. But Emet convinces me not to speak to Abel because of Simon's sensitivity about his adoption. He says Abel wants to ensure that Simon has a woman deserving of him. But Abel cares so much for all my daughters and treats them so well." He threw his hands up. "Why is he so against this?"

"It is strange. We sometimes talk about family and how much he and Leora enjoy spending time with all of you. Now that I think about it, sometimes he looks sad, like there is something he wishes to express but doesn't."

"Yes, he does the same with me. I know it is a lot to ask, but could you please help me find out if his feelings have changed?"

Josiah swallowed before speaking and leaned closer. "Zelo, I can see you are in pain. I don't want to upset my relationship with him, but I can try to see if he will open up about Mahlah."

"Thank you, Josiah. It is a key to my daughter's—and, I think, Simon's—happiness. Blessings to you. I can now go back to my daughters with hope."

The odor of burnt quail hung in the air. Milkah dropped the pan and hung her head.

"What happened?" Noa went over to help her.

"I burned it. I ruined dinner. I wasted it and disgraced Ima's memory. She would've reminded me to pay attention. Sh-she'd have ..." Milkah slumped onto a mat.

Noa scampered over. "Oh, Milkah, not to worry."

Abba lumbered in, his hands covered with aged scars from work, and sped to Milkah. "Is anyone hurt?"

Noa stood in front of Milkah. "It's my fault."

Hoglah and Tirzah added in unison, "No, it was my fault."

Milkah rose and stepped in front of Noa. "No, Abba, it was mine."

He lifted his hands wide. Noa thought he might yell, but he laughed. "I am proud of you, daughters." She thought it might be the first time Abba had laughed since the funeral.

"Oh, my daughters, you give your abba something to be proud of. I've a story to share with us all. It is my story." Abba motioned for them to gather around the table.

"I'm more than sorry I've not been here. It's been difficult for me, and I needed some time to myself. I wish for you to learn from my story about rising from defeat, from grief, and from mourning. I haven't spoken much about my first wife, Sara, and her death. It devastated me, so I engrossed myself in work where I could, for a moment, forget. The work consumed me, allowing me to bury my anger with God for taking her away. Why would our Lord strip me of all that I treasured?

"One night, I wandered past the camp with my bedroll, drawn to a lonely place under the stars with the firmament of heaven surrounding me. The full moon cast a luminous glow, bathing me in its warmth as if the sun engulfed me. I did not feel alone. Then, a still, small voice breathed on me. *'She is on her way to you. She will love God and she will love you.'* A shooting star streaked across the sky, carrying with it a joy that embedded in my soul. The presence of God enshrouded me—a gift, a genuine gift that whispered, *'You will marry again.'* I didn't quite believe it, but I learned to trust God. His plan for me was much more than I could've imagined.

"Your mother appeared a short time after this. God always brings light and a fresh path. It seems I need to learn this lesson again. We trudge through this desolate valley now, but we're together, and I will be here for you. I may need to slip away, but always, you are in my heart."

No one spoke, but a heavy veil had lifted, and a light entered their tent. Noa handed Hoglah her harp.

"Look up, and you will know," Tirzah sang as the others joined in. It was a moment that sustained them to start again.

Noa sensed enough time had passed. Before approaching all of her sisters, she asked Mahlah. Was it time to disperse Ima's things?

Mahlah agreed and motioned for their younger sisters to come together in front of Ima's open chest.

Sharing the shepherding of her sisters and surrendering control instilled peace inside Noa. Mahlah seemed ready to take on more responsibility since their mother's death.

"Noa and I feel sorting and sharing Ima's things would lessen Abba's pain, and maybe ours, too," Mahlah began.

"How do ordinary things become such a part of us? Why does a simple headscarf still smelling of her bring such tears?" Hoglah nestled one of Ima's scarves.

Milkah, her hair uncombed, plopped next to Tirzah. "A weight seems tied to my body, pulling me. Each step is an effort."

Noa bowed her head and asked God for the words to guide them. "I know we are all struggling. Perhaps we can dwell on the good things if we share a story. She always reminded us of our lineage and how we ought to behave. 'Remember Joseph.'" Noa raised her pointer finger, as her mother often did.

Hoglah grabbed Noa's finger, laughing. "Ima invoked Joseph's name more to me than any of you when I stepped out of the tent. Our neighbors must have thought we had a suitor named Joseph."

"Perhaps you should wear Ima's ivory headscarf, which was her favorite. Knowing our sweetest memory, we can help find something meaningful for each of us." Mahlah laid the scarf on Hoglah's shoulders.

"And also allow us to be generous. Do we agree, sisters?" Noa knew what she hoped for from her mother's treasures. Would it cause a challenge with Milkah?

As the sisters nodded, Hoglah wrapped it around her head.

Noa couldn't have planned it better, with Hoglah's buoyancy and Mahlah's guidance soothing their spirits.

"As for you, Milkah"—Hoglah presented the delicate material to Milkah as a servant would, wrapping it around her shoulders—"Ima allowed you to parade around in her woven shawl because you wanted to play the bride."

Milkah wrapped the shawl tighter. "I remember. You played my handmaiden and said, 'Your groom is coming for you, be ready.'"

They started clapping to a wedding song.

"I'd cherish Ima's sewing basket, grateful for how much she taught me," said Mahlah.

"That's fitting for you, for you've shared your expertise with us." Hoglah carried it over to her.

Noa glanced quickly at the item she prayed her sisters would approve and humbled her request. "I'd appreciate Ima's onyx necklace."

Milkah went and picked up the gleaming stone. "Hmm, I didn't think of that. It's quite dear. I'm surprised you chose it."

"It would feel like a hug from her," Noa said.

"Hmm." Milkah glanced around to see if her sisters agreed. "Be generous, Milkah," Mahlah chided.

Milkah nodded.

Hoglah presented the necklace to Noa, who secured it in a small leather pouch.

It was Tirzah's turn. "You've so many stories that I'll never experience. I miss what I don't have, what you've had with her." She choked on her words.

Noa glanced at her other sisters and nestled around her. "Oh, Tirzah, she so adored you. You filled her with such joy. Ima named you 'She's my delight' so you will always remember how much she loved you."

Each of them laid their items before Tirzah.

"You shall have them." Noa beheld each sister.

"You'd do this for me?" Tirzah put her bunched fist over her mouth. "No, I won't take your favorite memory of Ima. It means everything to me that you would offer your treasures."

"Are you sure, Tirzah?" Noa touched her cheek.

"Yes, I'm sure."

Noa selected a graceful gold cuff. "Why don't you have Ima's favorite bracelet, the one Abba gave her, reminding you you're loved every day?"

Tirzah tried on the priceless bangle as she scanned her sisters' reactions. When they consented, she twirled it on her wrist.

They reviewed the rest of Ima's things, and each revered their sweet keepsakes.

Noa's eyes prickled with tears. "I know that Mahlah and I are so proud of you, each giving with thoughtful grace. We will remember this for the rest of our lives. Ima would've been so happy to see how each of us came together. To know that we are there for each other, and always will be. I love you, sisters."

They came together in a circle. But as they sang the song Hoglah created for their ima, Noa's heart still ached. *Why is it a tragedy that reminds us to love one another?*

CHAPTER 10

Two Sabbaths passed as the sisters returned to a routine. But grief lingered like the embers of a smoldering fire. Noa did her chores by rote and today journeyed to the river. How could everyone still go on as if nothing had happened? She avoided the women and looked for Tikva, the midwife. She spotted Tikva bent over, rinsing some linens. "Shalom, Tikva. Can I talk to you?"

"I welcome a chance to rest. How is your father doing?" She squeezed the water from a cloth and spread it out on the rim of her basket.

"He's somewhat better, but it takes time. I wanted to ask you about my older sister. Do you have something that might heal her hip so she can walk better?"

"Ah, it's been some time since it first happened. She must try walking again to ensure she hasn't lost her ability. I have some ointment that I've just come to possess that may help, but it's too expensive for you."

"What does the ointment do? Then we can talk about the expense."

"Noa, what is the use if you can't buy it?"

Against her better judgment, Noa pulled out a leather pouch from her sleeve and revealed her mother's necklace. "It's onyx on a silver chain."

"It was your mother's?" Tikva rubbed her stubbled chin.

Noa nodded.

"You must love your sister very much. Would your mother want you to do this?"

"If it will heal her daughter. Yes, I'm sure of it."

The old woman stared at Noa. "Come to my tent, and you can give me the necklace. I'd put that away. When you come, I'll instruct you on how to use the ointment."

"Will it work?" Noa looked hard at Tikva.

"It's always in God's hands."

"I'll come later today." Noa flinched, hearing her father's words to leave emotion out of bargaining. But if the ointment worked, then it wouldn't matter. She'd stretch the truth and tell Mahlah that Tikva had gifted it to her in reverence for their mother. Perhaps a word game, but there was a gift involved. *Lord, without reservation, I give away this symbol of Ima so dear to me. Please let this ointment work for Mahlah.*

After their mourning period was complete, Assir persuaded Milkah to venture just outside the camp and to bring both Reba and Tirzah. He hoped to give her a respite from her grieving. Under a towering acacia tree that lent delightful shade, he set up two small, expensive rugs, arranging them within a short stone's throw of each other. Reba offered some apricots and water and then joined Tirzah, finding something to laugh about while watching them. Assir also presented a music scroll he'd promised to show Milkah.

"You're certain I'm not boring you?" Assir handed her the basket of apricots. He felt lighter than he had in days, for she didn't seem to remember her annoyance from the last conversation on her father's leanings. He opened the scroll and showed her what he was working on.

"Where do you come up with the ideas for verses and the music?"

"My youngest brother also loves to compose. He and I talk about ways to bring meaning to our worship. We listen to our elder Levites, hear their songs, and then try to come up with some of our own. We can spend hours writing together." Assir relaxed his shoulders, realizing he was feeling something he hadn't felt for a very long time—joy.

"Hoglah also loves to create music ... sometimes for the silliest things, but it keeps us all amused."

"Ah, we have an alamoth in the making."

"Alamoth?"

"It means a song to be sung by a female voice."

"She'll like knowing that, since she is always the one with a high range. I'll convey it to her."

Assir wanted to share more than knowledge with her. He wanted to support the faith she drew from her father. He glanced away. Why ruin this time together? He twisted the gold heritage ring his father reminded him of this morning, warning of his drained patience. Father would take the ring away if he weren't successful, which could mean being disowned. And if he were disowned, what could he offer Milkah? But should he convince Zelophehad to follow his father?

Milkah interrupted his thoughts. "Where will you live when we get to our Promised Land?"

"Ah, a great question." Assir smiled with relief. "The Levites don't inherit any land. We will dwell in cities. It's being determined now where each priest will live. Our Lord bestowed on us the honor of working for Him and deemed our inheritance to come from tithes as an offering to our Lord. I'm blessed to be in His service."

"I wish I could live in a city."

Would this be worth a try? As if something took hold of him, he blurted, "Milkah, perhaps your dream will happen. If you allow me, I would like to discuss something serious. It's about your father and my father."

"They know each other?" Milkah squirmed.

He read Milkah's reaction. Zelophehad must've spoken about his father. "They've met, but I wouldn't say they know each other, and maybe that's where the confusion lies."

"Confusion?"

"Your father should listen to what my father is proposing." Assir immediately regretted his sternness.

Milkah shot back, "I don't know who Abba listens to or what your father is proposing."

"But you should. Everyone in this community must choose." He tried to hold Milkah's hand.

She recoiled. "Choose what? What are you saying?" Milkah dropped her apricot and searched Assir's face.

"Milkah, you're a jewel any man would adore. I hope you understand my growing feelings for you, and I hope to speak with your abba about us. But first, he must choose, or this will never be." Assir stopped abruptly, surprised at his words. Where did they come from? Could he keep his place with the Levites and convince his father to betroth him to Milkah?

"Never be? Me and you? I don't understand. You want to marry?" Milkah's brows knotted with confusion.

"Milkah, there are so many things you don't know, which is why you must have someone to protect you." He again reached out for her hand.

Milkah extended her right hand, then whipped it back. "Assir, you're confusing me. What are you presuming? What do you and I have to do with Abba?" She withdrew from his hands.

Assir willed her to keep looking at him. *What am I doing? I don't want to convince Zelophehad.* "I can protect your abba and your family. Once you are safe, I can propose to him about us. You'll live in a beautiful city, far away from all this sand. I will always protect you. I love you, Milkah." There, he'd said what was on his heart. Father would never approve, but if Zelophehad came to his father's side ... *Is that the only way I can protect her?* Milkah's voice cut into this train of thought.

"Protect my abba and my sisters? I don't know what you think my abba needs to choose, but it scares me. You have said many things today that I didn't expect—especially a marriage proposal. I'm confused and think it is best now if I leave." Milkah rose and straightened her tunic, striding over to her sister and Reba. "Tirzah, we need to leave now."

Tirzah shot Assir a confused look. "Milkah, are you well? What happened?"

"Come, it is time for us to go."

Tirzah jumped up and looked back at Reba, shaking her head.

"Milkah, please, I'm sorry, don't go. I-I only want to help you and your family." Assir stood as Reba marched over to him.

"What have you done? Tirzah's my friend!" She punched her brother on the arm.

As he rubbed it, Assir knew he deserved that and much more.

Zelophehad waited till both Emet and Abel were out of the workshop for the day. He had stopped by Josiah's bench and asked him to stay a little longer. When no one else was left, he motioned for Josiah to join him. *Oh Lord, let it be so that Abel's heart has melted and he sees how right Mahlah and Simon are for one another.*

Josiah rotated back to ensure they were alone. His head pulled back as his shoulders pulled forward, and he licked his lips. "I'm sorry, Zelo. There is not much to share. I made enough innocent observations, but every time I mentioned Mahlah, he either returned to his current project, changed the conversation, asked something else, or lowered his head, saying, 'I don't know.' But again, he looked sad as if he were burdened with a secret himself."

Zelophehad pressed his weathered palms in a circular motion. "Emet is right, then. He's either too sad or embarrassed to utter it. It is the only thing that stands between us. I think he senses that. Oh, I had hoped for such a different answer. Thank you, Josiah, for trying. I know it must have been an awkward situation I put you in with your mentor. I hope you know that it was for the love of him, Simon, and Mahlah that I asked."

"You'll find the right husband for Mahlah. God be with you in your search."

While she foraged for kindling, Noa hadn't noticed the sun's position. Now she picked up her pace, or she would be late for the evening meal. Passing the back of the Korahites' tents, she overheard two men talking about Milkah. She glanced over and saw them sitting outside on mats under an awning. She shuffled quietly to the side, where they couldn't see. As she lowered herself to the ground, she shifted her unwieldy bundle of kindling closer to her body, holding it steady.

"Milkah believes Assir is pursuing her for marriage. We can learn a thing or two from our eldest brother. He said he was making progress in knowing Zelophehad's stance on Moses and converting him to Father's thinking because of Milkah."

"Abiasaph, our brother may be exaggerating. I would if Father ordered me to spy on someone and I had little to report. The smallest thing sets him on fire."

"Assir sounds sincere. Maybe he's fallen for her. Although it surprises me that Milkah wouldn't insist that he declare his interest to Zelophehad. It's not a good reflection on the Levites."

Noa's foot fell asleep. She stretched it out, and as she did, she slipped and dropped some branches. The commotion startled the two men, halting their conversation. She covered her head with her shawl and darted away, confident that if they got up to look, they could only determine that it was a female figure. Assir deceiving Milkah to spy on Father? If Milkah was putting them all in danger, should she expose her sister? She vowed to confront her first thing in the morning, away from everyone.

With Milkah's turn to fetch water, Noa volunteered to bring another jug and accompany her. Rehearsing her approach through a restless night, her anxiety grew over Milkah's unwitting involvement with Assir. Would her sister be truthful? *Will she trust me?* It would be a delicate balance.

"To what do I owe this kind gesture? Did someone declare how lovely I am, big sister, and you want to convey some of my attributes?" Milkah giggled.

Noa looked down, focusing on the path. "In a way, that's right."

Milkah stopped in her tracks. "It's not every day I get such a compliment from my sister. Who? What did they say?"

"It was Assir's brothers. They were conversing about you and Assir."

Milkah brightened. She hooked Noa's free arm in hers and strolled farther away from the family tents. "What did they say?" She beamed with anticipation.

She doesn't know. Milkah hadn't been this amiable with Noa for some time. *Should I bring up the brothers' conversation and ruin the bridge that just mended?* Noa grimaced.

"Well, what did they say? You're keeping me in suspense."

Noa saw the anticipation and hope in her sister. "Let me first ask how you've come to know Assir?"

"We've met a few times, on my way to do chores. He described his role in the Tabernacle and inquired about our family and Abba. He's quite handsome and so knowledgeable. I think Abba would like him. He thought it was a good idea for Abba to meet with his father, Korah. He also said he wanted to meet with Abba about something serious."

"Something serious?"

"I think he should talk to Abba about it." After briefly looking away, she squeezed her sister's arm, changing the subject. "I dream of a permanent home in a city, away from all this dusty wilderness."

"I'm trying to understand. You've never lived in a city, so how would you know you want that? And what does a city have to do with getting acquainted with Assir?"

Milkah stopped, unhooking from her sister's arm. Her smug smile filled her face. "Do I know something my sister doesn't?"

Noa swallowed and pasted on a smile. She lowered her jug and waved for Milkah to do the same.

"Our Lord assigned the Levites to cities as they serve Him. Assir will live in a city, as I wish to do."

Noa lowered her chin and peered up at her sister, keeping her question steady. "Assir attracts you because he'll live in a city?"

"It just so happens that Assir expressed the idea of a future with me just yesterday."

"How did this happen?" Noa knew Assir's charisma, along with his looks, could steal a young girl's heart. Would he be a good husband? *He'd be a good provider from the firstfruits tithings.* Perhaps the brothers' exchange was only hearsay?

"It was all proper. Reba and Tirzah joined us. He brought a music scroll to show me and some lovely apricots to eat."

"To show you where? I didn't see him come to our tent?" Noa kept her tone calm, belying her nerves.

"Just to the end of our tents, he laid out two beautiful rugs to sit on. Don't look so pale. Tirzah and Reba sat a stone's throw away, facing us."

Although her youngest sister and Reba were there, it was a stretch to be considered proper without an older chaperone. Noa's stomach lurched.

Milkah continued in her blissful ignorance. "Because of his role, I assured him our family is God-fearing. He even proclaimed he'd approach Abba to propose. You hold me in such suspense. What did Assir's brothers say?" Milkah nuzzled closer to Noa. "Please, before I burst."

Propose? Was he serious? *He should have come to Abba first.* She opened her mouth to speak, pausing to pray for the right words. "I'd collected an armful of sagebrush when I heard your name and crouched down to listen. Milkah, it was not very kind." Noa kept close, looking to see if anyone was around.

"So, it's gossip? Why would you stop and listen? I'm sure it's nothing more." Milkah flipped her hands in the air.

"Sister, please, I'm not saying this to hurt you. They bragged that Assir manipulated you by promising marriage, but he's digging for information about our father's loyalty to Moses. One brother even said you amazed him with your patience since Assir hadn't introduced himself to Abba." *I'm amazed too.*

"Stop. These are lies. I refuse to listen anymore. I'm confident Assir will make this right. There's no reason to mention this again, and without a doubt, don't speak to Abba. I am alarmed you would unveil such gossip."

"I can't promise." Noa felt squeezed into a vise. Wouldn't Abba want to know? Milkah was young and impressionable, but how could she not see the truth? Meet with Korah? *What has my sister been duped into?*

"You've never been on my side. You only want to please Abba."

"This has nothing to do with my feelings about Abba. It's about Assir luring you into something you may not realize is happening. I'm trying to help." She went to hold Milkah's forearms.

"Help like this, sister, I can do without." Milkah pushed her away, picked up her jug, and bolted toward the river.

For the next two days, Milkah avoided Noa.

CHAPTER 11

The back of Noa's tunic was already wet, and it was not yet the zenith of the day. She hadn't forgotten Abba's reprimand to make peace with Milkah. But how to do that now? She'd been tempted to spill out the cause of the tension, but she wanted to shield him from more worries. She sought Hoglah, hoping she would be a bridge to her younger sister and learn more about whether Milkah was being fooled by Assir. She quietly proposed to help Hoglah milk the goats. Noa picked up the two large, empty skins and waited for Hoglah outside the tent.

Hoglah approached, also carrying two skins, and joined Noa as they walked past the Benjamin tribes' tents to the Manasseh goat pen. "I know what you want to talk about."

"I knew Milkah would confide in you. Please, I know it might be uncomfortable, but I'm worried she could put herself in a troubling position."

Hoglah squirmed, rotating her body. "I don't want to betray her, but I'm worried too. First, Assir could do no wrong, but now she doubts him. Yesterday, she donned an old tunic and let her headscarf hang loose around her neck. She wasn't herself. The last time I saw her this upset, she scratched her precious mirror."

Noa shared a crooked grin.

"She told me she dreamed about his angular build, his consideration for her, his thoughtfulness." Hoglah copied Milkah's movements, swaying her hips and fixing her hair.

Noa leaned forward. "So thoughtful he didn't introduce himself to our father."

"I said as much. Then she cried and blamed herself. How could she be so blind? It didn't help that you were the one who told her about the brothers' conversation. It alarmed me when Milkah retold the conversations with Assir about his father and Abba."

"She could be putting Abba in a serious situation." An image of their abba defending himself and Korah shouting in front of Moses plagued Noa's mind.

"She admitted to deflecting the conversation and defending Assir's innocence when you tried to warn her."

"Because it came from me?"

"You two don't understand each other." Hoglah exhaled loudly. "How do you think she sees you?"

"Perhaps ... pushy, commanding. She's even called me a spare mother."

Hoglah snickered. "Perhaps appropriate sometimes?"

"You too?"

Hoglah shrugged her shoulders. "You can be stern with Milkah. She thinks you only dote on Tirzah and chastise her for caring about her appearance. But, in this situation, I professed you only tried to protect her."

"Thanks, I appreciate that."

Hoglah halted, looking sideways at Noa. "She's afraid you'll tell Abba."

"I can't imagine she would say anything to hurt his reputation. Did she?"

"She only expanded on how he told us stories about our ancestors, earlier times since we've been in the wilderness, and our commandment discussions."

"Good. I won't speak of this then." Noa returned to their normal gait.

"She'll avoid Assir for now. I suggested she practice with me on how to respond to him." Hoglah strode with a man's gait and mimicked Assir's absolutely straight posture. "It was the first time Milkah laughed in two days."

Noa stifled a laugh. "Good imitation from what you've told me. You're a wonderful sister, Hoglah. Let her know I will not speak to Abba, but also tell her to be careful not to share Abba's thoughts if she does speak to Assir. It's no doubt better coming from you. Did Assir share anything about what Korah wants from our father?"

"He said we must choose along with the whole Israelite community about something, but she wasn't sure of what the choices were. She couldn't help thinking about the marriage proposal. But now she sees that this choice may be something serious, and Assir was insincere." Hoglah clutched Noa's elbow. "What is happening to us that we would have to choose?"

"We can depend on Father. He'll protect us and keep us safe. Maybe Korah is jealous of Moses. Though who would follow a man who speaks against God's chosen leader? We should not worry. Thank you for trusting me with your concerns about Milkah and about ... me. I promise I'll be more mindful."

"I'm glad we talked." Hoglah tapped Noa's hand. "You're still going to help me with the goats, right?"

Noa raised her two large skins. "Yes. I don't mind milking our goats. Come, with the two of us, this will not take much time."

They walked the short way in silence. Noa reflected on all that her sister shared, but Korah concerned her most. There couldn't be many people listening to him. Abba had enough on his mind without worrying about Milkah, and since she was refusing to speak with Assir, it made little sense to bring this up. *I hope I'm right.*

"Are you sure it's my turn?" Milkah lay on her pallet. "It's so hot."

"Yes, Milkah, this is my third time reminding you. Please go. We're almost empty. When Abba comes home, he'll wonder why we don't have water with five able daughters." Noa rolled up a rug to shake outside. "Come now ..."

Milkah muttered to Hoglah. "I doubt he'll even notice."

"What did you say?" Noa snapped.

"Nothing."

Tirzah intervened. "I'll go. Don't argue anymore."

"No, Tirzah. It's Milkah's turn." Noa dropped the rug.

Milkah cajoled, "She's found some new friends. Would you deny her some fun? Let her take a leisurely dip in the water."

"Please, I want to go." Tirzah slid over. "Please?"

"Fine. Milkah, you can shake out the rugs with me."

But it was Noa who finished cleaning the rugs alone. Milkah had quit a while ago, complaining of the heat. As she scanned the horizon, to her horror, a spectacular display of dark brown clouds raced toward the encampment. She trembled as the rapid rise in temperature caused her to shudder. Then trumpets blared, with men shouting, "Ruah qadim. Sound the alarm, east wind." She struggled to gather two rugs, leaving the rest, and dashed to the tent. Mahlah, Hoglah, and Milkah stood at the entrance and yelled something.

"Is Tirzah back yet?" Noa screeched due to the vehement crackle of the wind.

"No. Should I go down to the river?" Milkah donned her outer tunic.

They carried the rest of the rugs inside and began to roll them up, staging them at the edge of the tent, preparing for the onslaught of sand.

"Where is Abba?" Noa yelled.

"With Uncle Emet." The color had drained from Mahlah's face.

"We must get these rugs positioned. All of you work together. You must stay here," Noa barked.

"You can't go out. The eye of the storm will be here any minute. You won't be able to see anything." Milkah gripped Noa's arm.

The tent shook from a booming clap of thunder. The fine sand and large clumps of dirt pelted outside the tent like the rumble of a herd of runaway camels.

Assir grabbed a walking staff and his goatskin cloak, observing with concern the approaching dark cloud. He remembered today would be Milkah's turn to go to the river. She'd avoided him after he pushed too far.

"Ruah qadim!"

The calls grew louder. He had to find her, so he bolted down a less-trodden path, bypassing the women running for cover. Heaving his breath, he heard earsplitting screams pierce the air from upstream. He squinted and could see the outlines of Reba and a young woman who looked like Milkah struggling in the water.

"Assir!" Reba screeched as she approached the hanging rug. He charged twenty feet over to her.

Even though he was now close enough to hear, she still shouted over the wind. "Thank the Lord. We need to hide under it." Reba pointed to the rug secured by a rope on the shore. The women hung it to separate a private area while they bathed. Reba pushed her wet hair back, her headdress missing.

With seconds to prepare, Assir darted to the shore and severed the rope. He caught one end, hauling his side down, then commanded, "Pull, Reba, Milkah!"

Reba strained to seize a corner of the soaking rug and tugged, falling backward. "It's Tirzah, not Milkah." Reba spat water out.

His body froze. Tirzah? She had been bent over in the water, her wet hair concealing her face.

"We must get to land. Reba, hurry, come quick." He loudly boomed his directive over the wind.

Reba startled him. "Assir! Grab her."

His one arm latched onto the rug, and the other stretched out. He couldn't reach her. "Tirzah, give me your hand. Hurry."

Tirzah inched her trembling hands toward Assir. Not covering her mouth, she choked on swallows of sand.

"That's it, I've got you."

Using the rug as a protective shield, they dragged it to shore just as the full force of the sandstorm struck.

Assir yelled over the powerful winds raging against them. "We cannot stay here, or we'll be buried. We must crawl to a safer place. Reba, keep the flap down as much as you can." He crawled forward, his hands bleeding.

"We can't see. We're blind. How do you know where we're going?" Tirzah gagged on her words.

"We must put our trust in God. He will lead us. Stay close to me." Assir begged God to spare them. As they scraped inch by inch over the rocks and sand, his knees bled. His heart wrenched when he heard Tirzah croak, "Abba, Abba."

Noa threw on her mother's heaviest kesuth, woven with close-knit goat's hair to protect from chilly nights and pelting rain. She prayed its length and hood would defend her. She circled her head with her father's mourning scarf so that only her eyes were visible.

Milkah begged. "It's not abated yet. Stay here."

"I'll wrap a rope around me and tether it to the tent. I won't go far, but I can shout and bang this pot so she hears a signal."

"You're impossible." Mahlah hobbled over to cinch the knots around Noa's waist while Milkah and Hoglah busied themselves with untangling the rope.

"Make sure the rope stays secure." Mahlah pleaded.

"Keep praying, sisters." Noa crept out, trying to keep the smallest opening of the tent flap, the sisters battening it behind her. The fine sand beat against her clothing like a thousand bees stinging in unison.

Her bravery evaporated. A suffocating brown haze emitted a musty, earthy odor that enveloped her along with a wind like nothing she'd experienced before. Even with her ears pressed tight by her scarf, the deafening sound vibrated through her whole body. She crouched, hoping this would lessen the force of the gale. *Lord, be with Tirzah and bring her home safe.* She hammered on one of Abba's tools, realizing no sound escaped the violent din of the storm. It was no use. She tugged on the rope, wincing in pain from her bloodied hands as she turned back. *Come back, sister, please come back.*

Startled by the loud pelting on the tent, Zelophehad bounded from his sleep. His grief had overtaken him when he'd returned to the workshop, and he'd taken refuge on Emet's sleeping mat for an afternoon rest, not wanting to alarm his daughters.

Emet and Adina were scrambling to secure rolled bedding to the tent's perimeter.

Zelophehad heard the screams. "Ruah qadim!" He bolted to the tent flap. "My daughters! I must go to them."

Emet grabbed Zelophehad's arm. "You can't go. It's upon us."

"Emet, I couldn't live if one of them perishes." He threw on his cloak. "I don't have my headscarf."

"It's foolish for you to go. It's impossible now." Emet blocked him from the opening.

Zelophehad swiveled toward Adina. "Do you have a sheer scarf to protect my eyes?"

She knelt at her dowry chest, pulling out a delicate scarf. "This was my mother's and is precious to me. May the Lord be with you."

"It is a gift I won't forget."

He secured the scarf, tucking it over his eyes, and strode to the tent door. "I must do this, Emet."

"God be with you, cousin." Emet quickly opened the flap.

The pelting sand momentarily blinded Zelophehad. *Lord, please guide me. Help me keep my daughters safe.* He squinted through the gauze veil, dimly seeing a man enrobed like a caterpillar cocoon made of goat skin groping toward him. In snatching him by the collar, he discovered it was Jonathan.

Zelophehad pointed to his tent, putting his arm around Jonathan's waist, ushering him on. They bent low and wobbled side to side from the thrashing squall. Struggling to untie the outer tent flaps, he thundered, "Daughters, are you there?"

He heard their muffled voices as Noa untied the last inner cords, and they stumbled into the tent. His daughters nosily gathered round, hugging them and shaking off their grit. He scanned the tent, dread gripping him like the panic when he awoke to Jeska's cold body. "Where's Tirzah?"

"She's by the river or somewhere in between." Noa stood close to him.

"Noa, grab your mother's cloak and stuff it in my leather bag. Milkah, fetch me two goatskins of water. Hoglah, find the extra strip of tent siding in the chest over there." They scurried to assemble everything. Mahlah grabbed the leather sack and helped Noa stuff the cloak in.

Jonathan cornered Zelophehad. "I will search with you."

"Jonathan, it will be too dangerous."

"We've no time to waste. It is why I am here—to ensure your daughters are all well. I knew you were not with them."

Zelophehad slid the goatskin leather satchel around his neck and handed the water skins to Jonathan. "I will not forget your coming at this hour."

The sisters wrapped the extra tent panel around them, with one end flapping over their heads. "May God protect you," they cried as they readied to secure the tent.

"We will be back. Don't, for any reason, go out." Struggling to gather his bearings, Zelophehad spied the brilliant light from the Tent of Meeting. *Lord, be our guide. Bring me to my daughter.*

CHAPTER 12

"Say it. I know what you're thinking, Noa. I should've gotten the water early in the day." Milkah paced back and forth.

Hoglah stopped cutting strips for bandages. "You couldn't foretell the storm."

"Aren't you going to hurl accusations?" Milkah scrunched her face, glaring at Noa.

"This isn't about you. We have Abba, Tirzah, and Jonathan to prepare for. Let's anticipate their needs for bandages and healing ointments. Keeping busy will help us, too." Noa set two mortars and pestles with large handfuls of hyssop and sage in front of Milkah and Hoglah. She took a large clean cloth, tearing it into strips while Mahlah rolled them.

As the minutes dragged on for what seemed like hours, the sand thundered so hard it rattled the tent, making it hard to hear anything else.

After all the preparations were done, Noa thought about what her abba would suggest to help give them hope. "Sisters, let us have a prayer vigil for the safe return of Abba, Tirzah, and Jonathan. Each of us will take turns praying and sleeping." But no one slept, each praying silently, huddling together. Noa's prayer for their safety combined with thoughts of guilt, asking for forgiveness, and wishing she could go back and change her decision to insist Milkah carry out her water chore. If she had, no one would have been in danger. Why didn't she insist?

Getting water now would be impossible, as these storms could last for days. A cloud of incessant, dense dust often hovered in the sky, confining everyone until the air became breathable. Noa's lack of supervision had put her family at risk. *Forgive me, Lord.* The night wore on.

At dawn, the wind ceased. Noa handed her sisters large wooden bowls to dig out the mountain of sand that blocked their entrance. "We must clear the opening." After an hour of digging, they tapped the top of the flap, and more sand cascaded, choking them with a haze of dust.

"Wait, shhh. I hear digging. Abba? Tirzah? Jonathan?" Noa's pitch rose with each name.

"We're here, all of us." Jonathan's utterance was low and garbled. "Untie the ropes from inside and take away the rugs. Never mind the mound, we'll step over it."

They flew to the ropes, sand flying to either side.

Noa choked at the sight of Tirzah—small, bruised, her eyes swollen shut.

Zelophehad carried her to his pallet. "Our dear heart is here, thanks to our Lord and Jonathan's bravery."

Noa's tears welled up. "Praise God you're all back."

Abba collapsed next to Tirzah. "Her scrapes and bruises need tending."

Tirzah attempted to straighten her torn tunic. She was almost unrecognizable. Her body was caked with mud, her hair in tangles, her belt and headdress gone. "I'm sorry I didn't return sooner. Reba and I were in the water for a swim, and then, then ..." Tirzah's bottom lip quivered.

Noa covered her with a blanket, holding her close. Even with the temperature raised from the sandstorm, Tirzah shivered. "You're here. You're safe now."

"Assir guarded Reba and me. Or father wouldn't have found us."

"Assir was there?" Milkah knelt next to the bed.

"He expected you and wanted to ensure you were safe. After unleashing the privacy rug, he dragged Reba and me under it. He battled the wind's mighty force to get us out of the water." Tirzah hiccupped.

Noa made way for Mahlah. "It's time for you to rest. We can hear all about it later. First, your wounds need to be cleansed, and then you can sleep. I'll make a potion."

Mahlah dipped a bandage in the little remaining water and, with a soft touch, pressed around one of Tirzah's swollen, bloody knees.

"You're in good care with your sisters. You'll be well." Her father cast off some sand like a dog who waggled emerging from the river.

"Jonathan, Abba, you're both hurt. Let me get you some water and ointment." Noa winced at the deep, bloodstained scrapes on their hands.

"Look after your sister with care. I'll let Emet know we're safe. He may have words for me about taking Jonathan. If it weren't for him, though ... No doubt God's hand guided this young man. Fetch me two tunics for us to change into. Your aunt will bandage our wounds."

Jonathan's whole body was a mask of mud. He leaned toward Mahlah. "Mahlah, Simon would've joined me, but a flying branch struck him on the way. With his eyes wounded, he couldn't see."

"Oh, please send us word about how he fares. We will pray for him. Thank you for telling me." Mahlah continued to clean and apply ointment to Tirzah's legs.

Milkah gripped two water jugs and headed for the opening.

Hoglah snatched one out of her hand. "Let's hope the river is clear. You can't carry both." They slipped out.

Before he left, Noa clasped her father and didn't let go. "You, Tirzah, Jonathan. My world."

He brushed her cheek. "We were not alone, for the Lord gave strength to Assir, Jonathan, and me. The light shining from the Tabernacle guided us. I'm so grateful to these young men. Without them, we wouldn't be here." Abba embraced Jonathan, patting his back. "God placed His hand on you. Your father and grandfather will be proud of the hero you are."

Noa couldn't restrain herself. She seized Jonathan's hands and squeezed them with all her might. "Blessings to you. My heart's so full."

"I will always be here for your family, Noa."

Abba coughed. "Your father and grandfather await."

Holding Reba by the waist, her arm slung around his neck, Assir waded through an avalanche of sand deposited throughout the camp. The sandstorm had knocked over tents and broken animal pens. The goats and sheep bleated with fear as they were herded back. Women and men shoveled, repaired tent poles, and yanked torn tent sections. Bruises covered his body as if he had wrestled all night.

When he arrived at the tent, his mother, alarmed by his appearance, insisted on bandaging Assir—lecturing him in a hushed tone about why he had endangered himself for Reba. He didn't dare confess that Milkah was his motivation for being at the river. Tirzah and Milkah must've changed places. Did Milkah suffer any harm? He ached to find out. After she cleaned and dressed his wounds, Assir poured water into a bowl and brought a clean cloth to Reba, who was sound asleep. His mother finally came over and also cleaned her wounds, but not as gingerly as she had for him.

"Your father and brothers are inspecting the damage to the Tent of the Meeting. Go to your father. He will be greatly relieved to know you are back."

He changed into an old tunic and headed toward the Tent, but when he saw the number of Levites circling around, he diverted to the river, where he spotted Milkah and Hoglah striding with determination. He limped on his injured leg to catch up with them but could only trail behind, close enough to hear their conversation.

"We could have lost her, and it would've been my fault," Milkah moaned.

"We've never endured a storm like this one. Look at all the damage. We're fortunate our tent withstood what it did. We must be thankful for God delivering her back to us."

"Will Abba ever forgive me?" Milkah wobbled on the uneven ground, almost falling into a mound of sand.

"Milkah, let's slow down. We need to be careful where we walk. Abba will forgive you. He's only concerned about Tirzah's healing."

"I can count on Noa to go to Abba. Forgiven, maybe, but not forgotten."

"Could you be judging harshly? She didn't say anything about blaming. Tirzah's safe. We need to gather water to keep her wounds clean, and then we can console and comfort her. We can sing to her."

"I've something better. I'll give her my mirror and brush."

Hoglah stifled a giggle. "A gift she'll know means a lot coming from you."

Agonizing pain gripped the back of Assir's thighs, yet his only desire was to hug Milkah, protect and comfort her. A branch cracked under his feet.

Hoglah turned toward him, then whispered in Milkah's ear as she steered her away. Milkah glanced at Assir, her eyes narrowed, her pupils like chips of flint.

His gut churned. *Why have I done my father's bidding to stand against Moses? Something I don't really believe. And now Milkah won't even speak to me.*

He sank to his knees. *Where are You, God?*

Zelophehad slept right through until the following day and rose mid-morning to bathe, returning from the river with gratitude that it could now be accessed. Adina set a large mug of brewed sage before Zelophehad and began rebandaging his wounds. "I thought a refreshing bath in the river would restore you, but you look troubled, Zelo. Is the pain bothering you? Drink this while it's hot—it will calm you."

"Adina, your healing touch is a gift to me. What troubles me is Korah's recruits casting aspersions against Moses. Korah shows no understanding of the sandstorm damage everyone is experiencing."

Emet peered up from his carving. "They're even meeting now at Korah's insistence."

With a nagging feeling growing in his chest, Zelophehad continued. "Korah is clever in his approach to his followers. He flatters people's vanity instead of being true to God's words. He tried to recruit me to persuade you, Abel, and others of our tribe to join him. Korah presumed we could influence other tribes because of our reputation and relationships in the workshop." Taking a deep breath, he silently thanked God that the estrangement from his cousin had ended and he could now get his counsel. After Jeska's death, Emet had been true to his word to be there for him.

"This sounds like treason, a rebellion within our community, a civil war. It's tragic that it has come to this." Emet's neck veins beat a pulse.

"Dathan invited me to visit with Korah before he has a gathering tonight of his supposed followers."

"You'll go? Why even consider it?"

"To learn how far this has spread. How many people has he poisoned with his words? Is he just bragging about his followers, or is it true? If true, it could end our community with brother against brother."

As the sun was setting, Zelophehad, flushed with anger from meeting with Korah, marched to Emet's tent at a pace a camel would've envied. He winced at every step from the pain that shot up his back after rescuing Tirzah. When he didn't find Emet, he barged into Abel's tent. The potent menthol aroma of baytheren and samwa invaded his nostrils, further annoying him.

Noa and Leora were picking off each plant's beaded and sticky leaves. Armloads lay on the table. He covered his nose, remembering that baytheren would ease Tirzah's upset stomach and the samwa would treat her wounds.

"Abba, what troubles you so?" Noa reeked of the plants as she bent to remove his sandals.

Zelophehad frowned. "Where is Abel? It is urgent."

"Noa, get your father water. He should be here soon. What is it? I'm guessing you met with Korah?" Leora cleared a space, grouped the fragrant herbs, and stuffed them into the two woven baskets.

Zelophehad did a double take. "How did you know?"

"Adina. She brought the myrrh I required for Tirzah's potion. Korah always blusters about what he's going to do. What makes this different?" Leora fiddled with a branch.

"This time it's serious. He's gathering notable tribe members from the community." Zelophehad threaded his fingers through his graying curly hair.

Leora shrugged. "It's mere talk."

"He betrays Moses and Aaron, and in total blasphemy against God Himself." He wiped the sweat from his brow.

"But Korah is Moses and Aaron's cousin." Leora passed a clean cloth to him.

"No matter. His delusional mind believes he deserves more, and it doesn't satisfy him and his sons with their God-given roles in the inner workings of the Tent. He says that Moses has gone too far."

Leora gasped. "I heard Abel sounding off about Korah, but nothing this drastic. Why has it come to this?"

"Korah planted these seeds of discontent long ago. He accused Moses of lording power over the people and said these decrees were created by Moses, not God. How can people be so gullible as to believe his fabrications?" Zelophehad rubbed the back of his neck.

Leora's fingers splayed out, covering her chest. "Oh, Zelo, this is frightening."

Noa cleared her throat. "I don't want to bring bad news, but I heard Korah's wife at the river today."

Zelophehad glared at her. "What did she say?"

"She rallied us together, she said, for an important announcement. She predicted Korah would soon be in charge, saying she awaited having her husband and sons to take back their rightful place."

"Back? Take back what?" He slammed his mug on the table.

Noa jerked but continued. "She said, 'When Korah rules, my husband and sons will finally stand where they belong, above the rest.' Several of us laughed. She spat with such vehemence and righteousness and said, 'You'll see. Mark my words.'"

"Prideful, jealous, full of self-ambition. Noa, the river allows gossip to travel fast with a potent effect. Warn your sisters to avoid all who speak Korah's rubbish. Don't let them have any friendships with their women or girls. Leora, I suggest you advise Adina to talk to her daughters-in-law."

"I will. I believe Tirzah is fond of Korah's daughter, though."

Before Noa could speak, her father scowled. "I am aware that Reba and Assir saved Tirzah and may have nothing to do with their father's motives. But for now, she must take leave from this friendship."

Noa nodded in agreement. "I've also befriended Reba, who seems alone in her family. It will be tough on Tirzah, especially after what they both experienced. But I'll help her understand. Do you believe Korah can cease his endeavors?"

"I'm afraid he is beyond reasoning. For all your sakes, stay away. Tonight, Korah is hosting a gathering with two hundred fifty of his followers and inviting Moses and Aaron to show their defiance against them. Yet it is not them he defies, but God."

Noa rubbed her arms. "This gets worse with each word. Two hundred and fifty followers? Will you attend?"

"No, of course not. But I haven't revealed the worst part. He's summoned the tribal leaders the day after tomorrow to confront Moses at the front of the Tent of Meeting."

"Can he do that? I thought only Moses or Aaron could proclaim a formal meeting?" Noa tugged at one elbow as her fist covered her mouth.

"Whether he can or not, he's going forward." Zelophehad rubbed both sides of his temples. Sleep would evade him tonight. "Don't share this with your sisters. I hadn't intended you to hear any of this. We're all recovering from the sandstorm, and grief is still close by.

"Leora, can you and Adina be with them for the next two days? Tomorrow we must be at the workshop. Only the men will attend the meeting the following day. None of our women should appear or sneak to the Tent. I don't care how much anyone wants to be there—especially you, Noa." He glanced over at her. "You can work outside on the tent loom. Do you understand?"

Before Noa could answer, her aunt did.

"I may have to tie Noa down." Leora aimed her quiver of a smile at Noa. "Sometimes you imagine the rules don't pertain to you."

"Comes from her mother's side." Zelophehad smirked.

Leora set her hand over his. "Hmm, maybe a little from her father?"

"Perhaps a touch." He looked directly at Noa. "Understood, daughter?"

"Uncle Zelophehad, is all well? Is Mahlah well? And Tirzah?" Simon fumbled in, his one eye bandaged and a black-and-blue bruise around his other.

"She's fine, as is Tirzah. But how are your eyes? That's some branch you chose to fight with." This was not the first time Simon had asked about Mahlah. *Why doesn't Abel see what a good match he'd be for her? It couldn't be because of Leora.*

"The branch won." Simon nodded to Leora. "Thanks to my mother, my eyes will heal."

"I appreciated your offer to join us and know you would've. I've taken enough of your good mother's time. She always calms me." He put his hand on Leora's shoulder. "Simon, walk with me. I have some news about the next two days that I'd like you to share with your father. Noa, arrange for your sisters to weave on the loom and explain why your aunts will join you."

After briefing Simon about the Tent meeting, he advanced to Emet's.

CHAPTER 13

"Tonight was all I hoped for with all my followers." Father paraded around the family tent. He swung his blue tallit shawl over his shoulders and swaggered from side to side like a peacock strutting before his intended mate.

Assir looked away, startled at his father's brazenness. His father, so full of himself, seemed to forget the recent disappointments of Assir's lack of progress with Zelophehad. He'd asked only his mother and him to be present. His brothers and sister were sent to another Levite's tent.

"Look at my beautiful tallit design. It is the exact opposite of Moses's instructions. He claimed God specified a garment should be white with blue tassels on the corners, and I made the whole garment blue."

Assir straightened, fixing his gaze on his father. "Moses said blue symbolizes the sea and the sky, and the sky resembles God's sovereign throne. The blue fringes remind us to observe all of God's commandments."

"My point. Why did Moses, Aaron, and Eleazar elevate themselves above us? I invited them to dinner but didn't give them their share of the priestly meal. My moment of triumph came when I signaled the men to reveal their all-blue prayer shawls while I taunted Moses with my loudest shout. Does a prayer shawl made entirely of blue require fringes?"

How could his father carry on with such blatant disrespect for their leader? Why thwart Moses's every step? *Is it not our Lord who speaks through him?*

His father glowed. "I taunted Moses, 'It's not God who made these rules, but you have elevated yourself as ruler and appointed your brother Aaron to high priest,' and all the men yelled in approval." He mocked Moses's stance, with his hand on his staff, and exaggerated his stutter, which had become less pronounced over the years. Only in times of frustration did it become apparent. "'You ar-r-r-r-gue we are h-h-h-holy, which s-s-s-sounds like you don't acknowledge the L-L-L-Lord. He gives us b-b-boundaries so we can respond with obedience. Why would you question His words? As a Levite, you have a responsibility to our c-c-community. Korah, are you able to change m-m-morning into the night?'" Father howled, almost choking.

"I dismissed him with the sounds of jeers surrounding him. No, son, this is where my leadership excels. We're all holy, and, as God's people, we're equal in holiness to Moses. He shouldn't be set up as better or as God's leader. Why honor his brother as the only one to enter the Holy of Holies? Moses says he only conveys God's decrees." He whirled in his shawl, leaning toward Assir. "I will do something about it."

Assir's mother, dressed in one of her many gauzy sheaths, caressed his father's arm. "Korah, why not assemble your followers and leave this band of wanderers? Select the wealthiest who still have their departing gifts from the Egyptians. Make them your community. Create your own rules from God, not the rules Moses portends come from God."

"Woman, haven't you understood? I'll wear the robes and golden breastplate in the Holy of Holies. The miracles I create with the Lord's staff will amaze the people. I will interpret the laws of our Lord." Father rocked back and forth on his heels, his hands jutting into his waist, and drew up close to Assir. "This is not to be repeated. I will tell the people what they want to hear, and they will reward me with loyalty."

That night, Assir lay awake, frantic about his father's assessment. With his father's plans, what would happen to Milkah and her family? Milkah continued to dodge him even after he saved her sister. Now he understood why. He'd been too emphatic in following his father's mission. He had to apologize, but then he'd have to disclose everything.

Zelophehad spent another night at Emet's, allowing Tirzah more time to recover. He returned early in the morning.

Tirzah didn't rise to greet him as she usually did. Instead, she relaxed with her legs on a pillow.

"How are you feeling, my sweet?"

"My sisters have cared so well for me." Tirzah brightened.

"Your knees. Are they healing?"

"The honey stopped the bleeding, though I'd rather have eaten it." She giggled. "My wounds are small enough, I didn't need any mending. The ointment Noa and Aunt Leora concocted will heal the rest. I am grateful to be alive. And you, how are your wounds?"

"I'm fine, little one. You make your father happy to see you well and at ease." Zelophehad lifted his arm around her.

Milkah wore a handed-down tunic, her hair pulled back and unadorned. "I, too, am grateful to you and Jonathan."

"We need to be thankful for our Lord's protection. I've much to do in the next few days and must leave. Your aunts will be with you, so please be mindful of them. I also set up the tent loom, and when you're ready, you can repair our tent entrance panel. You'll be in high demand from the storm wreckage. Aiding others will keep your heart and mind at peace. I'm sorry I can't be with you more, but I've important dealings at the workshop."

Hoglah edged next to Noa. "Is something bothering Abba?"

"I'm not sure. Perhaps it's the damage from the sandstorm." Afraid of what Hoglah might observe, Noa turned away.

"I heard it may be about Korah and his falsehoods. Abba said if you repeat a lie often enough, people believe it, and belief becomes the truth."

Noa turned back. "Where did you hear about Korah?"

Leora and Adina, their arms full of tattered tents, called out. "Shalom, girls, we're here."

Hoglah made a hmm noise in her throat. "Why has Abba sent both our aunts to be with us this morning?"

"They're here to assist us with all the work." Darting to her aunts, Noa hustled to unburden them, glad for the interruption to avoid talking about Korah.

Leora scrutinized their tent for signs of tears. "We've got much work in front of us. How is our patient, though?"

"I want to help." Tirzah quavered.

Leora hesitated mid-step. "Tirzah, stay put. Rest. We must organize everything. You can join us in a while." She kissed Tirzah on the forehead.

"Mahlah, can you gather the spun wool? Why don't we start on your flap first? Noa, Milkah, Hoglah, give me a hand." Leora pulled the shredded tent flap from the bent, splintered acacia frame.

Noa and her sisters dragged the battered flap to the loom.

Adina sat on a stool and spun the goat's hair thread onto a spindle. "You must thank your Abba for adding this canopy. The work is so much easier shielded from the sun's rays."

Although their tent had not sustained severe damage, some panels begged for mending. Due to the size of the loom, it required five of them to ensure a tight weave. The two ends and the center position required skilled weavers to keep the threads tight. Noa and Mahlah took the ends with Aunt Leora in the middle. Milkah and Hoglah were on the inside.

Milkah worked on the opposite side of Noa, for their relationship still required some attention. The family stories, the latest gossip, and many laughs created a camaraderie Noa enjoyed and provided a rest from all their troubles. They wove with their backs to the tent because of the sun's glare.

"What's all the laughter?" Tirzah bent to admire a large woven basket with its intricate design sitting at their entrance. "How beautiful. Aunts, did this come from you? How unique with its multicolored lid. We should learn how to design it. I'll bring it over."

The basket secreted a pungent, earthy scent. Inspecting the unusual oblong shape, Tirzah opened the lid and screamed, "Snake!" Petrified with horror, she quickly dropped the cover.

Noa bolted to Tirzah, yelling, "Step away!"

The snake reared his head and coiled back, ready to strike.

Noa snatched the thick lid and slammed it on top, smashing the snake into the basket. Tirzah collapsed into her arms.

"Oh, Tirzah, my sweet." Noa tugged Tirzah a foot away.

"Don't open it, don't," Tirzah howled, burying herself into her sister's chest.

A group of women from the surrounding tents scattered around. Noa handed Tirzah over to Mahlah. She circled those standing around, her hands flailing out, and shouted. "Whose basket is this? How did it get here? Who left it?"

The women retreated a step back, shaking their heads.

Noa ordered, "Hoglah, run to the workshop and get Abba." She lifted the water jug next to the loom and secured it on top of the basket.

"Are you hurt, Tirzah?" She knelt, examining her sister.

"No, but very scared." She clung to Mahlah.

Zelophehad, his cousins, Jonathan, and Simon arrived, thrusting the neighboring women aside. "What happened?"

"A snake hidden in that basket almost struck Tirzah." Noa pointed.

Zelophehad glanced at Tirzah, still buried in Mahlah's arms. "Is she hurt? Did it bite?"

"No, she's just terrified." Noa, at last, caught her breath.

He drew out his knife, as did his cousins. "Keep back, everyone. Jonathan, block the women."

"Abba, there are two snakes at least. One is dead, its head cut off." Tirzah squirmed out of Mahlah's embrace. "If it hadn't been for Noa—"

"Tirzah, you're safe now. Don't worry. What kind of snake? Was it large?" His voice soft, he looked directly at her.

"I-I don't know ... It had two horns sticking out of its head with brown and tan scales. It was curled around, so I don't know how large."

"Did you hear any sounds?"

"Yes, a rasping."

Zelophehad signaled to Emet and Abel. "Maybe a horned viper. Let's move it to the outskirts." He admonished the onlookers, "Return to your tents and don't follow. We will take care of this. Simon, remain here. I don't know how it got here, but I trust you to keep them safe. Jonathan, run to the shop and bring a few men and the long-handled hatchets.

"Emet, Abel, I will pick up the basket. You clear the path." Zelophehad set aside the water jug, clamped down the lid, and scooped up the basket. His cousins ran before him, threading through the tents to the perimeter.

Jonathan and two men met them there and lined up behind the basket.

They readied their weapons. Zelophehad tilted the basket in one move, removed the lid, and jumped back. No one made a sound. Jonathan walked toward the front of the basket. Zelophehad hissed, "Get back. Wait."

A moment later, a horned viper slithered forward. "It's more than an arm's length." Jonathan returned to the other side. "The other is dead."

"I'll go first. Be ready in case I miss." Zelophehad edged forward, raising a long-handled hatchet and, with careful aim, severed the snake's head. Convulsed with pain around his heart, he dropped to his knees. "Who would do this to my daughters?"

Jonathan charged over and dumped the basket's contents. Another horned viper lay in two pieces.

Intense heat pervaded Zelophehad's body. It must be Korah. No one else would endanger or create such devious torment. "Is this Korah's doing? To intimidate me? To scare me about not aligning with him?"

Emet stretched out his hand, helping him to his feet. "Korah might be angry because you rejected him, but would he do this?"

"I don't know. But this is enough." Zelophehad thrust his fists down. "I won't have my daughters threatened."

Abel turned away from the men so only Zelophehad and Emet could hear. "Should we go to Moses?"

Emet lowered his head. "We don't know who left this. Without proof, we can't accuse someone. First, let's search to determine if anyone saw something."

Assir stumbled toward them and, upon seeing the dead viper, moaned.

Korah's son—he must've known. *How dare he show up?* Zelophehad grabbed his tunic, "Did you do this? Did you scare my precious daughters?" He raised his fist and struck him hard.

Assir careened to the ground, holding the blood dripping from his nose.

Zelophehad picked him up, ready to strike again.

Emet pinned his arm. "Stop, Zelo. Let him speak."

Zelophehad shoved Assir back but stayed close. "What trickery is this? How did you know where we were?"

Assir bent forward, holding his nose with one hand. "I swear I didn't do this. It's why I'm here. Dathan and Abiram entered our family tent laughing and bragging that a dead snake would change your mind about joining my father. I only wish I'd discovered this last night so I could have prevented it. As soon as I heard, I scrambled to your tent. Your daughters told me where I could find you. I raced here as fast as I could. The basket was to scare you."

Zelophehad pulled Assir close. "To scare? A live poisonous snake is to scare?"

Assir shuffled back, begging Zelophehad to believe him. "They said nothing about a live one, I swear. I heard only that they wanted to scare you."

"You swear, huh? Look at what they did. You didn't know this last night?" He lifted his arm to punch him again.

Assir pleaded, "You've no reason to believe me. But I can't read the minds of men. They boasted about proving their loyalty to my father. I swear my father didn't know they were going to do this."

Zelophehad shoved him. "We must demand justice from Moses for the terror they caused."

Assir hung his head, barely speaking, "Moses is in prayer and ordered not to be disturbed. He's praying about tomorrow."

"Because of the meeting your father arranged. What will happen at this meeting?" Abel folded his arms.

"My father is deliberating with his inner circle. He plans to make a show of his followers to Moses, Aaron, and the community."

Zelophehad addressed his cousins, "We will seek Aaron or Joshua."

"They are both with Moses," Assir spoke even softer.

In one leap, he raised his fist to Assir. "If you're lying to us, I swear ... You will regret it."

"Zelo, let him go. He's just a fool." Emet grasped Zelophehad's shoulder and tried to turn him away.

He stepped back. "Go. Don't you come anywhere near my daughters."

"I promise you I will do all I can to ensure no harm befalls your daughters. I risked my life to rescue Tirzah. Be careful and watchful tomorrow. I fear my father has many followers." He held his head up to stop the bleeding and shuffled away.

Zelophehad barked at Emet, "Find out if Moses, Aaron, and Joshua are in seclusion."

"It must be the truth. Why would Assir expose himself and his father?" Emet said.

"I don't have the faith you do. I need to go to my daughters. Let's keep what's happened to ourselves. I will say someone intended to dispose of it, became afraid of the contents, and dropped it."

"Not sure they'll believe that." Abel collected the snakes and buried them. "Whatever tomorrow brings, we will face this together."

CHAPTER 14

The cool early morning air disguised the promise of summer heat. Yet heaviness and foreboding hung over Zelophehad as he trudged to Abel's tent.

Abel and his four sons waited for him. Alert but on edge, Abel asked, "How is Tirzah?"

"She's improving. Leora's lovely stories dazzled my young daughters' minds. Her spending the night was the right decision."

Emet and his five sons hustled from the workshop.

Zelophehad waved to gather them around him. "Do we have enough to go to Moses about what happened with my daughters?"

"Dathan can be reckless, we know. From what Assir said, it sounded like Korah didn't know about the actions," Emet said.

"I ask all of you to be aware and watch Dathan." Zelophehad's heart twisted in knots once again. "Come, we should go now. They were to approach Moses first thing this morning."

Assir waited on the path to the river. As soon as he saw her, he yelled out, "Milkah, please give me a moment."

She hesitated. "I can't talk to you, Assir. I promised Abba not to leave our tent this morning. The only exception is to fetch water. Now, I must return." She started to leave.

"Milkah, I vow to you this won't take long. Please."

She turned and scowled, full of judgment, showing she would not listen for long. "Why are you not at the Tent with your father?"

"I came to find you. I don't know where to begin." Assir's usual proud stance melted, his hands limp by his side. Should he get on his knees? He'd never felt so deflated.

"Be quick, Assir."

His heart skipped. He had one chance to make amends. "Milkah, thank you for not running away. How are you and your sisters?" He didn't divulge the altercation or his promise to her father.

"A snake delivered to our door? What omen is this? Who would do this? With Tirzah still traumatized, we kept our oil lamps burning all night to prove no snakes snuck in."

"I'm sorry for Tirzah and hope she'll erase it from her mind. Please, believe me. I had nothing to do with the snake. I'm grateful no harm came to any of you, and I owe you an apology."

"About the snake? You sent it?" She swung away.

"No, please. Let me explain." He dared to race after her and grabbed her arm.

She slapped his hand off. "You act genuine. But knowing your insincerity, I'm not sure what to believe from you. Including about the snake."

"I can understand why you feel this way. Please, just a moment." He hung his head.

"How can you explain your deceptive intentions?"

"Milkah, on my honor, I promise I will tell you everything. Can we sit here under this tamarisk tree for the shade?" He propped up his arm, but she refused it.

"What you want to say can be done right here because I won't be here long, and I certainly will not sit." She pointed to a spot three feet away for him to stand.

Assir stepped back and clasped his hands. "Milkah, I didn't know about the basket with the snake. I only told your father who planned it. But I want to apologize to you for something I did. This is hard for me to say. I've always honored my father. Since I was the oldest, he showered me with attention and mentored me on fulfilling my duties as a Levite. At first, Father was always faithful and diligent in his duties and training for the Lord. But when Moses chose Aaron as chief priest, it tore him apart. When Aaron donned the breastplate and he heard the bells from Aaron's special tunic, it gnawed at him like a decaying carcass.

"He became increasingly incensed about Moses and Aaron and lusted after their roles. His insatiable craving has devoured him to the point that I don't recognize my father anymore. It's as if a disease has overwhelmed his life. He talks about nothing else, and my mother's the same. She does all she can to encourage him. He's obsessed with allegiance to his cause. And he's banded together a following by using flattery and fear. He drives people away from Moses and God's teachings."

"So, I became part of this pretense to convince my father to believe in your father's plan?"

"I'm ashamed of what I've done. I beg your forgiveness. Please, with all of me, I regret what I did and how I treated you."

"Was it all a guise, asking for my hand?"

"Milkah, I admit at first it was to get information from you, but the more we got acquainted, the more powerful my feelings for you became. Please believe me," Assir begged.

She swatted his hand away. "I've thought about what to say to you. The snake incident instilled courage. My sisters and I survived it, and I will survive you. Decide where you stand, Assir. Where are your loyalties? As for me and my family, we will serve the Lord."

Assir started to reply, but Milkah hastened away.

The two silver trumpets blared a long, sustained note, summoning the entire community to the Tent of Meeting. Zelophehad stood ready. But the trumpets sounded different. This was not the usual sound of assembly, nor was it the sound directing which camp moved out first. This resonated more like the third purpose—preparing for war. *Are we at war?*

Zelophehad and his two cousins marched abreast, followed by Emet's and Abel's nine sons. His heart pounded with every step. The crowd had already assembled. At first, the hushed whispers turned louder, resonating like the hum of bees. Zelophehad and the men of his extended family assembled with the tribe of Manasseh.

Moses and Aaron emerged from the Tent of Meeting. Zelophehad's hands sweated as he elbowed his cousins to focus on their leaders. A sudden hush ensued when Korah and his lead conspirators, Dathan and Abiram, their shoulders back and chests puffed out, paraded in front of Moses. All two hundred and fifty of their coconspirators stepped forward.

Zelophehad choked. "Those are the appointed members of the council, all well-known community leaders." He also noticed two of Korah's sons had silver trumpets in their hands. They had sounded the trumpets.

Korah stationed his followers to repeat his words so the entire community would hear him. Moses usually arranged these meetings, but he didn't seem startled by the different speakers. *Rebellion!* Zelophehad's whole body quaked.

Korah glowered at Moses. "You have gone too far! The whole community is holy, and the Lord is with them. Why then do you set yourselves above the Lord's assembly?"

Outside of Korah's followers, the rest of the assembly gasped in unison and witnessed Moses prostrate himself on the ground—with another audible groan. No one could mistake Moses's humility.

Zelophehad muttered to his cousins, "Moses, may God give you the words now."

Moses arose, picked up his staff, his eyes of fire fixed on Korah and his followers. "Take censers and tomorrow put burning coals and incense in them before the Lord. The man the Lord chooses will be the one who is holy." Then his anger thundered with such vehemence, his face full of anger and frustration, "You Levites have gone too far!"

"He's giving them a last warning." Every fiber of Zelophehad's body strained.

Moses glared. "Now listen, you Levites! Isn't it enough for you that the God of Israel has separated you from the rest of the Israelite community and brought you near Himself to do the work at the Lord's Tabernacle? He has brought you and all your fellow Levites near Himself, but now you are trying to get the priesthood too. It is against the Lord that you and all your followers have banded together. Who is Aaron that you should grumble against him?" Moses pivoted and departed, leaving the crowd gaping.

The abrupt ending divided the camp into two vastly different moods. One part of the crowd huddled with their brethren and floundered away. The other strode with bravado, patting one another on the back and congratulating each other on their efforts.

Zelophehad overheard one of Korah's followers. "We will show Moses who is in charge and put him in his place. It will be a defining day. We will win our people's hearts." His ears rang with a high-pitched tone from the palpable tension. What would tomorrow bring?

Zelophehad's cousins instructed their sons to wait while they deliberated on what to say to the family.

"I am shaken by what we just witnessed." Emet scanned the surrounding men.

Zelophehad shook his head. "Korah's senseless accusations are dividing our community against one another by rewriting God's words. Surely, the Lord's wrath will be revealed tomorrow. My only hope is Korah and his followers will come to their senses, but it's unlikely. The damage is done. The conflict they have wrought will live with us long after tomorrow. Inform your sons, we will lead the conversation to prepare the women."

The three of them clasped each other's arms in silence.

When they arrived at Zelophehad's tent, the women sat working around the low table on various tasks. They quickly lifted and tied up the tent flaps to accommodate the men's return.

After the women resumed their places, Zelophehad and his cousins assembled before them. But before he could begin to speak, Jonathan arrived, heaving deep breaths. Zelophehad braced to learn the news. Had something else happened after the meeting?

With a quick greeting, Jonathan caught his breath. "It is good you asked me to stay behind, Uncle Zelo. Moses sent messengers and ordered Dathan and Abiram to come to his tent, and they—"

Zelophehad breathed a sigh of relief and interrupted. "Moses is trying one last time to prevent this insurrection against the Lord. What happened when Dathan and Abiram entered his tent?"

Jonathan shifted his feet. "They refused to come."

Zelophehad's hands flailed out, and he shouted, "Refused to come? What excuse did they give?"

"They said, 'We will not come! Isn't it enough that you have brought us up out of a land flowing with milk and honey to kill us in the wilderness? And now you lord it over us! You haven't given us an inheritance of fields and vineyards. Do you want to treat these men like slaves? No, we will not come!'"

He felt the room spin, disbelieving the words just uttered.

Zelophehad prayed for God to put the words in his mouth, bearing the responsibility of being the eldest. "Let us pray to our Lord, as Moses taught us.

The Lord bless you
and keep you;
the Lord make His face shine upon you
and be gracious to you;
the Lord turn His face toward you
and give you peace.

"Today, we will long remember. Korah, a leader from the Levite tribe, dared to come in front of the Tent of Meeting, in front of the entire assembly, to challenge Moses and Aaron for their positions."

Several of the wives stood, holding hands with their husbands.

Noa also stood. "What happened?"

"Korah garnered favor with his followers by his misguided beliefs. I fear that when young and old men have little to occupy them, they're susceptible to conspiracies. Korah attempted to entice me to join his rebellion. He hoped I would do so. He wanted me"—he glanced at Emet and Abel—"to convince my cousins and the workshop men to be a part of his deception. With fierceness, I opposed his lunacy. Tomorrow at the Tent, God will choose who is to lead."

"Who is to lead? It must be Moses." Noa stepped closer to him.

Zelophehad motioned to Abel and Emet. "Cousins, please continue." He stepped back and pressed his hands to his pounding heart. *How could this befall our community? After all we've been through, do we turn against one another?*

Noa handed him a cup of water. "Abba, you must sit down. This is too much for anyone to understand."

"Thank you, daughter. I will sit." *Oh, Lord, protect us from harming each other. May Korah see his error and give this up. Even now, I see that my refusal to join him led his champion, Dathan, to dispense that awful snake. Please, Lord, give Korah wisdom.*

When his cousins finished, Zelophehad rose to speak. "Tomorrow, no one will go to the Tent of Meeting except Emet, Abel, and me." Zelophehad scanned the younger males in the room while saying this. "Some of you will stay at the workshop to guard it. The rest of you should gather here tomorrow morning and wait for us. You're to remain here. Is this understood?"

Tirzah's face turned white.

"We will be together, Tirzah. We will be secure with our cousins here. I promise." Noa stood at attention like a soldier ready for battle.

Zelophehad ended the family meeting as he began—with the same prayer. When he finished, the extended family took their leave.

"My daughters, you must obey me." He locked his eyes on Noa. "It's important you honor my decision. Do I have your promise?"

The sisters dipped their heads. *Yes.*

"Noa, come outside with me." Zelophehad picked up two seating mats.

What did I do now? Does he not believe I'll keep my promise?

"Noa, my heart is heavy. With your mother gone, I need to know if something happens to me, that all of you will be safe. You're my strongest daughter. You remind me so much of myself, sometimes it hurts." Abba laid out the mats and had her sit opposite him. "We have a lot in common. I also rushed into things, spoke my mind, and didn't think about how my words hurt others. You see things in black and white, as I did, often making judgments too quickly, but doing what you believe is right. That's how you respond to challenges.

"When I was in Egypt, I did more for my fellow Israelites not by letting my temper flare in front of my enslavers but by outwitting them. In doing so, I saved many men from the whip and, in the meantime, taught them important skills. I admit I still struggle with my impulses and anger. That is how you get a reputation, as the Manasseh girls try to spread word of how volatile you can be, based on how you dealt with protecting Mahlah."

Abba's reminder of her reputation sank deep into her bones. Would she ever leave that behind? Noa opened her mouth to speak, but he held her chin gently.

"I know that is hard to hear, but how you deal with challenges is so important. Learn from me and the sinful mistakes I've made. Trust me, I have. God help you from knowing what I've done. My daughter, I hope one lesson I've taught you is how to get up from defeat—not only how to rise but how to live life and thrive. It starts by sharing everything with God. He seeks to guide us, even when we're ashamed of what we've done. He will forgive us when He sees into our hearts.

"I don't worry about you because you're tenacious and have become a great mentor to your sisters, living and embracing our faith. But you'll need help. Mahlah is wise, and she'll be good counsel for you. She's not impetuous like you. Listen to her and cooperate to lead your sisters." Her father looked up and let out a deep sigh. "I've waited too long. Emet is right. I should've arranged marriages already. I promised I would, but then the sandstorm, then Korah ..." He stared into the distance.

"Abba, why are you talking like this? Nothing's going to happen to you. Is this about tomorrow? Is this about the snakes?" Noa knelt before him, her thoughts scrambling to understand.

"I'm not trying to scare you. Someday, I will die, and yes, because of tomorrow, you should hear I have confidence in you. You'll face adversity, but you can lead your sisters through tough times. You're my ezer for them, a vital source of strength, which is why I'm sometimes hard on you."

"But, Abba, you'll be with us for a long time."

"Yes. I hope to be, daughter."

Heat permeated her body; her insides quivered. *Is he hiding something? Why did he clutch his heart?*

"Now, daughter, I know you mean to go to the Tent, but I'm holding you to your promise. Be here for your sisters."

Noa wondered whether she should reveal what had happened to Milkah. Would that disturb him even more? *But if I don't, will it be detrimental to all of us?* "I don't want to upset you, Abba, but Assir tried to convince Milkah to persuade you to join Korah and—"

"What?" Abba's jaw clenched. "The underbelly of Korah's web—it's unfathomable."

"I uncovered Assir's scheme and, as you suggested, attempted to reason things out with Milkah. It didn't go well. He'd filled her head with the idea of marriage; possibly he even meant it. But certainly, he didn't make his intentions clear to you. In the end, she believed me and refused any further communication with him." Noa omitted how Milkah came to this knowledge. "In the end, she did what was right."

Her father spat. "Despicable. She's too young to comprehend his scheming. It's good he's not here. I couldn't trust myself around him. I didn't see him today with his father, but when I do, I will have more than words with him." His lips became a thin, tight line. "Noa, Milkah needs your help. Promise me you'll let go of this pettiness between you. She only wants your attention. Give it to her." He squeezed her hand. "And now, it may be hard, but you need to sleep. We must be strong for tomorrow." He held her close. "I love you, daughter."

She wished the world could stop. Sheathed in her father's embrace, nothing could happen to her. For this moment, she could forget the severity of what lay ahead. She focused on his words about being the strongest. "I won't disappoint you. I love you, Abba."

Noa itched to divulge everything to Mahlah so she could never forget Abba's words, but her disclosure could put a wedge between them. Shouldn't it be Mahlah's place to be the protector, being the oldest? She tried to memorize what he said. *I am his ezer for my sisters? I know I am a helper to my sisters, but a vital strength? I am like him?* But he'd also said "impetuous ... sees things in black and white." *I still disappoint him. What did he mean by "God help you from knowing what I've done"?*

"What did Abba say that's bothering you? You're twitching in bed like ants are crawling in it. Settle, sister." Mahlah perched her head on her forearm.

"Sorry, Mahlah. I appreciate your offer to listen, but let's rest as best we can."

"Then visualize the stars Abba showed us, the Lord's love pouring out to give you peace."

Noa squeezed her sister's arm. "I'll try."

CHAPTER 15

The night dragged on as if it were a week. When dawn cast its light, Zelophehad dressed as he had the day before, in a plain tunic. Then he poured a cup of water he didn't taste.

Both Abel and Emet's families assembled outside his tent. Zelophehad hugged each of his daughters, thanked the sons and their families for remaining behind, and led his cousins to the Tent of Meeting. The trumpets blared. "This time, Moses's sons will have sounded the call." Zelophehad increased his pace.

He and his cousins lined up with the Manasseh community, seeking to distance themselves from Korah's followers. All two hundred fifty appeared, led by Korah, Abiram, and Dathan, swinging their incense-filled censers. The intense, pungent haze encircled them, causing Zelophehad to reel.

He cursed under his breath and growled to his cousins, "How brazen of Korah. What a scene with so many blue prayer shawls, parading forward with such swagger, all to defy our Lord."

Moses was not present. The murmurs swelled into loud grumblings, hurting one's ears.

Zelophehad positioned himself between Emet and Abel. "I'm certain Moses is on his knees offering one last humble prayer, pleading for the words in his mouth as he has done before."

"I hope he appears soon, or this could get out of control." Emet surveyed the entire surroundings.

Like a comet's tail, a bright blaze from the Tabernacle shot high into the sky, more intense than when Moses broke the tablets with the commandments. *Surely, we are in the presence of God.* The entire community quieted. Some kneeled, others stood stupefied by the terrifying and humbling power displayed.

Moses and Aaron emerged, prostrating themselves on the ground, appealing to God. Only those closest to them heard. The crowd understood that they were pleading for God's forgiveness.

Moses rose to his full height, holding his staff, and raised it. "Move away from the tents of these wicked men, or you will be swept away because of all their sins."

Zelophehad cried out, begging with his whole heart for the people to listen to Moses. To his relief, a majority stepped away. To his shock, Korah's sons slipped away from their father as Assir pulled back his two brothers. In his intense defiance, Korah didn't notice and continued to sneer at Moses. Zelophehad quivered from the horrendous thought of his family abandoning him.

Moses continued to address the community. "This is how you will know that the Lord has commanded me to do all these things and that it was not my idea: If these men die a natural death and suffer the fate of all mankind, then the Lord did not appoint me. But if the Lord brings about something totally new, and the earth opens its mouth and swallows them, with everything that belongs to them, then you will know that these men have treated the Lord with contempt."

The sky darkened to pitch-black, and the only light emanated from the Tabernacle behind Moses—God's light. A dampness pervaded the air. Suddenly, a noise bellowed deep underground, like a cascade of grinding rocks and cracking wood. The once-solid ground shuddered with ferocious intensity.

"Lord, have mercy on us." Zelophehad grabbed his cousins as they wobbled and crumpled to their knees. The ground swelled like an ocean with enormous waves as they tried to stand. Powerless against it, they huddled together, linking arms as many others did. No one could keep their balance. Everything around them bent in a fluid motion.

Moses, Aaron, and Korah remained steadfast, although shaken. A loud groan resounded from the earth as a laceration severed the ground at Korah's feet. Thrusting his censer above his head, he glared at Moses.

The laceration widened to an immense abyss as the earth ripped apart, shooting pillars of flames. A deep, acrid stench of sulfur and death permeated the air. In an instant, the earth swallowed Korah and all his 250 followers, and their tents with all their possessions. Horrific screams echoed downward into the bottomless abyss.

Emet grabbed Zelophehad. "We must leave now!"

"Wait!" Zelophehad pointed at Moses, who approached the rim of the abyss and peered down. He glimpsed Assir creeping toward Moses. "No, it can't be! Is he going to push him in?" He sprang forward, then stopped.

Assir removed his family ring and stretched his arm out over the abyss, dropping the heirloom into the crevasse.

As quickly as the earth opened, the ravine closed, leaving a haphazard scar on the dusty ground. A terrifying silence followed.

Moses knelt, stretching his hands on the closed crevice. "Why, Korah, why did you not obey our Lord?"

Emet and Abel moved forward to Zelophehad.

Mass pandemonium ensued, with men trampling over each other, shouting, "The earth will swallow us too!"

"Hurry! Our families will be desperate to know what has happened." Zelophehad charged them back to their tents.

Following members of the Manasseh tribe like a stampede of cattle, they barreled to the opposite side of the entrance. Others ahead of them raised the perimeter curtain, crawling under it to escape the maddening scene.

Their families waited outside Zelophehad's tent and surrounded them to hear what had happened. Zelophehad sought his daughters.

Tirzah spotted him and sprang into his arms, "Abba, we heard an unbearable noise. We were afraid our tent would fall from all the shaking."

Zelophehad clutched Tirzah and all his daughters as they clustered around him, willing his love to pour out to each of them.

The cousins did the same with their wives and family.

Zelophehad observed their anxious faces. "Let's go inside." He couldn't unsee Korah's utter destruction. What should he tell his daughters? *Lord, grant me the words.*

The devastating scene played before him, the agonizing cries echoed in his ears, and the foul stink of death saturated his clothes. He wavered with a heaviness in his limbs. "Korah and all his followers suffered their fate for contesting the Lord. The earth opened its mouth, split apart, and swallowed them, their families, their households, and all their possessions." His emotions quieted his words. "The earth closed over them, and they perished for their brazen defiance."

Tirzah blurted, "Why did God get so angry? I don't understand."

Zelophehad softened his voice to address his youngest daughter. "I don't profess to know all the ways of the Lord. God directed Moses to stop them from their fateful end. He forewarned them an entire day and night, allowing them to reconsider." Zelophehad's conviction grew more assertive. "Moses pleaded with them to honor the specific role and status God bestowed on them. He did not ask but ordered Dathan and Abiram to his tent to persuade them not to disobey our Lord. And even at the last moment, God commanded Moses to give a final warning. Some men listened and retreated, including Korah's sons."

Milkah flinched, her fingers covering her open mouth. She exchanged a glance with Noa. "Assir is still alive?"

"Yes. He pulled back both his brothers, and then afterward, he threw a ring into the abyss that took his father. It baffled me. I thought he was loyal to Korah." Zelophehad shook his head.

"Was Reba there? Is she alive, Father?" Tirzah clasped her palms together.

"She was not near her father or mother. Perhaps her brothers interceded. We will know in a few days." Zelophehad was thankful he'd listened to his heart and his faith. He waved Emet forward to continue.

Emet cleared his throat and, with a deep sigh, began. "We grieve for what happened and wish no one harm. We make choices in our lives. Will we choose a life following our Lord? Or will we choose a life based on personal prestige over others? This is a stern warning to anyone in a leadership position."

Zelophehad raised his arms. "We witnessed again the power of the Lord today. We must renew our faith and trust in His servant Moses. Yet I fear that some still don't believe God made this decision. As we left, we heard many men faulting Moses. We crept into the abyss of a civil war today. How many more would have died had Korah lived as he divided us against one another? For the next two days, we should stay close to our tents, come together as a family of faith, and abstain from any further rebellion. We will not participate in any discussions or actions of those who still question Moses. Agreed? Emet? Abel?"

The two cousins flanked Zelophehad. Emet affirmed, "We are a family. We've faced issues and quarrels in our past, but no one has ever questioned the faith of the grandsons of Gilead of the Manasseh tribe. We will follow our older cousin's plan. What we witnessed forces us to take stock of what we hold dear. What do we believe? Who are we? We can never forget where our salvation comes from. Each of us must reaffirm our faith in our one God who has appointed Moses as His mouthpiece." Emet embraced both his cousins.

"Well said, Emet. Together we stand with one another, faithful with all our hearts." Zelophehad clapped Emet's back. *I'm sorry, Lord, that it took disaster to finally bring us together.*

After a sleepless night, Assir's head pounded, and his mind raced with dire possibilities. His brother, Elkanah, always at odds with him in the past as they vied for Father's attention, made a truce with him. Assir worried about Reba, who had hidden behind a Levite's tent, witnessing the death of their father and mother. She'd not uttered a word since. They were orphans. *I am the head of the family.*

He replayed the events in his mind. He'd snatched his brothers from standing with their father. Elkanah and Abiasaph confided that they thought one of Father's devotees attempted a better view. Then, catching the terror in Assir's face, they followed him like sheep. He grasped his father's shoulder when the gorge burst dangerously close, but his father shrugged him off, defiant to the end. Could he have saved him? Had he wanted to? He knew when he took off the heirloom ring that he had made his choice.

One of the Levite elders, Tuvya, who'd been unpersuaded by Father, took pity on them, providing a small tent and warning them to stay in the tent for their safety. He would have manna and water delivered to them. But for how long? Would Moses condemn him and his siblings? Would the community ostracize them? Shaking his head, he sighed. It was time to convene with his brothers.

He waved them to the far side away from where Reba slept and motioned for them to sit. Their stares were blank, dazed. "I didn't sleep, brothers. I tormented myself about whether I could've held on to Father. I know most of me didn't try."

Abiasaph, the youngest, awoke from his fog and assured him, "Only if Father sought forgiveness from God, not from Moses, would it have saved him. It was not your fault."

"I thank you, brother, but it is something that will take time to sort out. The other weight on me is our situation. We're at the mercy of this community if we stay. We must go to Moses and Aaron. Only with their approval will we be able to remain."

Elkanah flapped his hands, shaking his head from side to side, "Why are you bringing up our future? I am undone. Are you not? We lost everything: our parents, our home, our possessions, clothes ... everything was in our family tent. We don't even own sackcloth for mourning clothes. Should we not rend these garments?"

Assir clutched him. "I know we've witnessed an unfathomable crisis without time to grieve."

"Grieve?" Elkanah shook Assir off, staring in disbelief. "We don't have a body to prepare. Mother and he didn't get a last prayer."

"A last prayer?" Abiasaph bared his teeth, glaring. "Do they deserve it? Father drove people to a fateful end. Mother goaded him into believing he was better than God. You say we're at the mercy of the community? What's wrong with both of you? Are you not fearful? Do you not comprehend what happened? We must pray for forgiveness, for we didn't stop our father and should have known better than to remain quiet."

Assir staggered with the sting of his brother's words. Guilt about surrendering to his father's demands and his deceit toward Milkah besieged him. His chest caved in as he bent forward. These burdens had blinded him. He couldn't make sense of it. Why was he saved? Why did he feel a mysterious hand on his shoulder pulling him back? God couldn't have forgiven him. Abiasaph was right. He knew better, maybe not at first, but as his doubts grew, he never confronted Father. *I was Father's fool, and I knew it. I didn't pray about it and left God out of it. Why didn't I listen to my inner voice bidding me to return to our Lord?*

Elkanah straightened his back. "We know our fifth commandment. Honor your father and mother. What do we do if our parents are not obeying the commandments?"

Abiasaph bunched his hands. "Both of them believed they deserved more, even at the expense of others. We know that in Egypt, they were part of the pharaoh's network of spies. They betrayed our people and boasted about being rewarded with special privileges. I'm ashamed of them."

"Ashamed? Assir is the one who should be ashamed. Doing Father's dirty work, prodding that daughter of Zelophehad. You're just like Father." Elkanah leaned down, grabbed Assir by the neck, and raised his fist to hit him.

All defense left him. "Go ahead, strike me."

Elkanah pushed him. "You're not worth it."

Assir went limp. Once Moses heard about his deeds, would they curse him like his father? Would someone also blame him for the horned snake at Zelophehad's tent? Guilt strangled him. "Elkanah, you're right. I'm not worthy, but I promise you I will try. We are all we have left, brother. I know I've wronged many. We witnessed God's wrath, and I vow to be an instrument of His will. We need to be together for this vow. Will you join me? Please? Would you join me in prayer?"

Elkanah started to shake his head but relented.

They bowed down on their knees. "Lord, our hearts and minds are in deep despair. We kneel before You, especially I, with my transgressions. Thank You for sparing us from the abyss, and may we find our way back to You and serve You all our days. I ask You to help me take care of my siblings. May I be a better man than I've been. Amen."

A rap came at the tent flap. "It is I, Tuvya. I must talk with all of you."

Assir quickened to open the tent ties. "Shalom, please enter."

Tuvya's dumbstruck appearance was like that of the men who witnessed Father's demise. He shoved the day's water and manna to Assir. Indicating for them to sit, his hoarse voice croaked between catching his breath. "You must not leave this tent. The people are still rebelling against Moses's leadership, claiming that they believe Moses killed Korah. Moses and Aaron are at the entrance of the Tent of Meeting, where these rebels have swarmed, and a leprosy has spread. Moses directed Aaron to make atonement for them—to bring his censer from yesterday with fire from the altar and lay incense on it. Aaron stands between life and death, halting the plague's spread.

But already thousands have died. Moses said he would call you when it was safe. Pray now for this congregation to come to reason and believe in God's choice. I must go and help where I can. Pray!" He departed quickly.

"Will our father's transgressions strike us with leprosy?" Elkanah moaned.

Abiasaph yanked his head into his hands. "Brother, do you not think of the thousands who have already died because of our father's insurrection? Will this ever end?"

Noa heard a loud lament coming from her father outside their tent, and before she could open the flap, her father reentered and hurriedly secured the ties.

"Abba, what is it?" Noa offered her arm to him.

He looked like he had aged at least ten years, with the gray hair at his temples spreading to all sides of his head. Two deep creases burrowed under his eyes, and several fine lines edged the corners. He took her arm, directing her behind the curtain away from his other daughters, who were resting from all the turmoil of the last day.

His labored breath divulged the urgency. "Jonathan came to ensure that we were safe. He relayed that Moses charged the Levites to go out and warn people to stay in their tents, because, as I predicted, some are still following Korah's insidious and destructive path." Her father looked defeated, his body sagging from the heaviness of Jonathan's message. "And our people are suffering the consequences, with a plague striking the remaining followers for refusing God's true servant."

"Oh, Abba, will we be affected?" Noa reeled and sat on the sleeping pallet.

He joined her. "Aaron stopped the spread, but we are still in a fog of fear. All we can do is hold on to our faith and pray God will sustain

His faithful followers. Noa, we cannot speak of this to your sisters. It is already too much for them."

Noa leaned against her father, and he put an arm around her, holding her tight.

At dusk the following day, Tuvya reassured Assir and his siblings that the plague had stopped the day it started, but over fourteen thousand people were dead. "God commanded Moses to ask the tribal leaders to bring their staffs, each with their names carved into it, and to place them in front of the Ark of the Covenant. God would choose the staff of the man to stop the grumbling against Moses and any further rebellions. Today, Aaron's staff was displayed as the only one blooming with ripe almonds. God's choice for administering the sacred Holy of Holies would only be for Aaron and his descendants.

"Moses has summoned all of you five days hence to honor the mourning period of your mother and father. I will come for you at the appropriate time."

"Thank you, Tuvya, you have been so good to us. You reflect your namesake. God is good, as you have done for us." Assir walked him to the opening.

Five anxious days passed, and Assir didn't dare open their tent for air, but only raised the outer edges two fists high.

CHAPTER 16

Tuvya escorted them to Moses's tent and left before they entered. Assir positioned his brothers and sister behind him as they humbly bowed. Relieved that he'd directed his siblings to adhere to the usual practices of mourning, they all had torn their only tunics. "Shalom, peace be upon you. It humbles us to be meeting with you."

Moses and Aaron sat cross-legged on a carpet at a long, low table where several scrolls lay scattered. Moses pointed to a place on the ground without cushions for them to sit.

A familiar scent of incense surrounded them. Many cushions, all different colors, sizes, and textures, lined the perimeter. Several oil lamps of various shapes hung from the tent posts. Moses, the last judge on issues, conducted meetings well into the night.

He and Aaron both appeared exhausted, with deep creases under their eyes and on their foreheads. The burden of leadership from this past week had taken a significant toll. Moses tapped Aaron's arm to begin. Aaron bowed his head. "Please join me in prayer. Lord, we come before You today. Our community is still faltering from the tragic event and acting out against Your words. We pray we would listen to Your commands, hold Your word in our hearts and lives, and live as You would have us do. Thank You for this day, and may we walk in Your path of righteousness. Amen."

After a moment of silence, Moses began. "Assir, why did you fall back and not stand with your father?"

Moses's tone sounded like the patience of a grandfather listening to his grandchild who broke something. Assir hadn't expected Moses to be so direct with his first comment.

"That morning, my mother dressed in her finest and cajoled my father to be extra careful with what he wore. She straightened his tunic, saying, 'We will show who should be God's spokesman and who should govern. Our sons will ensure the people revere our status.'"

Moses folded his hands in his lap. "Go on."

"My brothers and I have struggled with the fifth commandment of honoring our mother and father. Father bragged again about his defiant all-blue prayer shawl as we exited the tent. It triggered in me the other commandments I had witnessed him dishonor. 'You shall not bear false witness against your neighbor.' He'd scattered falsehoods about you and Aaron. 'You shall not covet.' He wanted to wear Aaron's vestments and be the only one allowed into the Holy of Holies. He'd also defied 'you shall have no other gods before me.' Father built himself up so much that he believed the Holy of Holies should be his domain. I followed along with much foreboding.

"I didn't understand my feelings until I witnessed you prostrate and heard your humble prayer. You shouted to move away, or we would suffer the same fate. Your countenance, your assertion, and your actions expressed the dire situation. I sensed a hand on my right shoulder, but turned and saw no one there. It might sound strange, but I perceived it as a sign and wrenched my brothers back."

"God seems to have been in many places that day," Moses reflected.

"Are you finished?" Aaron frowned.

"No. I'm ashamed to say, worst of all, my part," Assir added. "Father dispatched me to spy on Zelophehad from the Manasseh tribe by making the acquaintance of one of his daughters, Milkah. With no intention of proposing marriage, I was to convince Zelophehad to be my father's mouthpiece at his workshop. And I did what Father commanded without hesitation. Later, I tried to apologize to Milkah for not being honorable. She turned away, but not before expressing her and her family's conviction about her faith in God. Her certainty instilled a warning deep in my heart."

Elkanah kept his head down as he peered up, "We're ashamed of what transpired because we did little to stop our father."

Abiasaph mumbled, "We should have also perished. We didn't thwart these wrongs."

Reba quivered. "I, too, must confess. My father asked me to befriend Tirzah and Noa. In the beginning, I wanted to please him because it was the first time he had included me in something important. The daughters were the only people ever kind to me, and I miss their friendship. Once I suspected Father's cause, I ceased inquiring about their father. I didn't want to desert the only friends I had. I never shared all I discovered about Tirzah's family, but I'm not sure Tirzah will see it this way."

"Reba, I should have prevented this, my little sister. I'm sorry. I've wronged you, and I should've protected you." Assir felt the heat of shame rise on his cheeks as he watched his little sister stay true to herself.

"Perhaps in the future you'll give heed to your sister as she has shown great judgment." Moses raised his palm to Reba, who blushed. "God knows we are fallible. His forgiveness begins when we acknowledge our sins and accept responsibility for our misdeeds. Each of us must answer to our Lord with honesty, a contrite heart, and a genuine commitment to listen and do His works. God has spared each of you for some purpose. You now need to ponder, what will you do with this life He has given you?"

All of them bowed with their heads to the ground.

Moses reared. "Do not bow to us. Your posture is for God alone."

Aaron lifted Reba's forearm, helping her up. "Here, rise for us to give you a blessing." Aaron laid his hands on their bowed heads. "Lord, our God, we thank You for Your care, for the statutes to live by. We thank You for Your forgiveness when we fail. Please plant

Your will into the hearts of these young people. Steer them to Your path, and let them not deviate from it. Bless this family as they rise from the ashes and do Your work."

Assir's heart soared. There was light. He touched his heart. "I commit to you to lead my family on the just path. I swear it."

Moses raised his hands above them. "You will dedicate yourselves to our Lord. He's the one you want to commit to."

Assir linked elbows with his brothers and indicated for Reba to join. They professed, "We will."

"It is also important to address the wrongs done to Zelophehad's family." Moses looked directly at Assir.

"After meeting with you, it's foremost on my mind. We will offer our confessions of guilt and our sincere vow to make amends," Assir pledged.

"I'm not sure you'll repair this breach of trust. It will be hard to forget, but they may forgive in time. Zelophehad, his daughters, and the community will judge you because of your part in your father's scheming. You must help each other. Whatever grievances transpired between you are in the past. Learn from your parents' misplaced actions, but don't carry this burden. The Levite tribe will continue to provide some clothes, and you can stay in the current tent. You're a reborn family now. Contemplate your future with God."

"Your words humble us in gratitude, allowing us to stay. We hadn't considered anything more than meeting with you and Aaron about our futures. We will honor your advice."

"You and your brothers are to continue working with your fellow Levites. It will be challenging at first. They may assign you different roles until you can regain their trust. Your service will be a living sign of God's mercy."

Assir didn't hide his tears. Not being cast out and given the privilege of serving was beyond anything he could have hoped for. *A second chance? God hasn't condemned me?*

"Bless you, Moses."

Assir sent Elkanah to ask Zelophehad if he would meet with him the following morning. He was relieved that Zelophehad said yes. Assir practiced his words all evening and woke praying that his apology would be accepted. He selected a plain tunic from the clothes the family had received.

Zelophehad had arranged to meet at the entrance of the Tent of Meeting. Upon his arrival, Zelophehad's eyes bore into him.

Perspiration soaked Assir's tunic. "Sir, I thank you for meeting with me. I want to explain and apologize."

Zelophehad granted the slightest of nods.

"I'm here representing my family to make amends to you and your daughter."

Zelophehad brought up his fists at what this implied. "If you have touched my daughter ..."

"No. I never touched Milkah. We always remained in the community's view. What I did, though, was wrong. I did not violate your daughter's body, but I violated her trust. I don't use it as an excuse, but I was obeying my father's orders."

Zelophehad scowled. "What happened exactly?"

"My father wanted you to advocate his cause against Moses. Not being honest about my intent, I tried to persuade Milkah to share your views by making overtures for her hand. My abhorrent behavior torments me, and I'm so remorseful about what I've done. Yet what started with ill intentions changed as I learned more about your daughter. She's sincere, faithful, graceful, and loyal to you and all your teachings. Sir, on the day of the sandstorm, I ran to the river to protect Milkah. I care for her, and that's how I came to be there for Tirzah."

"I acknowledge you rescued my little girl and am most grateful. I recognize you risked your life, but it doesn't erase what you've done. Is this all you have to say?" Zelophehad's eyes narrowed.

Assir felt the daggers projected at him, almost halting him from continuing, but he knew he had to confess it all. He only hoped Zelophehad would give him time to express his gratitude for Milkah's faith and how it had saved him. "No."

Zelophehad's head jerked. "There is more?"

He swallowed, fighting the desire to lie. "My father enlisted my sister, Reba, to make friends with Tirzah for the same purpose. In my sister's defense, she conveyed no information because of your daughters' kindness."

Zelophehad spat his words. "I knew about Milkah as one of my daughters told me about this after overhearing your brothers. But Tirzah, not yet a grown woman, and deceiving her also?"

"My sister cares for Tirzah and Noa. I take responsibility for both Reba and myself. I'm sorry for the harm and damage we caused. Whatever it is that I or my family can do to rectify our grievous actions, we will."

"Reba cared and hoped to protect Tirzah and Noa, but you?" Zelophehad pointed at him. "You wouldn't do the same for Milkah?"

"I'm so ashamed. My sister is a better person than I am. I wish I had followed her inclinations." He wanted to run away to a place where no one could ever find him. He also mourned the lost love he knew would never come to pass.

Zelophehad glared at him. "I'll never know if you were part of that horrendous basket scaring my Tirzah. I won't speak for my daughters. It will be up to them to decide whether they want to speak with you in the future. For now, I insist you and your siblings stay away. I demand this from you."

"I swear to you I was not part of the basket. As soon as I knew, I rushed to try and stop it, but I understand and will obey your wishes."

Zelophehad's arms folded. "After all this effort you put forth championing your father's schemes, why did you not cleave to him and his beliefs?"

"That is the most important thing I also wish to express. Milkah opened my eyes with her sincere conviction and faith in God. She inspired me to stand up to my father and protect my siblings. I am so grateful to her, for she saved not only me but also them." Assir dropped to his knees. "I know I can never make total amends, but I give you my oath to be there for your family however I can."

"You will stay in the community?" Zelophehad raised his chin.

"Moses extended us the grace we don't deserve. My brothers and I will continue working with my fellow Levites. Not in our same positions for now."

"God and Moses have given you a gift. I hope you'll use it wisely."

CHAPTER 17

Noa couldn't help but stare at God's presence directing their next camp. Some months had passed since Korah's fateful day, and the community had returned to their daily routines. God beckoned them to advance with the billowy, milky white cloud towering above them. She pictured the upward, voluminous pillar like a pile of white, unspun goat's hair. Shaped like a funnel, the narrowest tip hovered above the Ark while clouds on top whirled straight up to the heavens. How could people not believe after living with this glorious luminescence for all these years? She wondered if it frightened strangers or might turn them away from their many gods.

The distinct blast from the two silver trumpets roused her from her daydream. The second one indicated the camp of Reuben should move out, which also encompassed the Gad and Simeon tribes. Even though they migrated many times, each journey was a significant undertaking involving tens of thousands of people in motion.

"Are we all prepared?" Noa didn't want to slow down the whole extended family.

Milkah completed braiding her hair and arranged one headscarf around her neck and another over her head. "More than half the camp departs before us, leaving us to bathe in dust. I understand why the Tabernacle and all the Levites go first, but why is our turn after the camp of Judah and the camp of Reuben?"

Hoglah tugged at Milkah's scarf and pretended to sprinkle dust over her.

Milkah pushed her away. "Don't."

Noa secured bedding in bundles with a leather cord. "At least we're not last, or we'd wade through a quicksand of dust. Sisters, there's still much packing to do."

Abba assigned everyone their decamping tasks. The contents of the extended family involved three large tents for Abba and his cousins and five smaller ones for Emet's and Abel's sons and their families. Father charged Abel with overseeing the workshop and Emet with overseeing seven tents, and he depended on Noa to organize theirs. He divided the heavier tasks to the twelve male second cousins, with the women dedicated to packing.

Noa struggled to fold two tent flaps. "With so much practice, it should be easier. What are these rugs doing here? We repaired these for Uncle Emet's friend. Milkah, you were to deliver these yesterday."

"I can do it now if you like." Milkah jumped forward.

"Oh, Milkah. There's still so much to pack." Noa swallowed hard. *Will my sister ever volunteer, or will I always have to nag her into doing something?*

"Let her go. It will be one less thing we pack." Mahlah continued packing the cooking utensils in a large basket.

Milkah turned to Noa and stuck out her tongue. "I'll be back, not to worry. You'll have plenty for me to do."

Noa staged the baskets of copper kitchen pots, utensils, and fire grid at the door, handing Hoglah and Tirzah a load to carry out to the waiting cart. They owned six carts: two for the workshop contents and four for the family tents and belongings. She followed, carrying the two small, rolled-up rugs.

"Your tent is the last tent loaded but always the first to be settled." Jonathan tightened the reins of the two ox-laden carts. "I reinforced the wheel spokes with acacia. We shouldn't have any issues with them this time."

"You always figure it out, just like father." Noa fingered the fine work. Jonathan radiated confidence. Her heart fluttered, enamored with how dependable, kind, strong, how—

"I fed and watered the oxen. So, watch where you're stepping." Jonathan patted an ox and fastened one more rope. "Stay close to the wagon on the sides. I'll keep watch for you."

She was glad he was attending to the ox rather than noticing the heat emanating from her face. "Thank you for watching out for us."

"And for you especially." Jonathan's hand grazed her cheek.

Noa cocked her head, feeling she could melt into the earth. She wished she could linger, but she needed to finish organizing her sisters.

The carts packed, Zelophehad lifted Mahlah onto the front wooden seat, where he had laid out a thick goatskin cushion. Jonathan leaped up to the other side, taking the reins of the oxen. Noa wished she could take Mahlah's place, but only pregnant, sick, impaired, or older women rode in the carts. She frowned at another reminder of the injury she'd caused her sister.

The day passed quickly compared to other, longer journeys. By late afternoon, they had made camp at Mount Hor.

"This is our thirty-third camp. By now, we should be adept at settling our tents. Who will be first this time?" Zelophehad teased.

"Uncle, this honor will remain with you." Jonathan and Simon, along with their older siblings, hauled the tent that had been packed last.

"Ah, so observant." Zelophehad laughed, patting him on the back, and unloaded the rest.

At sunset, one silver trumpet called the tribes' leaders to the Tent of Meeting. Zelophehad returned with the news: God had summoned Moses, Aaron, and Aaron's son, Eleazar, to climb Mount Hor the next day.

"We will assemble with the entire community to watch them go. It's a matter of respect and honor to the Lord and them." Zelophehad didn't mention Moses and Aaron's solemn demeanor.

"Father, does it remind you of when Moses ascended Mount Sinai?" Noa asked.

"When our Lord wants to communicate something significant, he sets Moses apart."

"Will they be gone for forty days again?"

"We will see. I am at ease. There's no one to stir up an anxious crowd like Korah. We will continue to pray for their return."

Late in the afternoon the following day, Moses reappeared only with Eleazar, who wore his father's garments, including the breastplate with the twelve precious stones. Moses ignored questions as he strode through the enormous crowd to the Tent. The trumpets blared their instructions to assemble. Speculation and whispers erupted throughout the throngs.

With a solemn frown, Moses leaned on his staff, his face contorted. Eleazar stood behind him, his eyes appearing red and raw. "My fellow Israelites, our Lord gathered Aaron to his people. God chose Eleazar, son of Aaron, to succeed his father as high priest."

Zelophehad's gaze briefly dropped to the ground. He empathized with Moses. "It's as if a part of him is missing. Moses and Aaron didn't always agree with one another, yet they suffered and accomplished much together. It weighs on him like a millstone." Zelophehad's bones ached, reliving memories of all he had lost: his parents, both of his wives, and his baby son.

Death also made one reflect on one's destiny. The reality of Aaron's death forced him to face his own. It was time once again to begin sharing stories of faith, ensuring his daughters knew their lineage and that they'd always be in God's care. Every night for the thirty days of Aaron's mourning, he chose a story to embed in his daughters' hearts.

"Sisters, there's no tent or weaving orders, and it's a mild morning with no wind. Mahlah and I thought it was perfect weather for us to clean the smaller rugs, a task I know you enjoy, especially Milkah." Noa tossed some goat twine to her with a teasing smile.

"Why do this now?" Milkah reclined on her pallet.

Mahlah stood over Milkah, handing her a sturdy acacia stick. Her hard smile and deep breath spoke loudly. "You griped about it being so musty inside. While setting up our tent, the men traipsed in a lot of sand."

Before Milkah could respond, Noa spread out some plain headscarves. "Here, sisters, I found some old headscarves, so you can spare yours. I bet we can finish before the noon sun."

Noa rolled up two rugs, hoping to inspire them. "Tirzah, will you help me tie the rope to hang the rugs? Hoglah and Milkah, can you roll up those three smaller ones? You'll work on the other side of us. Mahlah will join you." Noa winked at her sister, grateful Abba's sticks enabled her older sister's agility. She had become quicker in her movements and even stood for a while without them.

As usual, Tirzah jumped up first.

Noa and Tirzah chose an area between their tent and the back of Uncle Emet's side, away from his tent entrance. Still, they were careful not to splay the sand as they began beating out the apricot-colored rug with the sticks.

Once finished with their rugs, Noa's tunic drenched from their vigorous efforts, she jiggled the accumulated sand deposit from her headscarf. "I wonder how our sisters are faring. Did we beat them?"

"I'll go see." Tirzah pivoted to leave.

"We'll go together. Let's roll these up and bring them in." Noa shook out more dust from her tunic.

They heard their sisters singing inside.

"Look, Noa, they're already done!"

They both went over to where Milkah and Hoglah were smoothing out their three rugs.

"Well done, sisters! We just finished our two. Ah, time for a reward." Noa turned toward their cups, pouring some water. She followed with a plate of olives and goat cheese.

They'd just begun to eat when Emet barged in behind them, leaving the tent flap open.

"Shalom, daughters, you're all here. That is good, as I bring you a story and something important to show you." Emet secured a small bundle in his hand.

"Uncle Emet, please, would you like to sit and join us for something to eat? Would you like to wait for Abba to join us? He should be back shortly." Mahlah poured a cup of water.

"No, I came to talk to you. It won't take long. I'd rather show you." He took a large gulp of water. His stance cast a shadow on them, and his eyes, usually hooded and dull, sparked with a secret. Noa had never seen him so engaged.

As he peeled open each flap of the goat skin bundle, he lowered his chin, inspecting to see if they were watching him. After the last flap, he shifted the object above their heads.

"Uncle, you're teasing us. Please show us." Tirzah's upturned lips beamed brightly.

"Yes, Tirzah, it is time to show you." Uncle Emet's approach was the gentlest he had ever spoken. He lowered his hand with the broken object and circled his palm to each of them.

"Uncle, what is this?" Milkah stretched out to touch the colorful pieces.

He retracted his hand as if burned by her approach. "You shouldn't touch this. It is the remnants of Isis, the Egyptian goddess of life and magic. The Egyptians prayed to her for healing. They believed her to protect women and children and even bring the dead to life."

"Why is it in pieces?" Hoglah stared at the mangled figure of the woman. Her wings, detached and broken in two, shone brilliant colors of turquoise blue, red ochre, and burnished gold. A final piece lay beside it, a headdress of cow's horns surrounding a shape like the sun, also of shiny gold.

Mahlah's hands flew to her chest. "Why bring this here to us?"

"Because, dear nieces, this belonged to your father, your abba." With a flourish, Emet carefully deposited the cloth on the ground in front of them. He then flexed his fingers and curled them into a fist, offering a sneering smile that spread slowly over his face.

"Why would you imply this lie? Why besmirch his reputation?" Noa leaped up, standing between him and her sisters. The veins of her neck throbbed.

Her uncle didn't flinch.

"This can't be true. Uncle Emet, why would you hurt our abba this way?" Tirzah whimpered.

"Ah, your great abba didn't admit this to you. Then you should ask him before accusing me. I will leave you with what remains of Isis. He'll know when he sees it." Emet swiveled and marched out.

Tears dripped down Tirzah's cheeks.

"Don't cry, Tirzah. When Abba comes back, he will expose Uncle Emet's fictitious story. It's not true. This is a lie. Why is Uncle Emet so jealous of Abba? I can't imagine what else it could be. It's midday, he'll be here shortly to join us for a respite." Noa got up, sat next to Tirzah, and enfolded her in her arms. "You'll see. Abba will explain what these pieces are from."

A thick blanket of silence smothered the tent.

At the sight of Abba entering the tent, Noa drew a deep breath. She shook Tirzah from nestling against her. "Look, Abba's here." The agony of Emet's unfathomable little show would soon be erased.

Abba glimpsed his daughters surrounding the broken pieces of Isis spread on the floor. Everyone froze. No one breathed. Would he be angry, frustrated, or incredulous at this display? He was none of these things. He knew. *Please, Lord, no. He knew what it was.*

He folded in a heap, clutching his heart. No matter what it was, Noa ached inside. This wasn't the first time she'd witnessed his hand over his heart.

After what seemed like hours, he raised his head, and barely above a whisper, croaked, "Where did this come from?"

"Abba, tell us what Uncle Emet said about this is a lie. It wasn't yours. Tell us, Abba!" Milkah pleaded.

He pressed his fist over his mouth, stifling a moan. "I buried this earlier this year. I haven't seen it since. We've moved since then. I don't understand what it is doing here. Why would Emet dig this up and bring it to you?"

"Abba, what happened?" Noa fetched him his stool. He refused it, sitting on the rug.

"When your mother became ill, I was desperate. She was my reason for living as a man, a husband, a father to five daughters. I would give up my life to make her well again. I decided I should pray not only to our God but also to Isis."

They croaked at his admission.

"Yes, I know, it is a violation, a grievous sin. The Egyptians were so powerful, poisoning us with their gods and their beliefs. I'm ashamed to admit they were deep in our souls. Maat, the overseer of the Egyptian workshop, gifted me the statue when we departed Egypt. He declared her magical knowledge was more powerful than a million gods. He accepted that I didn't worship their gods, but declared that gold would command a bountiful price. I tossed it in with our tools and never used it or even acknowledged its existence. I forgot about it until your mother was sick."

Noa's stomach knotted. She choked back her nausea. What was he saying? What could he mean?

"Stop. I can't hear anymore ... all of our faith built on a bed of lies." Milkah picked up the broken remnants and threw them at her father.

Zelophehad pleaded, "No, my faith is true. I stumbled horribly, but I built my faith on our one true God, the dearest thing to me besides your ima and all of you."

"You deceived us. You put us and yourself in danger." Milkah's cheeks flashed a fiery red.

Noa grabbed Milkah's wrist. "Stop. Don't speak to our father this way." Would she have been tempted if Abba or Jonathan fell fatefully ill?

"Don't blame Milkah. I was so desperate, and I know I planned to sin against our Lord." Zelophehad hunched over. "Your mother found it."

A strangled chorus of "no" rang out.

"One day, I rediscovered it in the shop and hid it near our bed. I was despondent about my thinking of breaking the first and second commandments. She reminded me that our one true God must be at the center of our lives and charged me to seek Moses and the priests, and to offer the sin and guilt offerings. We smashed the statue into pieces, and she said to me, 'I forgive you, and I know our God will forgive you because you were tempted, but you returned to Him with all your heart.' She made me vow, no matter what happened to her, that I would worship no other God. I swore to her I would never again pray to anyone but our one God, and I have kept that promise. I am so sorry to hurt you now." His chin trembled as his shoulders curled in.

"You're not the father I thought you were. You portray yourself as faithful, but you did this." Milkah waved at the broken pieces. "I hate you." She bolted outside.

Noa's heart melted at seeing her father's anguish and contriteness.

"Go after her and remind her I love her and always will. I will bring it to Moses. I will go to the Tent and make my confession and sacrifice about bearing a false witness to you." His posture broken, he pleaded, "I beg you, in your heart of hearts, to know I love you, and I love our God with all my heart, with all my mind, and with all my strength. I'll stay with Abel tonight." He stored the pieces in the cloth, struggled to stand, and stumbled out.

An awkward, shocked silence pervaded.

Stunned, Noa put one foot in front of the other. "I'm going to find Milkah."

CHAPTER 18

Zelophehad reeled as he stormed to Emet's tent. *Lord, help me not kill him. Why would he hurt my daughters?* He stopped outside Emet's tent and took a breath. *Lord, please help me. My anger boils my brain, and I'm afraid of what I might do.* Zelophehad wailed. "Emet, come out. Now."

Adina opened the flap and tied it to the side. "Ah, Zelo. Shalom. Emet is not here. I think he may be at the workshop. Your face is the color of a hawthorn berry. It looks like Emet talked to you about your refusal to accept Simon as a husband for Mahlah."

"Wh-what did you say?" Zelophehad's skin crawled with multiple stings from imaginary scorpions. His legs became rubbery as he swayed, and he clasped the tent pole to steady himself.

"Oh dear, did I confide something he hasn't spoken about? Here, let me get you some water. Come in, Zelo." She tugged his arm and guided him to a seat.

Zelophehad pinched the bridge of his nose.

Adina set a filled cup in front of him. "Zelo, drink some water."

Reaching out, he took a sip. "Thank you, Adina. Let me catch my breath. But please go on with what you were saying."

"Abel told Emet he was going to ask you why you rejected Simon as a suitor."

"I rejected Simon?" A piercing tone rang in his ears. He stretched his hands to either side of his temples, then covered his mouth to prevent his agonized soul from spilling out.

Adina didn't seem to notice his pain. "Yes, we thought it was odd, as you are trying to get Mahlah married first. But when you shared that you thought Simon was born out of wedlock and was not from the tribe of Manasseh, Emet became so supportive of you and looked for suitors you would accept. I have to say, you are a hard man to please."

A cold heaviness smothered Zelophehad. He took quick breaths, panting in and out.

"Do you need some more water?" Adina took the water jug, then viewed the barely touched cup, picked it up, and handed it to him. "Zelo, take another sip."

Zelophehad's hand shook as he accepted it. He had to hear all of it. "Please go on."

She nodded. "Emet, being thoughtful of Abel, wanted to prevent his brother from getting hurt by you. He wanted to plead with you to accept Simon. Abel is very sensitive concerning Simon's adoption as he considers him his own son. He has made provision for an equal share of his inheritance with his natural sons."

Zelophehad coughed, trying to stand. "It seems Emet and I have much to discuss." With strength he didn't have, he muttered, "Adina, when Emet comes home, please have him meet me outside our community, where we killed the snake." An appropriate meeting place.

After coaxing and settling Milkah back to the tent, Noa's strained muscles propelled her to leave.

"Where are you going?" Tirzah disturbed the silence in the tent.

"I am going to the Tent to witness and uphold Abba." Noa departed before anyone could stop her.

She approached the outside Tent entrance and tucked herself behind a Levite's tent. She went unnoticed because of the census activity. Noa paced back and forth to keep her legs from being numb. An hour went by. She didn't know what to do. Should she approach someone? Reveal this dark secret about her abba, her hero? To whom? She twitched at the vision of the broken figure of Isis. *How could he have done this?* When Moses beheld the golden calf, he smashed the sacred tablets. How angry would he be with Abba? Would Moses condemn their entire family?

On spotting Moses advancing, leaning on his staff, Noa shuffled back a step, calming the flutters in her stomach. She smoothed her headdress and slid out from behind the tent.

"Shalom, daughter. What brings you here?" Moses rubbed the ridges etched into his forehead as if all his decision-making took a permanent home there. After the thirty days of mourning for Aaron, he still wore a mantle of grief.

"Moses, sir, I, I ..." Noa's mouth worked, but words failed her.

His beard was long and gray, his skin leathery, and his eyes deep set. The face that met with the spirit of God was now studying Noa.

"My daughter, what troubles you?" His deep resonance calmed her, penetrating her thoughts.

She straightened her back. "Moses, sir, my name is Noa. I am one of Zelophehad's five daughters. Has my father presented himself to you and Eleazar today?"

"Ah, Noa, I know of you and your sisters. No, he hasn't been here. Perhaps he's with Eleazar?"

"I've been here for a while." *Did Abba decide not to come?*

"Daughter, have you looked at the workshop? Perhaps your father is helping someone. You should not worry."

She studied the ground. "He told us he was coming to the Tent to ... to ..."

"Then he'll be here soon. I'll check with Eleazar and dispatch someone to your tent to let you know. Now be at peace."

Assir observed Moses lumbering from his chair at the Tent of Meeting, heading toward him.

"Did you ever converse with Zelophehad and his daughters?" Moses leaned forward, his gray bushy eyebrows raised.

He winced. "Yes, Moses, I spoke with Zelophehad. He warned me to stay away. I hope with time they may forgive me."

"A father's understandable response. You must continue to pray about this, and your actions must show your remorse and commitment. Now, have you seen him here today? Maybe with Eleazar?"

"No. Shall I inquire around?" Assir straightened and readied himself to leave.

"Noa, one of his daughters, approached me. She carries quite a burden. Is there news of anything about Zelophehad?" Moses rubbed his beard.

"Not that I know of."

"Assir, I would like you to be my assistant while we finish the census. We're very close. Perhaps this will help you reenter our community. Go to Eleazar and inform him you will be one of my messengers. Ask him also to send a message to the sisters saying Zelophehad hasn't been here."

Assir bowed low. "It is an honor I don't deserve. I, I will—"

"Assir, God's lesson showed His boundless care for us with our daily manna, His light above us at night, His cloud in the day. We must learn to do likewise for each other."

"Thank you, Moses. With this new duty and your words, you've given me a true gift. Both are planted in my heart." With a renewed lightness, he rushed to do Moses's task.

When Noa returned with no sign of Abba, Tirzah volunteered to look for him at their aunts' tents. She returned panting and out of breath, reporting their tents empty.

"I'll go to the workshop." Noa grimaced. "It's more likely he would be there." *Why would Father ignore his promise to sacrifice at the Tent?*

They could hear footsteps approaching and Leora's humming. Noa and Tirzah jumped to the entrance.

"How are my favorite nieces?" Her usual teasing would bring a laugh, as they were the only nieces she had.

"Aunt Leora, where have you been? I ducked into your tent and into Aunt Adina's, and neither of you were there." Tirzah appeared ready to cry.

"Let Aunt Leora come in and sit. Tirzah, please get some water for our aunt," Mahlah admonished her sisters.

Leora nodded her thanks to Mahlah. "What's all this fuss? Nothing can be so grievous. Where are your beautiful smiles?" Leora took a long sip of water.

Milkah blurted out, "Our father committed a terrible sin."

Leora frowned, her eyebrows knitted. "What could your abba have done to cause you such stress?"

Milkah hissed her words, "It was Father's love of Egypt. He had a statue of the goddess Isis, and when Ima was ill, he planned to worship our Lord *and* Isis."

Her stomach in knots, Noa wished she could comfort her sister's anguish. "Ima righted him before he worshipped the idol, and they destroyed the figure together. He buried it with Uncle Emet and Abel as his witnesses. He regretted his intent. Ima prayed over him for God's forgiveness and set him on the right path. Emet, for some strange reason, unearthed it. Abba left to bring the idol's broken remains to Moses. He promised to confess and sacrifice at the Tent of Meeting for bearing a false witness by not imparting his story to us."

Leora bobbed her head several times, her lips flattened. "I don't understand Emet's intent at all, but now I understand about your abba."

"What do you mean?" Milkah vented as if this were an accusation.

Leora stepped to Milkah and took her hands. "Your abba, like all of you, suffered through a grueling time after your ima's passing. He carried this deed like a donkey with a heavy load. At first, the tragedy of your mother's illness and her passing affected his health, but then I saw he bore guilt. Inconsolable, he believed God abandoned him not once, but twice, when his first wife died. I worried about his vigor deteriorating. But after the sandstorm and rescuing Tirzah, it tugged him back to life. He found purpose again by watching over all of you and keeping you safe."

"Keeping us safe by keeping an Egyptian idol?" Milkah let go of her aunt's hands.

Leora gingerly retook them. "He intended to do what was right. Your father asked Abel to gather two male goats from the family pen for a guilt and a sin offering. Something didn't seem right with such a significant sacrifice. Your abba said he would meet your uncle before sundown to go to the Tabernacle.

"We don't know what actions any of us would do, dear ones. Your parents loved each other like no marriage I've seen. The important thing is he came to his senses before he acted." She turned to leave, stopping at the entrance. "Please don't worry. I'll be back."

Zelophehad paced, talking to himself, as he tried to make sense of what had happened in the last hour. Could he wake up from this catastrophic torture?

Emet finally arrived with a swagger to his step.

Zelophehad held his hands at his sides, palms up, and opened and closed his mouth several times.

"The great Zelo speechless?" Emet taunted.

"Why ... Emet, why?" Groaning, he struggled to find a flicker of emotion in Emet's impassive expression. He looked down momentarily and beseeched him with a heat that entered his tone. "Why would you bring this up now, when you know Jeska prevented me from going astray? I buried it. You and Abel were my witnesses. I confessed to you, to Moses, and Eleazar, made the sacrifice, and did what Jeska asked—never to worship any other god but our faithful God. I thought we were forging a new relationship, you and I. After the sandstorm, snake, and Korah, what happened to all of that?"

"The infallible Zelo, whimpering like a child."

"Do you hate me so much that you would turn my daughters against me?"

"You've had everything come to you so easily. Let's start back in Egypt, where you wrangled a cush job and could have put me anywhere. And where did you place me? In charge of making leather. A stinking, filthy, body-crushing job." Emet clenched his fists, pounding them on his thighs as he thundered each word. "My arms burned and ached. I went to bed exhausted, hoping they would kill me. It would be better than doing that job. I convulse each time I smell leather."

"Emet." Zelo shook his head. "You live in the past. This has rotted in you for all these years?"

"You could talk anyone into anything, but you didn't. You let me suffer working that huge vat of urine to make the leather smooth. The stench of it still is in my nostrils."

"Emet, you were a bully to our own people, and the Egyptian chief wanted no dissension while we built his chariots. He knew you were strong, so he was the one who assigned you to the vats. The only way I could prevent you from building the bricks and help you escape the whip was through that job. It was the only one that he would agree to."

"Oh, you even believe yourself, Zelo." Emet jabbed a finger into Zelo's chest. "You then took Sara, the woman I would have married. And look what happened, she died giving birth to your only son. God punished you."

"Cousin, stop, please. I still carry the pain of losing Sara. For ten years, I grieved. I didn't want to go on." Zelophehad put his hands together in prayer in front of his nose and mouth and then hung them to his sides. "Thoughts of what it would have been like if she had married you haunted me. I suffered, Emet, please, let us put this behind us."

"I am not nearly done. Now we come to the desert, and you build yourself up again, on the backs of Abel and me in the workshop, where everyone knows the great Zelo, but do they know of your cousins who made it happen?"

Zelophehad grabbed his cousin's forearms. "Yes, they know both of you! And they would know more of you if you didn't hide in the back."

Emet snorted, snapping Zelophehad's hands away.

"You took a second wife who also adored you. When Jeska died, the tribal leaders even turned out to pay their respects because of their men learning all those skills. You can do no wrong, Zelo. No wrong."

"The Lord was gracious in giving me Jeska. A woman I didn't deserve."

"Certainly, a woman you didn't deserve. But now I've discovered that Simon wants to marry Mahlah, and my grandson, Jonathan, wants to marry your most outspoken and dominating daughter, Noa! This will not happen, Zelo!"

"What? Why wouldn't it? This is good news. I've thought this all along. We need to talk with Abel." A sliver of hope just out of reach was so close. *Adina had it wrong.* "I never shared with him what you told me, as you swore me to secrecy in honor of his protest that Mahlah wouldn't be a good match because of her impairment. But I knew these were not his true thoughts. I planned to speak with him today, regardless of my oath to you. We can clear up this misunderstanding." Zelophehad turned to leave. "Come, let us go."

"And he was going to speak with you about why you rejected Simon." Emet widened his stance and thrust out his muscular arms in front of Zelophehad.

"Rejected Simon? No, I never rejected ..." Zelophehad screeched, punctuating each word. "What ... are ... you ... talking ... about? What are you saying?"

"Zelo, *you* rejected him because he was adopted and lacked our ancestors' blood. You even thought of him as an illegitimate child. Your rejection crushed Abel, as he considers Simon his own son. He knew how strongly you felt about your heritage, but he couldn't understand why you wouldn't accept him. Yet, still, he loved you like a brother. Even with family, I had to compete with you. But you won him over in the way you do. I told him you had been through so much—with Jeska's death, the snake, Korah, for all of us, and your daughters discovering your Isis—and that he should leave it be. You're not the only one to feel strongly about heritage ... He will marry another tribal woman."

As if a horde of locusts attacked him, every pore of his body stung. His voice, a harrowing moan, shrieked, "Lies. All lies. These are *your* thoughts, Emet, not mine! Is this why you told my daughters about Isis? To distract Abel and me from talking? All this time, you prevented both Mahlah and Noa from marrying? You knew I didn't have much time left. I could have easily arranged betrothals for Hoglah and Milkah after my older daughters were married." Zelophehad's insides roiled with nausea, and his pores were covered with clammy sweat. He swiped his forehead and pleaded, "You have a wife and family who love you, only wanting some attention from you. You have so many blessings, so many sons, grandsons. Why would you do this? Why, Emet?"

"You've made me suffer all my life, and now you know what that is like."

"No. Emet. Please." Zelophehad felt his face droop. The world was spinning around, and his head pounded like a hammer whacking an anvil. Holding his waist and chest, he dropped to the ground.

Emet kneeled. "Zelo? Zelo?"

"What's happened?" Abel suddenly appeared and knelt next to Emet. "Adina said you were here. Zelo, Zelo, are you all right?"

Zelophehad's eyes fluttered, his words barely audible. "Tell ... tell my daughters I love them. Em, do what's right for—" And he was gone.

CHAPTER 19

"Where could he be? Aunt Leora said he hadn't been to their tent." Noa rubbed her hands along her crossed arms, and she headed to the door. "I have to go find him."

"No, we will wait to hear from Aunt Leora when Abba comes for Abel," Mahlah commanded.

"I can't. I … we need to find him. Please, Mahlah?" Noa pleaded.

Mahlah dipped her head. "You need to take Hoglah with you. Tirzah and Milkah will stay with me. Be back before the sun goes down."

"We will." Noa and Hoglah raced outside.

Their uncles headed toward them. Noa froze in place, watching their solemn approach. Something was wrong.

Abel snagged Emet's arm as if to hold him back.

What's wrong? What's happened?

She heard Abel as they came closer. "Please be gentle with them. They'll remember this their whole lives."

Emet shook off his brother.

Hearing their exchange, Noa screeched in near hysteria, "Where is Abba?"

Emet waved them back into their tent. "Let's all go inside." He paused after entering. His deep, low voice showed no emotion. "I am sorry. Your father was gathered to his people."

"What? Abba is dead? No, no, no." Noa backed away, struggling to remain standing. She heard Emet's words, but they made little sense to her. "No, it can't be true. Abba was just here."

Tirzah hiccupped with sobs and stumbled to Noa, who, crushed by the news, didn't move. She stared at Emet, voice shivering with a soft, shaky squeak. "How did he die?" She cradled Tirzah in her arms.

Abel stepped forward in line with Emet. "Zelophehad was more than a cousin. He was a brother. He was my best friend. I only got there for his last words."

Leora and Adina hurried in and stood by their husbands. The news traveled fast through the Manasseh camp.

Abel continued. "Your father said to tell you he loved you." He looked at his brother and shook his head. "I know Emet exposed the Isis statue he dug up, but your Abba buried that long ago. Emet and I were with him when he did. He told us then about his love for God, your mother, and all of you. After he confessed and made a sacrifice in front of Moses, he requested we witness the destruction and burial of it. He prayed and cried for forgiveness. I know he truly felt this. I hope in time you can forgive him, as we did." Abel's tears welled. "With all his strength, his message to you was love."

"Daughters, you knew your father wasn't to enter the Promised Land after God's edict." Emet surveyed each of the daughters. His lack of empathy left Noa stunned.

"What are you saying?" Tirzah hiccupped again.

"He never told them, brother." Abel stepped in front of Emet and raised his arms to prevent Emet from speaking. "Your father was twenty when we left Egypt, and when the spies came back and convinced Moses not to go forward into our sacred Promised Land, our Lord decreed that all those over twenty wouldn't enter."

"Father talked about this." Noa pushed the back of her hand over her nose. "But not about he himself being twenty. How could you, Uncle Emet, alarm us with this now?" Noa seethed, wanting to ask him to leave.

Abel glanced back at his older brother. "Don't, I'll answer that. Dear ones, your father never told you because he didn't want to worry you. The Lord was gracious to him. Many of his peers have already passed away. The Lord had a purpose for him. He saved little Tirzah, made you strong after your mother's death, and told you stories to follow our faith. Your abba wanted you to know God as he had." He grasped Emet's elbow, pushing him toward the tent opening. "We must leave to bring back your father. Your aunts will assist you with the preparations. May God comfort you with His love and compassion. May you see through your despair how much your abba loved you. We will bring two of our sons to help carry him."

Frozen in position, muscles weak, Noa stared after them. Nothing made sense.

"The last thing I said was 'I hate you.'" The color drained from Milkah. "I yelled it, not bearing to look at him, and left. I'll never be with him, hug him, or understand why. Never." Milkah melted to the floor.

Leora shrouded her with a blanket, stroking her head. "Your father understood your response. He never dreamed of hurting any of you. All he ever desired was for you to know his love."

Noa and her sisters surrounded Milkah. Together, they cried until there were no more tears.

Leora directed the sisters to rest in her tent. She and Adina would prepare the body. "Uncle Abel will deliver your father's sacrifice after his ritual cleansing."

"It will give us some peace. Is Emet not going with him?" Noa pursed her lips.

"It's better this way." Leora squeezed her hands.

Aunt Adina stiffened. "I am sorry, girls. I will try to change his mind."

"Sometimes our deepest wounds prevent us from healing. I hope he'll allow himself to heal," Leora said.

Noa ground her teeth. How could Emet dishonor her father's dying wish to go to the Tent to offer his sacrifice?

Noa lumbered through the day in a daze. She had sent their younger sisters to Aunt Leora's tent to wait until late afternoon, when the burial would take place. Aunt Leora and Aunt Adina offered to prepare Abba's body for his final rest, sparing Noa and Mahlah from a task they couldn't imagine. It would mean that their aunts would be considered unclean and would have to undergo purification, as they all had to do with Ima. Out of kindness and consideration for her and her sisters, they deemed it an act of family to help. The purifying process had to be done within seven days, or one would be cut off from the community. Abba said these laws are meant to emphasize the sanctity of life, acknowledge that God is our source, and come to Him with clean hearts.

Noa prayed she could bring a clean heart, but her rage seemed only to grow. Why did Uncle Emet dig up and then keep that horrid abomination of a statue? *And then bring it to us when Abba wasn't here. How can I even look at him?*

Their aunts asked them to ready their tent for visitors, helping to focus them on a task. Noa's thoughts haunted her through the afternoon—from feeling absolute shock that her abba was gone, to his admission, to anger at her uncle. Her head throbbed.

Late afternoon, the sun was at three-quarters in the sky. Her aunts signaled it was time for the men to enter. Jonathan, Simon, Abel, and Emet carried Abba's bier. The sisters trudged behind them in the funeral march, greeted by hundreds of mourners. Some of Noa's pain dissipated with the support from the people. Men waved their tools, and women, grateful for the skills their husbands and sons had learned, stood with them. Her heart swelled with comfort from the sincere looks and the number of people who paid their respects. After their week of purification, they returned to their tent, which was also purified with the water of cleansing.

At her mother's funeral, Noa and her sisters didn't know all the traditions and protocols, but with no new distractions, the strain of loss had overwhelmed her. She loved her parents but cherished a special bond with her father. And they were now alone, orphaned.

When evening came, Noa cleaned the table after the neighbors' visit and found everyone asleep except Mahlah. "I never understood why we had so many funeral customs until I lived through two of them. Without them, we would drift like sand in the wind, nothing bringing us together. We somehow braved this day, but I don't accept what's happened."

"Thank our God for the gift of sleep. Look at our sisters. They're at peaceful rest." Mahlah stretched her back from hours of sitting.

"I wondered how I'd make it through. At one point, all I wanted was to disappear. My thoughts are so jumbled, and they keep circling back to Uncle Emet. I am outraged about his dragging that Isis statue to us. How dare he dig it up when Abba had him witness his atonement! I can't help but think, was he the cause of Abba's death?" Noa appreciated being able to let her guard down with her sister. She'd stayed strong for her younger sisters all last week. But now her fury engulfed her.

"I, too, had those thoughts. All of us are still in shock. As hard as this is, you must focus on our sisters. We cannot change what has happened to Abba. And it is unfathomable about Uncle Emet's actions, but this, too, we cannot change. Noa, I need you to help shepherd them—they need us. Tirzah seems to have withdrawn within herself. Milkah is in much pain with the last words she spoke to Abba. Hoglah is concealing it all. They'll need our compassion."

"Abba said you are a wise counselor. I will try, sister." Noa blew out her cheeks. "Shall we go outside? There's so much heaviness in here."

Mahlah grasped her walking sticks while Noa lifted a stool. The camp was quiet. With no breath of wind, the mild evening contrasted with the day's turmoil.

"Ah, I needed this." Mahlah muted herself in deference to the neighboring tents.

"What heartened me were the little things. Did you notice Jonathan's attentiveness to Tirzah? He wouldn't leave her side, even hugging her when she cried and letting her nap on his shoulder."

"The many stories of Abba's teachings to the men and the boys stirred me. A man named Edar related that he owned nothing to barter, but he and his son would work in the shop for tools. Father instructed them to fashion some tent poles, a table, and a loom. When they finished, Abba surprised them not only by giving them the tools they had earned but also by providing all the items they had constructed. Edar later discovered that Abba found out what items the family needed. He vowed he would never forget father's thoughtfulness and, when he could, would pass the kindness to others."

"My grief eased even with those who shared no story but just their compassionate expressions. One man clutched my hands in his and was about to speak after I greeted him, but tears rolled down his leathery cheeks, attesting to his whole story. It moved me so much." Noa hoped Milkah had found some peace from hearing the many stories.

"Our father was a special man. More than we ever knew."

"Did God forgive him?" Noa muttered.

"I pray with all my heart. I believe God already forgave him for Isis because Ima showed him the light, returning him to trust God even after her death. He made the vow and kept it."

"It's been on my mind, strangling me like gnarled roots. By you expressing it, I feel a heavy weight lifted."

"Remember, he also said, 'God looks at our hearts.' Abba believed in God's faithfulness, no matter if he wasn't to live in our land. As for not confessing about Isis, maybe we put Abba on a high pedestal.

The important thing is that he listened to Ima's guidance and didn't proceed with his intent. Our father was human. He made mistakes. Did we think he was without blemish?"

Was Mahlah's last statement meant for her? Did Noa idolize him? Too much strain to consider now. "I'm thankful Uncle Abel will present Abba's sacrifice, even if Emet won't."

"It will help, especially Milkah. She carries an awful burden of guilt and regret."

"I can't imagine the unbearable ache if my last words expressed rage to anyone, much less Abba. I've empathy for her and am wondering the best way to convey it. We now have a better understanding of how Abba dealt with Ima's passing, how he became absorbed in his work and sought time away from us. I—"

Mahlah interrupted her sister. "Our sisters require a steady hand. Together, we shall give patience and encouragement. You understand? I know you long to take Abba's place in the workshop, to get away like he did when Ima died. But even if Uncle Emet allowed it, now we must bind together."

"Mahlah, sorry, I wasn't thinking about the workshop, only how to turn to tasks to deflect the pain. I won't disappoint you or Abba. I know we are needed. But we, too, will need to find our way through it. I'm still having trouble acknowledging it. How can everything change in a moment? Both Ima and Abba?"

"If our parents taught us anything, it's about faith and trust."

"I've been seeking words to pray but am not finding them." Noa lifted her palms and shrugged.

"Your spirit will carry your prayers. Share your feelings with me or Aunt Leora, but please be mindful of how you affect our younger sisters. They depend on us."

She'd hoped Mahlah would provide some relief, but their conversation only added to the hole in her heart.

Late the next afternoon, Noa heard a commotion outside the tent. The long line of visitors separated, clearing a path for Moses, and the visitors inside departed. Only Noa, who had briefly met Moses, had been this close to their revered leader.

Tirzah knelt, but Moses intervened. "No, my daughter, no need for this." Though he was advanced in years, his posture was erect like a youth. His plain brown robe was woven of fine linen cloth.

Mahlah offered him her low stool.

"Thank you, but I'll stand. Why don't you all sit here in front of me?"

Noa viewed her sisters. *What must they be feeling?* Mahlah's brows raised in uncertainty while Hoglah and Milkah shot each other worried glances. Tirzah stared wide-eyed.

"Peace be unto you, daughters. Your Uncle Abel delivered your father's sacrifice and disclosed what happened. When your father lived in Egypt, he convinced the guards to recruit more Israelites and, in doing so, saved many lives. He was a good leader of men. He imparted his knowledge, preparing many with skills for our new world."

Noa slightly bowed. "Your kind words about Father deeply touch us." Tirzah, Milkah, and Hoglah relaxed their tense postures.

"We've all sinned. We're all sinners. Your father's intent was wrong to violate our first and second commandments, which is why he hid this from you, to protect you. Your uncle said he loved your mother like his own soul and would've given his life for hers. The Egyptian culture left a haunting mark on those who came out of that land. I know, for I was once an Egyptian prince. People the world over sought Egypt's knowledge in medicine, construction, and water irrigation. One could not help but be in awe of their temples. This generation who came out of Egypt witnessed daily miraculous signs from our God and yet couldn't leave their past behind. They choose not to believe in our mighty Lord but in what they experienced long ago."

Noa breathed a heavy sigh, hearing Moses, their esteemed leader, describing Egypt as Abba had. But did he still condemn him?

"What we know is our God requires a loyal and repentant heart. He gave us rules to live by, accepting that we will sometimes fall. Knowing this, He sought a way to forgive us. Your father admitted his temptation, and thanks to your mother, he didn't succumb, then made a sacrifice by confessing his transgressions. He swore never to resort to Isis or any god and committed to ensuring you knew only our one true God. I prayed over him and extolled how the Lord peers into our hearts."

"Why didn't he tell us?" Milkah crossed her arms.

"There's so much that has happened to all of us. Korah's rebellion, Aaron's passing, your mother's death, the sandstorm that almost took several lives, including, I understand, Tirzah's. Your father endured many things. Each of us will have challenges in our lives. But the Lord sends people into our lives when we lose our way. We're all tempted, but how we respond is in our power. Your father is now in God's hands. He chose the righteous path and confessed it when the time came. His intent in offering another sacrifice was to honor his love for you while admitting he had kept it from you. Daughters, our God is loving and forgiving. Let us pray together.

"O Lord God of heaven, I beseech You to give serenity to these five sisters and grant them peace. Let them be still and hear the solace in their hearts only You can give. Let them preserve all the lessons their parents imparted and learn from their mistakes, so that they may not turn away from Your commandments. O Lord, let your ear be attentive to the prayer of your servant."

"We thank you, Moses, for your thoughtfulness in coming at this time of our grieving." Noa rose and stood tall, her sisters joining her. "Your compassion and sharing of your own story humbles us. Your words about our abba and prayer over us are like a balm to our wounds."

Moses lifted his hand, blessed them, and left.

What an honor for Moses to comfort us in our own home. Moses indicated that God forgave Abba. She hoped Milkah would feel a measure of relief and heal.

CHAPTER 20

The week after their mourning, Emet barged into the tent early. "Mahlah, Noa, I come to inform you about your futures."

Noa stopped preparations for another day of visitors. "Now, Uncle Emet?" Hearing the stories about their abba's kindness and generosity had buoyed them. Uncle Emet's declaration would replace the fragile spirits of her and her sisters. For the last six days, she'd thought of only the next moment before them.

Emet pointed to the privacy curtain, waving to Noa and Mahlah to pull it down.

Noa covered her throat with a scarf, feeling a knifelike sensation choking her. This did not bode well. What could be so important that it required privacy from her younger sisters?

"I am next in line as kin, so I am responsible for you and your sisters. I'll be arranging marriage contracts. We will not wait for our arrival in the Promised Land. You all should be married by now. We may wait two years for Tirzah. In the meantime, we will school her to be a proper wife."

Mahlah's mouth dropped open. "Uncle, what are you saying?"

Noa dared to lay her hand on his arm. "We appreciate you coming here to discuss our futures, but we're still in mourning. Please, Uncle, you know a year hasn't passed since our mother's funeral. We wish to wait a full year, to honor our father. Please let us return to preparing for today."

Emet smirked. "I'll go. Abel will be here today, as I must oversee the workshop. We won't wait a full year, as you are orphans now. I will give you two more Sabbaths, and then I will return." Emet abruptly turned and stormed out, leaving both sisters speechless.

"What happened in there? Are you coming out to tell us?" Milkah rapped on the divider.

Mahlah grasped Noa's hand. "We must be strong."

Noa raised the curtain rope, grasping it to prevent herself from falling. Her gut clenched. Uncle Emet had no intention of doing what was right by them, but what was convenient. Her commitment to Abba to protect her sisters coursed through her blood. She pivoted away from the others to compose herself. *Lord, please give me wisdom and help me to—* Suddenly an idea flashed into her mind. An audacious idea that would change her sisters' lives. What if? *Lord, did You give me this idea?*

"What was so important that Uncle Emet wanted the curtains drawn and left in such a huff?" Tirzah wrung her hands.

Noa breathed deeply, exhaling through her mouth, and signaled for her younger sisters to draw near. How Mahlah and she answered would affect them. *Lord, please help me be calm.* She mustered a sympathetic smile. "People will be here soon to share their memories of Abba. Let us be mindful of their stories, honoring him."

Tirzah bit her fingernail. "But should we be scared of what Uncle Emet said?"

"He was stating his concern for our futures without our father." *Forgive me, Lord, for recasting my uncle's purpose.* Mahlah's request to be strong for her sisters fortified her. She closed her palms in prayer. "Let us give thanks for this day in front of us. Should we share our prayers to encourage one another?"

Noa corralled them into a circle, holding hands, and, with a grateful smile, nodded to Mahlah to start.

"Dear Lord, thank You for everyone who shared stories about our father. For our aunts and family who have supported us over the past few days. We thank You for Abba's heart and what he contributed to this community. Although he didn't have a son, he cared for each of us as if we were his firstborn. He gifted each of us with his love and his stories." Mahlah turned to Hoglah.

Hoglah's chin trembled, "I thank You, Lord, for my father, who taught me to think for myself and not be afraid to speak even though I challenged him with my humor."

Afraid her emotions would consume her, Noa looked up, which helped her keep from shedding tears. *Lord, give me words of compassion to ease their minds.* "I thank You, Lord, for our abba, who taught us about being a family and for Your presence with us, no matter what valley we are in. Teach us to be thankful for all You've given, especially to 'look up and know' that You will watch over us always."

Milkah was quiet before her turn but then blurted out, "Abba teased me about my name, Queen. But he made me feel special. He made me feel loved."

Noa glanced up, catching Milkah's attention. Smiling, she raised their joined hands, reminding Milkah this was a prayer.

"Lord, I thank You for Abba's love. I hope he knows how much I loved him and hope You have forgiven him, and he has forgiven me." Milkah's petition was a bare thread.

Noa softened her gaze at the pain imprinted on her sister. She displayed no finery, her hair pulled back in a plain leather tie. It was agonizing to watch her, to feel the depth of her regret.

Tirzah bit her lip but found the words to pray. "I'm jealous, Lord. Forgive me. I have not spent as much time with our father as my sisters. I long for both of my parents ... It hurts my heart, hurts my body to my bones."

Noa squeezed Tirzah's hand, her sister's words taking root in her body. Somehow, she would shield them from their uncle's plans. "Lord, we come to You with our hearts in different places, with questions on our minds that may not be answered right away. We trust You to bring healing, to know we are not alone." She envisioned God's light guiding them, as it did for Abba, to save Tirzah. Praying together released a tranquility she hadn't felt since Uncle Emet's despicable revelation.

Noa woke with her bedding soaked, cringing at the thought that her uncle would parade their intendeds before them, whatever betrothals he had concocted. Even though the seven days of mourning and another Sabbath had passed, they continued to greet more visitors, with their aunts checking on them. Their aunts meant well, but it was exhausting. She needed to work out her idea but had to focus on her sisters' lives first, distracting them from the grief that pervaded their days. She remembered Abba's words, *"You're the strongest. I need to know they'll be safe."* She wouldn't let him down. Grieving—and her idea—needed to wait.

She woke early to gather their daily provisions. Mindlessly humming, she picked up the seedlike manna, grateful she didn't have to think about collecting too much. They'd created a special basket, which, when full, measured seven omer portions to obey God's daily allotment. She marveled at how Mahlah could vary the preparation, sometimes baking it like little cakes, its oily texture making a rich, creamy taste. Other times, she'd grind and boil it with fresh coriander or thyme or create wafers that tasted like honey. Most mornings, they ate it raw, with delicious goat cheese on a satisfying crunchy surface. Her belly growled, thinking about the morning meal, and she picked up her pace.

"Thank you, Noa, for taking my turn and humming about it." Milkah joined her sisters around the low table, rubbing her neck, and yawned. "What is making you happy?"

"It is a new day that our Lord has given us and has provided us with a way to help us from our grief. After several days of soliciting whether anyone needed a repair, I have good news." Noa leaned in and spread her fingers on the table. "We have orders for three small tent flaps. With us working together, it should not take much time."

Milkah's jaw set, and she waved her arms. "Three tent flaps. On top of all the new things we are doing, you add more?"

"It will do us good. You'll see." Noa rose from her place and strode to the basket of goat's hair.

Milkah darted over to Noa, standing in her way. "You could've asked us, Noa."

"I thought you would be happy for us to do something together. Before we say no, let's try. I'll fetch the canopy to protect us."

She stepped to the side around Milkah. "I'll be back soon. Please, it will be good for us to work together." She sped to the workshop. Before she entered, she swallowed. It was her first time visiting the workshop after her father's death. *This is for my sisters. I'm watching over them.* Noa would be strong. She knew her sisters were complaining, but they would see. *It will help us. Won't it?*

Relieved Uncle Emet wasn't present, she acknowledged no one, and proceeded to the rear of the tent, where the canopy and loom had their corner. She put her hands on her hips and scowled. Wood boxes, planks, and long, thin tools thwarted her efforts. Determined, she rummaged through the clutter and sighted the four main acacia poles. Hauling one out, she dragged it to the back of the workshop exit, but it snagged, and with a thud, she tripped.

Jonathan approached and stifled a laugh. "Where are your sisters?"

She dusted herself off. "I'm trying to set up the loom to entice my sisters to work on our new tent orders."

"Shouldn't you wait a little? It's only been a litle more than two weeks. Are your sisters ready for this?" Jonathan positioned himself between Noa and the fallen pole.

She froze. It was one thing to be berated by Milkah, but to have Jonathan question her plans? She didn't expect the tears and wiped them away. "I'm doing what my father asked of me. Just before Korah's insurrection, he entrusted me to watch over my sisters if anything should happen to him. I'm trying to help them."

"You don't have to do it all alone. Besides, the last time you wove on the loom, you discovered the snake. Will it bring back terrible memories? Has enough time passed?" Jonathan picked up the pole and handed it to her.

His touch, along with his intense, caring eyes and sheepish grin, disarmed her. She longed to fall into his arms. She wished to forget the pledge to her father, but it bound her to honor the mantle he'd placed on her. "Jonathan, your words are true. But I must do this. I promised him, and I must live up to my promise."

"If I can't persuade you, may I help you before you're buried in sand?" Jonathan pointed to the side of her tunic.

She shrugged a reluctant nod and dusted off more sand.

"Noa, I will always help you. I hope you know that. I'll always be there for you. We will set it up here, but far enough away that you can enjoy your women's chat."

"You mean so you won't hear us all." Noa leaned in with a sliver of a smile that tugged at her lips.

He called out to his brothers and, with haste, set up both the sun canopy and the loom a stone's throw from the workshop.

She wished he'd linger. *He cares for me*. She replayed his words again. If only she weren't so driven. Maybe they would have talked longer.

"Noa, you look so far away." Jonathan touched her cheek.

"Thank you, Jonathan. You've helped me more than you know." She called out to his brothers. "Thank you for setting this up. You made it look so easy. I'll go fetch my sisters." She looked one more time at Jonathan and placed her hands over her heart. "Your words earlier are in my heart."

"And mine."

Her step became lighter as she sauntered toward the family tent. As she neared, she heard Milkah complaining.

"She's impossible, ordering us around. Tent flaps. What is she thinking?"

Mahlah answered with a smooth, sure voice. "Everyone heals differently. We need to give her a chance, too. Let's try to do as she asks."

Noa appreciated her older sister's support. *Why can't everyone see I'm trying my best to help us?* She swallowed her words on entering and attempted to cajole and praise each of them.

And to Noa's relief, working on the looms contributed some lighter moments from their grieving. For a while, Jonathan and his brothers remained, encouraging them. Their stories enabled the sisters' first sounds of laughter since Abba's death.

Noa glanced at Jonathan and mouthed, *Thank you.*

His tender gaze sent waves of emotion through her body. With his support, she would get through this time of grief. *Thank you, Lord, for Jonathan.*

When Noa climbed into bed, her body melted into her pallet, her mind free from the words exchanged with Milkah.

CHAPTER 21

Noa woke with energy, bolstered by her sisters' weeklong work on the tent panels.

The loom set up near the workshop yielded more than she expected. They had completed the original tent orders, as well as one additional one, all thanks to the encouragement from Jonathan, Simon, and two of their friends.

"Sisters, you've encouraged me over the last week. I wanted to ask for your help with our chores, as we've not been as consistent in doing them." *With me doing many of them.* "You have your choice to gather manna and any herbs that may be found first thing in the morning—the coolest part of the day, and before the manna melts. We need to fetch water both in the morning and late afternoon. Our goats need to be milked twice a day. We also need help finding kindling and cleaning the dishes. We can all appreciate Mahlah always doing the manna preparation, but I'm sure she wouldn't mind help. I know milking goats isn't one of your favorites, so I'll go. While I am gone, could you all do one of these things?" Noa picked up the milking bucket and skins and left.

On her return, she surveyed her sisters chatting, with none of the chores completed.

Milkah came within inches of Noa, her body shaking with rage. "Why is it always you? Why are you giving orders? Who made you master of this home?"

The other three sisters peered up. Mahlah didn't interrupt.

"What are you saying? I don't give orders. All I'm doing is ensuring we each contribute to keep us going as a family." Noa reddened like the blood of a lamb. Her idea of being right about her judgment melted away.

"No, that's not what you're doing. You think you are Abba's overseer and can order us around. Just because you were his favorite doesn't mean you are him. Can any of us compete with you?" Milkah threw her brush across the room. An ugly scowl momentarily diminished her beauty. "Have you ever thought of Mahlah? She's the oldest. Do you show her respect for her role?" Milkah's fury hardened. "No. Your only thought is for Tirzah, who's young and doesn't know any better."

Tirzah leaped forward, but Mahlah snatched her back.

Hoglah stepped over to Milkah, grasping her arm. "Milkah, calm yourself."

Ready to explode, Noa caught the defiance in Tirzah's stance. Her little sister, poised and ready to fight Milkah on her behalf, melted her heart. She felt only shame. To bring her other sisters into this was unfair. Milkah still wrestled with guilt about Abba, which was why she was lashing out. She should comfort her, but the rebuke kindled a fire. Curtailing her reaction by shrugging, she muttered, "Your words are hurtful, Milkah. You who wouldn't wear a tunic because it was mine, who hounded Ima for a new one. Who, because of your beautiful hair," Noa made an exaggerated gesture as she lifted her hair, "begged to be excused from dusting all the sand out of the tent? Who refused to—"

"Just like you to change the subject," Milkah spat out. "You won't acknowledge what I've said. Come down from your hilltop to hear our ideas to get things done. You're not our ima or abba. It is *not* you who decides. It is us *together*."

Defeated, Noa's body trembled, turning limp. "Fine, Milkah, you do it then." She sulked out and scurried toward her aunt's tent, her head spinning when she collided with Jonathan.

"Noa, what's wrong?" Jonathan stepped back, momentarily holding her shoulders to steady her.

Why did it have to be Jonathan? If only she could melt into the ground and not hear her sisters' words. She wanted to run from him and not divulge her scathing exchange with Milkah. But his touch calmed her. Being in the open, no one could misconstrue any improprieties. Though right now, she didn't care if it raised eyebrows.

"What has caused you such dismay?"

Noa wheezed. "Milkah ..."

"A sister's squabble?" Jonathan cocked his head with a quizzical smile.

"Milkah accused me of being an overseer, casting me as a master over everyone—that I don't consider any of them, especially Mahlah."

Jonathan had the slightest smirk. Noa's jaw dropped. "You too. You think I am—"

"Master of tasks? Direct? Who doesn't let anyone get in your way with *your* plan, like this whole last week?" Jonathan crossed his arms.

Milkah's assessment jabbed her, but from Jonathan, her skin tightened. *I thought he liked me*. Didn't he care for her? What did he mean, "like this whole last week?" *My sisters enjoyed the weaving.*

"Noa, let's walk a little further and sit under the palm tree." Jonathan pointed to a shady spot.

Noa moved without thinking.

"You've been like this since you were young."

"Been like what?"

"I've watched you grow into a beautiful young woman who takes on so much responsibility. Your father, who had longed for a son, molded you into someone he could trust. He knew he wouldn't be here for you in the Promised Land. It's why he was so hard on you and asked you to be strong. And why you react—because he thrust you into being an adult before you finished childhood. You assumed you had to protect Mahlah after the accident, and so you adopted the mantle of the oldest. When your mother became ill, you divided the chores. You even put yourself at risk by saving Tirzah from the snake. And thank God you protected Tirzah, or we may have lost her."

Noa's brows cinched together. *What is he saying? I wanted to help Abba.*

Jonathan briefly touched her shoulder. "And even now, after losing your dear father, you haven't given yourself time to grieve as you concentrate on your sisters first."

Her mind whirled with betrayal from his matter-of-fact scrutiny. Her mouth dry, she felt an intense thirst. She latched on to the one thing she could respond to. "I, my sisters, all respect each other."

"They do, but one must earn respect to be a leader."

"I wasn't being a leader. I was trying to guide them as my father requested."

"It's a challenging position your father put you in. He relied on you to care for your sisters, but also just to be their sister. Every day, you worry about getting everything done, which only aggravates you and prompts you to try even harder. Maybe the only solution is to ask your sisters for their ideas. Use their suggestions, even if you have a better way. You've been so good at teaching Tirzah and protecting Mahlah. It would help you slow down and not be frantic to fix everything. You need to be a sister and not act as their mother or father."

Noa's mind raced. Did she mean nothing to him? Why couldn't he see her side? Maybe ... maybe all along, he had his eye on Queen Milkah. Could it be Milkah in that picture he drew?

Jonathan studied her face, as if he were reading her thoughts.

A tingling in her fingers and toes caused a chill. "You've believed this about me for a while?"

"You're so brave, Noa, and you always try to make things better. All of us, at one point, realize something unpleasant about ourselves. But you do something about it."

A trickle of perspiration dribbled down her back, his assessment contributing to her unease. "What do you think is unpleasant about yourself?"

Jonathan blushed. "That's a story for another day. Now, what will you say to your sisters?"

"I must figure that out." She pinched her bottom lip.

"Good. Would you like some company?"

"No. I must do this alone. Jonathan, you've been ... been ..." She didn't know what to express. Dazed, she plodded without direction to the end of the Manasseh tents.

Milkah was one thing, but Jonathan, too? Her senses turned inside out. *Jonathan sounded like an older brother, not someone interested in me as a wife. Or does he care so much that he wanted to help me?* She kicked a stone, stubbing her toe.

With a painful grimace, she reiterated his words over and over. A terrifying realization dawned on her. It was true. Abba had expected much from her. He'd said Noa was the strongest and had relied on her. *But I wanted to help. I wanted to earn back his love for what I did to Mahlah.* Past scenes and voices inundated her. Times when she'd asked—or was it *told*?—her sisters to do the chores. Something shattered inside, and her whole body convulsed, shaking. Perhaps being Abba's favorite had challenged her to put him above everyone and do whatever she could to please him. Milkah was right. *I see what needs to happen and act without thought.*

Arriving at the end of the tents, she walked a little farther toward a view of the mountains around a jutting boulder to be alone in peace. She shut her eyes and began a rhythm of deep breathing, calming herself. Opening her eyes to the sharp rocky peaks, deep wadis, and steep, rugged slopes, she marveled at the resplendence of God's creation.

She dipped her head. "Lord, thank You that I can see and behold Your abundance. I come hoping You will give me vision on my path to do Your will, not mine.

"I never recognized how I'm perceived. Coming from Jonathan, it's like wiping a dusty mirror clean and seeing myself face-to-face. I feel like a piece of wood in a vise—crushed. I don't know, Lord, even what to pray. Help me. Correct me when I surge ahead, thinking I'm right and not considering others. I love my sisters. We're all we have.

There's so much to be mended between us. Grant me patience and the desire to hear what they say. Forgive me, Lord. Let me realize I don't have to do everything myself. Guide my path, gird my mouth, my heart. Give me not only the words but also steer my actions.

"Lord, I believe You instilled in me an idea about how to safeguard my sisters. It is a daring idea. It will take much courage and fortitude from me and them. And Lord, please let me know if Jonathan will be my intended. Was it out of friendship or love that he spoke to me today? Whatever the outcome, let me accept it, as my heart feels torn in two, with hope and fear."

She waited in silence. Nothing. Was God there? Was there an order of prayers that got answered first? If so, she would be at the very last of the list—Moses, Eleazar, the Levite priests, tribal leaders, fathers, and mothers. Her shoulders folded. "Lord, I may be last, but I hope You can find a way to guide me." The white translucence of the setting sun's rays glistened through a scattering of clouds, creating beams of light separated by shadows. "I wait for You, Lord, when Your shadows will be illuminated and make my path clear."

When she returned to the tent, everyone slept in their corners. Only Mahlah was awake, her oil lamp still lit. "Do you want to talk?" she mouthed in a hushed tone.

"Thanks, Mahlah, for waiting, but I'm exhausted and need sleep."

"Sleep well, sister, for we'll need our wits about us. Uncle Emet sent a message that he would visit tomorrow afternoon."

"The last thing we need is to expose our sisters to his plans. We should meet with him alone. I'll coax Simon to bring our sisters to the goat and sheep pen for the shearing."

A gentle smile flickered on Mahlah's lips. "Even now, when you're so low, you shield your sisters. Your big heart will restore the rift with Milkah. I know you might not believe it, but trust your steps ahead. The Lord will guide you. Be at peace."

Noa's throat thickened. "Thank you, Mahlah, for your words, especially for our Lord's guidance. I am ... blessed with your wisdom, your care, your words of comfort. I treasure you not only as my sister but as my dearest friend."

Wrapping herself in her warmest outer robe and scarf, Noa tiptoed out before anyone was up. She needed to be alone, her mind overflowing with apprehension about her uncle's plan. *If he marries us right away, except for Tirzah, she will live under a much stricter interpretation of our rules than Father's, and I can't shield her.* Her skin prickled. She pulled her rope belt tighter.

Milkah's and Jonathan's words still roiled within her. Larger than making amends, how could she change who she was? She passed by the goat pen, and they thought she had come to feed them and started bleating. "Hungry, are you? Me too, but not for food. Just be patient." A corner of her mouth lifted. Patience.

The dawn shifted her thoughts to the seed of the idea she believed came from the Lord. She carried a skin of water and headed in the opposite direction from the day before, finding a secluded spot along the river. Instead of pouring out to the Lord again, she sat still. The river gurgled over the rocks, composing soothing music from the earth, and the scent of crisp morning air revived her. The horizon revealed streaks of the softest colors—pink and the lightest blues—with a golden dome rising, stretching out its rays and unveiling the majestic mountain ridges.

Encouraged by God's beauty, the tension left her body, and she surrendered to the surrounding scene and released all thought from her crowded mind. Would God answer her today? Lacing her fingers behind her head, she felt secure for the first time since Abba's death. She imagined her father with God behind him, placing a hand on his shoulder. Abba's sign cheered her on, encouraging her not to be afraid. She reveled in the solitude and drifted into a deep sleep.

A screeching wheatear woke her. The sun continued to bathe the surrounding peaks. She squinted toward the rocky outcrop of fallen rust-colored boulders on a flat plateau, where she spied several stone nests. A white-crowned blackbird sounded her alarm call, her flared wings warning her neighboring wheatears of the danger from the falcon's approach. Suddenly, four wheatears rallied around her—their loud, short whistles and flapping wings beating—and scared off the falcon five times their size. They were small yet defiant, protecting the carefully crafted stone nest layered with twigs—which warned of the sound of yet another predator, snakes.

Noa raised her chin to the sky and laughed. *Is this Your message?* Could it be? Was that her answer? Could five small birds, their sweet sound known as the bird of happiness, protect themselves? "Oh Lord, thank You! Thank You!"

A sense of calm and ease infused her with hope. God would put the words in her mouth. Ready to encounter her uncle, she rose, reached up to stretch her body, patted down her tunic, and hummed on her way back.

It wasn't hard to convince Simon to invite her younger sisters to the goat and sheep pen. His bashful, ruddy square face brightened when she told him how it would help Mahlah. He accompanied her back to the sisters' tent, bringing four bone spindle whorls to her older sister. The discs maintained the spindle's speed, making it easier for Mahlah to turn the raw goat and sheep fibers into yarn. Noa hid her smile at her sister's reserved manner, which dissipated into a gentle laugh as Simon spoke softly into her ear, a friendly ease enveloping them. *Please, Lord, make Uncle Emet's marriage choice be Simon.* She could only hope.

Mahlah asked Simon to keep their sisters busy for at least two hours. A challenge arose in convincing Milkah, who protested, but when Simon suggested she could supervise her two sisters, they headed off to the pen wearing their oldest tunics.

Noa concentrated all her energies on Uncle Emet. *How does my idea work with his?* Or didn't it? *Patience.*

Emet strutted into the tent at the appointed time.

Noa had set a blanket in Father's place.

He eyed her, casting the blanket aside. "I have good news. I am arranging marriages for each of you. Where are your other sisters? I requested they be here."

Mahlah poured Emet a cup of water. "We wanted to meet with you first so we can help them understand your decisions. We're all still grieving."

"Uncle Emet, it is not yet a full month since our father left us. Can we at least wait until next week?" Noa kept her request respectful and soft.

"It takes time to negotiate these marriage contracts. I'm here to apprise you, not get your permission. But if you're here to help, then fine. I'll go through each one." He didn't look at either of them and muttered his first arrangement. "For you, Mahlah, I've chosen Nahash from the Reuben tribe. He's older and has six children who will help tend to the chores."

But then, flashing with pride, he looked at Noa. His voice regained its vigor. "For you, I've chosen Merari from the Simeon tribe. I know him for his strict adherence to the law. After your father's teachings about the law, you should have a firm hand to continue guiding you." Emet tapped his fingers together.

Noa caught her breath. Merari? No, it couldn't be. Nahash? No, it must be Simon for Mahlah.

"For Hoglah, I chose Jeremiah from the Benjamin tribe for his serious nature to curb her nonsense. I promised Tirzah to Zebediah, who is only twelve, a little younger than she, but comes from a wonderful Ephraim tribe family." Then, with a pause and some bravado, he continued. “And for Milkah, I’ve chosen Jonathan from our Manasseh tribe.” Emet drew a long drink.

Noa, dumbfounded, turned away. Her sister to marry Jonathan? Her breath caught in her throat. Uncle Emet disregarded Abba’s desire for her and her sisters to marry within a single tribe, preferring the tribe of Manasseh. With these matches, they’d live in distant regions. Would she ever see her sisters again?

Merari? Uncle Emet confirmed that he wouldn’t be anything like Abba or like Jonathan either. Her uncle omitted Merari’s much older age, his known bitterness, and his lack of humor. She envisioned a stilted, hollow life with no joy. Milkah married to Jonathan? Her stomach churned bile up her chest. Mahlah to marry that crabby old man Nahash? He was at least twenty years older than Mahlah. His older children, another nightmare. And what of Simon? His feelings for Mahlah grew deeper with each visit. She didn’t know Jeremiah or Zebediah, but with her uncle’s other choices as a sign, she dreaded the rest.

Emet snarled, squaring his shoulders. He’d completed what he had advised Abba long ago, to marry them off as soon as possible. It was clearly his vindication. Why did he rush this? Did he hunger to receive the bride-price for each of them?

“As you are orphans, I’ll petition to excuse the yearlong betrothal time and arrange them to happen in six months. I will bring your intendeds to you next week.”

Noa took shallow, rapid breaths. She relived the pelting sting of the sandstorm. Tightening her fists, she hid them behind her back, convinced now to go forward with her idea. She bowed her head and spoke with the utmost care to be deferential. “Dear Uncle, can we please wait until the end of the month before confirming with the families?”

Emet grunted. “I’ll give you till the end of the month, not a day more.”

Noa's heart froze until he departed. And then she could hear it hammering.

Mahlah burst into tears.

This can't be. She kneeled before Mahlah, caressing her hand. "I am dazed. I can't imagine how you feel. Nahash? He's not worthy of you. We must challenge this."

"It's worse than anything I could imagine for each of us. And what of Milkah and Jonathan?" Mahlah wiped her tears with a soft wool cloth.

"I'm drowning in it all. Nothing of what Abba desired for us." Should she speak of her idea? She wanted to spill it out, but something stopped her. Instead, she jumped up and hugged her. "I've an idea that could save us. Give me a little more time. For now, let us trust that we're in God's hands and that He wants us to be in fruitful marriages. Before I leave, can I bring you anything?"

"A new uncle would suffice."

CHAPTER 22

Bursting to reveal her bold idea, Noa persuaded Aunt Leora to accompany her outside the camp. She resorted to pushing her aunt's elbow, edging her forward from greeting the neighbors on the long walk. Hands sweating, Noa rocked back and forth on her toes as her aunt pulled out a blanket. A burning sensation engulfed her chest. She stared at the ground, unable to force her gaze on her aunt. *Lord, please give me the words. I need her to bless my plan.* Without waiting for Leora to spread the blanket, she looked around to ensure they were far enough away from anyone.

"Aunt Leora, I've always appreciated your counsel. I have an idea and want your advice." She caught her aunt's eye. "But I must warn you, I've made up my mind to do it."

Leora laughed and touched Noa's shoulder. "Oh? You have an idea. You will do it no matter what I say, but you seek my advice?"

"That didn't come out quite right." Heat coursed through Noa's body as familiar red-hot blotches flashed on her cheeks, neck, and chest. She hated her body's reaction to her emotions.

"I would agree with you."

Noa straightened, summoning a definitive boost to her confidence. "What I mean is, I believe my sisters and I must do something dramatic and controversial. You might say daring, or our futures ... would be ... would be ..."

"I knew this blanket would come in handy. Let's sit. I can't wait to hear what you've already decided on." Leora displayed the look that said, *You are my favorite niece, but sometimes you stretch my feelings.*

Noa noticed the concern in her aunt's furrowed brow as they laid out the blanket.

"Aunt Leora, please be patient with me. I'm worried that what my sisters don't understand is that now, with Ima and Abba gone, we would be a burden to you, Uncle Abel, and Uncle Emet. You have your own families to attend to." Noa rubbed her upper arms, warding off a creeping tightness. "Moses called for a new census to prepare us for the upcoming conquests and to apportion the property of our long-awaited Promised Land. With no brothers in our family, it will not include us."

Leora raised her palm. "We'll do our best for all of you. We're family. Emet might be difficult sometimes, but he'll do what's proper. As he's the eldest in the family now, it is his responsibility to ensure you're all taken care of."

"Oh yes, Uncle Emet believes we should all marry as soon as possible." *It's not the right time to speak of his betrothal plans.*

Leora covered her mouth and gasped. "When did he say this?"

"He informed Mahlah and me last week that he was arranging marriages, and today he announced who they are." She bit her lip.

"Emet—such a foolish man."

Noa's voice croaked. "What about Abba's name and his lineage? He instilled in us respect and love for our heritage as descendants of Joseph, the tribe of Manasseh. *The* Joseph, the one who ruled Egypt when Pharaoh bestowed on him authority over everything." Of course, her aunt knew the lineage well, but her father's lessons drove her to repeat it.

Leora focused on the distance.

"Aunt Leora, are you listening?"

"Emet and his timing—not sure I can make sense of it." Leora shifted her gaze to Noa. "You are your father's daughter. I once prodded him on why he insisted on emphasizing his lineage. He wanted you all to know that whatever hardships befall you, like

Joseph, our Lord is on your journey, and never to doubt He's with you."

Noa wouldn't rush into her next piece of the puzzle. She leaned forward to whisper. "That's comforting to hear, and I believe the Lord is with me. I have prayed about my idea. It's been on my mind since Uncle Emet discussed our arranged marriages. Because Abba had no sons, we will not inherit his lands. The leadership will allot the land to the closest of Abba's kin, Uncle Emet and Uncle Abel, and other cousins. I know this may sound ungrateful, and that's not what I want to convey.

"Without land as an inheritance, our father's lineage will be forgotten. This is about honoring our father, his story, and the testimony of his life. This is not about competing with our uncles, but this is our father's inheritance of the Promised Land from God. Does God not have compassion and justice for women and young girls? Should daughters have a right to inherit their father's property and not burden another's family? Or do we rush into ill-matched, discordant marriages?" Her lip and chin trembled. She had divulged most of it, and by revealing it, some of the pressure lifted, like steam evaporating from an uncovered boiling pot.

Leora fanned herself. She gulped, "Noa, dear, I know you feel adamant about this, but that is not how things are done. You'd have to ... you'd have to approach Moses himself, and I'm sure he would uphold the laws God has given him."

"I intend to ask Moses, Eleazar, and the tribal leaders. I would ask them to consider our situation. I hope my sisters will join me, for I'll need their consent. It would be wrong to do it without their knowledge."

"What you're suggesting is unheard of. No one has ever challenged a male's right to inheritance, nor has any daughter dared to come forward. I didn't expect this. Oh, Noa, this is too much. Have you considered the reactions from the tribal leaders? They may interpret this as heresy or, even worse, think you bring shame to the Manasseh tribe, Zelophehad's name, and our extended family. Would they compare it to Korah's rebellion?"

Noa sagged like an ox carrying a heavy burden. She'd hoped for a better response. Her sisters would react even more vehemently to her proposal. "I admit it's a lot to digest, and that's why I wanted your counsel. There is no intent to cause harm to our extended family. We don't want to turn people against Moses, as Korah did. It's about our faith in our God. He's merciful and attends to all His children, men and women alike." Her throat dry, her hands shook at each point. Considering her aunt was a friendly audience, she wavered on the battle before her.

Leora pinched the skin on her leathery neck. "Moses explained God's directive for the census and how to distribute the land. There was no reference to fatherless daughters. Would an all-knowing God not plan for this?"

"If that was so, why petition God with any prayer? Should we not seek what's in our hearts?"

Leora leaned in, and though no one was there, she whispered. "You've overwhelmed me, my dear niece. Can I confide this to your Uncle Abel?"

Noa furrowed her eyebrows. "Until I am sure, please don't share it."

"I understand. Have you spoken to anyone else about this? Jonathan?" Leora smiled.

"Only you. I wouldn't do that now."

"What do you mean?"

"Uncle Emet intends to give Milkah's hand to Jonathan."

Leora put her fist over her mouth, bumping her hand forward and back. "Oh, that brother-in-law of mine."

"Jonathan must've asked for Milkah." Noa turned her palms up and out. Defeat thumped on her chest.

"I'm sure he doesn't even know, as Emet's mentioned nothing to Abel."

"For Mahlah, he has chosen Nahash, whose name couldn't be more appropriate. He's a snake."

Leora put her hand to Noa's cheek. "And for you?"

"He has chosen Merari, another name well chosen. *Bitter*. I believe joy and humor have no part in his approach to life. His judgment is of the strictest means." She recited the other two intended betrothals.

"My word, this is more than I could've predicted. You have such burdens to carry, my beloved dear." Leora leaned over and hugged Noa.

"I haven't approached my sisters about this, but I should prepare more thoroughly after your reaction. I believe God would grant our request, as it's not only for us but for any daughter orphaned."

"Who is to fathom how our Lord would rule? You're wise to continue praying for discernment. Let's reflect on it overnight. I'll keep it to myself until tomorrow."

At the sight of the overturned water jug the next morning, Milkah scolded, "What's wrong with you today?"

"I'm sorry. I didn't sleep last night." Noa righted the jug.

"You must replace it. It's my day, but since you are at fault ..."

Noa donned her headscarf, took the jug, and started for the door.

"You appear confused. Noa. Should you rest before you go?" Mahlah said.

"I'm fine. I'll go. I'm sorry, Milkah." She slipped out of the tent and meandered toward the water.

Leora called out. "I've been waiting for you, for I've thought of nothing else since our conversation, and it seems you haven't either."

"There are so many emotions bubbling inside." Noa put her free hand to her chest. "I prayed, but something prevented me from listening to what the Lord might say. The same fears circled like a fly hovering around an oil lamp."

"My body is a little older than yours, so I had no trouble sleeping." Leora chuckled. "But I'm troubled by my dream from last night."

"A dream?" Noa recalled Tikva, the midwife, explaining how dreams were a window into a person's soul and the future. "What was it about?" Noa leaned closer to listen.

"I saw a ladder that stood on its own. You were at the bottom, ascending it. A crowd corralled it, jeering and laughing. A man hollered, 'How will this ladder stay upright without leaning on something?' Nothing deterred you. You offered your hand to Mahlah, and she climbed up with no impediment, followed by Hoglah, Milkah, and Tirzah. Somehow, the ladder turned sideways, and you all stood holding hands. Then I woke up."

Noa envisioned the entire dream before her. *Could this be a sign from the Lord?* She lowered her jug and enfolded her aunt in a hug. "What a blessing. I believe my sisters and I are meant to do this together. Our Lord braced the ladder, a symbol of faith. He will hold us up. He will turn this life around for me and my sisters. What a gift, this dream."

Leora pushed back, wringing her hands. "I'm not sure I should have told you. What if it doesn't go as you plan, and perhaps this dream is terrible advice? We should alert Uncle Abel, who will be at the Tent of Meeting. He could help temper any reactions from the men."

"Let me ask my sisters. I won't do anything until I speak to you again. Please, for now, keep your dream between us."

"As you wish. I hope I served you well and did not put you in any danger."

"Don't worry. I'm going to clarify the laws of inheritance with Assir."

Leora's eyes narrowed with distress. "Is that wise? Your choice mystifies me because he caused such damage to your family. Your father wanted nothing to do with him."

"He approached me several times to do more than apologize, seeking redemption. I'll be careful not to specify why I'm asking." She reassured her aunt and spoke firmly, shutting out her fears.

Noa sprinted to Assir's small family tent while rehearsing her questions. Slowing her pace as she approached, doubts crept in. Was it wise to approach him? Was she still as impetuous as her father contended? She bit her nails and longed for a sign. A light to know that she pursued the right path. *Guide my feet, Lord.* A slight relief uplifted her as Assir came around the corner on his way to the Tent. She'd rather avoid Reba and his brothers.

When he saw her, he stiffened and shuffled back a step. "Welcome."

"Shalom. I've some questions and was hoping you could answer them." Noa steadied her nervous fingers.

"I have waited to be of service to you and your sisters. What are your questions?"

"We've no news of the completion of the census and the allotments of the Promised Land. Can you explain the distribution?" She threaded the question while scanning Assir's response for any adverse reactions.

"Not what I imagined you'd ask." His head flinched back. "The census counts every household male, each inheriting land according to the number of men in a family. Your Uncle Emet discussed it with me yesterday, as he is arranging marriages for you and your sisters, save Tirzah."

She looked sideways, trying not to show her annoyance. "But if father were alive, they'd allot him land?"

"Yes, as the only and eldest son of Hepher, he'd inherit a double portion," Assir confirmed.

"A double portion, so if we were five sons?" Noa covered her mouth, trying to hide her surprise.

"The oldest would inherit a double portion, and the rest would get a portion, so they divide the inheritance into six portions. Mahlah, if she were a male, would get two, and the rest of you as males would get one portion."

"Why is that?"

"The firstborn stands in his father's stead with expectations to carry the family name forward. His responsibilities include caring for their mother and any unmarried sisters. He assumes the duties and mantle of supporting the whole family. The firstborn carries important obligations."

"It's a burdensome obligation. How does the land get divided among the tribes?" She tugged her ear.

"Each tribe will get an equal portion of the land. Locations with excellent sources of water or grazing will be smaller because they must have equal value to other locations. Moses has appointed Joshua to lead this effort with the help of the priests at the direction of our God. The land will be allotted by lottery and dispensed again according to the number of males in their family who are twenty years and older."

Noa squinted while trying to digest the allotment ramifications. "Thank you for your explanation."

"Nothing more? I can offer more than a knowledge of our laws, but I'm glad you're satisfied." He bowed his head.

She risked her next question, hoping it wouldn't reveal her audacious plan. She needed to clarify one more point. "If there is no son and only daughters, what happens to the father's name? His lineage, his heritage?"

Assir slumped, and his mouth twitched. "A father's name would be forgotten. Each person's name and legacy are tied to the land that our Lord has promised to us. It is why God instructs us not to sell it, because it is His, and we are His tenants."

"Assir, so much to know. Thank you again." She turned to leave.

He called after her, "Noa, please, can I ask you something? Reba is desperate to visit with Tirzah. My father never explained to her why he commanded her to befriend your sister. Once she surmised his reasons, she revealed nothing. She cherished how kind and generous you both were to her and hoped you'd be her first genuine friends. Would you consider giving her a chance again?"

She cringed, sympathizing with Reba's predicament of being orphaned and with three demanding brothers. "And how have you and your brothers been treating her?"

"It's a fair question. My life changed the day we lost Father. Unlike my brothers and me, Reba knew right from wrong from the beginning. We respect her and try to be attentive and helpful to her."

"I'm relieved to hear it. Losing your parents, no matter how you felt about them, is heartbreaking. Without a last goodbye there is even more anguish." Once tall and proud, Assir's stance now hung like an old man's sagging skin. He'd lost everything, and he and his siblings were outcasts.

Assir clutched his arms to his sides and blurted out, "I didn't send the snake. Believe me. I rushed to your father to explain how Dathan and his brother Abiram planned it to prove their loyalty to him. I only wish I had known ahead of time so I could have prevented it. It convinced me my father incited people to go to any length to achieve his goals. Milkah saved my life and my siblings' lives by shining a beacon of truth into my heart. Her witness strengthened me as she stood firm in her faith—a bright, burning light. We owe your family so much, especially Milkah."

An overall heaviness encircled Noa. Pain from missing Abba, his death, Uncle Emet's plans, and the scare from the frightening snake. She shook her shoulders and directed her attention to his words about Milkah. "It seemed strange to risk your life, saving Tirzah, and then try to hurt any of us. I'm glad you discovered there's more to my sister than just her beauty. Knowing Tirzah, she'll welcome Reba back."

He regained his composure and straightened his long frame. "Bless you. I understand why Reba admires you. Please don't worry. Your Uncle Emet will take care of you and your sisters."

"Yes, of this, there is no doubt." *He'll marry us off as soon as he can.* He wouldn't consider marrying Noa to Jonathan. Jonathan was for Milkah. Milkah. She'd saved Assir's life. *I've been so absorbed with my idea that I haven't apologized to her after she yelled at me for rushing them into repairing the tents.* How could she suggest her daring plan when Milkah was so angry?

Dusk approached, and a sliver of a moon appeared as Noa hurried to one of the visiting vendor carts. Looking at the promise of the evening, Noa imagined pouring Aunt Leora's and Assir's conversation into the long-handled star dipper in an upright position and then, a couple of days later, having it dip back its contents to her. For now, she needed to focus on Milkah. How could she show her sincerity? Words were words. What would Milkah hold dear? Perhaps the intricate braided belt she'd worked on for many months? She'd designed its pattern of turquoise, carnelian, and onyx from the share of her payments from their weaving. She had planned to wear it on her wedding day. Like a splash of cold water awakening her, she nodded and envisioned Milkah's delight over a gift from Noa's heart and hands.

Should she confess to Milkah alone or with all her sisters? They all deserved an explanation and apology. She bartered one of her smaller turquoise stones for some raisin cakes from a merchant. She paid a king's ransom for something simple, hoping it would show her remorse. She would accompany it with hot, steeped habek, the sweet-smelling wild mint that was Milkah's favorite.

With her plans completed, she concentrated on her apology. Her gift, the tea, and the cakes would mean nothing if she didn't show who she really was.

CHAPTER 23

What's all this? It's not a feast day." Tirzah stared at the raisin cakes on the table that Noa had decorated with a little yellow rabil flower.

"Raisin cakes ... they look delicious." Hoglah dove into a cake.

Milkah's piercing look almost scuttled Noa's budding endeavor. She positioned herself across from her. "Milkah, come. This is for all of you. Please come and sit. I will pour a drink for us."

Her sister sauntered over and slumped next to Hoglah.

Noa poured each a cup. "I want to apologize. I rush into things, not realizing that my well-intentioned actions can be wrong. All of you've received my strong-willed efforts. I mean well, but how I carry myself may seem to be forceful."

"Seem to be?" Milkah huffed, glaring at her sister.

She needed to make this right. Her father's words floated in her mind. *"Milkah only wants your attention."* Noa touched her shoulder, remembering his sign. "I owe a specific apology to you, Milkah. What you said about my demands and how I've been especially hard on you is true. I am sorry and hope to change."

Milkah crossed her arms, tilting her head. "Yes, go on, you hope what?"

"I was so upset when I left, I collided with Jonathan and confessed what you said." Noa paused, her fingers fumbling, and then opened them up. "He agreed with you."

Snickering, Milkah jutted her chin. "I admire him even more."

"Your words shook me, but when he expanded on it—"

"He told you more?" Milkah perked up, and she snatched a raisin cake with glee.

Noa's cheeks burned. It was her moment of truth, with no turning back. "Yes, and I felt turned inside out. You were right. I tried to be Abba and Ima, too, when she became ill. You were correct about Abba entrusting me to watch over all of you, and I wanted to prove to him that I was worthy because of my secret, which I should have admitted long ago."

"Secret? There's more for you to confess?" Milkah dropped her cake.

Mahlah stood up straight, holding her hands out. "No, don't. You don't have to share this."

"I am the reason for Mahlah's injury." Noa leaped up, bringing her hands to her heart.

Milkah's rage thundered. "You kept this from us? You're the reason our older sister leads a life of pain? A life of—"

Mahlah stretched out her hands. "Stop. I insisted that Abba, Ima, and Noa vow never to speak of it. It was an accident. She didn't mean for it to happen, so we won't discuss this." She turned her focus to Noa. "Noa, we agreed."

"How can an injury like this be an accident? What did you do, Noa? And why would you forgive her, Mahlah?" Milkah pounced from her seat, jolting upright.

"There was nothing to forgive, as it was an accident. Noa was trying to protect me. Milkah, don't blame her, please. I never have." Mahlah stood between them.

Noa stepped to the side, looking at Milkah. "I've lived that accident over and over, pleading to take it back and remove the pain I caused. Ever since, I wanted to make it right, to fix what I broke. Do you see? It's why I stepped in to help Mahlah and take on things she couldn't do because of me. And I longed to meet Abba's expectations to earn his trust, so I persisted in getting things done. The more I could do, the happier he would be, and the more I would make amends. In my haste to cover up my guilt, I forgot the most important thing—to love each of you with compassion. It's not an excuse for my actions, which I recognize now. Abba cautioned me to make peace with you, Milkah. Those were the last words we spoke to each other." She took a step toward Milkah, her chin quivering. "I am sorry I mocked and scolded you. You are so beautiful—fairer than any other Hebrew woman. It was my terrible attempt to emphasize that you're more than your beauty. All I ever wanted was for you to know you are beautiful inside and out. To be yourself and not rely on your appearance. You're so much more."

Noa's words hit Milkah like a physical blow. She bent over, gripping her stomach, and a raw sound ripped from her mouth. "All ... all I ever wanted was some light shining on me. Each of you commanded our parents' attention. Mahlah, for your wisdom and expertise in weaving. Hoglah, for your enchanting singing, song creations, and as the keeper of Abba's stories. Noa, for being so capable. Tirzah, for your effervescent spirit and innocence. But for me, my appearance is all I have. How else was I to be appreciated in this family? All of you have talents to offer, and I don't. It's why I teased you the most, Noa. Master of everything. I kept teasing you because at least you paid attention to me."

Noa enveloped Milkah in a mighty hug with the love she had withheld.

Milkah pushed her away.

Desperate to remove her sister's pain, she approached Milkah again and put her arm around her. "You've accomplished something none of us has. You saved someone's life."

"What are you saying? Whose life?" Milkah's voice was an octave higher.

"Assir's. I met him today. He proclaimed that you let a beacon of truth enter his heart right before his father perished. Milkah, you saved his life because of your testimony of faith. Sharing your beliefs without fear and giving up your dream of living in a city inspired Assir to make the right judgment."

Milkah's lips parted slightly. "He admitted that?"

"Assir, his brothers, and Reba would be dead if you had not stood by your faith. You saved their lives. I have profound admiration for what you've done, and I'm so proud of you."

Mahlah stepped forward and put her hand on Milkah's shoulder. "Something good came from your broken heart."

Hoglah's lithe body swayed, clapping and encouraging Milkah to join her, but she remained in place. She sang out in her clear, melodic voice, "A song for my sisters! It's called, 'What a Day It Has Been.'"

> What a day it has been, as for tomorrow we shall see.
> But today, my beloved sisters made amends and set us all free.
> Milkah is a hero with four lives saved.
> We celebrate her faith for being so brave.

Hoglah encouraged Mahlah to clap and grabbed Tirzah by the hand, singing.

"We can count on you to bring us joy." Tirzah giggled. "Your talents amaze us."

"Thank you, Hoglah, for your endearing and true song. Do you think so, Milkah? Can you forgive me?" Noa bowed her head and stretched out her hand.

"I accept your apology. Thank you for sharing what Assir said about me and for your kind words. I will wait to witness a change in you, but it's a start." Milkah raised her eyebrow.

"I've something for you." Noa sprang to her bedroll and pulled out a cloth wrapped with a leather tie. She motioned for Milkah to sit and, squatting down, handed it to her with both hands.

Milkah unwrapped it and held it up. "It's beautiful, but this is your wedding belt. I can't take this from you." She laid the precious gift in her lap, folding it back in the cloth.

"I want you to have it. My words you may forget, but a gift of love you'll always have." It was much more than surrendering a stunning belt to make amends. She'd shed tears imagining Milkah's wedding day to Jonathan, giving up her dream to the Lord. It was a true gift of her heart.

Milkah gingerly held it. "It's the most beautiful one I've seen. Thank you. I'll cherish it and your words today."

Tirzah took Noa aside. "Such a burden you carried for so long. It's such a gift. Milkah must know how much you love her."

"I've not been a good example to you, my sweet."

"You have, though. You've shown me how to get up from a mistake. How to own my actions and make things right." Tirzah caressed her sister's hand.

"I thought I let you down." Noa choked up.

"It's a more important lesson to right a wrong than always being right. I love you, Noa."

Noa squeezed her sister so tight that she squealed. "Assir also asked if you would befriend Reba again."

Her sister jumped at the chance. "Can I go now?"

"Not tonight. Tomorrow, I have something important I'd like to discuss with you all. Let's wait a little. All right?"

Tirzah nodded her head. "Can you give me a hint about what it is?"

"Something that will be wonderful."

Noa sensed a change, especially after Milkah offered to brush her hair before bed. Her body felt lighter, released from her long-kept secret and the responses from Milkah and Tirzah. She tried to dwell on these thoughts, but the sad resignation about Jonathan and the angst about sharing her idea swallowed her mind.

The next morning, Noa returned from getting water, surprised to see the tent empty. She sighed with relief. Mahlah ventured out more, using her walking sticks to visit with Aunt Leora. Uncle Emet soon would announce his betrothal choices, and with the daunting task of warning her sisters and convincing them of her idea, she needed to gain Mahlah's support. She waited for her return.

After describing her audacious plan, Aunt Leora's dream, and the wheatear birds scene, as well as answering her many questions, Mahlah agreed without hesitation. Her older sister also advised being patient in explaining it, for it would ask much from each of them to first understand and then carry it out. Noa, buttressed by her wise and steadfast sister, prayed that the idea would be this agreeable to her other sisters.

Together, they decided to wait till the end of the day to build on the brokered truce between Noa and Milkah, spending the rest of the afternoon with their younger sisters. Once Noa volunteered and finished clearing and cleaning the dishes, she approached the dinner table. *Please, Lord, put the words in my mouth.* "I would like to have a sister's meeting for an important decision. We must discuss—"

Milkah interrupted her. "Must we do this now?"

"I know we still grieve for our father, but we must decide what path our lives will take." Noa continued in a softer tone. "It's imperative for our future, or I would postpone it." Her younger sisters lowered their heads.

She slowed her pace. "Moses commanded the tribal leaders to conduct a census, and it is almost at its end. Our wilderness journey will end soon, and we will explore a whole new world—God's gift of the Promised Land."

Milkah propped her head with her fist. "We have some excitement about our future, even with our grief. Why so serious and not grateful?"

"Because we won't be part of this census. Our law designates that only males may inherit." Mindful of her tone, Noa rehearsed her words so as not to be condescending or belittling.

"Why? I'm confused," Hoglah said.

"It's about a male's family name being carried forward to sustain his lineage. Upon the death of the male head of the family, the sons will inherit the property, guaranteeing it will remain in their tribe." Mahlah stepped in to explain.

"Then what will happen to us?" Tirzah's feet tapped.

Noa hesitated but replied, "All of Abba's inheritance will be divided among our uncles. As daughters, we will not inherit any of the Promised Land."

Milkah stood, defiant. "You didn't answer. What does it mean? What will happen to us?"

"It is as if we are widows, relying on our extended family or marrying as Uncle Emet deems."

"Wouldn't they take care of us? Although with five of us, it could be a burden for them. What about our dowries?" Hoglah trembled.

"We own valuables traded to us for our tent-making, but not enough for all five of us. Sisters, I have an idea and hope you'll consider it." Conscious of their extended family and neighbors passing by, Noa lowered her voice even with the tent flaps closed. "Moses instructed the tribal leaders about inheritance laws. He declared that if a man dies and leaves a wife with no son, then the man's brother must marry her so she can have a son to carry on the lineage of her dead husband's name. He decreed this three weeks ago."

"But it's not the case with us. Why bring this up?" Milkah frowned and left the table.

"I know it's not the case. But it made me think about how laws can change. I'm suggesting we petition for our father's inheritance to guarantee his lineage so Abba's name will not disappear."

Mahlah waved Milkah over. "Names are remembered in genealogies, songs, and blessings to future generations. Remember all the stories Abba taught us about our lineage? It is how we honor and learn from those who've gone before us. It's about continuing Abba's memory and place in the Israelite story of our ancestry, from his father Hepher and grandfather Gilead." They all joined in, murmuring,

"Son of Makir, son of Manasseh, belonging to the tribe of Manasseh, son of Joseph."

Mahlah continued. "Each night, we listened to him detail where we came from and how our ancestors surmounted tragedies through their faith. Without this lineage, can you imagine how these stories would survive for future generations? Noa proposes we appeal to secure our inheritance of this new land where we will build homes for our families. The most important purpose is to ensure our father's name is not forgotten."

Tirzah squirmed with bewilderment. "I don't understand. If we don't do this, then Abba's name won't exist?"

Noa took her hand. "If we receive Abba's inheritance, we will own the land in his name. When we marry, our firstborn will be of Zelophehad's lineage, and our children will inherit our land. Otherwise, it will be transferred to our uncles, and only their names will be perpetuated." She described Leora's ladder dream and her interpretation of it, hoping to instill assurance. "I have faith in our merciful God. He will brace this ladder for us. I believe with all my soul this is an act of faith that we have a place in God's plan for us."

Milkah dove to Noa, shouting, "How do you know what God wants for us? Did He instruct you to do this? Are you as grand as Moses?"

Noa backed away, feeling a blow to the brittle relationship they had just begun. "No. Our parents raised us with strong convictions, teaching us to have a place at the table. Remember all those Sabbaths where we debated God's laws? How we learned to defend them or question them?"

Milkah shrugged. "All based on falsehoods. We all know Father believed in Isis."

Noa's skin prickled. "Yes, Abba faltered, but he believed in God and returned to Him, even knowing he would not get to our Promised Land. He not only instilled respect for our heritage, but all his stories are about how God is always with us. He taught us reverence for God's many gifts. Remember the stars he loved so much? He loved God with all his being. All he said about his faith is true. Abba and Ima admitted how being exposed to four hundred years of Egyptian rituals and customs influenced their entire generation." Noa's eyes implored Mahlah's support.

Mahlah continued reinforcing Noa's thoughts. "We cannot judge him. Ima reminded him of his faith in our one God, and he recognized his sin for thinking of praying to Isis. God places people in our path to help us and to ensure that we stay true to our Lord's teachings. Ima was there for him, as we are now here for each other."

"We should demand Abba's rightful inheritance." Hoglah knotted her fists.

"What? You're like Noa, acting on emotions. Hoglah, you don't know what could happen to us." Milkah glared at her.

Hoglah jumped up, putting her finger in the air. "Yes, we should. We will petition Moses, Eleazar, and the heads of the tribes at the Tent of Meeting, while they are all assembled."

"Have you gone mad? They won't listen. Why would they? They're concentrating on completing the census. In front of the Tent of Meeting? No. It is simply wrong. Women don't do this." Milkah glowered at her sister.

Hoglah approached Milkah, her palms facing up. "Why should we be bereft of the right to our lineage? Why should our father's name vanish? As directed by our great ancestor, Joseph, we carry his bones for burial to the land of his fathers. Our Promised Land. It's our heritage too, to cherish and love this land."

Noa, amazed and grateful for Hoglah's response, knew this was far from over.

Milkah bent down to where Noa was sitting. "You think they'll allow us to speak? We've no say in this. Hoglah, this will not happen." She flung her arm, pointing at Noa. "We know of her brazenness, but you speak with such conviction."

Noa plunged on. "God directed Moses to follow specific laws of inheritance to ensure a family's lineage. Which is what we desire, isn't it?"

Milkah stomped her foot. "This will destroy our reputations. What man will want to marry us? And if our firstborn is not from our husband's lineage, then why marry any of us? Coming before the Tent of Meeting to state our demand? This is not a simple request. They could stone us. Do you dare to do this after what happened to Korah? I'm shocked you would consider it. Mahlah and Hoglah, have you fallen under her spell?"

Noa cringed. When Milkah discovered that Uncle Emet had chosen Jonathan for her betrothal, she would be furious to jeopardize it and would never agree to Noa's plan. Would Milkah ever forgive her? Was she wrong for not informing Milkah about Jonathan? "Korah incited the leaders and their tribes against God and His statutes. We don't lead people down a destructive path. We petition God to advocate for his daughters."

Milkah raised her hands with a stopping motion as if to prevent any more words from coming forth. Her intense, wide-open stare unnerved Noa as she continued, "You think our almighty God didn't consider this situation? How foolish you are."

Tirzah stepped forward between Milkah and Noa. "What if we discuss a compromise? Why confront everyone at the Tent of Meeting? What assurance do we have that they'll even listen to us? Why don't we seek the individual who can make this decision? Moses. Then we won't bring much attention to ourselves."

Tired and worn out, Noa stopped the conversation. "We have a lot to consider. I suggest we pause to reflect on our thoughts and refrain from discussing this with anyone yet. Let us promise not to share our discussion."

Milkah rose and stood nose to nose with Noa. "You already broke this by talking to Aunt Leora. It's always good for you. Anything you do is fine. It was only yesterday that you apologized to me and said you would no longer be commanding us. This is your best behavior?"

"I deserve that, but I'm not acting rashly. Instead, I am seeking your advice and counsel to make a joint decision," Noa whispered.

"You promise it will be a joint decision?"

"You have my word. I suggest we wait three days, for it is a big decision. We could fast tomorrow, ponder our thoughts, and pray for guidance. We can discuss it further on the second day, and on the third day, we will make a decision. Agreed?" All but Milkah nodded their heads.

Hoglah turned Milkah away and whispered, then turned back to Noa. "She agrees."

CHAPTER 24

The next day, Noa, relishing her earlier mornings for time alone, grabbed a skin of water and hastened toward the outside of camp. Passing by Aunt Leora's tent, she missed a small crevice and lurched forward, landing on all fours. She fumbled in the dirt, her hands and her one knee on fire, her palms layered with fine pebbles, and blood seeping into her ripped tunic.

"I heard some commotion. What happened? Let's get you inside." Aunt Leora supported her waist, and they hobbled in, Leora placing her on a padded sleeping mat. "Quite a fall. Where were you off to? This will hurt a bit." Leora cleaned her wounds with water and hyssop oil. She found her basket of wrapped, soft wool bandages.

Noa moaned, hunching up her shoulders. Her headscarf shifted, and she pulled it up, sensing a bruise on her forehead. She hesitated to speak—the plans for her precious morning, to be apart for discernment, dissolved. "I was searching for answers to what I ... what we should do. Am I doing God's will for me and my sisters, or am I plowing ahead doing my will and then seeking God's permission?"

"What do you think?" Leora asked.

"How can I be sure it's His will and not my own?"

Leora finished cleaning the wounds, covering them with more hyssop ointment, and wrapped a fine linen gauze around each one. "Keep your leg up with this extra pillow under your foot. Do you know the hyssop plant? It sprouts a hairy stem boasting bright blue, purple, or white flowers. Distilling the plant produces a potent oil that keeps wounds from infection." Leora pointed to her knee. "You remind me of this plant. Your hair sticks out from under your scarf.

You can be potent in your words and actions, but when you distill them down, you mean it all for good, and"—Leora stroked Noa's hair—"you're lovely as a flower."

Noa tucked her hair into her headscarf. "So, I am a hairy weed?"

"Did you listen to what I said?"

"I know I can be direct, and I mean to do what's right. But I've started to doubt."

"Life brings ups and downs. We fall, we hurt, but the Lord watches over us. Our skin heals with the wonders He planted for us. Was your fall a sign? Do you have doubts with fears growing? Your inner voices warn, 'No, you can't do this.' My dream coaxed you, and now you wonder. What does your heart say?"

Noa added a small mat behind her head, raising herself to see her aunt better. "Sometimes I'm certain, and then not. How does God speak to you?"

"First, I listen to my inner voice, mulling it over. I prayed about my advice to you and suddenly remembered what my mother would say, 'Wait three days, and somehow the answer will come to you.' What are you smiling at?"

"You must have told me this before. We will make our decision on the third day. How else does God talk to you?"

"God communicates to us through people, through nature, and through amazing coincidences—which I believe aren't coincidences."

Noa again had a broad smile. "Yes, Auntie. This happened to me!" Noa shared the story of her falcon and wheatears.

Leora jolted her head back. "Hmm, that is some coincidence."

"Do you ever hear 'no' from God?"

"I hear that it's my choice, but it's most often clear what the better path is, and sometimes I accept it, and sometimes I don't. It's the gift of making decisions with the responsibility that comes with owning them. Remember your father's story of Moses saying no to God when he didn't want to go to Egypt? God told him, 'I will put the words in your mouth and Aaron your brother's mouth.' Trust God to be with you every day. He will let you know if you're off the path."

"Korah believed he followed a holy path."

"Korah listened to his ego and fixated on being God's chosen one by the injury of others. He chose the wrong path, and God cautioned him many times, but he didn't heed the warning. I'm afraid your walk is not a good idea today, but you can stay here and ponder. I'll go visit your Aunt Adina, and I'll let your sisters know you will stay here for tonight."

Noa massaged her leg. "I love you, Aunt."

Noa leaned back, grateful that God had gifted her with such a wise aunt. *Lord, You've given me the dream from my aunt, the startling scene of the wheatears, this idea inside that doesn't seem to go away. I humbly ask that what You bestowed on Moses—putting words in his mouth—You will do for me. And if I am wrong, please guide me.*

Noa whispered to Mahlah as she helped roll up her sister's bedding. Her younger sisters had already done theirs and were on to the other morning chores. "A thought came to me in the middle of the night about how we can make this decision." Noa quickly explained her idea, and then they joined the others.

After a breakfast of goat cheese and manna wafers, the sisters positioned themselves in a circle on their most comfortable mats.

Mahlah chose where their father used to sit. "Sisters, we spent our day apart, and now it's time to share your reactions. We will start with prayer. Holy Lord, we thank You for this day. Please be with us as we decide our path forward. We thank You for giving us our perspectives and ask for continued wisdom and courage to do Your will. Let us respect one another, and may whatever we decide be pleasing in Your sight. Amen." Mahlah glanced at Noa.

Her heart swelled full of gratitude for her older sister. Her simple elegance and quiet guidance testified to the difference in their approaches.

Mahlah continued. "I've given this much consideration, as you all have. Noa proposed to us a momentous decision even as we grieve the tremendous loss of our father. We stand at a precipice with a choice to make. Each of us will speak, but whatever our decision, we must all agree, not two out of five or even four out of five. We must be of one mind. We may feel frightened, but as sisters, we must all agree on our outcome."

Noa cleared her throat. "Mahlah, before we start, I promise that whatever is decided, I will, without objection, accept the decision. I trust our decision will be the best because we honor each other." As much as she believed hers was the right course, she surrendered the outcome. They were all in God's hands.

Tirzah yawned, blinking slowly, and she peered at her oldest sister. "Mahlah, what do you think?"

Mahlah smiled. "We influence each other, so to help us discuss this without sway, Noa and I created an idea this morning. We suggest each of you take one of these stones." She laid out five of them. "Once you have your stone, we will turn away from our circle. Put the stone in your right hand if we should ask for our father's inheritance and extend his name. If you disagree, hold the stone in your left hand. Close both hands, so we don't know where you placed your stone."

Reaching for a stone, they turned away, then back.

Tirzah turned a shade of pink as she drew her lower lip between her teeth. Noa glanced at the others, who sat cross-legged, shoulders straight. *So much pressure on Tirzah for this decision. She always wants to please all of us.*

Mahlah directed, "On the count of three, open your hands. One, two, three."

Noa, Hoglah, and Mahlah opened their right hands. Milkah clutched the stone on her left, and Tirzah dropped it before her.

A loud silence filled the room. Mahlah assessed, "We have three sisters who agree to come forward, and one sister says no."

Milkah crossed her arms. "It would be senseless."

"And one sister is?"

Tirzah grabbed the stone and put it between both palms.

Noa touched her little sister's fist. "My little duck, you dropped your stone? You held it in the middle?"

Tirzah shrugged, clutching her hands.

She choked with a lump in her throat, knowing she was responsible for causing this stress. Tirzah didn't trust herself yet, was only trying to please everyone and not focusing on her own opinion.

Hoglah hopped up and gushed, "I have an idea. Why don't we pretend we've all revealed the stone in our right hands and, together, imagine a plan? Then, we'll vote again for a final decision. Would this help?"

Milkah straightened with her most regal pose. "This was supposed to be a day to discuss the idea, not to decide, but I will play along."

Hoglah twisted toward her with a little bow to Milkah. "Thank you, Queen Milkah."

Noa could have kissed Hoglah. Milkah would enjoy being one of the deciding votes with Tirzah.

Tirzah blurted, "Yes, a great idea."

"Let's form a picture. We arrive hand in hand at the Tent." Hoglah acted as if she were strutting to the Tent. "They'll stop to find out why we've come. Then, we would address our speech to Moses. Who should say it?"

Noa eased back in her seat, laughing to herself as she had never pictured Hoglah contributing in such a forceful way.

"It should be Mahlah. She's the oldest," Tirzah said.

"I'm good at persuading. Perhaps I should, as they'll listen to me." Milkah raised her chin high.

"It's not a command. We will need to request, dear Queen." Hoglah rolled her eyes and again bowed. Milkah tossed her comb, just missing Hoglah.

"We're pretending, yes?" Milkah threaded her fingers through her hair.

Noa, seeing this could spiral out of control, interjected. "The solution is simple. We will all speak." Assured by Leora's dream, she knew each one would share the reward. And, with a breath of angst, she admitted they would all share the consequences.

"Even me? I'm the youngest. They won't listen to me." Tirzah shrank in her seat.

"Yes, even you will play an important part." Noa squeezed Tirzah's hand, who glowed from her older sister's encouragement.

Seeing that Hoglah enjoyed being the ringleader instead of her two older sisters, she glanced at Mahlah to know if she agreed. Mahlah waved to Hoglah to continue.

Hoglah grinned to regain her role. "Let's start again. What should we say to convince them to grant our request? Mahlah, what do you think?"

"We must start by saying who we are. We are the daughters of Zelophehad, son of Hepher, son of Gilead, son of Makir, son of Manasseh, son of Joseph, and then say our names."

Noa had prayed and rehearsed different ways to speak about Abba. "Yes, that is right, it is all about our heritage—that is why we come to them. Many will remember that Abba mentored men for all the tribes, fortifying their skills for our Promised Land. We must address Abba's death, as that's the reason we are there. We must admit that Abba died for his sin as did all who were twenty years or older coming into the wilderness." She read their even expressions. No one objected.

"And we should address that Abba was not a rebel. He took no part in Korah's insurrection, and he led our entire family to distance ourselves from that fateful day. We know Moses is aware, but the rest of the community may not be." Noa paused, not wanting to overwhelm them.

"That is important," Mahlah added. "We can start by saying who we are and why we've come, but he was not among Korah's followers."

Hoglah added, "We must condemn Korah's actions. We should say, 'Who banded together against the Lord.'"

"Hoglah, that is a good idea. Thank you for your contribution. The next part is important ... about what we want and why." Noa's breathing became steadier.

Tirzah drew up her slight frame, unwavering in her eye contact with Noa, and firmly asserted, "'Why should our father's name disappear from his clan because he had no son?' That's why we're asking."

Noa hugged her. "Tirzah, you're getting good at this game."

Tirzah's shoulders dropped from her ears. She softly swayed as if listening to one of Hoglah's songs. It looked like Tirzah would vote yes. Milkah's cold manner remained firm. She would need to play a part, or it wouldn't be a unanimous decision. Would she add anything to what they should ask? She was the last one to convince. A silence fell over the room. Everyone looked at Milkah.

Milkah declared, "'Give us property among our father's relatives.'"

Noa gasped at her sister's clarity. The inheritance was about the Promised Land and what was allotted to each family. Where Milkah began and ended amazed her. She played the queen. Noa comprehended Jonathan's and Leora's observations and sage advice to encourage her sisters to be a part of the plan. Moved by Milkah's assertion, tears formed.

"Noa, remember, this is just a game. I haven't said yes. We will hear all of our opinions." Milkah tossed her hair back.

Hoglah coughed. "We need a decision. Do you agree, Milkah, my queen?"

Milkah nodded ever so slightly.

"Let's take our stones in our hands again." She handed each one the deciding stones. "Turn away, then back around, and everyone opens their hands. Are you ready? One, two, three."

Noa gazed at Milkah and Tirzah, as the decision depended on their commitment to the plan. All but Milkah opened their hands. Tirzah didn't hesitate, holding her right hand, palm up, beaming with her decision.

Milkah held both hands out, her fists closed, and scrutinized Noa.

"You're keeping us in suspense." Tirzah squirmed.

"You promise if I say no, you'll never bring it up again?" Milkah angled her chin up with her neck exposed, her lips closed tight.

Noa held her breath until that moment. *She'll vote no because of me.* She saw it in Milkah, her unfavorable decision made. Defeated, Noa tendered a slight nod. "I promise."

Milkah pulled back her left hand and opened her right. A collective gasp filled the tent.

"You're not the only one who cares about Abba's lineage. I made my decision in his honor."

Noa melted and enveloped Milkah with all her might.

Milkah rested her hand on her shoulder. "You're our sister, right or wrong. We will stand by each other. Abba would want that."

Hoglah tossed the comb back at her. "Queen Milkah, you sure know how to captivate an audience. What a scare."

Milkah swept both arms wide around them. "They will hear what we sisters have to say."

Hoglah jumped up and down.

Noa's mind raced. *Thank you, Lord, for guiding Milkah. She said yes. We've come a long way, but many more details still need to be discussed. Should I push this now?* "This is a tremendous decision. Each of you humbles me, and I am grateful for how we came to this point. And yet, we still have some planning to do."

Milkah whined, "What now? Sister, can we take a moment to celebrate?"

"Of course, forgive me. Let's stop for some water, and we still have some raisin cakes to share."

Over their repast, they couldn't help but discuss what would come next.

"Who will say what?" Hoglah began.

"What's your suggestion, sister?" Noa beamed, enjoying Hoglah's enthusiasm.

"We can go from youngest to oldest, saying what we would prefer." Hoglah twinkled with the attention.

Starting with Tirzah and proceeding to Mahlah, they kept the sentence each offered when envisioning their petition.

They planned to spend the next day preparing, bathing in the river despite the chilly water, and straightening the tent for the expected family to join them in celebration. Noa chuckled to see the different energy in the tent. No quarrels, no spats. Each of them working together. She heard Tirzah rehearsing her line, and each time, her posture straightened further. As the day flew by, a quiet resignation entered as the night approached.

CHAPTER 25

In the morning, Mahlah softly called out from behind the closed curtain. "Noa, come here. I need your help."

Noa hastened to her sister. What could be wrong? The sisters insisted that Mahlah sleep in their parents' bed because of her condition. She must've maneuvered the curtain last night. But how?

"I have a surprise for you, sister."

Already dressed in one of Ima's tunics, Mahlah had arranged her hair. Something had changed about her countenance. She stood with perfect posture, joy exuding from her whole being. How could she act so happy when facing the eventful day ahead?

"You're beautiful, but something more. You're joyous. What is it?"

Mahlah waved her back.

Noa cocked her head and retreated five steps. Her sister advanced toward her.

"Your limp—it's gone! You're walking without your sticks. What happened?" She leaped, embracing her sister.

"Shhh. Don't bring our sisters in yet. I wanted to be certain. Thanks to God's healing, I'll walk unaided to the Tent."

"What a blessing. I'm overjoyed. Come, let's share this wonderful news." *How could this be?*

"No, wait. I've something else I must reveal. Sit here on the bed with me." Mahlah's exuberance changed to a pained gaze.

She rushed to her sister. Why worry about such good news? "What's happened?"

"It's time for me to air a secret, especially after you confessed to Milkah." Mahlah took in a deep breath, releasing it quickly. "I never liked my name, Mahlah. I sympathize with our parents' choice, reminding us of our blessings, no matter the circumstances. But to be named Mahlah? Sick? Weak? Fat? I hated being the center of ridicule. The day you defended me and almost knocked out five supposed friends, I admit I was ready to do the same. Only when I realized you could hurt someone did it dawn on me to stop you."

"I am so sorry. If only I didn't—" Noa paused and silenced herself. *If this is part of her healing, I will listen, Lord. Allow me to aid my sister, even though this is hard to hear.*

"No, don't. No apologies. That's not the reason for reliving this. After I fell, I cried for several days, feeling weak, wondering if I would always be a cripple. Then I considered. I won't have to go to the river or ever hear cruel jokes again. I could stay in this tent, and with all the practice, I would become a good weaver. Abba encouraged me to venture outside, and when he presented me with the sticks, I reacted with false joy. He knew in his heart I hid away in this tent. It was selfish of me."

"I would've protected you." She ached for her sister, hiding all these years. Words hurt. Words could worm their way into the very fiber of one's being. She reflected on her name, Noa, meaning "movement" or "motion," which was fitting. Why did her parents name her sister Mahlah? She wouldn't like the name either.

"I had to work this out for myself. As the oldest and with our tradition, I felt the burden of inhibiting all of you from marrying, as no one would deem me a good match. I know Abba contrived to wait for the property allotments because he couldn't find anyone who would take me."

"That isn't true. You know how strongly he believed in keeping us together so we could live near each other." Noa squeezed Mahlah's hands.

"I came to believe that, but you're getting ahead of my story." Mahlah laughed with mirth.

Noa's pulse quickened. What would make her laugh now?

"You bartered with Tikva, our trusted midwife, for the exorbitant clay and malachite healing ointment. You traded Ima's necklace for it."

"It was worth it, sister." Noa lifted her palm, gesturing to her sister's legs. "But how did you find out my secret?"

"Tikva wouldn't have given this for free, so I admit I checked your hiding place, and it was gone. But let me finish. I never used it."

"What?" She shook her head. "I don't understand."

"When you surrendered your precious gift of Ima's for the healing ointment, I had to confront my fears. You've carried a yoke of guilt for some time, which wasn't fair of me. It's why I told you over and over not to discuss it. You didn't mean the accident to happen. It is I who ought to apologize. I prayed not for my healing, but for yours. It forced you to assume my responsibility as the oldest. I should've protected you, not the other way around."

Noa's mind clouded with confusion from her dizzying happiness at Mahlah's healing to the sadness of her confession and apology. Until that moment, she hadn't realized the tremendous weight of responsibility that had shaped her. But not only the responsibility. It was the guilt. The guilt of seeing her sister cooped up all these years. *But she is apologizing to me?* With mixed emotions, she replayed the scene that changed everything.

"Stop imagining it. It was an accident. You paid for it all these years because of my cowardliness, which I regret. Can you forgive me?"

"I don't know what to say. I'm so happy you can walk. That's the most important thing." She shifted her legs on the bed. Would Mahlah have carried the joy and burden of being Abba's favorite if she'd healed sooner? How different would her life have been?

"And?"

"I'm trying to absorb and sort out my feelings." Distracted by the confession, Noa focused on the discarded sticks. "I don't understand. How did you walk without the ointment?"

"God inspired me with the strength to overcome, but you were the impetus. I can never repay all your years of effort, but I couldn't let you lose a cherished memento from Ima. Because of your genuine, unselfish act, I forced myself to shuffle going back and forth in this tent to strengthen my legs. I prayed for God's mercy, envisioning our Lord laying his healing hand on my head."

Noa opened her mouth, but Mahlah continued. "There's more." Her sister nabbed something from under the pillow and extended her hand over Noa's. "When I saw this was gone, I called on Hoglah to find Tikva." She laid the precious onyx necklace in Noa's hands.

"Ima's necklace." She clutched it to her heart, forgetting the pressure, the weight, the mold that had formed her. It melted away, knowing her sister's true healing, both physically and mentally.

"You bought the ointment as a genuine act of sacrifice, reminding me to trust God. I love you so much for standing by me."

Not only a treasured gift from her ima, but also a gift of her sister's healing and Noa's freedom from guilt. Forgiven. *God, I am humbled by Your countless gifts. Thank You for the relief of leaning on Mahlah and for how I can partner even more with her in safeguarding our sisters.* God had answered her prayers. "How could I not be happy for you?" Noa kissed her on the cheek.

Mahlah beamed. "There's even more."

"More? What could be more?" She laughed.

"I told Aunt Leora my secret, and she acted as my lookout and chaperone as I attempted to meander outside on uneven ground to ensure I could manage. She sent Simon over with a donkey, and he easily picked me up and transported me to the outskirts. He showed such patience that it made me laugh. When I stumbled, he made me feel comfortable being me, with no awkwardness at all. He demonstrated some of the training routines he and Jonathan had to do in preparation for serving in God's army, which strengthened their legs and arms. It took weeks of practice. After the second month, he declared his love for me, saying he couldn't be happier. At first, he hesitated, as he assumed I would reject him because of his adoption. Even though Uncle Abel vowed an inheritance for him, just like his other three sons, he didn't feel worthy. He said he took a chance because of our time together and wants to marry me, declaring it didn't matter if I could walk."

"Of course it doesn't, not to Simon! What is not to love? No wonder you're glowing." They both started to laugh.

"What's going on in there?" Milkah rapped on the curtain.

Mahlah put a finger over her lips. "Let's not mention Simon now. It may be just a dream if Uncle Emet prevails."

Noa cupped her hands together, palms up. It was a secret code they'd had as children, meaning they were in God's hands. Then she shouted, "Mahlah has something to show you. Open the curtain."

Milkah, Hoglah, and Tirzah lifted the curtain and circled around the bed.

"You must go over to the table." Noa spread her arms to accompany them to the other side.

Mahlah straightened her shoulders and glided over.

All three of them raced to meet her halfway.

"No sticks." Hoglah spun around her.

"You're walking." Milkah joined Hoglah.

"I knew this would happen someday," Tirzah gushed.

"You did?" Mahlah said.

"Yes, I felt God would put His hand on you and heal you. At least that's what I prayed for."

Mahlah embraced Tirzah. "I have you to thank?"

"God and me." Tirzah glowed.

"And someone else, our sister Noa," Mahlah said.

"You don't need to." Noa curled her hands around her middle.

Mahlah insisted and recounted her story of healing. "I thrust the eldest role on Noa, who only tried to live up to our father's bidding when I should've been the one to do so. It grieves me how I affected our family. However, I make this commitment to all of you to take on my responsibilities, which I should have done long ago. We owe her our gratitude. I will join Noa in helping to keep you safe."

Milkah folded her arms and smirked. "Now we have two of you ordering us about? You still need to be just our sisters."

"You're in safe hands with both of us." Mahlah smiled.

"Such a gift before our momentous day. This must be a sign from God." Noa danced, waving everyone to join her.

But Hoglah raised her hands, waving her two older sisters over. "It is. And yes, we need to celebrate again, but we still have more to plan." She went to the table and presented a hot cup of habek to Noa and Mahlah, inviting them to sit.

Milkah put her hands on her waist. "Oh, now there are three of you ordering us around."

Hoglah cleared her throat and waited for her younger sisters to join her. "While waiting for you for breakfast, Milkah, Tirzah, and I discussed where we should stand tomorrow at the Tent of Meeting."

Noa covered her smile with her hand. *God has more than just a plan for me to grow with this bold petition. He's leading all of us.* She looked admiringly at Hoglah. "Well done, you three. That is important." She tapped her forefinger over her mouth. "Let's make a map." She set three small stones apart in a row. "Here we are, the Manasseh tribe between the Ephraim and Benjamin tribes on the opposite side of the Tent entrance." She put a cup to show the location.

"We should scout out the path for tomorrow. Milkah, will you take Hoglah and Tirzah with you to the Tent? Pay attention, as we will follow the same way tomorrow. As soon as you come back, we can complete our map."

Her younger sisters, already finished with breakfast, donned their headdresses and hurried out.

"We were worried about you. You've been gone for a long time." Noa put down her weaving and joined them on the family rug.

"I'm glad you sent us today, for it's a much longer walk than I expected. The Tabernacle is dazzling—God's cloud emanating from it even more breathtaking." Milkah's radiant glow reflected her awe.

Hoglah picked up the stones, laying them down as she described the path. "We will head north to the neighboring Benjamin tents, then east to Dan's tribe. The tribal standards identify the start and end of each. After that, there is the smallest section of the Asher tents, and then the largest ones are Naphtali and Judah. It took quite a while to get there."

Milkah took a stone and positioned it. "We proceeded as far as we dared at the Tent entrance without being noticed. The men concentrated on the census with loud discussions bursting from all sides."

"I overheard one man speak about his unborn child." Hoglah donned a deep sound from her throat. "My wife is six months pregnant. She bore five sons, and this one will be a son as well. You should include him in the census."

"Did he get his way?" Noa raised an eyebrow.

"The Levite priest said the census was for men over twenty. Otherwise, every pregnant woman would claim a son, and he would be born at twenty." Hoglah laughed.

"And no one spoke of women or daughters?" Noa thrust her hands upward.

"No, not a word."

"What else did you observe?" Warmth spread over her as she listened to her sisters' excitement. This was good. The excursion built on their courage and confidence. Their daring plan was enough to worry about without fearing where they should go.

Tirzah lifted twelve stones and placed them as she spoke. "Each tribe flies their heritage flag, six on either side leading up to the Tabernacle curtain. They gather on carpets with a small, low table, a scribe, and a Levite priest."

"Where do Moses and Eleazar preside?" Noa knew where they should focus.

Hoglah moved two large stones at the top. "They sit on red carpets nearest the Tabernacle. If there's a disagreement the Levite priests cannot settle with the tribal leaders, they approach Moses for judgment."

Milkah plopped a bowl on the top of their map. "An old woman told us about a bronze basin behind Moses where he and Eleazar wash their hands and feet before entering the Holy of Holies. We saw the veil before the Holy of Holies shimmer with its vibrant colors of deep blue, purple, and scarlet. She said the blue represents the color of heaven, purple for royalty, and scarlet for man's blood."

"As soon as you enter the Tent of Meeting, there's a large bronze altar for the sacrifices." Tirzah wedged a stone onto their map.

"Good job, sisters. The most important thing is for Moses to hear us. How far is the last tribe from the Tabernacle?" Noa pointed to where they sat.

"Should all the men hear or only Moses and Eleazar?" Tirzah asked.

"All," Mahlah and Noa said together.

"This decision will affect the shares of land not just for us but for all brotherless daughters. For some, it will be threatening," Mahlah said.

Noa frowned at her sister. "But there will be fathers who will welcome this change."

"Is this what it will be like?" Milkah shook from side to side, simpering, "You two advising us on either side?"

"We can stand here at the second tent canopy nearest Moses." Hoglah positioned five stones. "We won't say a word until we're all together. It'll be enough commotion to cause the men to gather around us. Perhaps Tirzah can lead us in?"

"Tirzah, it's a lot to ask of you." Noa raised her eyebrows.

Tirzah threw her shoulders back. "I will lead my sisters because I believe God is with us."

"You're very brave, and our parents would be very proud of you for your faith." Noa realized that she wasn't the only one forced to grow up fast. Her little sister had experienced more in one year than she had in her entire lifetime. *She is stronger than I even imagined.*

The enormity of their plan descended on them like an avalanche of stones, with not a word spoken or dinner to be touched. Each laid out their best tunic, and they prepared each other's hair. They planned to wear the only other leather sandals they owned—the ones reserved for weddings and funerals. While each of her sisters rehearsed their lines, Noa imagined the potential consequences, as she thought her sisters might be doing as well.

No matter what happened, Mahlah's healing of her body and heart elated her. Mahlah would not settle for Uncle Emet's miserable choice, believing her infirmity prevented childbearing. She'd live an abundant life with vital, charming Simon. *Somehow, it will happen.*

Noa knelt, her sisters joining her. "Let's pray before we sleep. Dear Lord, we give thanks for answering our prayers for healing, especially Tirzah's prayers, for our sister Mahlah. We dance with joy for her fresh path ahead. You know our hearts and how we loved our parents. Tomorrow, we come before our Hebrew leaders and ask You to put the words in our mouths. Please give us the courage to honor our father's name. Dear God, we are thankful and nervous all at the same time. Instill a confident spirit within us, and let our words prompt reverence to You and our lineage. Amen."

"I have a song for us. It will complement your prayer." Hoglah strummed her harp. "I was so excited. I couldn't sleep last night, so I created this song. It's called 'Voices in the Wilderness.'" Her eyes sparkled, and she sang with a soft, yet sure, voice.

The daughters of Zelophehad learned his stories well.
He inspired them to love our God, his heritage to tell.

We come to honor our father's name, to keep it and preserve.
We state what's in our humble hearts unto the God we serve.
Our voices in the wilderness, let them hear what we convey.
Give us the words to speak. Lord help us, we pray.

Noa floated over to hug her sister. "That was beautiful, Hoglah. You captured it so well. Shall we sing this together?"

The sisters' harmonies always stirred her, underscoring how each contributed to a synchronized, joyful sound.

"And now, Mahlah, can you share a short story with us before we go to bed?"

"You remember the story of our ancestor, Joseph? He was his father's favorite, which made his brothers very jealous, and they found a chance to sell him into slavery. They told their father, Jacob, that Joseph had been killed by a wild animal. He ended up accused of a crime he didn't commit and was imprisoned. But God gifted him with the ability to interpret dreams, and when Pharaoh sought a diviner, Joseph told him what his dream meant. Pharaoh rewarded him. So, our ancestor, a Hebrew prisoner, became the overseer of all of Egypt. Now, Joseph had a choice when he met his cruel brothers, and God instilled in him the courage to forgive them. God reunited him with Jacob, his beloved father, who adopted Joseph's sons, Manasseh and Ephraim. We're like Joseph, with many struggles, yet God prevailed for him, and we believe as he did, that God meant it for a good purpose so that he could preserve the lives of many people. We do this for the great lineage of Abba. Be of good courage, sisters."

Each said, "Amen."

But even with the reverence from the evening, her sister's confidence, and God's grace in healing Mahlah, Noa's unease grew, and she struggled with sleep.

CHAPTER 26

The crisp autumn air burst into Noa's lungs and sent a chill through her body, but the early morning sun promised warmth. Was it her imagination, or did the cloud over the Tent of Meeting glow brighter?

She pulled back the tent flap, reentering the family tent and waving her four sisters to circle her. "Don't be afraid. Don't look left or right. Look forward. Whatever they say, don't be dismayed. My dear ones, we've made a daring decision together, and today, we'll make ourselves heard at the Tent of Meeting. We trust our Lord will be with us. Remember Abba leading us with Moses's blessing? Say it over and over."

As agreed, Tirzah proceeded first, followed by Noa. The other three proceeded from youngest to oldest.

They wove their way through the organized maze of Manasseh's tribal tents. The sounds of the Israelite community having a typical day—women's chatter, bleating sheep, and laughing children—tempted Noa to turn back from what they were about to do. She shivered, remembering Milkah's fiery words shouted at her only three days ago. *"This will destroy our reputations. What man will want to marry us? Do you want us to challenge our laws before the sacred Tent of Meeting? No woman has ever asked this before. They could stone us. You dare to attempt this after what happened to Korah?"*

Like wildfire through parched grass, heat ignited throughout Noa's body. *Did I force my sisters to make this decision?* She shook her head. No, they had all agreed. *Lord, please put the words in my mouth to lead them. I can't lose my courage now.*

A woman working on her loom called to them. "Why so dressed up? Where are you going? To a wedding?"

Noa's finger crossed her lips. "Something special, but it's a secret."

Children skipped along and badgered them with questions.

When they came to the Benjamin tents, an elderly man, flanked by five young boys, blocked their path. Tirzah peeked up at his hefty frame. "We're going to the Tent of Meeting. Would you like to join us?"

The elderly man and five boys blocked their path. Tirzah couldn't march on. They had practiced what they would say at the Tent of Meeting, but not on the walk there. A younger woman grabbed his arm. "Father, these are Zelophehad's daughters. Maybe they have a message to deliver. Let them pass."

Disgruntled, he stepped aside, huddling and speaking with his grandsons.

Row after row of tribal tents. *Will we ever get there?* A pebble snuck its way into her sandal. She shook her foot, hesitant to stop, as she observed the older men scrutinizing Milkah.

Women from the Dan, Asher, and Naphtali tribes crossed their arms and shook their fingers. Noa's chest tightened when a Judah woman stomped alongside them, blaring her warning. "Only men can present their lineage for the census."

Noa's tunic, now soaked under her arms, clung to her. How could news of their walk spread so fast? The old man must have sent his grandsons ahead to try to stop them. She bowed to the woman and forced herself to remain calm. "We thank you for your concern. Ours is another matter. Shalom." She squeezed her shoulders together, straightening her back, and gently nudged Tirzah forward.

After a couple of steps, Tirzah stumbled.

Noa caught her before she fell. *I should have gone first. It's too much for her.* But her brave little sister had insisted on leading them.

Tirzah quivered and looked to the ground.

Will my sisters lose their confidence in front of Moses, the priests, and all the tribal leaders?

Noa lifted Tirzah's chin. "You are so brave, leading us all. I am so proud of you. You've given me the strength to bring us this far and reminded me to trust our Lord for every step. Would you like me to lead now?"

Tirzah hugged Noa and scooted behind her.

Noa turned to her sisters, her eyes gleaming. "Let us thank our fearless Tirzah. She's given more than she will ever know, boosting our determination. Let us go."

She quickened their pace with a decisive stride.

As they drew closer to the Tent, they heard the tribal leaders bellow.

"You there, Shem, son of Jared, wait with your father. It's not your clan's turn yet."

Another man roared, "It's my turn next."

"We will get to you, be patient," a harsher voice volleyed.

Noa stopped in front of the entrance. "Sisters, gather round me." She raised the corner of her mouth. "They'll be so busy arguing, they may not notice us at first."

"Oh, they will notice us." Milkah coyly raised her shoulders.

Hoglah elbowed her. "Must you always remind us of your beauty?"

"Sisters." Noa raised her hands between them and grabbed Milkah's hand. "We are here to honor our father. He is with us as our Lord is with us." Noa grabbed Mahlah's hand. "Will you lead us in prayer?"

Mahlah clasped Tirzah's hand, and Hoglah completed the circle.

"Sisters, I've never been more thankful for our family. Each of us has given so much to reach this decision." Mahlah peered from Noa to Milkah, who dipped their heads at each other. "Let us be assured we are not alone. Let us say the blessing Moses taught us."

The Lord bless you
and keep you;
the Lord make his face shine on you
and be gracious to you;
the Lord turn his face toward you
and give you peace.

They stood holding each other's hands.

"Stay here for a moment. I will see to our entrance." Noa broke away and scanned the courtyard. Eleazar, the high priest, resplendent in the gold chest plate embedded with twelve precious stones, stood just before the magnificent Tent curtains. Hanging from five towering gold posts, embroidered winged cherubs floated on a heaven of blue, purple, and scarlet fine linen. Moses appeared in front of the imposing curtain. He held his staff, the one given to him from the Lord. His curly silver hair encircled his weatherworn face. What would this man who talked with God say to their audacious request that had never been asked before?

She'd seen the cloud above the Tabernacle her whole life, but to see it this close stunned her. They stood in the presence of God.

She couldn't breathe.

She turned and eyed her sisters. When all nodded, she led them forward.

Since the men focused on their tribal leader and priest, they hadn't been noticed yet. Noa breathed a little easier. When they passed the second of six awnings, some men lunged up from their tables as the sisters neared Moses. Others pointed. A few gasped. Would they make it to their planned spot?

Her knees locked. Could she take another step? She spotted the Manasseh flag raised over near her uncles, who were deep in conversation with their backs to them. She willed herself to see Jonathan. His eyebrows raised. *What will he think? Will he even talk to me after this?* She turned away, not answering his questioning eyes. At the fourth awning, Noa waited for her sisters to flank her. She focused on Moses, who examined a scroll in deep conversation with Eleazar.

Assir's heart leaped when he saw Milkah, who looked more beautiful than ever.

He tapped Eleazar and pointed to the daughters, causing Moses and Eleazar to glance up.

"What do we have here?" Moses dropped his scroll.

Eleazar murmured, "Perhaps they're still concerned about their father's death? Assir, go to the Manasseh tribe. Ask their uncles why they're here."

Not knowing whether Zelophehad's family would deign to speak with him, Assir acted as if he were a messenger from Moses regarding the census. *Why did Noa inquire about inheritance?* And would Emet and Abel now blame *him* for their impertinence? He stood close to the Manasseh tribe's canopy to discern if they knew the reason for the sisters' arrival.

Emet and Abel, their backs to the disturbance and surrounded by their sons and grandsons, hadn't noticed the sisters, but when they saw other Manasseh men looking away from the table, they swung around.

"What are they doing here?" Emet blared. He sprang up and hurried to the front of their canopy. Abel dashed to his side. Assir edged closer to listen.

"I don't know. I'm as baffled as you. Jonathan, Simon, do you know anything about this?" Abel yelled over the commotion.

They both shook their heads.

"We must prevent them from making fools of themselves before they embarrass our families." Emet strutted forward. Abel grabbed his arm.

"Emet. Stop. You'll make it worse and bring attention to yourself. Let us listen. Perhaps they came to thank Moses for visiting after their father's funeral. You don't want to interfere with their gratitude."

"Abel, let go of me. I'll put a stop to this! They'll learn a harsh lesson after this is over, I promise you!"

Assir hurried back and repeated what he saw and heard to Eleazar.

Standing in the middle, Noa grabbed Tirzah's and Milkah's hands. "We must wait for Moses to recognize us. I know it's hard, but be patient. 'Look up.'"

They joined hands, completing their lyric, "And you will know."

Moses surveyed each of the sisters and confided a comment to Eleazar. He pushed back from the low table and picked up his staff to rise. He never took his eyes off them. As he did this, the men closest to them ceased their negotiations and edged closer. A whir of sarcasm surrounded them.

"Are you lost, young women?"

"Didn't you know your family men are here?"

Uncle Emet stormed in front of the sisters. He thrust up his hand and spit out his words. "Why are you here? There is no place for you. Turn around and go home now." He jerked his arm up and pointed to the entrance.

Noa's sisters blanched. Tirzah hunched her shoulders and pressed her elbows into her sides, making her body as small as possible. *What did I get them into?* Would her sisters run? *I must protect them.* Noa stepped forward to confront her uncle when Moses struck his staff three times.

Tirzah huddled toward Noa and gripped her hand so hard that Noa's hand throbbed.

Noa's sense of calm evaporated like rain on a steamy day. The silence was deafening. Had she led her sisters to disaster? *Lord, is this your sign? Should I beg Moses for forgiveness and insist he give whatever the punishment is only to me?* Dazed, she raised her eyes to Moses. The man who spoke to God bent forward and peered into her soul.

Moses deepened his tone. "Stand back and let them speak."

Emet's rage darkened to a violent purple, and he turned to Moses. "But they should not be here. They are still in shock over their father. Let me counsel them, please."

"What do you have to fear from five young women?" Moses waved his hand. "Go back and join your tribe."

Noa's sisters, with beads of sweat covering their foreheads and upper lips, looked at Noa for direction. It was as if time stood still. The men had quieted. She swayed from the intense woody smell of the incense. Dazed, she glanced at Moses, who nodded slightly and lifted his palms to encourage her. The face of God's messenger compelled her.

Just then, two eagles circled above the Tabernacle. Noa lifted her head and whispered to her sisters. "Look! Remember Abba's sign of an eagle? God sent two. Don't be frightened, sisters. We were meant to be here."

Her sisters looked up and at each other, smiling the widest grins.

Noa squeezed Tirzah and Milkah's hands, who passed the signal for them to start.

Noa inhaled a deep breath and began loud and clear. Her sisters' voices at first wavered but gained more surety as they spoke in unison. "We are the daughters of Zelophehad, son of Hepher, son of Gilead, son of Makir, son of Manasseh, son of Joseph." They each spoke their names. "Our names are Mahlah, Noa, Hoglah, Milkah, and Tirzah."

Tirzah let go of her sister's hands and took a step forward.

The men leaned in.

Standing tall, she asserted, "Our father died in the wilderness."

Mahlah followed. "He was not among Korah's followers, who banded together against the Lord."

The men suddenly stood motionless. The Israelites would never forget Korah's confrontation.

Emet scowled. "What are they getting at?"

Noa heard her uncle and feared he'd interrupt them again.

Hoglah continued, "But he died for his own sin and left no sons."

Noa felt a surge inside her. She took Tirzah's hand, her eyes glistening. "Why should our father's name disappear from his clan because he had no son?"

Murmurs came next.

"What are they saying?"

"What's this about?"

"How dare they come here?"

To Noa's right, Uncle Abel and Jonathan restrained Uncle Emet.

Milkah shone in her ivory tunic, adorned with the belt that Noa had made. Her turquoise headdress accented her fair complexion. She slanted her chin down, then raised her head and scanned the whole gathering. Her eyes then focused on Moses, and with a slight bow of her head, she took Noa's hand and proclaimed, "Give us property among our father's relatives."

Pure silence ensued. No one moved. Noa looked at her sisters' expressions—relief, gratitude, defiance, and assuredness.

One man picked up a rock and threw it at their feet. The men barked all at once, emitting a frightening rumble.

Tirzah's clammy palm shook her older sister's hand. "Will we die?"

Noa defiantly kicked the stone aside, squeezing back, hoping it would instill her sisters with resolve and hide her feelings. Would this be the first of many and the end of their lives?

Moses lifted his arms and bellowed, "Silence." He strode over to the daughters. They formed a semicircle around him. The men leaned forward to listen, but Noa guessed they heard only the gentle flapping of the colorful linen canopies.

"You are brave to come here before the whole assembly and raise an important question about a daughter's inheritance. I cannot make this decision alone, but I will confer with our Lord. Don't talk to anyone. Go back to your tent. Have your extended family bring you what you need for the next few days, as this community will not decide, but only God. Be still. When I have an answer, I'll send for you."

The sisters bowed their heads to Moses, then Noa whispered to her sisters, "Be brave. Stay close behind me and in front of Mahlah. Do as we did before. Look up and know." She hastened and secured Tirzah's hand. Her other hand waved through the swarm of men who confined a narrow opening as she continued her persistent pace. A sea of fiery expressions and enraged shouts taunted them. She must get them to safety. Many older men and women lined the way back to their tent. They pointed and shouted as the news spread. But she saw and overheard one man nudge another to say, "Yes, what about my daughters?" In the din of the confusion, Noa clung to her father's memory. *Be at peace, daughter. God is with you.*

Assir felt his hair lifting from his arms and the nape of his neck. Did Noa implicate him about offering this effrontery to God's law? Would they yet banish him from the Israelite camp?

Moses crossed his arms over his chest and shook his head while studying the sisters as they departed. The men taunted them, separating for a scant alley, barely making room for the sisters to exit. Men clustered around Moses, speaking at once.

"You declared God's details about inheritance as law. Why address this?"

"You can't grant this to them."

"This is heresy."

Discontent raged. Some spoke in favor of preserving a family's lineage. Others were indignant, admonishing Moses that this would change their sacred laws. To his right, a loud argument ensued between Abel and Emet and their sons. It seemed Jonathan and Simon were the most vocal in favor of the sisters' request.

Moses again raised his hands for silence. "This is God's decision and only God's."

Eleazar stepped forward. "God entrusted you with the instructions to divide the land. Wouldn't this authority include divining this decision? Why shouldn't you make it?"

Moses arched his eyebrows, holding Eleazar's elbow. Assir bowed his head to hear this intimate conversation. "Eleazar, you should know the answer. God encourages us to seek advice to make our path clear and involve Him in our lives. You stand at the Tent of Meeting in front of the Holy of Holies, where God desires to be at the center of our lives. Son, never forget to seek God's will in your life."

If Moses said anything more, Assir didn't hear, as the crowd vented their vehement opinions.

Moses's lips flattened. "Enough. I'll commune with the Lord, and whatever He decides, we will obey. Leave, go back to your tents. We will reconvene when I have an answer." No one spoke. He strode toward his tent, stopping at the brass basin to wash his hands and feet. Eleazar accompanied him.

Assir followed to assist with a towel, keeping his head lowered.

"Moses, I can attend with you if you wish," Eleazar offered.

"I thank you for your offer, but this demands time with God alone. Your moment will come."

Assir remained motionless until they both passed by. *What will the Lord command Moses? Will they question me? Lord, You know my heart. Please guide me so I may protect my siblings.*

CHAPTER 27

Noa predicted they would relive the last three days—especially this morning—over and over. And now, the excruciating wait for God's decision for their lives to be decided. She heard Abel and Leora's voices—a welcome interruption.

"Daughters of Zelophehad, we are here to celebrate with you." They carried in a jug filled with goat's milk and a small basket of dates. Abel's broad smile beamed. "You honored your mother and father today. You supported one another with each of you being heard. It sprang from all of you, not one deciding for the others."

"Thank you, Uncle. We've all learned so much. We're recovering from our momentous morning and are relieved to hear your thoughts." Like a small opening drifting apart on a cloud-filled day, his reassurance came as a ray of light shining through the oppressive fog of Uncle Emet's condemnation. Her Uncle Abel, like Joseph, believed good could always be found, no matter the circumstances. She received the basket and kissed him on the cheek.

Milkah linked her arm with Noa's, effusing a warm acknowledgment. "It was a formidable decision, but Moses, the Levite priests, and all who were present heard our voices today."

"Abel, you haven't complimented Mahlah on her walking without aid," Leora said.

Abel waved Mahlah to him. "It's beyond my joy. Your father and mother would be so happy. How did you hide it from everyone?"

"Aunt Leora kept watch at our tent so I could practice. I knew she would keep a secret." Mahlah blushed.

"Aunt, you astound us all the time. This day would've been momentous for Malha's healing alone." Noa nodded to Leora.

Their aunt filled their cups, looking from one to the other. "I wish I'd been there. I love that Tirzah was allowed to go first. I imagine she quieted them so fast they became intent on listening."

"I'm still reeling from it, especially after Uncle Emet demanded that we leave. I wouldn't look at him for fear I'd forget my words. The men cocked their heads closer when I spoke, giving me confidence without quivering." Tirzah, with a flair, bowed.

Leora clapped and added, "Such courage to address Moses, Eleazar, the leaders, and the assembly of the twelve tribes at such a crucial time. I'm in awe of your bravery, and despite Uncle Emet, you found the fortitude to continue. Every tent will retell the story of these sisters, much to the chagrin of many men and your uncle."

Abel passed the dates to Noa. "Yes, you could have sought Moses alone. Why speak to everyone and at the Tent?"

Hearing Jonathan's words in her mind, Noa pointed the credit to her sisters. "Hoglah suggested the Tent of Meeting because it affected not only us but all the tribes. She also helped us reach a joint decision. Mahlah brought up the issue of Korah. Milkah advised what we were petitioning, and Tirzah agreed to start."

"Noa played the most vital role by bringing us the idea. She changed our lives." Milkah took a little bow to her sister.

"Let's hope so." Goosebumps galloped up and down Noa's arms. This time, the heat that flushed over her warmed her. She wished the moment wouldn't end, that she could always feel so close to her sisters.

A loud bark came outside their tent. "It is I, Asher. May I enter?"

Noa hadn't seen her cousin Asher, Uncle Emet's youngest son, in quite some time.

He didn't wait for an answer and stormed in, wiping the sweat from his forehead. "What audacity. How dare you?"

Noa imagined none of her uncle's family approved of their actions. If this was how his son reacted, she dreaded Emet's arrival.

Abel cleared his throat. "Welcome, Asher. You come to congratulate your cousins?"

"Not quite, Uncle. Moses disbanded the census for the day, thanks to you." He glared at Noa. "How will this work? What a crazy idea. And of course, if granted, which is preposterous, you must marry within the tribe of Manasseh otherwise …"

"Asher, we did this to honor our father's name and his lineage. We want his inheritance to be within the tribe of Manasseh." Noa dipped her chin.

Asher's fists jutted into his waist, and he rocked back and forth on his heels. "God will condemn your ridiculous request, so there is nothing to plan."

Leora stood between Asher and the daughters. "Asher, that's enough. We don't know what God will decide, and for you to pass judgment is beyond arrogant. Now I suggest you take your leave as we all will and let these fine young ladies get some rest."

Asher pivoted and sprinted out.

"Thank you, Aunt, you're a blessing to us." Noa craved rest from the strain of their daring words, Emet's obstruction, the threats, and the stone thrown at their feet. It was time for everyone to leave. "We don't know when Moses will call us back. He instructed us not to leave our tent or roam about, as this is God's decision, not the community's." Noa squinted. *I won't even think that God's answer would be no.*

"Restraining the people's many opinions will challenge him." Leora rose to leave. "We will supply food and water for the duration. Abel and I will return for dinner. Our sons will help. Come, Abel, let us leave these young women in peace."

After a fitful rest, the sisters picked up their weaving except for Noa. She rubbed her bottom lip as her mind wandered. She'd get up, walk to the entrance, look left and right, and return.

"Noa, we will know when Moses calls us back. They'll come for us. Now, come join us again," Mahlah called.

"Of course, I was just stretching." Noa prayed the answer would come soon. Waiting could lead to imaginings she didn't want to think about. She joined her sisters and asked Hoglah to retell the story of their morning again.

Leora, Abel, and their four sons hosted a lively dinner, bringing manna, goat cheese, and olives. Simon and Mahlah talked quietly together.

Leora stood, gathering her empty vessels. "I'll bring more of this tomorrow. Tonight, you'll find sweet sleep from exhaustion." She bowed her head. "Let us pray. Lord God, these five daughters of Zelophehad, with faith in their hearts, bravely came forward before the Tent of Meeting to honor their father. May the words of their lips be pleasing to You. We trust in Your care for all daughters. These daughters made their request with reverence, reflecting their love and respect for You and the memory of their abba. May they accept whatever Your answer is with grace. Amen."

Abel, Leora, and their sons said their goodbyes. As soon as they left, Emet and his sons whirled into the tent without removing their sandals and dragged Jonathan behind them. Abel and Simon reentered and charged in front of the daughters. Emet's nostrils flared.

Abel greeted Emet with warmth and the full honor accorded to an older brother. "Brother Emet, so glad you're here to celebrate our dear nieces by bringing your sons and grandson Jonathan. Come and sit. We can all enjoy your acknowledgment of their bravery."

Emet's furor raged. "It has taken me all day to calm down. I spent most of it demanding an audience with Moses. Abel, your head is in the clouds."

Perhaps receiving Uncle Emet's wrath would require more courage than approaching the Tent. Noa snuck a peek at Jonathan to gauge what was to come. His furrowed brows didn't give any reassurance. An audience with Moses? *What does that mean?*

"Were you lying to me this morning? Did they forewarn you about this outlandish ploy they performed today?" Emet slammed his fist down on the low table.

Abel forged a smug smile. "No, I didn't know. The first I heard of it was when they came forward."

"At least I don't have to lecture you," Emet conceded. "I'll address this to Mahlah and Noa, as you are the oldest. Why did you not consult me or Abel? And why make a spectacle? Why the Tent, of all places? Why not Moses alone? What am I saying? You shouldn't have been there at all. This is an insult to our family. You've shamed and endangered all of us. Do you have any idea of the consequences of your actions?"

Noa would address her uncle. She stood as straight as she could, Mahlah by her side. Before either of them could utter a syllable, Tirzah jumped in front, taking a large step toward him. "Uncle Emet, we're happy to have you in our home."

Mahlah stepped beside her little sister. "Uncle, it was a big decision. We did not make it in haste."

Hoglah followed. "We discussed it and allotted ourselves three days to determine whether we would go forward."

Milkah tilted her head and, raising it, gazed into Emet's eyes. "Uncle, your cousin, our father, loved and valued his lineage. Night after night, he regaled us with stories of our heritage to fortify us. You and your family have heard these stories, too."

Noa, bursting with pride in her sisters, continued, "Our reason for asking is simple. We believe in our Lord and trust God's mighty hand to preserve our father's heritage. We anticipate the Lord will grant it for us and all daughters with no brothers."

In complete silence, everyone stared at Emet.

Abel opened his mouth to speak, but Emet raised his hand. "I am not addressing little girls anymore, including you, Tirzah. But it doesn't matter if you're going to be stoned."

"We understand the risk we took. Our faith and trust will guide us, whatever the outcome." Noa shook off her fear.

Abel seized Emet's arm, pulling him back. "Your uncle and I will leave you to your prayers. No more questions for them today. Come, Emet."

Emet threw off Abel's hand. "This is not finished." He stomped out.

Jonathan bowed his head and departed with the others.

The sisters heard the men arguing as they took their leave. Both Noa and Mahlah shuffled their sisters to bed. "Let's get some sleep. We won't persuade Uncle Emet to change his mind. Instead, let us dream of our Lord pouring out His care to us from his dipper of stars." Noa tucked Tirzah into bed, caressing her cheek. "Good night, my dear one. Try to sleep. It's been a big day."

Once all was quiet, Noa crept to the entrance. She discovered a small slit in the tent's flap and peeked out. Emet and Abel were still there, alone.

Even in the dark, Emet's face bore a scarlet hue. "Brother, what's wrong with you? I rushed to speak with Moses to express their mistaken foolishness, but I didn't get a chance. What possessed you to congratulate the daughters? They usurped the portion which would have come to us. Are you so enamored of your nieces you didn't ponder this?"

"We're kinsmen and obligated to share with them anyway."

"Yes, share, but not an entire inheritance. They would get a double portion, because Zelophehad was the firstborn son." He sprayed spittle as he yelled. "They are girls. They have no reason to do this."

Abel hung his head. "This is about you not getting a double share? We have our own inheritance. We're counted in the census. These girls have lost both their mother and father. Don't you have any pity?"

"You want to dismiss everything." Emet rubbed his hands through his matted hair. "Zelophehad and his imperial heritage. He neglected to tell his daughters the entire story. How many times have we heard, 'The daughters of Zelophehad, son of Hepher, son of Gilead,' on and on, until mighty Joseph? Joseph." Emet hissed. "The truth is, Joseph's father, Jacob, our illustrious great-grandfather eight generations ago, overlooked Manasseh, who should have received the first-born blessing. Instead, Jacob bestowed the privilege on Ephraim, the younger brother. Jacob didn't change the blessing even when Joseph corrected his father for his failing eyesight. We built our family history on arrogance, with our tribe spurned of status."

"Emet, you're forgetting the most important part of this story. Jacob adopted both his grandsons, Manasseh and Ephraim, as his own sons. Joseph's offspring received an honor no other grandson had by doing so. It's why we now have twelve tribes of Israel. Don't you accept God's hand in this?"

Emet mumbled, "What I know is Zelophehad didn't share all of this with his precious daughters."

Noa controlled her urge to open the flap. How could he talk about her father this way? It took all her will to stay still and only listen.

Abel countered, "I was there when he did. He has five daughters. Not sons. Daughters. He instilled in them a sense of themselves and taught them about Joseph and how he advanced to prominence despite the direst circumstances. It was about showing them an example of great faith, bravery, intelligence, and determination to trust God with their lives. With no sons, Zelophehad tried to prepare them."

"He had us to rely on. We would protect them." Emet flinched his hands, batting away the comment.

"Emet, brother, God blessed you with so much in life. You have a devoted, loving wife, five grown sons with wives, and grown grandchildren. You and your sons will have land of your own. What more could you want?"

"I don't know why I'm even discussing this. We will wait until the Lord gives an answer, which I am sure will condemn them."

"Brother. No. We should not regard it this way." Abel grasped Emet.

He swatted him away.

"Emet, if our Lord answers yes, we must celebrate with them. And if it's no, we must not abandon them. Is it in your heart to embrace them, no matter the consequences?"

"Either way, this will not be fortuitous. God will judge against them, and it will ruin any chance of good marriages. Who will want Noa, who has clearly demonstrated what I've felt all along, an outspoken woman who has now instilled this in her sisters? It's already an embarrassment for the entire Manasseh tribe. You're mad to think the Lord will say yes. But with a slim chance, if yes, you realize this not only affects Zelophehad's daughters, but it will change the course of inheritance for all families. How will our fellow Israelites accept it? We will be outcasts. Either way, it will be harmful to our reputation."

"Are other families in the same situation? If you had only daughters, wouldn't you want this?"

"I don't have daughters. I have sons. I'm taking care of our nieces. I have arranged marriages for them." Emet turned slightly away from the tent, and Noa shifted from peering out to her ear on the slit opening.

"Ah, I thought you might confer with me about this. As you know, Simon wishes to marry Mahlah. I'm sorry I didn't get to speak with Zelo about it, but I think he warmed to the idea."

Emet coughed and cleared his throat. "Hmm. Yes, that is a good idea. I had other plans, but this will do."

Noa gulped. *Did I hear that right? Did Emet change his heart?* He'd never considered Simon.

Abel straightened and released his breath slowly. "Did Zelo speak of this?"

Emet put his arm around Abel's shoulders, "Yes, Abel, he did. I was waiting for the right time."

"Well, this is the right time, brother. This will surely comfort them, as it does me. Let us share this good news." Abel squeezed both sides of his brother's forearms.

"They've gone to sleep. Let's give them rest. We can wait till after the Lord's answer, which we know will be to refute their request, and this will be able to encourage them."

Abel shook his head, releasing his brother. "Even in good news, you drown a flame. Do you recall why they petitioned so that Zelo's name wouldn't disappear? Do you recall your promise to Zelo that you would be there for him after Jeska died?"

Emet looked away.

"Emet, we don't see eye to eye on this. If Zelophehad were alive, he would be proud, and I am too. We must do what's right and just for them. May you wake in the morning with a new light. Good night, brother. Shalom."

A long silence followed, then Emet murmured softly, "Shalom."

Moments later, Emet commanded. "Noa, wake up. I must talk with you."

She quickly leaned back from the flap opening. *Was it true? Mahlah and Simon?* She fumbled putting on her cloak, jamming her feet into her sandals. "Yes, Uncle." She held off a smile to hear the good news.

"I know you put your sisters up to this ludicrous spectacle. You will go to the Tent and inform Moses of your misjudgment. You will confirm I have arranged your marriages and rescind your request. Accept this shame you've caused to the Manasseh tribe and rectify it."

Noa swayed, her head throbbing. Not what she expected. "Uncle, we're honoring our father so his name will not be forgotten. We trust and believe God will give us this land to preserve the legacy of his faith."

"Legacy of faith? To honor a father who once possessed an Egyptian idol? I am now head of this family and will run things differently. You'll plead with Moses. In return, I'll undo the marriage contract to Milkah and bequeath you to Jonathan instead. That should give you plenty of reason to change your mind."

She bent forward as if a donkey had knocked her in the stomach. Simon and Jonathan? Reeling, her head snapped back. "What? You'll grant my marriage if I rescind our request?

"Not only revoke your request, but you will also beg forgiveness from Moses. Say it was a foolish idea that you led your sisters into, and you've come to your senses. Do you think our Lord will consent to your nonsense? Then you're a fool—worse than your father. Why would God say yes to this? There's no reason for God to render a positive judgment. When Moses announces God's decision, you will suffer the repercussions. They will stone you if you don't do as I say."

Bile rose from Noa's stomach. She covered her mouth.

"I could've saved you if you had come to me first, but you didn't. This is the only way I can protect you now. One last motivation for you. I know you didn't care for my choice of husband for Mahlah. I'll change that, too, and give her Simon."

Is this why he changed his mind? He was dangling what she wanted most, trading it for what was paramount to him—his standing with the leaders and the definitive thought that they shouldn't have dared to ask.

"We will go to Moses before he assembles the community. I will come for you. Be ready at the break of day. Noa, will you choose a life following our Lord? Or will you choose a life based on personal prestige over others?"

Emet left like a sandstorm, leaving her insides scattered in tatters.

CHAPTER 28

Noa crumpled to the cold ground, and the night air chilled her body. *Lord, have I not done Your will? Should I revoke what we said? The consequences are enormous. Jonathan, the dream of my heart, to be mine. Mahlah with Simon, as she desires. Why this choice? Lord, what should I do?*

Mahlah lifted open the tent flap. "Come in. Let us lower the curtain so we don't disturb their sleep."

"Did you hear it all?"

"It was hard not to."

They dropped the curtain.

"I feel frozen in place, like I can't move. I'm stunned by what he said about God, about you, about Jonathan. Endangering you and our sisters. What have I done?" Noa sank next to her sister.

Mahlah stroked her hair. "You didn't jump into this. You reviewed it with Aunt Leora and me and even sought Assir. After listening to Milkah's and Tirzah's worries, you paused for three days for us to pray. You would've abandoned your idea if we, as sisters, had not agreed. We deliberated this together. Don't doubt God was in our planning."

"That won't matter when they stone us."

"Noa, why did we do this? We did it to preserve our father's lineage. We searched our hearts and decided because we trust in God. One can have faith, but it takes complete trust to follow our path."

"I don't presume to know God's answer." She lay her head on Mahlah's shoulder.

"No, you don't. You can trust God no matter what the answer is. Our Lord will not cast us aside."

"What about you? What if Uncle Emet insists that you marry Nahash? I would live all my days regretting you being yoked to that awful man. Besides, you love Simon, and he loves you."

"Uncle Abel reminded me I could refuse Emet's proposal. Not often done, but I can do this, even if he believes it would tarnish future marriage prospects. I have faith that Uncle Abel will step in to offer a marriage proposal for me to Simon."

"Of course, Uncle Abel would honor both of you. He would be the only one to persuade Uncle Emet. What a relief."

"You have a much dearer situation with Jonathan."

Noa felt like a messy, snarled clump of tangled wool before it got carded, entwined with fragments of dirt and twigs. "I have what's left of this night to make such a decision. Mahlah, what should I do?"

"Do you wish to give this up and plead to Moses that we were mistaken? The foundation for our decision is trust in God. Do we believe our Lord will grant us our desire to honor our father?"

"I thought God would, but I'm shaken to my core after Uncle Emet's verdict. Is this a warning from God that we shouldn't proceed? Is this like Moses's warning to Korah that he had gone too far?"

"Abba believed in trusting God, even in dire situations. Joseph may have wavered, but he put one foot in front of the other because he chose God's path. Do not lose faith now. Your substantial decision is about Jonathan. If you rescind our request to Moses, you'll be betrothed to him. If you don't, Uncle Emet will give Milkah to him. Could you live with Milkah as his bride, surrounded by children they sire?"

Noa stared at the curtain. How ironic that she and Milkah had achieved a truce, a new start of being genuine sisters. And now? Could she ever control her emotions around either of them? Could she avoid them? She pictured Jonathan's reassuring eyes, their ease with one another, his drawings, his work, his encouragement, his sense of humor ...

"Should we have a sister meeting in the morning? No one could blame you if you followed Uncle Emet's proposal. Milkah would understand."

"To claim rights to Jonathan sounds so selfish, but if I'm honest, it's what my heart desires. What about Father and his heritage?" Noa frowned, sighing deeply.

"I'll pray for you. The answer will reveal itself to you by morning. Trust in God, sister. No matter what, we can trust in the answer God gives you." Mahlah helped Noa remove her outer tunic and tucked her into the other side of the bed. "Shalom."

"Shalom, Mahlah."

Sleep? How could she sleep? She considered each sister's reaction. Mahlah would be faithful, endorse her decision, and never criticize her, no matter the outcome. Tirzah, so young and devoted, would also support her. Hoglah would do what Milkah did. Would Milkah be angry that she didn't marry Jonathan? She remembered the day that Milkah lingered with her tunic open and teased him. Would Milkah resent her for life? Noa remembered Milkah before the Tent of Meeting, commanding the men's attention, where she'd mesmerized them with her regal poise. She had reviewed them as if they were her subjects. Then, with a deferential nod to Moses, she began her speech. It had sent chills down her back to recognize her sister's power. Would Milkah be resentful of her caving to her uncle's demands? *Lord, I seem to be at Your door, desperate for advice moment by moment. Make my path clear. Amen.*

The cooing of turtledoves woke Noa. She stared at the ceiling. Mahlah wasn't beside her. She practiced in her mind what to say to her sisters. Her sisters were up whispering. Did Mahlah relate what happened? She threw on her tunic, knocking over a basket.

"Someone is up," Hoglah sang out.

The heavy curtain raised, and her younger sisters piled onto the bed.

"I told them some of your burden, as we should carry this together," Mahlah said.

Noa shivered. *What did she leave out?*

Milkah laid a hand on her heart. "I won't accept Uncle Emet's marriage proposal to Jonathan. I couldn't do that to you."

Dazed by such an unexpected outcome, she lost her balance and joined them on the bed. "You will? I mean, you won't accept?" Noa squeaked.

"You're my sister, and we have only begun our friendship. Marrying the man you love wouldn't be wise." Milkah shrugged and laughed.

"What? Are you sure?"

"I couldn't. Knowing each time we get together as a family, you and Jonathan would wish it to be different. No, I desire someone who dotes on me. I'm sorry you suffered last night."

Noa hugged Milkah with such force they fell back on the bed. "You would do that?"

"I didn't know I could reject a marriage proposal until I heard Mahlah's declaration that she would refuse Nahash. Uncle Abel told her how it could be done. It was a simple decision then for me."

"I'm overwhelmed. Thank you, Milkah. I didn't expect this."

"We are sisters, after all."

"Uncle Emet promised more last night." Mahlah glanced at Noa.

"Why even discuss it now? It's over." *I should be happy about Jonathan.* But would Uncle Emet keep his commitment? *Perhaps he went alone, supposing I'd refuse.*

Mahlah began, "Uncle Emet proposed he would reconsider my engagement and would choose someone better suited for me and also for Noa to marry Jonathan."

"What?" Milkah withdrew her arm.

Mahlah continued, "All this if Noa would accompany him this morning and rescind our actions yesterday. He directed her to declare we were happy with the marriages he could arrange and that we were too young and naïve to request something so grand from God. He insists he is saving us from being stoned."

"That is not right." Milkah squealed. "He knows a marriage to Jonathan is what you've longed for. Here I thought I was giving you a gift."

Tirzah scrambled from the bed and stamped her foot. "It isn't fair."

"He's head of the family, enabling him to make these decisions." Noa exhaled through clenched teeth.

"This means you'll marry Jonathan? But you don't seem happy about it." Hoglah's forehead wrinkled.

Noa's chin dipped. "I know I should be. I prayed last night for God's wisdom. When I woke this morning, I felt no closer to a decision."

"Sisters, whatever she chooses, we will uphold it. Right?"

Before they could respond, Noa gulped. "Thanks, Mahlah. But there is no choice. I'm sure he charged to the Tent to see Moses without me. He stole it from us."

Hoglah clasped her hands under her chin in a prayer gesture. "What if he didn't? What if he's coming still?"

Milkah added, "And if he went, would Moses grant him an audience?"

Hoglah challenged, "There are so many ifs. We should decide. Will you declare to Moses that it was a mistake? Or will we listen to God's decision?"

She needed to confess what their uncle predicted. "Is this God's way of signaling to us he's not pleased with our request? After Uncle Emet's warning of being stoned by the crowd, if God denies us, should we rescind what we bravely proposed? Are any of you in doubt?"

Hoglah's eyebrows raised. "If you recant, you'll marry Jonathan. Are you seeking permission so you can be with him?"

"No." Noa offered a wistful smile. "Be truthful. Did I push you into this?"

"Shall we get our stones out again? Do we listen to what God tells Moses or recant?" Hoglah grabbed them from the table.

Noa caught a sunbeam flickering through the top of their tent. "Wait. You just said the answer. What difference would it make if we rescinded our request? God will answer Moses. We must put our trust in the Lord."

"You'll give up Jonathan?" Milkah tipped her head to the side.

"Mahlah shared the right story last night about Joseph. If I had been him, I might have doubted after being sold by his brothers and sitting in prison, but he trusted. God guided his life's journey. You've given me such a gift this morning. Milkah, your sincere generosity, Mahlah for sharing my situation with everyone, and all of you defending me. I believe God has a path for us, no matter how dire the circumstances."

"Are you sure of your decision?" Mahlah looked at Noa.

She nodded. "I am sure, and we as sisters will trust God for the right outcome for our lives. We will listen to what the Lord decrees with no reservations."

Tirzah, Hoglah, and Milkah had woken early and set out the manna, water, and goat's milk Leora had left earlier to break their fast. But hardly anything was touched. Noa's hands shook, trying to open and secure the tent flap back so they could spot Emet's approach. *He'll be here anytime now*. But it was Adina who headed toward them instead. Leora must've seen her bustling by, because she rushed to catch up and grabbed her sister-in-law's sleeve. "What is it, Adina?"

Adina pulled away, marching past, and swept by Noa into the tent. Her "Shalom" sounded more like an arrow hitting its target.

"Girls, I'm here to warn you …" Their aunt blinked back tears. "Your uncle departed early this morning for the Tent. He wants … he wants all of you … to remain here until he comes for you."

Adina sounded as if she had rehearsed Emet's message.

"Aunt Adina, what is he doing at the Tent?" Noa already surmised the answer.

"I'm sworn to your uncle's confidence. I'm sorry, I am." Adina slouched, the veins in her wrinkled skin flushing like the lasting embers of a fire. She about-faced and departed.

"I'll be back," Leora pledged.

Noa planted herself at the tent door with her sisters close behind. They didn't have to wait long, as the light of the morning sun still cast long shadows when Leora strode in as fast as her plump body could, humming a joyful tune.

"Aunt Leora? What's happened?" *What's changed that she is humming?* Noa's emotions jarred like the first time she mounted on the back of a camel, which propelled her back when he bent down and thrust her forward as he rose.

Leora motioned for Hoglah to shut the opening.

"Let me catch my breath. Some water, please." Leora plopped on the nearest rug mat, a peal of laughter reverberating in the stillness of the tent.

"Aunt, are you well?" Noa wondered if she should stir some rabil in the water to calm her.

"Never underestimate women." She gulped the water and leaned forward. "Before I explain what's making me giddy, I have a question. Have you girls decided what you'll do?" Leora surveyed each of them.

They all babbled at once.

Milkah raised her hands for everyone to stop. "Noa, you speak for us."

Noa's eyes shut for an instant, warmed by Milkah's offer. "We have. Together, we will trust and hear God's decision."

"I expected this. Admirable decision, Noa—especially with Emet's allure of a proposed marriage to Jonathan. Now that I know, I'll offer my story."

Noa nibbled her bottom lip. "How did you discover Uncle Emet's plans?"

"Last night, Abel recounted his conversation that took place outside your tent. I came back to comfort you, but saw Emet assailing you. I wanted to intercede but thought listening to what he spewed was wise. When he finished, an idea dawned on me. Abel, my boys, and I devised a diversion to stop Emet from going to Moses. We will feign a fire at the workshop, forcing Emet to rush to extinguish it."

Noa's mouth dropped. "A fire? Aunt Leora, with all the tents nearby, that could be disastrous."

"We have firepits at every tent. We've laid kindling in a deep hole a distance from the workshop and lugged the water jugs from our tent. I directed my sons to the river last night to fill them." Leora clunked down her mug in determination.

"Wait, I don't understand. When will you start it?" Noa envisioned flames engulfing the workshop. What danger would it bring?

"Emet announced to Abel that he was going to the Tent at sunrise. Abel dispatched a messenger to Assir, instructing him that under no circumstances should Emet receive an audience with Moses. But you know your Uncle Emet will stay until he is heard."

"Why Assir?" Milkah tugged on her ear, her brows squished together.

"Moses has appointed him one of his messengers during the census. So he is very close to the Tent of Meeting. Now, let me get to the best part."

Milkah looked like she'd been given a new headdress. "Yes, please, Auntie, what is the best part?"

"Whenever the decision is made and the trumpets sound, calling the community together, my sons will start a small, contained fire. You will go to the Tent of Meeting, but head away from the workshop.

Three of my sons will stay and watch the fire, and Simon and I will already be waiting outside the Tent of Meeting. Then, we will beg Emet to save the workshop. By the time he returns, Moses will have declared the Lord's decision."

Mahlah cleared her throat, her words almost imperceptible. "But what if the decision is not made today and Uncle Emet forces Noa to rescind our request?"

Leora's kind, gentle voice sounded like an extension of her pleasant humming. "This is where our faith comes in. God will find a way. Whatever the decision, no one can stop our Lord from hearing His judgment."

Noa's thoughts swirled. They were hard to follow. *Can this work?* It sounded like an idea she would have devised, but not one that her gentle, pragmatic aunt would. "You believe in us? You, Uncle Abel, and our cousins? Aunt Leora, this is humbling, and it just might work."

"That's one way to deter Uncle Emet." Hoglah snorted.

CHAPTER 29

The morning sun rose as the brilliant light from the Tabernacle faded—the white, puffy cloud taking its place. Assir busied himself near the Tent entrance, pondering Abel's message. *"If you ever wished to make amends to Zelophehad's daughters, you'll follow my instructions. Do not, for any reason, allow Emet to meet with Moses."* Brother against brother. But which side should he choose? The daughters were now Emet's responsibility. He'd exposed his fierce anger and desperation to obstruct the daughters from uttering even a word. And now, frustrated that he didn't get to speak to Moses, he vowed to return early to wait for an audience. He guessed that Emet, like some Israelites, expected God to judge against the daughters. Assir wanted to protect them, but was he going against God's will? Assir flashed back to his father, plummeting into the abyss with the deep, acrid odor of the earth permeating the air. Defiant to the end, his father extended his shoulders back, his chest jutting. *"Father, step back!"* Assir had shouted.

Abiasaph shook his arm. "What's troubling you? Did the messenger bring bad news?"

Assir explained how Emet demanded to speak with Moses, and Abel demanded that he be barred. "Even if I could do something, I'm not high enough up in rank to interfere with whom Moses meets."

"But you could influence Eleazar, who manages Moses's day."

"What should I do?" Assir rubbed his hands.

"The question is, how will God judge? If you're wondering who to please, we learned this so well. Have you prayed about it?"

"No, I've only reflected on Abel's words."

"I'll keep watch for Emet. Spend some time here and listen for your answer."

"How will this work, Aunt Leora? What if Uncle Emet sees us? What if he doesn't respond to the fire?" Noa and her sisters dressed in their best tunics again, hoping Moses had received God's decision.

"The workshop means as much to him as it did your father. He'll let nothing happen to it. When the trumpets sound, we'll wait for the community to gather, and then you'll leave. By that time, we will summon your uncle."

Noa, her mouth parched, gulped. "What if they can't find him in the crowd?"

Leora cast Noa's comment aside with a wave of her hand. "Assir will help us. He wishes to atone for what he did. You inspired me when you went to speak to him about inheritance laws."

Milkah smiled at Noa. "He does? She did?"

"Before talking with you about the idea, I needed to know what the law said. Assir was eager to help, and yes, he wished to be forgiven. Remember what I said about you saving him from his father's fate?"

Milkah nodded.

Noa shifted back and forth on her heels, reflecting on her aunt's wild idea. "If meant to be, it will be."

Abel called outside their tent. "It's Jonathan, Simon, and I. May we enter?"

Milkah opened the flap. "Shalom, you are welcome here."

"Shalom, wife and my beautiful nieces. Your aunt described the plan?"

Noa's gaze clouded while the room spun. Jonathan, her beloved. Unsteady on her feet, she swayed, trying to find her balance.

Jonathan rushed to Noa. "Are you well?"

"She's fine, young man. She carries a heavy weight." Leora poured some water and handed it to him.

He extended the cup, touching her fingers. "Here, drink this."

She wanted to declare how much she loved him, to let him know how difficult her decision was. Would he ever speak to her again?

"Don't worry. Our plan will work. We will be ready whenever the decision comes. You will hear God's judgment at the Tent of Meeting." Jonathan pushed a wayward strand of hair from Noa's temple.

Abel coughed, diverting attention away from Noa. "I'll accompany you to the Tent. Don't worry, we've been very careful. Simon and Leora will find Emet. She can be quite persuasive."

Noa tried to concentrate on Uncle Abel. Jonathan's tender touch, those reassuring hazel eyes. He didn't know. *I'm sure of it. He's here to uphold us in trusting God as we do.* Noa beseeched God. *Lord, You know my heart. I love him. If he's not to be mine, give him to someone who will love him as I do. Strengthen my resolve in what I started. Your will be done, not mine.*

Assir set a water pitcher on a table outside the brilliant curtains that lined the sanctuary's front. Moses was forbidden to enter the Holy of Holies, but God had granted him access to the outer chamber before the innermost room. How long would it take Moses to receive an answer? It could be days before he appeared. What if this put his role at the Tent in jeopardy? *Lord, I promised to obey Your commandments, to tell no lie or bear false witness. Strengthen me to follow Your path.*

In a short while, Moses came out of the Tabernacle, stretched, and yawned. "Assir, good, you're here. Advise Eleazar to sound the trumpets. I have God's decision, and I shall announce it as soon as possible so we can complete the census. Everyone should hear the verdict so there is no confusion. Send a message to the daughters. I'll remain here until then." Moses drew some water and pivoted back into the outer court.

Assir dashed to follow Moses's instructions. He looked to the right to see if Eleazar was in his usual place, but he wasn't there.

He launched forward, but Emet blocked him, gripping him by the shoulders.

"Did you relay my request to Moses? It's most urgent."

"I, I haven't had a chance."

Emet raised his hand to shade the sweltering sun and scrutinized the front of the Tabernacle. "When you see Eleazar, announce I am waiting."

Assir nodded and sprinted to finish Moses's tasks.

The trumpets resonated two long, precise blasts.

Noa swallowed. "Moses is summoning the community together."

Leora rose and proffered her hand to Mahlah. "Let me help you up, my dear."

"Thank you, Auntie, but I can do this on my own now."

A messenger yelled, "Daughters of Zelophehad, Moses requires you at the Tent of Meeting."

Hoglah furled back the flap. "We are the daughters of Zelophehad. We are ready."

"Come, daughters, affix your headdresses. We will wait a few moments before you leave." Leora straightened Tirzah's headscarf.

Noa motioned to Leora.

Leora turned away from her nieces and approached Noa. "You don't have second thoughts, do you?"

"No, I've yielded my will to God's. But ..."

Leora grabbed her hand. "What is it, my love?"

"I'm thankful to Uncle Abel for escorting us."

Milkah edged over to where they spoke. "But we need to do this alone."

"Yes, Aunt Leora, can you help us?" Hoglah touched her aunt's arm.

"I'll inform Abel that you want to stand together as sisters for your judgment. He can guard your backs, which will help in case Emet returns."

Noa's heart felt like it would explode. *The moment is here. The Lord decided, and now we will face the consequences. I must remain calm.* "Sisters, Aunt, Uncle, Jonathan, Simon, thank you for believing in us. The last two days have felt more like a year. Bless you for your trust in our God. May we cling to our faith and abide in His power."

Assir stationed his brothers, Elkanah and Abiasaph, on either side of the Tent to watch Emet, who wouldn't leave his place by the Tabernacle entrance. Moses wouldn't appear until the crowd finished assembling.

Assir straightened the outer curtain. Eleazar must be with Moses, as he hadn't appeared all morning, relieving him of delivering Emet's message. After some time of the trumpets sounding, Simon, a son of Abel, and Leora, Abel's wife, appeared. They jostled through the crowds, searching left and right. Assir signaled for his brothers to join them and find out what they wanted. Elkanah intervened and guided them to Emet. Assir overheard parts of it.

"I'll stay, Uncle, I promise, but you're the head of the shop now. It's urgent. You must direct everyone." Simon blocked Emet's view of the Tabernacle.

"Where's Abel? Where are my sons? Or your sons, Leora?" Emet pushed Simon aside.

Leora stepped in front of him. "My sons are trying to extinguish the fire. I know not where your sons are."

Assir approached. "Sir, I couldn't help overhear. I know you are desperate to speak with Moses. If you state your reasons, I'll forward them to him. He's been in the Tabernacle all morning, only coming out to request an assembly meeting."

Simon grabbed Emet's arm. "Maybe what Moses will address doesn't involve the daughters. You'll be back in time. Please, hurry."

Emet knocked his hand away and again came inches away from Assir.

"Beg Moses to delay his proclamation for the Lord's judgment until I return." Emet then added, "So I can protect the girls. Swear to me you'll do this."

Assir's neck became taut, and he rubbed the pulsing veins. Emet didn't want to "protect the girls." *He only wants to protect his standing in the community.* He had to think fast. "I swear, but I may only get to Eleazar."

"Tell them both." He glared at Simon and Leora. "We must find my sons so I can return." Emet huffed and plowed through the crowd, paying no heed to whom he pushed out of his way.

Noa took the lead this time, but would they encounter Uncle Emet? If they did, it would unnerve her sisters. She also wanted to shield them from vile utterances. She slowed her stride to allow her sisters and Uncle Abel to keep up with her. Tirzah followed behind her, then Hoglah, Milkah, and Mahlah, with Abel at the end. She focused ahead, watching for signs of Uncle Emet or his sons. They were on opposite paths to the Tent, so they shouldn't see him. They were just moments away from hearing the decision.

As they passed many tents, those not attending spoke their mind.

"The audacity."

"The Lord be with you."

"Who do you think you are?"

Noa turned back to offer Tirzah her hand.

Tirzah flexed her fingers. "Trust, sister."

Buoyed by her bravery, Noa started singing the Lord's Blessing, and her sisters and some of the community joined in. As they approached the Tent, the crowd parted to let the daughters go forward. Noa whispered words of gratitude. They had made it this far. Perhaps the Israelites were also eager to hear the verdict? They received a very different reception from the day before. There was an eerie silence, but lots of indignant stares.

The twelve tribe leaders and Eleazar stood at the front of the Tabernacle. Moses hadn't appeared yet. Noa searched the crowds for Emet, who was nowhere in sight. She spotted Assir, who nodded, raising her hopes. The callers standing on platforms interspersed throughout the space would repeat the original message, disseminating it to the back.

A priest led them to the very front. The chill of the cool morning air offered little relief, the back of her tunic wet with perspiration. She whispered, "Look up." Together, the sisters responded, "And you will know." They stood abreast, intertwining their hands, their posture transformed to a composure of competence, certain of their faith.

Assir peered over the crowd in front of the Tent. Emet shoved people aside, and his five sons followed in his wake. Emet glowered at him, holding up his fist. Assir wished he could hide. *Oh no, he's coming for me.* The soothing tinkling of the unique golden bells sewn on the bottom of Eleazar's garment distracted Assir as he appeared in his stunning turban, ephod, and breastplate.

"Every time I move, I hear this beautiful sound, God's gentle reminder of my duties. Why are you here, my son?" Eleazar asked.

"May I please speak with you, Eleazar? It's urgent." Assir dared to rotate him away from the crowd.

"Is this regarding Zelophehad's daughters?" Eleazar examined his hunched shoulders and creased forehead.

Assir bowed his head. "Yes, Emet, their uncle, is fighting his way here. He wants an audience with Moses before he declares God's proclamation."

Eleazar rarely laughed, but he chortled. "They still don't understand." He shook his head in disbelief. "No one will stop Moses from speaking what the Lord decrees."

"He made me swear to approach you and Moses. Early this morning, I received a message from Abel, his brother, urging me to prevent any audience for Emet."

Eleazar waved his hands over the breastplate. "And the reason for this?"

"I'm not sure, but I believe Emet feels this will bring shame to the Manasseh tribe."

"I understand."

A wave of relief washed over Assir. Not only had he made an oath and kept it, but he had also honored Abel's request by assisting the sisters. Emet made his way to the front, approaching Eleazar.

"Shalom. I trust that Assir told you about my message. I must confer with Moses." Emet, dripped with streaks of black sweat and reeking of smoke, bounded to the Tent entrance.

"Assir informed me. Moses is still in the Tent. When he emerges, I'll convey your message. Now, please join with the others in the crowd."

"It's important. The honor of my tribe is at stake." Emet jutted his chest.

Eleazar nodded and waved him back.

Assir watched as Emet turned and spoke with his sons. They moved to the front of the Manasseh tribe.

Moses strode out, raising his staff. Eleazar spoke to him, but he shook his head. No. Moses spotted Emet and gestured for him to remain in place.

As Emet opened his mouth, Moses leaned on his staff. "I say, 'Don't talk about this,' and the Israelites do the opposite."

The crowd responded with nervous laughter.

Noa, rooted in her stance, squeezed her two sisters' hands.

"My fellow Israelites, two days ago the five daughters of Zelophehad came forward here at the front of the Tent of Meeting. They petitioned for their father's inheritance to honor and perpetuate his name."

Some in the crowd murmured words of disapproval.

Moses raised his staff again for silence. "Even though we have yet to conquer our Promised Land and are not in full possession, they come with conviction as if they already own it. They came forward in God's faith for all His children, men and women alike. They declared their trust in a virtuous and caring God. What would have happened to the generation who left Egypt if they had believed as these young women do? Would we already be enjoying the land of milk and honey? Do you perceive the serenity exuding from them? They are ready to accept whatever God's judgment is."

Noa nodded at Moses. They were ready to face God's answer.

"Some advised I could make this decision, as our Lord appointed me to conduct the census to allot property. I reminded our leaders that we ought always to seek our Lord's guidance, and whatever the outcome, we would obey it. You've discussed this all night while I spent the night communing with our Lord, and He has given us His answer. Our Lord decreed, 'Say this to all the people.'" Moses paused until the rustling stopped, and it was silent.

Even though Noa and her sisters displayed confidence and faith, they tightly squeezed each other's hands.

Moses handed his cane to Eleazar, raised his palms, and sprightly beamed, "God said, 'What Zelophehad's daughters are saying is right. You must certainly give them property as an inheritance among their father's relatives and give their father's inheritance to them.'"

Noa heard the gasps from the crowd.

Tirzah jumped up and down. Hoglah moved the sisters into a circle, smiling, crying, and marveling at the announcement. Noa kneeled, and her sisters followed. "Mahlah, please lead us in giving thanks to the Lord."

Mahlah whispered, "Thank You for Your grace in bestowing our father's lineage and inheritance. We commit to revere this land and live under Your commands." The daughters stayed kneeling and said, "Amen."

Moses continued to detail inheritance laws, but it was hard for Noa to hear more until Moses said, "'Say to the Israelites, "If a man dies and leaves no son, give his inheritance to his daughter."'"

Noa observed Moses searching for someone. She followed his gaze to Uncle Emet's ashen face. Moses spoke as if to him alone. "Do not discuss alternatives or possible different situations. The Lord commanded this, and we will obey His ruling."

She couldn't discern Emet's reaction with his head bowed. Was he angry, mad, embarrassed? No matter what, he would make his thoughts clear. Would he be as demanding as last night? Would this inspire him to keep his word about Jonathan? *But I sacrificed that promise to honor my father*. She wouldn't let Emet's reprisal ruin this momentous decree.

A gentle breeze refreshed her. *"He is on his way to you, he will love God, and he will love you."* These were the similar words Abba had heard before he met Ima. A calmness of hope filled her.

A multitude of feet pounded the ground, raising dust as the crowd showed the ultimate endorsement to the proclamation.

Back from the extinguished fire, Jonathan, Simon, and his brothers circled the sisters, congratulating their good fortune. Simon, his brawny arms stretched out to Mahlah, flung her up into the air, both ringing with peals of laughter.

Noa's smile couldn't be any broader. Jonathan sprang forward and squeezed her hand. He was coated from head to toe in black ash.

"I would do the same, but I am covered with embers. I heard the last part when Moses—"

"The fire. Oh, yes. Is everything fine? No one got hurt?" She'd forgotten about the fire scheme. It felt like a month had passed, not just a short time ago.

He answered by twirling her around, soot and all. "Everything is wonderful."

Noa laughed despite the fact that her best tunic was now darkened.

Uncle Abel beamed with pride. "We'll celebrate to honor your faith and courage."

As they floated back to their tent, many well-wishers said their congratulations, and some just stared. Nothing could interfere with Noa's joy, but she didn't strut with pride. She met people's stares with a soft, kind expression, repeating, "Shalom, peace to you."

The extended family grouped outside their tent. "We'll let you settle, and we'll be back later with refreshments. Celebrate among yourselves." Uncle Abel waved all his family to follow him.

The sisters cheered. "Thank you for helping and supporting us today."

Jonathan and Simon lingered, and Noa and Mahlah steered them to the side.

Simon folded his arms, leaning his head toward Jonathan. "Will these sisters consider speaking with us now that they're landowners?"

"I'm not sure about that. Ladies?" Jonathan exaggerated a bow, with Simon following his lead.

Noa leaned against Mahlah. "What do you say? Do we acknowledge these cinder servants?"

"They have yet another deed to do." Mahlah pretended to wave a scepter in her hand.

"And what may that be, fair maiden?" Simon raised his head.

Mahlah tapped Simon on the shoulder with the imaginary scepter. "Thwart Uncle Emet and his plans for our futures."

"That may be harder than the fire," Simon acknowledged.

"We will plan our rebuttal until this evening, then." Jonathan bowed low, Simon joining him.

Noa melted into her sister's arms, sharing her hope and joy with the one who believed in her. "Perhaps we can have a double wedding. It's so close to being true."

Tirzah came between the sisters and hooked her elbows into theirs, Hoglah beckoning them to come inside.

When they entered, they jumped up and down. Hoglah danced. "I can't believe it. I know I should, but I can't."

Milkah dove into the softest cushion. "We were so intent on the asking that I'm not sure we contemplated the judgment."

Hoglah settled beside her. "Our hope and faith said yes, but until Moses spoke, my insides were jumbled."

Milkah continued, "We will start a new life, a life with property, where we can build a home, raise a garden, have a bed on which to lay our heads and never move again with thousands of others, and no more"—she shook her head, and all the sisters repeated—"sand everywhere."

Hoglah added, "We will have children, God willing, and we'll have such stories to impart to them."

"But first, we need to get married." Tirzah giggled.

"What about Uncle Emet's ideas about our marriages?" Milkah fanned herself.

The merriment stopped like someone being woken from a sweet dream.

Noa hugged herself. "Not to worry. We will marry within the Manasseh tribe and live near each other, as Abba dreamed."

"We will have many suitors, given we have our property." Milkah sighed.

"Milkah, you'll have many suitors, whether for property or not," Noa said. "But we won't have to hurry. Remember Abba saying that the Lord answered his prayers more than he could've imagined. And so it is with us. We can receive our property, and when satisfied that the right man has come along, we will make the right choice unencumbered. This ruling is a genuine gift from our Lord."

"We've two sisters that may already know the right one has come along," Milkah teased Mahlah and Noa.

Noa avoided the subject. "We'd better straighten up with so many people coming tonight."

CHAPTER 30

The evening sported a magnificent, clear sky, with not a cloud to be seen. The stars shone throughout the firmament like oil lamps celebrating the news. As if God Himself honored them with congratulations, the fire emanating from the Tabernacle seemed to burn with extraordinary brightness. With most of the extended family in attendance, the sisters tied up the sides of their tent, allowing fresh air to waft over so many people, bringing a soothing coolness. The noise level swelled to a high decibel, punctuated by laughter and congratulations. Although Noa enjoyed those in attendance, she kept glancing at the entrance, waiting for Emet and his family to arrive. Would he relent? Would he be happy for them? Or would this kindle even more anger?

A voice called out, "May we join your festivities? We come bearing celebration gifts."

Noa looked twice. She didn't recognize Reba, who was wearing one of Tirzah's ivory tunics. The tunic fit her perfectly, and the bright amber headdress complemented it, creating a lovely combination. Someone had arranged her dark cinnamon hair with just a peek showing on her forehead and cascading ringlets down her back. No tangles or straggling ends. Assir had regained some of his assurance but not his bravado. They entered bearing pomegranates and dates.

"Oh, Reba, you look lovely." Tirzah stretched her hand up high, signaling Reba to turn around.

Reba blushed and twirled in front of all the sisters. "It's all because of you, Tirzah. You insisted on giving me your tunic and headdress."

She fanned out her hands around her head. "I've never seen such a delicate hair adornment. It's beautiful, isn't it?"

"It should be. The headdress is mine." Milkah snickered.

Noa flashed her a frown.

"And I'm so delighted to see you enjoying it that I want you to have another, as it suits you so well." Milkah handed her one of her favorites.

Noa put her hands on her sister's shoulders, leaned in, and with the softest voice, whispered, "You continue to surprise me, Queen Milkah."

"Thanks to you, Reba is a new person. I thank you all for what you've done for her." Assir handed Milkah an overflowing basket of dates.

Noa put a protective arm around Milkah. "Thank you for your generous gifts. We enjoy Reba. She's always welcome here. If you can spare her, she can stay with us whenever she wishes." Noa glanced at Tirzah's broad smile.

"I doubt my brothers can manage for more than an hour without me, but they will." Reba grabbed Assir's hand and pushed him forward. "My brother has a special gift. He's written an alamoth, a song composed for female voices, and he'd like to debut it tonight."

"How very thoughtful. Will you sing it for us? Come, everyone, let us listen." Milkah waved to everyone to be quiet.

"Will the surprises ever end?" Noa waved Assir forward—a song from a Levite. *I couldn't have imagined this day. My cup runneth over.*

Assir unrolled the scroll and looked at the sisters. "My brothers and I composed this and offer it in honor of your great trust and faith in our Lord. I'll recite it first and then sing it. It will sound much better when you learn and sing it."

God is our refuge and strength,
an ever-present help in trouble.
Therefore we will not fear, though the earth give way
and the mountains fall into the heart of the sea,

though its waters roar and foam
and the mountains quake with their surging.
There is a river whose streams make glad the city of God,
the holy place where the Most High dwells.
God is within her, she will not fall;
God will help her at break of day.
He says, "Be still, and know that I am God;
I will be exalted among the nations,
I will be exalted in the earth."
The LORD Almighty is with us;
the God of Jacob is our fortress.

The sisters picked up the melody and harmonized with Assir. When they finished, everyone applauded.

"What a beautiful song." Noa wanted to pinch herself for the continual joys. "We wish you and your brothers inspiration for the many songs you will write to praise God."

At that moment, Emet strode forward. He must have entered while all ears were riveted to Assir's song. Adina was by his side, their five sons behind them. Noa gulped. Her pulse quickened as she led him into the gathering, showing him deference as the head of the family. He followed her, holding Adina's hand. Would he accept the outcome? Once they'd arrived among the others, Noa noticed that neither a smile nor a frown replaced his usual grimace. Noa's neck and shoulders tightened.

Emet coughed to get everyone's attention. "Unlike Zelophehad or my brother, I am not used to speeches or flowery words. Or Assir, who offered a meaningful song. You know what happened today?"

Some nervous giggles escaped.

Noa stiffened. What could he mean?

"I mean with the fire," Emet stated.

Noa, Mahlah, Jonathan, and Simon stepped forward, ready to block him from the group.

Emet motioned them back. "I need to speak."

They withdrew but didn't sit.

"The fire was a diversion to prevent me from speaking with Moses. I'm astounded my family would go to such extreme efforts to deceive me. I learned many lessons today, especially from my wife. Few things in life bring more happiness than having someone by your side to face challenges together and to guide you back when you've lost your way, like your ima did for your abba. By God's grace, my wife is that someone." Emet drew Adina close. "She has my heart and soul, and today, I commit to being the husband she deserves."

Adina cuddled into him. "You big ox. You're the love of my life. All I ever wanted was your love." Adina leaned into her husband, and they kissed.

Abel chuckled. "You have a way to go, brother. I'm here to hold you to your word."

"I deserved that. Now, about the fire." He shifted Adina's hand.

Abel bolted forward.

Emet held up a hand. "Brother, let me finish. What I also learned is the story of passion for family. To set a fire? That's daring. You amazed me with the preparations, ensuring its containment, gathering water in the middle of the night."

Noa's body eased a bit, waiting for the rest to come.

Emet refocused his attention on Jonathan. "Tremendous efforts from all of you, especially my grandson, Jonathan, with more at stake than any of you. My wife reminded me of the lengths someone will go for love, no matter the cost. It's been right before me, but I couldn't see how much Jonathan loves Noa. But your abba knew it. Even though Jonathan knew I would be angry with him, he detained me longer than any of you did. I discovered he'd considered I might disown him."

Noa glanced from her uncle to Jonathan. Anticipation and hope dangled like a tight weave inside her. What did he say about love, no matter the cost? He wouldn't renounce him now. He wasn't angry and seemed in control.

Emet released Adina's hand and waved to the entire room. "And you missed Moses's declaration, all to bar me from speaking to Moses."

Jonathan stood straighter, looking ready for a blow.

Noa stiffened, the tension burning. What would he say next? She and Jonathan inched closer to Abel.

"I had planned to come here to unfurl my anger, to renounce all of you except my immediate family. But my wife challenged me: 'You must live up to your name's meaning: Truth." Emet put his arm around Adina's waist and drew her close. "She said, 'Who are we to question God's judgment? Our Lord has spoken, and we should rejoice in God's care for these daughters.'" He then took in the entire room, acknowledging each family member, then landed on Jonathan. "What was I thinking? I knew very well Moses would only proclaim what God had told him. I'm glad you prevented me from shaming myself, our entire family, and our tribe."

"Thank—" Abel began.

"I'm not finished, Abel."

Noa rubbed her neck. Couldn't he have stopped there? Would he still ruin it?

"Mahlah, Noa, Hoglah, Milkah, and Tirzah, you are dearly loved. I apologize for causing you such distress about your abba. It was wrong. Very wrong. He was a good and faithful father, and like all of us, he made mistakes in judgment, just as I have done and did with you. Your father and I had a long history, and I admit now I was jealous of him to the point of taking it out on him and all of you. I hope you will forgive me, and I hope that you see he even left you with a lesson on how to find your way back to our one God. And it shows in your actions. Your faith humbled all of us, especially me."

Adina looked up and whispered something to Emet.

"Ah, yes, thank you, wife. I am ashamed to say that I mocked Zelo a lot, but mostly about why he drummed our heritage into you. What would it matter to girls—"

Adina cleared her throat.

Emet smiled ruefully at his wife, then turned back to the daughters. "To you young women? When you marry, you will take on your husband's heritage. Why memorize …" Emet waved to the sisters to join him in saying, "'The daughters of Zelophehad, son of Gilead, son of Hepher, son of Makir, son of Manasseh, belonging to the tribe of Manasseh, son of Joseph'? Now I see how Zelo planted something crucial for all of us, sons and daughters alike. To honor and learn from those who've gone before us. I only regret that I didn't emulate his teaching to my sons. But my deepest regret is that I'm sorry I couldn't apologize to him for my stubbornness and for so many other things. And so, with this, I now want to be a better father and uncle, and that begins with no marriage contracts from me."

The tent erupted into applause. Noa, Mahlah, Jonathan, and Simon sighed as each couple hugged one another.

Abel cleared his throat, looking at Noa and Mahlah. "Yes, my wife informed me there already seem to be matches in the air."

Noa placed her hands on her chest. "I don't think any of us expected that speech, Uncle Emet. I'm overjoyed and still taking it all in. Thanks to Aunt Adina's wisdom and for all of you believing in us. Now, please help us celebrate with these refreshments that you have brought."

Jonathan raised her hands in his. "It was more than my conviction about you and your sisters. It was about—"

Tirzah unhooked their hands, "Sorry, but Noa, you must acknowledge our uncle's good wishes."

She pushed Noa toward the gathering around Uncle Emet and Aunt Adina. Noa looked back and mouthed, "I must … Please remember what you wished to say."

The celebration continued, with several young and not-so-young men calling on the sisters. Uncle Emet stepped forward to address them, but Mahlah advanced. "I can talk to them, Uncle."

Noa held her breath. How would he react?

"Gentlemen, you may speak to the firstborn, Mahlah." Emet waved them toward Mahlah.

Noa, along with many in the tent, gasped. *Lord, thank You for changing his heart and for his confession to You and us. And most of all, I am grateful for Abba—and now he will be remembered always.*

"Thank you, Uncle, and thank you, sirs, for coming and celebrating with us. We'll wait until we're allotted our Promised Land before considering marriages. With my uncle, we can discuss dowries, and maybe whether it should be a groom-price instead of our traditional bride-price." Mahlah chuckled. "But for now, we're thankful and appreciative of God's vision for our future."

The four sisters clustered around Mahlah.

Noa began, "We're proud of you, sister, for taking such a bold step."

"It's what we accomplished together." Mahlah put her hand around Noa's waist. "Abba is smiling at us. His dream to have us be there for one another will come true."

"We're forever changed and for so many reasons, in a good way—our confidence, our faith, our relationships. And forgiveness for our father and a cherished love for his protection." Milkah squeezed Noa's hand.

"Each of us grew in ourselves and together." Noa cast her eyes on Tirzah. "It's about our collective and individual courage." She shifted her gaze to Mahlah. "And rising from defeat and fears." She next studied Hoglah. "Being taken seriously by our leaders." Smiling at Milkah, she said, "And being recognized for more than beauty." Her voice quivered. "And for me to be still, listen patiently in waiting, and trust our Lord to answer our prayers." She looked down briefly. "And about trying to be a dutiful sister, not an extra mother."

Her sisters joined in her laughter.

"It all began with you, Noa." Tirzah gazed at her sister.

Milkah leaned her head to Noa and nodded toward Johnathan. "Someone wants to talk to you."

He stood by himself, trying not to watch the sisters. "Go."

While many people celebrated their promising new future, Noa accompanied Jonathan outside.

"I couldn't wait to be with you. Sorry if I interrupted your sisters. You all look so happy. How are you feeling?" Jonathan no longer sported smudge marks from the fire. He was dressed in his nicest tunic and belt, and the glow from the pillar of fire accented his strong figure.

Noa's heart radiated with joy at having Jonathan all to herself. "It's hard even to describe ... I have a multitude of emotions. One minute, I want to shout for glee, another cry, another, I am dumbfounded."

"Why dumbfounded? You had faith our Lord would grant your request."

"I think I did. I show more bravado than what I feel inside. I had faith to petition the request, but I was astounded that God granted it, not only that, but also by the way God said it. 'What the daughters of Zelophehad are saying is right. You must *certainly* give them their inheritance.' I can't get over it. I am ..."

"Speechless? You seem to be doing well. You realize that every man, woman, and child is humbled by what God decreed. Did you change His mind? Or did He encourage you to trust Him so that this story would be told to future generations?" Jonathan edged up against her.

Noa flinched, shaking her head. "Jonathan, that is too much. I'm humbled and grateful that our Lord planted the seed and persisted, guiding me even when I doubted I was doing His will. God is listening to us, even those considered weak or who don't seem to deserve a seat at the table."

"I don't think anyone would think of you or your sisters as weak. And now everyone knows that daughters are at the table."

"Like my father said, 'Our Lord's plans are larger than we can ever imagine.' I will never be nervous again to share my thoughts and dreams with God." Noa gazed up at him. *He knows me so well. The good parts of me and the ones requiring some mending.* Through all of Noa's challenging situations, Jonathan had been her best friend.

"Besides changing God's mind," Jonathan smirked, "what are you happiest about?" He smiled, squeezing her hand.

"Changing God's mind? No, I only shared my fears. I think it was He who nudged me. I don't know, that's too big a question. I'm happiest about how Moses announced it and the complete silence that followed. And then the community stamping their feet was so wonderful. Our life will not depend on the kindness of our aunts and uncles, however generous they may be. Abba passed on the importance of heritage, and now we can rest assured that he'll not be forgotten."

"You are as luminous as our Tabernacle light."

"There's more ..."

"There's more gratitude?" A small smile tugged at his mouth.

"So much more. I don't think I'll come down from this cloud soon. Mahlah's healing. Isn't it miraculous? Her happiness with Simon, her dreams coming true, so many gifts. It's also about all my sisters. We weren't always in agreement about coming forward."

"Why doesn't this surprise me? What you, as sisters, accomplished required an enormous amount of unity and courage."

Something else shone in Jonathan's eyes. What was it? Happiness for the outcome? Yes, but more. Was it a mixture of pride and admiration?

"I'm so proud of you ... no, that's not the way to express it. I respect you ... I admire you ... I ... I ... have a gift I made for you." Jonathan removed a rolled-up scroll from his satchel. He presented it with both hands.

"One of your drawings?" Noa clasped her hands together. Her mouth hurt from smiling at all the blessings, yet there was a special gift from Jonathan. Her pulse picked up a beat.

"Open it."

She untied the leather string and unrolled it with care. "It's magnificent. You captured it perfectly." In her hands was a drawing of Noa and her sisters, their backs to the viewer, hands intertwined, standing tall before the Tent of Meeting. One could feel the enormity of their action as the men crowded around them. It depicted both Moses and the leaders as blurred figures. There was a light surrounding the sisters, beaming from the sky. "Jonathan, such an incredible gift. I'll treasure it always."

She couldn't contain herself as she gazed up at him. But she came to an abrupt stop. "One last gratitude."

Jonathan had prepared for an embrace. He dangled his arms by his side and grinned. "One last gratitude and then ..."

"I hope it's not the last one." She leaned into him for a moment and then sat upright, bringing her palms together. "To know we contributed to others with the same destinies is humbling. No brotherless daughter will ever be afraid of how she is to live. We were doing this for our father's name and our future, but we didn't comprehend that our Lord would decree this is now part of our laws."

Jonathan's grin widened, and he looked like he would burst with pride. "They will remember the daughters of Zelophehad for many years to come. All thanks to your faith and your vision."

She beamed. "I've learned to seek God's guidance and to trust even in dire circumstances. If it is our Lord's will, our paths will be guided. I hope our story will instill faith, and someone will say many years from now, 'The daughters of Zelophehad came forward.'"

AUTHOR'S NOTE

The biblical story of Zelophehad's five daughters lay on my heart for over thirty-five years, ever since I first heard it at the Network of Biblical Storytellers International Conference, where Tom Boomershine, the founder, opened my eyes to experiencing Scripture in a new way. He invited us to study the story's context deeply, to hold it in our hearts and memory, and then to tell it aloud—so that it might live within us and be shared with others. For me, that method brings the Bible to life as it was first told.

It was a challenging story to tell due to their unfamiliar heritage and the daughters' names. In just eleven verses of the Old Testament (Numbers 27), these daughters dared to do what no woman had done before: They stepped into the sacred space before the Tent of Meeting, where women held no authority; stood before Moses, Eleazar, the Levite priests, and Israel's leaders; and asked for an inheritance in their father's name. They risked rejection from the community, ridicule, and even the possibility of being stoned. And yet, they asked.

I found myself wondering—what made them so bold? How old were they? Did all five agree? Did some hesitate? What gave them the faith to believe that God would hear them?

The verses of Zelophehad's daughters highlight their courageous appeal, while the text offers limited narrative detail. Through extensive historical, cultural, and scriptural research, I have sought to faithfully reconstruct their world—honoring the biblical record while imaginatively exploring what might have shaped their boldness.

It is not certain how old the daughters were. Scholars note that their names appear in the Numbers 26 census with parentheses ("Zelophehad had no sons ...") and debate whether this means they were counted among those over twenty, fit for war. Some stated they were in their forties. Others suggest the parentheses indicate that it was an afterthought, added as a response to an unfortunate situation. The average age for marriage in ancient times was fifteen. With five daughters, it would have been highly unusual for all of them not to be married if they were older.

Although most English Bibles and older Hebrew translations spell Zelophehad's daughter's name as *Noah*, the same as the male figure of Genesis, the Hebrew text reads *Noa* (נעֹהָ), meaning "movement" or "motion." I chose the original Hebrew form of her name to help distinguish her from *Noah* of the flood story.

Scripture records that Zelophehad "died for his own sin" (Numbers 27:3), though it does not specify how. While some scholars suggest different causes, I chose to frame his death within the larger judgment on Israel, that all men over twenty exiting Egypt would not enter the Promised Land. They refused to trust God after the report from the twelve spies and wanted to choose a leader to take them back to Egypt. The daughters had to love and honor their father, or why would they ask for his name not to be forgotten?

In my research on Zelophehad's lineage, I discovered that he was an only son, but he had several cousins. For the sake of the story, I limited his interactions to only two cousins. For the daughters, I refer to these second cousins as "Aunt" and "Uncle" to reflect respect and the closeness of family bonds.

Tent of Meeting and *Tabernacle* are used interchangeably. The Tent of Meeting is where Moses met with God in a simple tent outside the Israelite camp. After God's designed, portable structure was built, it was called the Tabernacle, which housed the Holy of Holies. The Tent of Meeting now referred to was where the priests ministered and where the community gathered for significant matters.

The timing of Korah's insurrection occurred earlier in the Bible. In my retelling, I placed their petition in the shadow of Korah's rebellion, highlighting their bravery and revealing that they acknowledged the consequences of their actions. They trusted God's justice enough to ask anyway.

At the end of the story, Assir offers an *alamoth*, a song composed for female voices. This is partially quoted from Psalm 46, which notes that it is "Of the Sons of Korah." We do not know why Assir and his two brothers were saved from their father's demise. Several hundred years passed from Korah's death to the time when the eleven psalms credited to the sons were written. Could one of these have been created earlier and passed down orally? I included this to emphasize how faith and story can echo across generations, transforming a legacy of rebellion into one of faith and dedication.

With their trust in God, the daughters' actions changed the course of history by setting a precedent for inheritance. For the first time, if there were no sons, women could inherit and own property, which is known as the Mosaic law.

I also wanted to explore how we make decisions. How do we discern whether we are following God's will or pressing our own desires? How do we find the courage to step forward, not knowing the outcome, especially in a patriarchal society like the daughters experienced? I've come to believe that even when we take a wrong turn, God will guide our steps.

This story carried me through my thirty-five-year journey in corporate work. Each time I opened the door to the executive boardroom, I whispered, "The daughters of Zelophehad came forward," reminding me that I, too, had a place at the table.

My prayer is that this book will inspire you as their story inspired me—to live with courage, faith, and hope, trusting in God's guidance on the path before you.

GLOSSARY

Alamoth: A musical term for high-pitched voices or instruments.

Baytheren: Desert plant used for its soothing and cleansing properties.

Censer: A small vessel used for burning incense during worship, particularly by priests.

Ezer: A Hebrew word meaning "help" or "helper."

Holy of Holies: The inner, sacred chamber of the Tabernacle where God's presence dwelt.

Keriah: The Jewish ritual act of tearing one's garment as a sign of mourning or grief.

Korahites: Descendants of Korah, a Levite clan, who served in worship roles.

Malachite: A valuable green mineral known for its rich coloration of green.

Matzevah: A standing stone or pillar erected as a memorial or marker.

Mekonenot: Professional women who performed laments during mourning rituals.

Mount Sinai: Where Moses received the Ten Commandments and the covenant law.

Omer: An ancient dry measurement and the daily portion of manna in the wilderness.

Pillar of fire: A visible sign of God's presence guiding the Israelites by night.

Promised Land: The land promised by God to Abraham's descendants, later known as Canaan.

Rabil: Fragrant desert plant used for medicinal purposes and as a beverage.

Ruah Qadim: Hebrew for "east wind," symbolizing power.

Samwa: A desert herb or plant, often associated with fragrance or healing.

Shema: The foundational Jewish declaration of faith beginning with "Hear, O Israel ..."
Tabernacle: The portable sanctuary where God dwelt among the Israelites.
Tamarisk: A resilient desert tree or shrub with feathery leaves and deep roots.
Tent of Meeting: Where Moses met with God before the Tabernacle was built. Later, the Tabernacle was referred to as the Tent of Meeting.
Wabau: A Hebrew narrative term meaning "and they came" or "and they entered."
Wadi: A desert valley or riverbed that fills seasonally with water.
Wheatear: A small, agile desert bird often noted for its distinctive colors.

DISCUSSION QUESTIONS

1) What did you find to be the most significant theme or message of this book? Did it change your perspective or deepen your understanding of anything in Scripture?
2) Which sister was your favorite? Which sister did you most relate to and why? Do you think the order of birth influenced their personalities?
3) How did the main characters grow and change over the course of the story? Did their growth feel earned and believable to you?
4) The sisters experience rivalry—Noa with Milkah and Noa with Mahlah—for different reasons. What were those reasons? Did it remind you of your own experiences?
5) What's the difference between Korah questioning authority and Noa questioning it? How do their motivations and outcomes compare?
6) What was the most surprising element of the book for you—a plot twist, a character's decision, or a new idea that you hadn't considered before?
7) The daughters required a unanimous vote before approaching the Tent of Meeting. If you were one of them, what would you have chosen? In your own family or friend group, how do you make decisions—by majority vote or total agreement?
8) By approaching the male leadership to secure their father's land, how do the daughters of Zelophehad manage individual courage with the injustice and the patriarchal inheritance structures of their time?
9) Zelophehad instills in his daughters a love for God, their family heritage, and creation's beauty. Did your parents, family members,

or guardians impart lessons about heritage, faith, or creation that shaped you?

10) Noa has an assertive personality. Do you think this came from her own nature or from Zelophehad's charge to protect her sisters? How do you personally discern whether you're following God's will or your own?

11) Four thousand years ago, marriage, children, and household management were expected roles for women while men led tribes, commanded armies, or learned a trade. Noa pushes against those boundaries. Have you ever experienced a glass ceiling?

12) What did you like best about the book? What did you like least?

13) Would you recommend this book to others? Why or why not?

ACKNOWLEDGMENTS

The seed for this story was planted decades ago when biblical storytellers Tom Boombershine, Tracy Radvosevic, and Dennis Dewey sowed the idea of Zelophehad's daughters in my heart through the Network of Biblical Storytellers International.

That spark stayed alive until I discovered Tessa Afshar's *Pearl in the Sand*, which, with her encouragement, awakened my longing to tell this story. After I shared my first draft outline with thirteen POVs (points of view), Tessa's gentle wisdom guided me with grace and humor. This book wouldn't have been born without her inspiration, mentorship, and wise counsel. Words can not fully express my gratitude for her generosity and belief in this story, from its inception to the final pages.

A huge thank you to Andrea Doering. Every writer should be blessed to have an editor like you. Your skillful expertise and keen observations gently guided my story to its true potential. I am forever grateful. Thanks to my copyeditor, Julie Davis, for your insightful attention to detail. You helped the story shine while still keeping my voice.

Many companions have walked this path alongside me. Lucinda Secrest McDowell, Codirector of reNEW writers' retreat (how I miss your presence in all our lives), who opened doors and made amazing introductions. To Rachel Britton, who carried on as reNEW's Director, ensuring a safe harbor to learn for first-time writers. Heidi Chivaroli, for your encouragement both by example and by support in so many ways. Thank you for all the lessons you imparted. To Lori Roeleveld, who at reNEW offered to read my first draft and poured courage into the next revision. To Edie Melson, whose excellent mentoring inspired my author social media journey by first asking what my "why" is for pursuing this.

Thank you to the Redemption Press team, especially Jennifer Fedler, who is a fantastic project manager, and Athena Holtz for her early involvement. Tiffani, thank you for your creativity and care in capturing the daughters so beautifully in the cover design. I'm also appreciative for the great support of Sara Cormany, Claire Tucker, Anastasia Corbin, and Ray Dittmeier.

To my Seeds of Faith board of directors, Reverend Dr. Constance Pak, Dee Jae Diliberto, Leslie Kle, and Marie Abbondondolo, who believed in and supported me as both a storyteller and a leader. My Seeds of Faith book groups, with their shared stories and insights, gave this novel depth and heart. Your insight and friendship have been a gift.

A huge thank-you to the teachers for all the support from American Christian Fiction Writers, Blue Ridge Christian Writers' Conference, She Writes for Him, and Northwestern Christian Writers Conference, whose classes and critique circles sharpened my craft and built friendships that will last far beyond this book.

Thank you to Rabbi Irwin Huberman for sharing your passion for the Torah and opening your library and *The Torah and Commentary*, which grounded this story in its sacred roots.

To Cher Gatto, who organized my critique partner group of Desiree Future, Stephanie Goddard, and Kathy O'Malley, and for their countless hours of listening, refining, and encouraging. To Karen Porter for wise guidance and encouragement. To Barb Roose for the encouragement you offered early in my journey. To Mojdeh Hassani and Fredda Klopfer, my sisters in our Daughters of Abraham Group, who reminded me that stories bridge worlds. To Stacy Ladyman and Maureen Miller for generously sharing their publishing journey and offering lots of support! Special thanks to Amanda Greaney for her invaluable administrative and launch support. Your creativity and encouragement have helped my blogs, newsletter, and this book reach readers in ways I could not have on my own.

To my friends at church and Kiwanis, who listened, prayed, and never stopped believing. Thanks to Kim, Lauren, and Sara for sharing what it's like to live with all sisters.

To Ashley and Kris, Cliff, Jeff, and Leah—each of you holds a piece of my heart. Your love, support, and encouragement have carried me more than you know.

This book would not exist without the steadfast love of my husband, Roger—my best friend, coeditor, cheerleader. You kept me fed and laughing through *every* draft for the last seven years and reviewed and edited each one! You tolerated my many hours at the computer and listened to me talk about these characters so much that you started talking to them, too, even creating songs about them! When I was stuck on a new beginning for the book, you brought forth the inspiration and words! No love song or poem could ever capture how deeply I cherish you. I am forever grateful for every step we've taken and all those still ahead in writing our story together.

Lastly, I thank God for making a way in the wilderness—for this novel and for me. I will carry the lessons of this journey always—above all, the call to trust.

Trust in the LORD *with all your heart and*
lean not on your own understanding;
in all your ways submit to him, and he will make
your paths straight. (Proverbs 3:5–6)

ORDER INFORMATION

To order individual copies go to
redemption-press.com/bookstore

For discounts on bulk orders
send an email to
bookorders@redemption-press.com.
subject: bulk orders

www.ingramcontent.com/pod-product-compliance
Lightning Source LLC
LaVergne TN
LVHW100514110826
845146LV00002B/634

* 9 7 9 8 9 9 5 4 1 9 6 0 0 *